Daniels se...

Magic Bites

'Splendid . . . an edgy dark fantasy touched with
just the right amount of humor'
New York Times bestselling author Patricia Briggs

'Andrews' edgy series stands apart from similar
fantasies . . . owing to its complex world building and
skilled characterisations'
Library Journal

'Andrews shows a great deal of promise. Readers fond of
Laurell K. Hamilton and Patricia Briggs may find her work a
new source of reading pleasure'
SFRevu

Magic Burns

'With all her problems, secrets and prowess both martial and
magical, Kate is a great kick-ass heroine, a tough girl with a
heart, and her adventures are definitely worth checking out'
Locus

'*Magic Burns* hooked me completely. With a fascinating,
compelling plot, a witty, intelligent heroine, a demonic villain
and clever wry humour throughout, this story has it all'
Fresh Fiction

Magic Strikes

'Andrews' crisp dialogue and layered characterisation
make the gut-wrenching action of this first-person thrill
ride all the more intense. Place your book orders now;
it's wort'   ...penny!'

Also by Ilona Andrews from Gollancz:

Magic Bites

Magic Burns

Magic Strikes

A Kate Daniels Novel

Magic
Burns

ILONA ANDREWS

First published in Great Britain in 2010 by
Gollancz
An imprint of the Orion Publishing Group
Orion House, 5 Upper St Martin's Lane, London WC2H 9EA
An Hachette UK Company

3 5 7 9 10 8 6 4 2

A CIP catalogue record for this book is available
from the British Library

ISBN 978 0 575 09394 2

Printed in Great Britain by Clays Ltd, St Ives plc

The Orion Publishing Group's policy is to use papers that are
natural, renewable and recyclable products and made from wood
grown in sustainable forests. The logging and manufacturing
processes are expected to conform to the environmental regulations
of the country of origin.

www.ilona-andrews.com
www.orionbooks.co.uk

To the late David Gemmell.
You have inspired me with your books.
It was my dream to meet you,
and I deeply regret your passing.

CHAPTER 1

THE PHONE RANG IN THE MIDDLE OF THE NIGHT. THE magic wave was in full swing, and the phone shouldn't have worked, but it rang anyway, again and again, outraged over being ignored, until finally I reached over and picked it up.

"Yehmmm?"

"Rise and shine, Kate." The smooth cultured voice on the line suggested a slender, elegant, handsome man, all things that Jim was not. At least not in his human shape.

I clawed my eyes open long enough to glance at the windup clock across the room. "Two in the morning. Some of us sleep during the night."

"I've got a gig," Jim said.

I sat up in the bed, wide-awake. A gig was good—I needed the money. "Half."

"Third."

"Half."

"Thirty-five percent." Jim's voice hardened.

"Half."

The phone went silent as my former Guild partner mulled it over. "Okay, forty."

I hung up. The bedroom lay quiet. My curtains were open and moonlight sifted into the room through the metal grate shielding the window. The moonlight acted as a catalyst and the metal bars glowed with a weak bluish patina where the silver in the alloy interacted with the ward spell. Beyond the bars, Atlanta slept like some hulking beast of legend, dark and deceptively peaceful. When the magic wave ended, as it inevitably would, the beast would awaken in an explosion of electric light and possibly gunfire.

My ward wouldn't stop a bullet, but it kept the magic hazmat out of my bedroom, and that was good enough.

The phone rang. I let it ring twice before I picked it up.

"Fine." Jim's voice had a hint of a snarl in it. "Half."

"Where are you?"

"In the parking lot under your window, Kate."

Calling from a pay phone, which shouldn't have worked, either. I reached for my clothes, left by the bed for just such an occasion. "What's the gig?"

"Some arsonist wacko."

FORTY-FIVE MINUTES LATER, I WAS WINDING MY way through an underground garage and cursing Jim under my breath. With the lights knocked out by magic, I couldn't see my hand in front of my nose.

A fireball blossomed in the pitch-black depth of the garage. Huge, churning with violent red and yellow, it roared toward me. I jumped behind the concrete support, my throwing knife sweaty in my hands. Heat bathed me. For a moment I couldn't breathe, and then the fire hurtled past me to burst in an explosion of sparks against the wall.

A thin gleeful cackle emanated from the garage depths. I peeked out from behind the support in the direction of the sound. Nothing but darkness. Where was the tech shift when you needed one?

Across from me at the next row of supports Jim raised his hand and touched his fingers to his thumb a few times, imitating an opening and closing beak. Negotiate. He wanted me to engage a lunatic who had already turned four people into smoking meat. Okay. I could do that.

"Alright, Jeremy!" I yelled into the night. "Give me the salamander and I won't cut your head off!"

Jim put his hand over his face and did some shaking. I thought he was laughing, but I couldn't be sure. Unlike him I didn't have the benefit of enhanced night vision.

Jeremy's cackle reached a hysterical crescendo. "Stupid bitch!"

Jim peeled himself from the support and melted into the darkness, tracking Jeremy's voice. His vision worked better than mine in low light, but even his sight failed in absolute darkness. He had to hunt by sound, which meant I had to keep Jeremy talking. While Jim stalked Jeremy's melodious voice, Jeremy, in turn, stalked me.

Nothing to worry about, just a homicidal pyromaniac armed with a salamander in a sphere of enchanted glass and intent on setting what's left of Atlanta on fire. The main thing was to keep the salamander's sphere safe. If that thing broke, my name would be more famous than Mrs. O'Leary's cow.

"Damn Jeremy, you need to work on your vocabulary. So many good names to call me and the best you could come up with is bitch? Give me the salamander before you hurt yourself."

"Suck my dick . . . whore!"

A tiny spark flared into existence to the left of me. It hung suspended in the darkness, illuminating both the scaly outline of the salamander's mouth and Jeremy's hands clutching the glass sphere with white-knuckled need. The enchanted glass parted and belched the spark. The air hit the tiny packet of energy and the spark exploded into a fireball.

I ducked behind the support just as the fire smashed against concrete. Flames shot past on both sides of me. The acrid stench of sulfur stung my nostrils.

"That last fireball missed me by a mile. You shoot blanks with your other salamander, too, Jeremy?"

"Eat shit and die!"

Jim had to be close to him by now. I stepped into the open. "Come on, you sniveling shit for brains! Can't you do anything right?"

I saw flames, lunged to the side and hit the floor rolling. Above me the fire howled like an enraged animal. The handle of the knife burned my fingers. The air in my lungs turned to heat, and my eyes watered. I pressed my face into the dusty concrete, praying it didn't get any hotter, and then suddenly it was over.

Screw this. I jumped to my feet and charged in Jeremy's direction. The salamander flared within the sphere. I caught a flash of Jeremy's crooked smile above the glass. It wilted as Jim's dark hands closed around Jeremy's throat. The arsonist slumped, ragdoll limp, the sphere rolling from his weakened fingers . . .

I dived for it, caught it three inches above the cement, and found myself face-to-face with the salamander. Ruby-red eyes regarded me with mild curiosity, black lips parted, and a long, spiderweb-thin filament of a tongue slithered from the salamander's mouth and kissed the sphere's glass in the reflection of my nose. Hi, I love you, too.

Gingerly I got to my knees and then to my feet. The salamander's presence tugged on my mind, as eager to please as an overly enthusiastic kitten arching her back for a stroke. Visions of flames and heat wavered before me. *Let's burn something* . . . I slammed my mental shutters closed, locking her out of my mind. Let's not.

Jim relaxed his hold on Jeremy and the arsonist sagged to the ground like a wet blanket. The whites of his eyes stared at the ceiling from his slack face, caught by death in a moment of utter surprise. No pulse check needed for this one. Shit. There goes the capture bonus.

"You said it was a live-preferred bounty," I murmured. The living Jeremy was worth a lot more than his corpse. We'd still get paid, but we had just waved a third of the money goodbye.

"It is." Jim twisted the body on its side, exposing Jeremy's back. A thin metal shaft, tipped with three black feathers protruded from between Jeremy's shoulders blades. Before my mind had the time to digest its significance, I hit the deck, cradling the salamander. Jim somehow got there before me.

We stared into the gloom. Darkness and silence.

Someone had taken out our mark with a crossbow bolt. Could have taken us out, as well. We had stood by the body for at least four seconds. More than enough time to squeeze off two shots. I touched Jim and touched my nose. He shook his head. With all the sulfur in the air he probably couldn't smell a skunk if it sprayed him in the face. I lay very still and tried to breathe quietly. Listening was our best bet.

A minute dragged by, long, viscous, and silent. Very slowly Jim shifted into a crouch and nodded to the left. I had a vague feeling the door lay to the right, but in the darkness with some unknown crossbowman waiting, I would trust Jim's senses over mine.

Jim grasped Jeremy's corpse, slung it over his shoulder, and we took off, bending low, running fast, him ahead and me, half-blind in the gloom, slightly behind. Concrete supports flashed by, one, two, three, four. The tech hit, and before I could put down my raised foot, the magic drained from the world, leaving the battered technology in its wake. The fluorescent lamps in the ceiling blinked and snapped into life with a buzz, bathing the garage in a weak man-made glow. The black rectangle of the exit gaped ten feet before us. Jim dived into it. I lunged to the left, behind the nearest support. The salamander in the globe stopped glowing and went to sleep, looking like a harmless black lizard. My long-range weapon was tuckered out.

I set it down on the floor and slid Slayer from its sheath. Salamanders are overrated anyway.

"He's gone," Jim said from the doorway and pointed behind me.

I turned. Far at the back, the concrete wall had crumbled, revealing a narrow passageway probably leading up to the street. He was right. If the bowman wanted to take us out, he had had plenty of time to do it.

"So he sniped our mark and left?"

"Looks that way."

"I don't get it."

Jim shook his head. "Weird shit always happens around you."

"This was your gig, not mine."

A shower of sparks fell from above the door and a green EXIT sign burst into life.

Jim stared at it for a moment, his features twisted in a distinctly feline expression, disgust and fatalism rolled into one, and shook his head again.

"Dibs on the bolt in his back!" I called.

"Be my guest."

Jim's pager went off. He checked it and a familiar neutral mask slid onto his face.

"Oh no, you don't! I can't carry him by myself."

"Pack business." He headed for the exit.

"Jim!"

I killed the urge to throw something at the empty doorway. Served me right for taking a job with a guy who served on the Pack Council. It's not that Jim was a bad friend. It's just that for shapeshifters, Pack business always took precedence. On a scale from one to ten, the Pack was eleven and everything else a one.

I stared at a very dead Jeremy lying like a sack of potatoes on the floor. Probably a hundred and fifty pounds, dead weight. There was no way I could carry him and the salamander at the same time. There was no way I could leave the salamander unattended, either. The magic could hit anytime, setting the little lizard ablaze. Plus, the sniper might still be around. I needed to get out of here, and fast.

Jeremy and the salamander, each worth four grand. I no longer did a lot of work for the Guild, and gigs of this size didn't come my way too often. Even split in half with Jim, the bounty would cover my two mortgages for two months. The thought of leaving four grand on the floor made me physically ill.

I looked at Jeremy. I looked at the salamander. Choices, choices.

THE MERCENARY GUILD'S BOUNTY CLERK, A SHORT, trim, dark-haired man, stared at Jeremy's head on the counter. "Where is the rest of him?"

"I had a slight logistics problem."

The clerk's face split in a wide smile. "Jim took off on you, didn't he? That will be one capture ticket then?"

"Two tickets." Jim might be an asshole, but I wouldn't screw him out of his share. He'd get his capture ticket, which entitled him to his half of the bounty.

"Kate, you're a pushover," the clerk said.

I leaned over the counter and offered him my best deranged smile. "Wanna push and see if I fall over?"

"No thanks." The clerk slapped the stack of forms on the counter. "Fill these out."

The inch-thick stack of paperwork promised to occupy me for a good hour. The Guild had pretty lax rules—being an organization of mercenaries, they took keen interest in profit and little else—but death had to be reported to the cops and thus required red tape. The small significance of Jeremy's life was reduced to the price on his head and a lot of carefully framed blank spaces on a piece of paper.

I gave the top form the evil eye. "I don't have to fill out the R20."

"That's right, you work with the Order now." The clerk counted off eight pages from the top of the stack. "There you go, VIP treatment for you."

"Yipee." I swiped my stack.

"Hey, Kate, let me ask you something."

I wanted to fill out my forms, go home, and take a nap. "Shoot."

He reached under the counter. The Mercenary Guild occupied an old Sheraton Hotel on the edge of Buckhead and the clerk's counter had been a lobby bar in that previous life. The clerk pulled out a dark brown bottle and set it in front of me with a shot glass.

"Why, no, I won't drink your mysterious love potion."

He guffawed. "Hennessy. The good stuff. I'll pay for the info."

"Thanks, but I don't drink." Not anymore, anyway. I still kept a bottle of Boone's Farm sangria in my cabinet for a dire emergency, but hard liquor was right out. "What's your question?"

"What's it like to work for the Order?"

"Thinking of joining?"

"No, I'm happy where I'm at. But I've got a nephew. He wants to be a knight."

"How old?"

"Sixteen."

Perfect. The Order liked them young. All the easier to brainwash. I pulled up a chair. "I'd take a glass of water."

He brought me water and I sipped it. "Basically the Order does the same thing we do: they clear magic hazmat. Let's say you've got a harpy in a tree after a magic wave. You're going to call the cops first."

"If you're stupid." The clerk smirked.

I shrugged. "The cops tell you that they're busy with a giant worm trying to swallow the federal courthouse, instruct you to stay away from the harpy, and tell you they'll come out when they can. The usual. So you call the Guild. Why wait, when for three hundred bucks a couple of mercs will bag the harpy with no fuss and even give your kid a pretty tail feather for his hat, right?"

"Right."

"Suppose you don't have three hundred bucks. Or suppose the job is code 12, too nasty for the Guild to take it. You still have a harpy and you want her gone. So you call the Order, because you heard they don't charge that much. They ask you to come to their Chapter, where a nice knight talks to you, gets your income assessed and tells you good news: they're charging you fifty bucks because they've determined that's all you can afford. Kismet."

The clerk eyed me. "What's the catch?"

"The catch is, they give you a piece of paper to sign, your plea to the Order. And there in big letters it says that you authorize the Order to remove any threat to humanity that arises in connection with this case."

The Order of Merciful Aid had chosen its name well. They provided merciful aid, usually on the edge of the blade or by the burn of a bullet. Trouble was, sometimes you got more aid than you wanted.

"Let's say you sign the plea. The knights come out and observe the harpy. At the same time, you notice that every time you see the damn thing, your elderly senile aunt disappears. So you watch the old lady and sure enough, the magic wave hits and she turns into a harpy. You tell the knights you want to call the whole thing off—you love your aunt and she does no harm sitting in that tree anyway. The knights tell you that five percent of harpies carry a deadly disease on their claws and they've determined her to be a danger to humanity. You get angry, you yell, you call the cops, but the cops tell you it's all legal, there is nothing they can do, and besides the Order is part of the law enforcement anyway. You promise to lock your aunt up. You try a bribe. You point to your kids and explain how much they love the old lady. You cry. You beg. But nothing helps." I drained my glass. "And that's what it's like working for the Order."

The clerk poured himself a shot and tossed it down his throat. "Did that really happen?"

"Yep."

"Did they kill the old lady?"

"Yep."

"Jesus."

"If your nephew thinks he can do that, tell him to apply to the Academy. He's at a good age for it. It's hard physically and the academic load is pretty big, but if he has the will, he'll make it."

"How do you know?"

I swiped my stack off the counter. "Back when I was a kid, my guardian enrolled me. He was a knight-diviner."

"No shit. How long did you last?"

"Two years. Did well on everything except mental conditioning. I've got authority issues." I waved at the clerk and took my paperwork to one of the tables in the gloom.

Truth was, I didn't do well. I did great. Tested right off the power-scale. Got certified as an electrum-level squire. But I hated it. The Order required absolute dedication, and I already had a cause. I wanted to kill the most powerful man in the world, and that kind of desire leaves little room for anything else. I dropped out and went to work for the Mercenary Guild. It broke Greg's heart.

Greg had been a great guardian, fanatical in his determination to protect me. For Greg, the Order was a place of safety. If my target found out I existed, he'd kill me, and neither Greg nor I had enough power to resist him. Not yet anyway. Had I joined the Order, every last knight would protect me against this threat. But it wasn't worth it, so I parted ways with the Order and never looked back.

And then Greg was murdered. To find his killer, I went to the Order and maneuvered myself into their investigation. I found the murderer and killed him. It was a grisly, nasty affair, now called the Red Point Stalker case. In the process my Academy record came to light and the Order decided they wanted me back. They weren't subtle about it, either. They made up a job—a liaison between themselves and the Mercenary Guild—promised me Greg's office, his files, authority to handle minor cases, and a steady paycheck. I took it. Part of it was guilt: I had shunned Greg after dropping out of the Academy. Part of it was common sense: I had mortgages on both my father's house, near Savannah, and on Greg's place here in Atlanta. To give up either one would be like ripping a chunk out of my body. Guild gigs paid well but I had a small territory near Savannah and a big job happened there maybe once every six months. The lure of steady money proved to be too strong.

My affiliation with the Order wouldn't last. But for now, it worked. I had yet to default on either payment and once I filled out these forms, I'd ensure I could cover my bills for another month or two.

After writing my merc ID number ten times on every imaginable piece of paper, I was treated to a "check yes or no" questionnaire. Yes, I acted in self-defense. No, I didn't believe excessive force was used in subduing the suspect. Yes, I perceived the suspect as presenting imminent threat to myself and others. By the time I reached the "fill in the blank" portion my eyes needed match sticks to stay open. In the "state the suspect's intent as perceived by you" section, I wrote down, "Intended to burn down the city due to being a complete crackpot."

When I finally stepped out of the Mercenary Guild's heavy, reinforced steel doors, the sky was pale gray with that particular color that usually meant the sun was rising. At least

I had the bolt from Jeremy's back. And I was three hundred bucks richer, thanks to my advance. The rest of the money would have to wait until the cops approved the kill. By the time I got to the intersection, I had the advance divided between various bills. I still had it—if I thrust my hand in my pocket, I would feel the soft paper of four worn fifty-dollar bills and five twenties, and yet the money was already gone.

The great mystery of the Universe.

TWO HOURS LATER, I STUMBLED INTO THE ATlanta chapter of the Order, bleary-eyed and armed with a huge mug of coffee, the mysterious bolt wrapped in a brown paper bag and tucked securely under my elbow. The office greeted me with its plethora of vivid color: a long hallway with gray carpet, gray walls, and gray light fixtures. Ugh.

As I stepped in, the magic hit. The electric lights went out. The bloated tubes of feylanterns flared a gentle blue as the charged air inside them reacted with magic.

This was the third wave in the last twenty-four hours. The magic had been going crazy the last couple of days. Shifting back and forth like it couldn't make up its mind.

The faint clicking of an ancient typewriter echoed in the empty office, coming from the secretary's nook by the door of the knight-protector. "Good morning, Maxine."

"Good morning, Kate," said Maxine's voice in my head. *"Rough night?"*

"You could say that."

I unlocked my office door. The Atlanta Chapter of the Order made an effort to appear as inconspicuous as possible, but my office was small even by their standards. Little more than a cube, it was barely large enough to house a desk, two chairs, a row of filing cabinets, and some bookshelves. The walls showcased another radiant shade of gray paint.

I paused in the doorway, arrested in midstep. I had inherited the office from Greg. It had been almost four months since his death. I should have gotten over it by now, but sometimes, like this morning, I just . . . had a hard time making myself enter. My memory insisted that if I stepped in, Greg would be there, standing with a book in his hand, his dark eyes reproachful but never unkind. Always ready to pull me out of whatever mess I had gotten myself into. But it was a lie. Greg was dead. First my mother, then my father, then Greg. Everyone I ever cared about died violently, in a great deal of pain. If I took a moment to let it sink in, I'd be howling like a Pack wolf during a full moon.

I closed my eyes, trying to clear the memories of the office and Greg within it. Mistake. The image of Greg only got more vivid.

I did a one eighty and walked down the hall to the armory. So I was a coward. Sue me.

Andrea sat on a bench cleaning a handgun. She was short, built with strength in mind, and had the kind of face that made people want to tell her their life stories in a checkout line. She knew the Order's Charter front to back and could rattle obscure regulations off the top of her head. Her radios never lost contact, her magic scanner never malfunctioned, and if you brought her a broken gadget, she would return it the next day fully operational and clean.

Andrea raised her blond head and gave me a little salute with her hand. I shrugged a little, feeling the reassuring weight of Slayer, my saber, in its sheath on my back and waved in reply. I could understand the metal addiction. After the little adventure that had landed me this job, I was loath to part with Slayer. A few minutes without my blade and I got edgy.

Andrea noticed me still looking at her. "You need something?"

"I need to ID a crossbow bolt."

She made a come-here motion with the fingers of her left hand. "Give."

I gave. Andrea removed the paper, took out the bolt, and whistled in appreciation.

"Nice."

Blood-red and fletched with three black feathers, the bolt looked about two feet in length. Three inch-long black lines marked the shaft just before the fletch: nine marks in all.

"This is a carbon shaft. It can't be bent. Very durable and expensive. Looks like a 2216, designed to bring down medium-sized game, deer, some bear . . ."

"Human." I leaned against the wall and sipped my coffee.

"Yeah." Andrea nodded. "Good power, good trajectory without any significant sacrifice in speed. It's a man-killer. Look at the head—small, three-blade, weighs about a hundred grains. Reminds me a lot of a Wasp Boss series. Some people go for mechanical broadheads, but with a good crossbow the acceleration is so sudden, it opens the blades in flight and there goes your accuracy down the drain. If I were to pick a broadhead, I'd pick something like this." She twisted the bolt, letting the light from the window play on the blades of the head. "Hand sharpened. Where did you get this?"

I told her.

She frowned. "The fact that you didn't hear the bow go off probably means it's a recurve. A compound crossbow 'twangs' at release. Can I fire it?" She nodded at a man-shaped paper target pinned to the far wall, which was sheathed in several layers of corkboard.

"Sure."

She put on gloves to keep the magic residue to a minimum, took a small crossbow off the bench, loaded, swung it up, and fired, too fast to have aimed. The bolt whistled through the air and bit into the center of the man's forehead. Bull's-eye. And here I was, unable to hit a cow at ten yards with a gun.

The feylanterns flickered and faded. On the wall, a dusty electric fixture flared with soft yellow light. The magic wave had drained and the world had shifted from magic back to tech. Andrea and I looked at each other. Nobody could predict the duration of the shifts: the magic came and went as it pleased. But the waves rarely lasted less than an hour. This one had been what, fifteen minutes?

"Is it me, or is it shifting more than usual?"

"It's not you." Andrea's face looked a bit troubled. She freed the bolt. "Want me to scan it for magic?"

"If it's not too much trouble." Magic had the annoying

tendency of dissipating over time. The sooner you could scan your evidence, the better your chances of getting a power print.

"Trouble?" She leaned to me. "I've been off-line for two months. It's killing me. I have cobwebs growing on my brain." She pressed her finger below her right eye, pulling the lower eyelid down. "Look for yourself."

I laughed. Andrea worked for a Chapter out West and had run into some trouble with a pack of loups raiding the cattle farms. Loups, the insane cannibalistic shapeshifters who had lost the internal battle for their humanity, killed, raped, and raged their way from one atrocity to the next, until someone put the world out of their misery.

Unfortunately, loups were also contagious as hell. Andrea's partner knight became infected, went loup, and ended up with two dozen of Andrea's bullets in her brain. There was a limit to how much shapeshifters could heal, and Andrea was a crack shot. They relocated her to Atlanta, and although she didn't have any trace of Lycos Virus in her blood and wasn't in any danger of sprouting fur and claws, Ted kept her on the back burner.

Andrea took the bolt to the magic scanner, raised the glass hood, slid the bolt onto the ceramic tray, lowered the cube, and cranked the lever. The cube descended and the m-scanner whirled.

"Andrea?"

"Mmm?"

"The tech's up," I said, feeling stupid.

She grimaced. "Oh, Christ. Probably won't get anything. Well, you never know. Sometimes you can pull some residual magic imprints even during tech."

We looked at the cube. We both knew it was futile. You would have to scan something really saturated with magic to get a good m-scan during tech. Like a body part. The m-scanner analyzed the traces of residual magic left on an object by its owner and printed them in a variety of colors: blue for human, green for shapeshifter, purple for vampire. The tone and vividness of the colors denoted the different types of magic, and reading an m-scan correctly was practically an art form.

The traces of magic on a bolt, probably held very briefly, were bound to be miniscule. I knew of only one man in the city who had an m-scanner high-speed enough to register such slight residual magic during tech. His name was Saiman. Trouble was, if I went to him, it would cost me an arm and a leg.

The printer chattered. Andrea pulled the print out and turned to me. Her face had gone a shade whiter. A wide slice of silvery blue cut across the paper. *Human divine.* That in itself was not remarkable. Anybody who drew their power from deity or religion registered as *human divine*: the Pope, Shaolin monks, even Greg, a knight-diviner, had registered silver-blue. The problem was, we shouldn't have been able to get an m-scan at all with the tech up.

"What does this mean? Is the residual magic just incredibly strong on this thing?"

Andrea shook her head. "The magic waves have been really erratic lately."

We looked at each other. We both knew what rapid-fire waves meant: a flare. And I needed a flare like I needed a hole in the head.

"You have a petitioner," Maxine's voice said in my head.

I grabbed my m-scan and went into my office.

CHAPTER 2

I LANDED AT MY DESK. A FLARE WAS COMING. IF normal shifts were magic waves, a flare was a magic tsunami. It started as a series of shallow magic fluctuations, quickly falling and rising, but never leaving the world. During those short waves, the magic didn't completely fall, coming back stronger and stronger until it finally drowned us in an enormous surge.

Theory said that magic and tech used to coexist in a balance. Like the pendulum of a grandfather clock that barely moved, if at all. But then came the Age of Man, and men are made of progress. They overdeveloped magic, pushing the pendulum farther and farther to one side until it came crashing down and started swinging back and forth, bringing with it tech waves. And then in turn, technology oversaturated the world, helped once again by pesky Man, and the pendulum swung again, to the side of magic this time. The previous Shift from magic to tech took place somewhere around the start of the Iron Age. The current Shift officially dawned almost thirty years ago. It began with a flare, and with each subsequent flare, more of our world succumbed to magic.

Weird shit happened during the flares. The magic surge only lasted two to three days, but those days were killer. For a moment I wished I was still just a merc. I could go home and wait all the craziness out.

A woman appeared in the doorway—my petitioner. Slender and elegant in that willowy way of tall and naturally slim people, she wasn't simply attractive, she was gorgeous: beautifully cut Asian eyes, perfect skin, full mouth, and blue-black hair that spilled over her shoulders in a glossy straight wave. Her dress was black and clingy. Her shoes made my calves ache.

And she looked familiar, but for the life of me I couldn't recall where I had seen her before.

"Kate Daniels?"

That's me. "Yes?"

"My name is Myong Williams."

We shook hands awkwardly. "Please, sit down."

She sat in the client's chair and crossed one lean leg over the other in a whisper of fabric.

"To what do I owe the pleasure?"

She hesitated, unconsciously repositioning her legs to better show them off. "I've come to ask you for a favor."

"Of what nature?"

"Personal."

She fell silent. We'd reached a standstill.

Something clicked in my brain. "I remember where I've seen you before. You're Curran's . . ."—*lover, mistress, honeybunny*—"significant other." Dear God, what could the Beast Lord's concubine possibly want from me?

"We're no longer together," Myong said.

Her problem wasn't connected to Curran. Good. Great. Fantastic. The more distance that lay between me and the Beast Lord, the better it was for everybody involved. We had worked together during the Red Point Stalker case and almost killed each other.

Myong shifted in her chair, adjusted the hem of her dress with a casual swipe of her fingers, and furrowed her meticulously waxed eyebrows. "You and Maximillian . . ."

The mention of Max's name brought a bit of unease. I had thought I was over him. We had met during the investigation of Greg's death. He was handsome, smart, occasionally kind, and very interested in me. I had wanted . . . I was not sure what the hell I had wanted. Intimacy. Sex. Someone to come home to. It didn't end well. In fact, he probably hated me. "Max and I are also no longer together."

Myong nodded. "I know. We're engaged."

I didn't quite catch that. "Who?"

"Maximillian Crest and me. We're engaged to be married."

The world had just stood on its ears. "So let me get this straight. You and my—" Ex-boyfriend would be inaccurate since technically we were never a couple. "Could have been" boyfriend was plain stupid. "You and Max are an item?"

"Yes."

Awkward, to say the least. I felt no jealousy, but talking to her made me uncomfortable and I couldn't pinpoint why. I forced my lips into a smile and leaned back. "Congratulations. What do you want from me?"

Myong looked uncomfortable. "It's customary to ask Curran's permission."

"You mean he has to approve your marriage to Crest? Even though you and Curran are no longer together?"

"Yes. I'm a member of the Pack."

That explained things. Curran ruled the shapeshifter Pack with an iron fist. Every shapeshifter in the Southeast called him lord. Unless that shapeshifter was a loup, in which case he usually didn't have a chance to call Curran anything before the Beast Lord ripped him to pieces. I looked her over and arched my eyebrows. "Fox?"

She sighed. "Everybody thinks that. I turn into a mink."

I tried to imagine a weremink and failed. It would appeal to Crest, though. "You still haven't told me why you're here."

"I asked Curran," she said.

"And he said no?"

"No. He didn't say anything. It's been two months." Myong leaned forward, hands folded together. "My alpha refuses to broach the question to Curran. I was hoping you could ask my lord for me."

"Me?"

"You have a certain amount of influence with him. You saved his life."

You want me to ask your ex-lover/homicidal shapeshifter who scares me shitless to let you marry my "ex–could have been" boyfriend? You've got to be kidding. "I think you overestimate his opinion of me."

"Please." Myong bit her lip. The fingers of her left hand

gripped and twisted the fingers of her right, exposing the small jagged white line of a scar on her wrist. Left-handed. She had slit her own wrist, probably with a silver blade—a dramatic gesture and completely futile. It took more than a three-inch cut to bleed a shapeshifter dry. She was looking at me, seemingly unaware of what her hands were doing. "Max said you would understand."

Oh, hell. He didn't come himself, though, did he?

I glanced at her. She looked off-balance, almost as if someone had knocked her legs out from under her, but she hadn't hit the ground yet. I had seen precisely the same look on her face before, three months ago. It had happened right after the Red Point Stalker called the Pack Keep. Curran and I had finally figured out who he was, and he wasn't happy about the situation. The Stalker had held a phone to a woman's mouth so Curran wouldn't miss a single whimper and tore her to pieces until she died. The woman had been one of Curran's former lovers. I had sat in on the call and as I was walking back to my room, trying not to cry, I saw Myong through an open doorway, hugging herself, that very look of utter helplessness contorting her face.

With this recollection, a feeling flooded me, a feeling of being too dumb to see what was under my nose, of being scared, hounded, and alone, dashing about the besieged city, blundering from one mistake to another while all around me people died. It grabbed me by the throat. My pulse raced and I swallowed, reminding myself that it was over. Back then, when I was drowning, Crest offered me a straw, and I almost dragged him under with me. He deserved to be happy. Without me.

"I'll ask," I said.

She exhaled. "Thank you."

"I don't know if I can convince Curran. Your lord and I have a tendency to infuriate each other." And every time we met, something of mine got broken. My ribs, my roof, my hammer . . .

She didn't hear the last part. "I know we can. Thank you so much. We're so grateful."

"Incoming," Maxine's voice warned in my mind.

A familiar lanky figure appeared in the doorway of my office. About five ten, he wore pale jeans and a light T-shirt. His brownish hair was cropped very short. He had a fresh, clean-cut face and velvet brown eyes framed in embarrassingly long eyelashes. If it wasn't for the promise of a masculine square jaw, he would be bordering on "pretty." On the plus side, if he ever had to fight through a room full of adolescent girls, he only needed to blink a couple of times, and they would all faint.

But his prettiness and smoky eyes were misleading. Derek was a killer. He'd seen more suffering in his eighteen years than some people packed into half a century and it had sharpened him to a razor's edge. I hadn't seen him since Red Point, when my big mouth managed to get him sworn to protect me with a blood oath. Curran had since released him from his oath, but a pledge sealed in blood didn't just go away. Its aftereffects lingered. That had been the first and last time I would ever screw with the Pack's hierarchy.

"Kate, hello." Derek said mildly. "Myong? What are you doing here?"

Myong jumped off her chair and cringed. Her shoulders hunched, as though she were expecting a punch, her head drooped, and her knees bent. She looked down on the floor. Had she been in her animal form, I'm pretty sure she would have peed herself.

Alrighty then, I guess we knew who stood higher in the Pack's chain of command.

"You don't have to answer him," I said. "Information disclosed to a representative of the Order is confidential unless subpoenaed by a court of law."

She just stood there, watching the floor. It was too much for me.

"You may go," I said.

She fled the office. A second later the door leading to the landing clicked closed behind her. I bet she was running down the stairs to the outside. Hopefully, she wouldn't break her legs in those stilettos. Her bones might take a whole two weeks to heal.

"May I come in?" Derek asked.

I pointed to one of the two client chairs. "Why is Myong scared of you?"

He sat and shrugged. "I can only guess."

"Do."

"I work for Curran directly now. She's probably afraid I'll snitch, because I think I know why she was here."

"Will you?"

He shrugged again. "It's her own affair. Unless she starts plotting some harm to the Pack, I'm not interested. Coming here wasn't her idea anyway. She's very passive."

"Oh?"

He nodded. "That asshole made her do it. I always said he was a slimebag."

"Your opinion is duly noted." Thank you, boy wonder, for the editorial on my "almost could have been" boyfriend. What would I do without the moral compass of a teenage werewolf?

"Why didn't he come himself? Shouldn't he be here saying, 'Hey, I know it didn't work out between us, but I need your help?' His ego's so big, he sent his fiancée to beg his former girlfriend to arrange his wedding. How weak is that?"

Pretty weak. "Not another word."

Derek sat up a little straighter. Yellow rolled across his eyes and vanished. That wasn't normal.

I pulled Slayer from its sheath and ran my finger along its length. The opaque, almost white metal of the saber nipped at me with faint magic teeth. Definitely a flare. Shapeshifters had trouble controlling their emotions during the flare. Great, just great. Perhaps Curran could be emotionally detached about this wedding problem? Ha! Who was I kidding?

"You look good," I told Derek.

"Thanks."

"You never come to visit me, though. Are you in trouble?"

"No. Is the room secure?"

"You're in a Chapter house of the Order. You can't get more secure."

He reached behind him and pushed the door closed. "I've come to extend a petition from the Pack."

I don't want to work with Curran, I don't want to work with Curran, I don't want to work with Curran. "I'm sorry, I didn't hear that right. I thought you said the Pack wanted my help?"

"Yes." Little tiny sparks danced in his eyes. "We were screwed and he didn't even kiss us first."

"How tacky of him. And this 'he' would be?"

"We aren't sure," Derek said carefully. "But you have his bolt on your desk."

I leaned forward. "Do tell."

"Let's just say that this morning one of our teams was jumped by a man using this specific type of bolt. He has stolen Pack property and we want it back."

"Aha. Why me?" The last time I checked, the Pack preferred to take care of their own problems. Hell, they didn't even admit to having problems most of the time.

"Because you have contacts we don't." Derek permitted himself a small smile. "And because if we start turning the city inside out looking for this person, certain parties will wonder why and the rather embarrassing facts of the theft might come to light. We don't want to air our dirty laundry in public. The Order always helped us without undue publicity."

Great. The battle was lost. Greg was the only person within the Order who had earned the Pack's trust. Now since he was dead and I had earned Friend of the Pack status, that trust naturally extended to me. The Order wanted to keep an eye on the Pack, I knew that much. Something told me the knights would view this petition as a wonderful opportunity to do just that.

"What did the crossbowman take?"

Derek hesitated.

"Derek, I'm not going to hunt I don't know whom to retrieve I don't know what. What did he take?"

"He jumped a survey team and took the maps."

I almost whistled, except that my Russian father would have risen from his grave and smacked me for whistling indoors. The Pack maps, legendary in quality, precise, up-to-date, with all the new neighborhoods and power zones clearly marked, every alley explored, every place of interest indicated.

I knew at least a half a dozen people who'd give their left nut
for a chance to photocopy the bloody things.

"He must have balls," I said.

"He did look male."

"Description?"

"Very fast."

"That's it? That's all you got?"

"Very good shot."

I sighed. "Who did he shoot?"

"Jim."

Oh shit. "Is he okay?"

"He was shot four times in less than two seconds. He isn't
very happy about it. A bit tender in places. But generally he'll
be okay."

My brain put the pieces together. "After our mark went
down, Jim got a call from the survey team. The crossbowman
tailed Jim, jumped him, incapacitated the survey team, and
stole the maps."

Derek's face radiated all the joy of a man biting into a
lime.

One hell of a trick, tailing my former partner. "Just out of
curiosity, how many people are in a survey team?"

"Four."

Five with Jim. "And you let him get away?"

"He just disappeared."

"I guess the shapeshifters' sense of smell isn't what it used
to be."

"No, Kate, you don't understand. He vanished. He was
there one moment and then he was gone."

I couldn't resist. "Like a ninja. In a puff of smoke."

"Yes."

"So you want me to track down a supernaturally fast sniper
who can disappear into thin air, retrieve your maps, and do it
so nobody finds out what I'm doing or why?"

"Exactly."

I sighed. "I'll get the paperwork."

CHAPTER 3

WHEN YOU DON'T KNOW WHAT TO DO NEXT, GO back to the beginning. I had no name, no description, and no place to start looking for the mysterious sniper, so I figured the garage where Jeremy almost toasted us was my best bet. Since the magic was determined to fluctuate and I didn't fancy being stranded, I decided to take a horse from the Order's stables, located a block away.

Turned out I wasn't the only person who had noticed the magic craziness. The stables were nearly empty, and all my regular choices were out. I entered on foot and left atop a red molly. Her name was Ninny, she was fifteen hands tall, and as she braved the downtown traffic with nary a twitch, I began to see the wisdom of mule breeding.

The shortest route to the garage lay along Interstate 85 through the heart of the city. In happier times, the view from the highway must have been breathtaking. Now both Downtown and Midtown lay in ruins, battered to near rubble by the magic waves. Twisted steel skeletons of once mighty skyscrapers jutted like bleached fossil bones from the debris. Here and there a lone half-eaten survivor struggled to remain upright, all but its last few stories destroyed. Shattered glass from hundreds of windows glittered among chunks of concrete.

Unable or unwilling to clear the rubble, the city grew around it. Small stalls and stands had sprung up here and there along the twelve-lane highway, selling everything from fake monster eggs to state-of-the-art miniature palmtops and precision firearms. The palmtops rarely worked even when tech was in full swing, and the monsters sometimes hatched.

Horses, mules, camels, and bizarre vehicles all attempted to negotiate the crowded road, blending into a huge multicolored crocodile of travelers, and I rode within it, bathed in the animal smells, choking on automobile exhaust, and assaulted by gaggles of vendors each trying to scream themselves hoarse.

"Potions, potions, cure for arthritis . . ."

". . . the best! First two are free . . ."

". . . water purifier. Save hundreds of dollars a year . . ."

". . . beef jerky!"

Beef. I bet.

Twenty minutes later we left the highway's noise behind by way of a wooden ramp and trudged down into a tangle of streets collectively known as the Warren.

Bordered by Lakewood Park on one side and Southview Cemetery on the other, the Warren stretched all the way to McDonough Boulevard. A few decades ago, the area had been included in the South Urban Renewal project, its layout redesigned to accommodate several large, sturdy apartment complexes and new two- and three-story office buildings.

In the years since the Shift, when the first magic wave hit the world, the Warren had grown poorer, tougher, and more segregated. For reasons unknown, magic displayed a selective appetite. It chewed some buildings into rubble, while leaving others completely intact. Walking through the area now was like trying to make your way through a war zone postbombing, with some houses reduced to refuse, while their neighbors stood untouched.

The garage where Jeremy had lost his life sat sandwiched between a bank and an abandoned Catholic church. Three stories high and three stories deep, stained with soot and missing its roof, the garage jutted like a burned-out match of a building. I dismounted and tied Ninny to a metal beam protruding from the wall. Nobody in their right mind would try to steal a molly with the Order's crest branded on its butt. The Order had a nasty habit of magic-tagging their property and there was nothing the street life disliked more than finding a couple of knights full of righteous anger on their doorstep.

Inside the garage, the air smelled of chalky powder, the familiar dry scent of concrete turned into dust by the magic's ever-grinding wheels. I took the stairs down to the bottom floor. The spiraling levels of the garage had crumbled in places, letting enough light filter down to dilute the darkness to a weak gloom. The stench of sulfur nipped at my nostrils.

I found the big black stain on the wall and backtracked from there, until I came to Jeremy's headless body. The Gray Squad must have been overloaded with cadavers this morning—they should have taken his body to the morgue by now.

I walked the perimeter of the room until I found the fissure in the wall we had seen last night. I stuck my head into it: dark and narrow, smelling of damp clay. Most likely this was the way the bowman had escaped.

I pulled my saber out and ducked into the tunnel.

BEING UNDERGROUND WAS NEVER ON MY "THINGS to do for fun" list. Being underground in the dark for what seemed like an hour, with dirt crumbling onto my head, walls rubbing my shoulders, and a sniper possibly waiting on the other side ranked right up there with getting a face full of giant toad vomit. I had only gone up against a giant toad once, and the nightmares still made me gag.

The tunnel turned. I squeezed around the bend and saw light. Finally. I stood still, listening. No metallic click of a safety being released. No voices.

I approached the light and froze. A huge chasm carved the ground before me. At least a mile wide and close to a quarter mile deep, it started a couple of yards from my feet and stretched forth for a good two miles, veering left, its end lost behind the bend. Piles of metal refuse lay in heaps along its bottom, giving slope to sheer walls. Here and there clusters of thick metal spikes punctured the trash. Razor sharp and shiny, they curved upright like the claws of some enormous buried bear, rising to three times my height. Above this baby Grand Canyon, two tall storklike birds surfed the air currents, circling the gorge as if they rode an invisible aerial calliope.

Where the hell was I?

Below, at the very bottom of the chasm, a large metal structure slumped among the iron debris. From this angle, it looked like some giant with a sweet tooth had gotten ahold of a metal hangar and squeezed its sides to see if there was cream filling inside. If I needed a place to hide, I'd be in that hangar.

One of the birds swooped in my direction. A bright spark broke from its orange wings and plummeted down, slicing into the ground a few feet below with a heavy metallic clang. I negotiated the knot of crooked rusty pipes and climbed over to where it had fallen. A feather. A perfectly shaped bird feather, red at the root and tinted with emerald green at the edge. I flicked my fingers at the shaft. It chimed. Holy crap. Solid metal, shaped like a knife and sharp like a scalpel. A feather of a Stymphalean bird.

I pulled my knife out of its sheath on my belt and pried the feather out, managing not to cut myself. A bird straight out of Greek mythos. At least it wasn't a harpy. I stuck the knife into a spare loop on my belt, slid the feather into the sheath, and started down the slope. Mythological creatures tended to occur in bunches: if there was a Russian leshii in the forest, in the nearest pond you'd likely find a Russian vodyanoi. If there was a Greek bird in the air, some Greek critter would surely jump me in a moment. If my luck held, it wouldn't be a handsome Greek demigod looking for the love of his life or at least his love of a couple of hours. No, it would be something nasty, like Cerberus or a Gorgona Medusa. I gave the hangar a suspicious glance. For all I knew it was crammed full of people growing snakes instead of hair.

Midway down the slope, the Universe treated me to another magic wave. The wind brought a whiff of an acrid, bitter stench. In the distance something thumped like a sledgehammer hitting a drum with mind-numbing regularity: *whoom, whoom, whoom*.

Five minutes later, sweaty and covered in rust stains, I reached the hangar. Soft voices filtered through the metal walls. I couldn't make out the words, but someone was inside.

I put my ear against the wall.

"What 'bout my mom?" A thin, high-pitched voice. A young girl, probably an adolescent.

"I gotta split." Slightly deeper, male. Heard it somewhere before.

"You promised!"

"The magic's cresting, okay? Gotta split."

Young voices. A boy and a girl, talking street.

The only available door hung crooked and would make noise when I tried to open it.

I kicked the door in and walked inside.

The hangar was empty, save for a huge heap of broken wooden crates. Sunlight punched into the building through the holes in the roof. The hangar had no floor, its dented metal frame resting on packed dirt. In the very center of the dirt sat a perfect ring of barely visible white stones. The stones shimmered weakly, wanting very much to be invisible, trying to slide out of sight into nothing.

An environmental ward. A good one, too.

"Anybody home?"

A kid stepped out from behind the crates, dangling a dead rat by its tail. He was short, starved, and filthy. Ragged clothes, patched, torn, and patched again, hung off his skinny adolescent frame. His brown hair stuck out in all directions like the needles on a hysterical hedgehog. He raised his right hand, fingering a knotted hemp cord, from which dangled a dozen bones, feathers and beads. His shoulders were bony, his arms thin, yet he stared at me with unmistakable defiance. It took me less than a second to recall that stare.

"Red," I said. "Fancy meeting you here."

The recognition crept into his eyes. He lowered his hand. "Sokay," he called. "I know her."

A dirty head poked above the tower of crates and a thin girl climbed into view. Ten, maybe eleven, she had the waifish sort of look that had little to do with her petite frame and everything to do with being underfed. A wispy cloud of grimy hair framed her narrow face, making the deep circles around her eyes seem even deeper. She looked tainted with adult skepticism, but not beaten yet. Life had abused her and now she bit all hands first and looked to see if they offered food later. Her hand clutched a large knife and her eyes told me she would be willing to use it.

"Who are you?" she asked me.

"She's a merc," Red said.

He reached inside his shirt and pulled out a stack of papers, held together by a string. He dug in it with dirty fingers and deposited a small rectangle in my hand. My business card, stained with the brown whorls of a thumbprint. The print was mine; the blood belonged to Derek, my werewolf boy wonder.

Derek and I had been trying to drag ourselves home after a big fight that hadn't gone too well. Unfortunately, Derek's legs had been torn open and Lyc-V, the virus to which shapeshifters owed their existence, decided to shut Derek down so it could make repairs. When we met Red, I was trying unsuccessfully to load my bleeding, unconscious sidekick onto my horse. Red and his little band of shaman kids helped, and I had given Red my card and a promise of help if he should need it.

"You said you'd help. You owe me."

Now was not a good time, but we didn't often get to choose the time to repay our debts. "That's true."

"Guard Julie." He turned to the girl. "Shadow her, sokay." He darted to the side and out the door. I followed and saw him scrambling up the slope like a pack of wolves was snapping at his heels.

CHAPTER 4

"BASTARD!" THE GIRL YELLED. "I HATE YOU!"

"Any clue why he took off in a hurry?"

"No!" She sat down cross-legged on the crates, her face a picture of abject misery.

Alrighty then. "I take it you're Julie."

"You're real smart. Did you figure it out all by yourself?"

I sighed. At least she had dropped out of street speak for my benefit.

"Just because my boyfriend thinks you're all that, doesn't mean I'm going to listen to you. How are you going to guard me? You don't even have a gun."

"I don't need a gun." A small hint of metallic sheen within the crates caught my eye. I approached the pile. "Any clue what I'm guarding you from?"

"Nope!"

I peered into the space between the crates. A broken bolt, stuck tight in a board. Blood-red shaft. The fletch was missing, but I bet it had three black feathers. My bowman had been here and had left his calling card.

"What are you doing?" she asked.

"Hunting."

"Hunting what?"

I wandered to the ring of stones, crouched, and reached for the nearest rock. My fingers slipped through it. Whoever set this ward really didn't want his hiding spot disturbed. But the trouble with wards was that sometimes they didn't just hide. They also contained. And a ward of this caliber could contain something nasty. "Where are we?"

"What are you, retarded?"

I looked at her for a second. "I came through a tunnel from the Warren. I don't know what neighborhood this is."

"This is the Honeycomb Gap. Used to be Southside Park. It pulls metal to itself now. Gathers the iron from all over—Blair Village, Gilbert Heights, Plunket Town. Pulls it all into itself, the iron from all the factories, from the Ford Motor plant, cars from Joshua Junkyards . . . The Honeycomb's right above us. Can't you smell the stink?"

The Honeycomb. Of all the hellholes, it had to be the Honeycomb.

"What are you doing here?" I asked.

She stuck her nose in the air. "I don't have to tell you."

"Suit yourself."

I pulled Slayer from its sheath.

"Whoa." Julie crawled forward on top of the crate tower and flopped on her stomach so she could get a better look.

I put my hand on Slayer's blade. Magic nipped at my skin, piercing my flesh with sharp little needles. I fed a little of my magic into the metal, aimed the tip of the saber toward the stone, and pushed. Two inches from the rock a force clutched at Slayer's tip. Thin tendrils of pale vapor curled from the sword and the magicked steel began to perspire. I gave it a little more of my power. Slayer gained another half inch and stopped.

"I'm looking for my mom," Julie said. "She didn't come home on Friday. She is a witch. In a coven."

Probably not a professional coven. The daughters of professional witches had more meat on their bones and better clothes. No, most likely it was an amateur coven. Women from the poor side deluding themselves with visions of power and a better life.

"What's the name of the coven?"

"The Sisters of the Crow."

Definitely an amateur coven. No legitimate witch would name a coven something so generic. Mythology was full of crows. With magic, you made sure to cross all your t's and dot your i's. The more specific, the better.

"They met here," Julie volunteered.

"Right here?" I fed a little more power to the sword. It didn't bulge.

"Yeah."

"Did you ask the other witches about where your mom might have gone?"

"Gee, I'd love to, except none of them came back."

I paused. "None?"

"Nope."

That wasn't good. Entire covens didn't just disappear into thin air.

"I'm going to break this ward. If something ugly comes out of there, run. Don't talk to it, don't look at it. Just run. You got me?"

"Sure." Julie's tone plainly pointed out that she'd have to be crazy to listen to some idiot woman who doesn't even have a gun.

I dug my feet into the ground and pushed, putting all of my weight behind the hilt. The blade quivered under the strain. It was like trying to push a baseball into a wall of dense rubber, but giving the saber more power would leave me too drained to defend myself against a magic attack.

Sweat broke on my forehead. Oh, screw it.

I shot my power through the blade. With a sweet whisper, Slayer cleaved through the invisible barrier. Steel struck stone with a loud clang and the white rock slid an inch out of its place.

A shudder ran through the circle. The stones blinked into reality and I scrambled to my feet. Brilliant light rippled through the air above the broken ring, a silvery aurora borealis gone mad as the forces held captive in the ward flailed, unleashed. The glow flared and streamed to the ground in a torrent of pure white. The ward burst. The magic aftershock pulsed through the building and caught me in a dizzying whirlpool. My teeth chattered, my knees shook, and I clutched at Slayer's hilt, trying to keep the saber from slipping from my trembling fingers. Julie cried out.

So much power . . .

Viscous drops slid from Slayer's metal, evaporating in midfall. I felt it too, a fetid smear staining the building—the magic of undeath. There was enough of it to make a layman vomit. I turned to the circle. A dark hole gaped in the broken ring of the stones. I leaned over the edge and glanced into the black hole, grimacing at the reek of rotting flesh emanating from the moist earth.

Deep.

So deep I didn't see the bottom.

The walls of the shaft were smooth and even, punctuated by roots severed cleanly at the edge. The hole stank of damp soil and moldering bodies. I picked up one of the stones and ran my thumb over its smooth surface. Rounded and pale, like a pebble from a river bed.

No mark, no glyph, no sign of a spell. Just a ring of white stones that no longer hid a bottomless hole in the earth. The Sisters must have let something into the world, something dark and evil and it claimed them for its own.

Julie sucked in her breath. A corona of dark spills appeared around the hole. With a faint buzz, a fly landed on the nearest stain, closely followed by another. Blood. Impossible to say how much—the ground had soaked up most of it. As I looked at the blood circle, I noticed three impressions in the ground, each a small, roughly square hole in the dirt. I connected them in my head and got an equilateral triangle with the pit smack in the middle. Three staffs arranged in a triangle to summon something? If so, where did they go?

The heap of crates behind the hole shivered, as if about to melt with Julie on top of it. With a faint magic tremor, a skeleton materialized right below the kid, nailed to the crates by four crossbow bolts.

"Freaky," Julie said.

No kidding. For one, the skeleton had too many ribs, but only five pairs attached to the sternum. For another, not a shred of tissue remained on the yellowed bones. If I hadn't known better, I would've said it had weathered a year or two in the open somewhere. I leaned closer to examine the arms. Shallow bone sockets. I was no expert, but I'd guess this thing could have bent its elbows backward. At the same time, I'd probably dislocate its hips with one kick.

"Your mom ever mention anything like this?"

"No."

The bolts anchoring the skeleton were red and fletched with black feathers. One punctured the skeleton through the left eye socket, two went through the ribs on the left, where the heart would be if it was human, and one between the legs. Precision shooting at its best. Just to make sure the odd humanoid aberration doesn't get away, always pin it through the nuts.

I grabbed a crate from the pile, planted it in front of the skeleton, and climbed atop it to get a better look. Fewer of the neck vertebrae fused than normal, which provided for a greater flexibility of the neck, but made it fragile. No incisors, no canines, either. Instead I saw three rows of teeth, long, conical, sharp, used to puncture something struggling and keep it in the mouth.

The crate snapped under me with a loud pop. I dropped with all the grace of a potato sack, grabbing at the skeleton on the way down. My fingers passed through the bone and snagged a bolt. I landed on my ass in a pile of shards, the shaft in my hand and light powder on my fingers.

A hole gaped in the skeleton's left side, between the third and fourth rib. It held for a second, grew, melting, and then the entire skeleton imploded into dust. The dust outline lingered in the air for a moment, taunting me, before melting into the breeze. "Shit!" There goes my evidence. Smooth, Kate, real smooth.

"Was this supposed to happen?" Julie asked.

"No," I growled.

A round of enthusiastic applause echoed behind me. I jumped to my feet. A man stood leaning against the wall. He wore a leather jacket that wanted very much to be leather armor. The business end of a crossbow protruded over his left shoulder.

Hello, Mr. Bowman.

"Good form!" he said, clapping. "And a lovely landing!"

"Julie," I said, keeping my voice level, "stay put."

"No need to worry," Bowman said. "I wouldn't hurt the little lass. Not unless I had to. And maybe if I was really hungry and there was nothing else to eat. But then she's so thin, I'd be picking out bones from between my teeth all day. Hardly worth the trouble."

I couldn't tell if he was kidding. "You want something?"

"Just came to see who troubled my bolts. And what do I find? A mouse." He winked at Julie. "And a woman."

He said "woman" in the same way I'd say "Mmmmm, yummy chocolate" after waking up from hunger pains and finding a Hershey bar in an empty refrigerator. I flicked my sword and backed away a bit so the hole would be to my right. If he knocked me into it, it would take me a long time to climb out.

The man approached. He stood tall, at least six three, maybe six four. Broad shoulders. Long legs in black pants. His black hair fell in a tangled mess on his shoulders. It looked like he might've cut it himself with a knife and then tied a leather cord across his forehead to keep it somewhat pinned. I looked at his face. Handsome bastard. Defined jaw, chiseled cheekbones, full lips. Eyes like black fire. The kind of eyes that jumped from a woman's dreams right into her morning and made trouble in the marriage bed.

He gave me a feral grin. "Like what you see, dove?"

"Nope." I hadn't had sex in eighteen months. Pardon me while I struggle with my hormone overload.

Shave that jaw, brush the hair, tone down the crazy in the eyes, and he would have to fight women off with that crossbow. As it was he looked like he prowled in dark places where the wild things were and they all ran away when they smelled him coming. Any woman with a drop of sense would grab her knife and cross the street when she saw him.

"Don't worry. I won't hurt you," he promised, circling me.

"I'm not worried." I began to circle, too.

"You should be."

"First you say I should, then you say I shouldn't. Make up your mind."

Drops of water slid down his jacket. Judging by the light stabbing through the holes in the roof, the sky was clear. No hint of moisture in the air. Suppose Derek's intel was right. Suppose he did teleport. How would I keep him from disappearing?

The man spread his arms. I didn't like the way he moved, either, light on his feet.

"What's with the cute shoelace on your head?"

"What this?" He flicked the end of the cord with his finger.

"Yeah. Rambo called, he wants his bandana back."

"This Rambo, he a friend of yours?"

"Who's Rambo?" Julie asked.

If a cultural reference flies over a man's head, does it make a sound if nobody else gets it? I had never managed to watch the whole movie—magic always interfered, but I had read the book. Maybe after the flare cut out and tech reasserted its dominance for a few weeks, I'd dig the minidisc out and watch the darn thing from start to finish.

The bowman took a step, and I pointed Slayer's business end in his direction. "No closer."

He took another baby step forward. "Sorry, my foot slipped." Another step. "Sorry, just can't keep the bloody buggers under control."

"Next one will be your last."

He rocked forward and I almost lunged.

"Uh-uh-uh." He shook his head in mock disappointment. "I didn't actually step, see."

Julie snickered.

He raised his hand in a peaceful gesture. "You need to relax a bit, dove. Like Mouse over there. You trust me, don't you, Mouse?"

"Nope!"

"Ahhh, I'm hurt. Nobody likes me."

I knew he'd move a fraction of a breath before he started. Those eyes gave him away. He lunged, missed, and found Slayer's tip at his back.

"Move, and I'll cut your liver in half."

He spun toward me, and my saber glanced off metal. Chain

mail under the jacket. Crap. Steel fingers clamped my sword hand, keeping it pinned. He turned and stabbed the rigid fingers of his right hand under my breastbone. I shied away from the stab to lessen the impact—it still hurt like hell—and grabbed his right wrist, jerking him toward me. For a second all of his weight rested on his left leg and I kicked it out from under him. He crashed to the floor and dragged me down with him, his fist locked on my sword hand. I hit the ground, letting go of Slayer. My hand slipped between his fingers and I rolled into the clear.

Half a breath later we were both on our feet.

"Pretty sword," he said, twisting Slayer to catch a sun ray. The light danced on the opaque blade and sank into the black chain-mail shirt now showing below his jacket. "Why no guard?"

"Don't need one."

"Is it any good?"

I kicked a strip of leather I'd sliced off. "You tell me."

His hand went back to check his chain shirt, and I kicked him, aiming for the throat. He caught my foot with a grunt, and dumped me on the floor. His knee pressed on my neck. He'd set a trap and I'd walked right into it. The light was shrinking. I could barely breathe.

"You kick like a mule." He grimaced and ground his knee harder. I wasn't getting enough air. He had my right hand pinned, but not my left. I bent my left hand, and a cold sliver of the silver needle slid into my palm from the leather wristband. "But I've been at this a lot longer . . ."

I drove the silver needle into his thigh.

His thigh muscle contracted. He grunted and fell off me. I leaped to my feet and kicked him in the face. It was a solid kick and it connected. He sprawled on his back, blood running from his nose. I dropped next to him, slid my leg under his arm, and clenched it with my other leg, bending the arm backward in a classic shoulder lock. He growled. All I had to do was scissor my legs, and I'd dislocate his arm, and I still had both hands free.

I zipped his jacket open, looking for the maps.

"Wrong zipper," he gasped. "Try lower."

"In your dreams." I reached into the inner pocket and pulled a plastic pack free. The maps. "Stealing's a crime. Thank you for returning the Pack's property. Your cooperation has been noted."

He looked me straight in the face, smiled, and vanished.

I scrambled to my feet. The red bolt punctured the dirt between my feet, catching me on the way up. I straightened very slowly.

He stood a few feet away, pointing the crossbow at me. It was loaded. The hand-sharpened bolt head stared me in the eye. I couldn't dodge a crossbow bolt from nine feet away. Not even on my best day.

"Hands where I can see them," he ordered. I showed him my palms, the Pack maps still securely clutched in my right hand.

"You cheated!" Julie's outraged voice rang from above. "Leave her alone!"

His nose no longer looked broken. No blood, either. Wonderful. Not only could he teleport, but he also regenerated while he did it. If he started spitting fire, we'd be all set.

Keeping his crossbow leveled, he reached down to his thigh and pulled my needle out with a wince. "That hurt."

"Serves you right," Julie yelled.

"I suppose you're rooting for her?"

Julie's eyebrows rose in trademark adolescent scorn. "Duuuuuuuh."

"Don't make me come up there." Steel vibrated in his voice and Julie ducked behind the crates.

"Leave the kid alone," I told him.

"Jealous? Want me all to yourself?" He jerked the crossbow right a little. "Turn around."

I turned my back to him, expecting the bite of a steel bolt head between my shoulder blades any moment. "Very nice," he said. "Turn around again."

I turned around to see him frowning. "I can't decide if I like the back view or the front one best."

"How about a view of my sword up very close?"

"That's my line, dove."

His leer left no doubt as to the meaning of his "line."

"Turn around again. That's a good girl."

I heard him walk toward me. *That's right, come closer. I'm very helpless. With my hands held up and everything.*

"Nothing funny," his voice warned in my ear. "Or next time I pop in, I'll pin your lass to those crates."

I clenched my teeth and stood still.

"You broke my ward. I'm put out—those bitches are hard to pin down and now I'll have to do it again. I should put a bolt through your neck." His fingers brushed the back of my neck, sending shivers down my spine. "But I'm a nice guy. I'll give you a piece of advice instead: gather your kid and go home. I'll even let you take the maps back to the furries, since you fought so hard for them. Stay out of my way from now on. This isn't your fight and you're in over your head."

"What fight? With whom? Who are you?"

"I'm Bran. The hero."

"The hero? Humility is a virtue."

"So is patience. And if you're patient and lucky, you might just be the girl I bed on my last night in town."

His hand squeezed my ass. I spun about, intending to punch him in the nose. The hangar lay empty, except for the gossamer trail of mist. It lingered for a long breath and then dissipated into the breeze.

I battled a very strong urge to kick something.

Julie stared at me from the crates. "He went poof."

"Yes, he did."

"He likes you. He grabbed your butt."

"Next time I see him, I'll cut his arm off. We'll see if he can grow it back."

I glanced to where the skeleton once hung. The bolts were missing. How the hell did he manage that?

All my precious evidence was gone. I didn't even have a chance to m-scan the scene to get a fix on what kind of magic was used. All in all, this had not gone very well. I didn't have a clue as to what was going on, and I'd just had a conversation with the guy who could explain everything and learned absolutely nothing. Except for the fact that I had a shapely ass. Healthy self-esteem is a good thing. If I didn't have any, I'd be beating my own stupid head against the first available hard surface.

"Are you leaving now?" Julie asked from the crates.

Hell no. Nothing that involved several women missing, a bottomless pit ringed in blood, and an inhuman skeleton could possibly amount to something benign. And Mr. Grab-ass apparently wanted to keep me as far away from it as possible. I wondered why.

"You want to find your mom?"

"Yeah."

"Do you want my help?"

"Sure."

"You know who was the head witch in the coven?"

"Esmeralda."

Esmeralda. Oh boy. "Where does she live?"

"The Honeycomb."

This just got better and better. "Climb down. We're going to pay her a visit."

CHAPTER 5

WE CLIMBED UP THE SCRAP-METAL EVEREST, WITH
me leading the way and Julie slightly behind. Her breath was
coming in ragged gasps. Too little food. Julie wasn't much
stronger than a mosquito. In fact, if a big one rammed her, she
might fall over. She didn't complain, though.

About halfway up the slope she finally gave in. "How far?"

"Keep climbing."

"I just want to know how far!"

"Don't make me turn this car around, missy."

"What does that even mean?" She mumbled something
else under her breath but kept moving.

The edge of the Gap crept closer. The rhythmic *whoom*,
whoom, *whoom* grew louder. Had to be a beacon of some sort.
I climbed onto the narrow ledge and reached for Julie. "Give
me your hand."

She stretched a matchstick arm. I grabbed her wrist and
raised her over the jagged remains of the refrigerator onto the
ledge next to me. She weighed next to nothing. "We'll take a
little break."

"I can keep going."

"I'm sure you can. But Honeycomb isn't a nice place. By
now someone probably knows we're here and they have a welcoming committee prepared."

"Oh boy! They'll throw us a party!" She sat in the dirt.

Heh. I sat next to her. "You're not from there, by any
chance?"

She shook her head. "No. I'm from White Street."

White Street got its name during the snowfall of '14, which

refused to melt for three and a half years. When a street can hold three inches of powder despite the hundred degree heat, you know it's packing some serious magic. Anybody who could afford to move did.

"How old are you?"

"Thirteen. I'm only two years behind Red."

Looking at her, I would've guessed eleven tops. "How old is your mother? What does she look like?"

"She is thirty-five and she looks like me only grown up. I have a picture at home."

"So what do you know about the coven? Who did they worship? What sort of rituals did they do?"

Julie shrugged. In front of us the gorge stretched into the distance, bristling with spikes and rusty iron. Thin tendrils of mist clung to the steep slope. A deep threatening growl echoed from the walls, too far to be a threat. The Stymphalean birds answered it with their screeches.

"Did you know the birds are metal?" Julie said.

I nodded. "They're Greek. You know who Hercules was?"

"Yeah. The strongest man."

"When he was young, he had to go through twelve challenges . . ."

"Why?"

"His dad's wife made him temporarily insane. He killed his family and had to atone by serving a king. The king very much wanted to kill him so he kept thinking up more and more difficult challenges for Hercules. Anyway, the Stymphalean birds were one of the challenges. He had to drive them away from a certain lake. Their feathers are like arrows and their beaks are supposed to pierce the strongest armor."

She looked at me. "How did he do it?"

"The gods made him some loud clapper things. He wrapped himself in the skin of an invulnerable lion and made noise until the birds flew away."

"Why is it in those stories that the gods always pull your butt out of trouble?"

I got up. "It helps if the king of the gods is your dad. Come on. We've got to climb and I'm pretty sure your dad isn't a god, is he?"

"He died," she said.

"I'm sorry. My dad is dead, too. Now climb, young grasshopper, so your kung fu won't be weak."

She braved a crumpled barrel. "You are so weird."

You have no idea.

TWENTY FEET BELOW THE LIP OF THE GAP, I FELT THE Honeycomb. Above us magic twisted and streamed, boiling in a chaotic frenzy, its intensity spiking hot enough to scald. The magic field felt me and spilled over the edge, sending thin currents toward me like invisible lassos. They licked me and fell short. That's right. No touching.

The magic waited, almost as if it were aware. Up top, where it boiled, I would create one hell of a resonance and that was never a good thing. The Honeycomb couldn't touch me, but it didn't like me and it would keep trying. The sooner I got out of there, the better.

I climbed over a water heater, twisted and crushed like an aluminum can, and pulled myself over the edge. Before me the bloated trailers, contorted and rippling with strange metallic bumps, clung to one another. Some had merged into hives, some three trailers high, and a couple joined ones looked identical, like two cells caught in the middle of mitosis. A few sat on top of each other, hanging at precarious angles yet apparently steady. Long clotheslines ran between the trailers and freshly washed garments flapped in the breeze.

I pulled Julie up. She winced as the magic smashed against her body. The currents wound about her . . . and calmed. It was as if she suddenly wasn't there. Interesting kid.

"You been here before?"

She shook her head. "Not this deep."

"Walk where I walk. Stay away from the walls. Especially if you see them get fuzzy."

We started through the labyrinth of trailers. A long time ago the Honeycomb was a mobile park retirement community called Happy Trails or some such. It sat just under the Brown Mills Golf Course, across the Jonesboro Road. At first it had survived the magic waves pretty well, and when the cheap project apartments east of it crumbled and split, a slow but steady trickle of homeless refugees filled the mobile park. They pitched tents on the manicured lawns, bathed in the communal pool, and cooked on the outdoor grills. The cops chased out the squatters, but they just kept coming.

Then one night the magic hit especially hard, and the manufactured homes warped. Some expanded like glass bubbles, some twisted, others stuck together merging into hives. More yet divided and grew additions, and when the dust finally settled, a fifth of the inhabitants had vanished into the walls. To the *Outside*. Nobody could ever figure out what the *Outside* was, but it was definitely not anywhere in the normal world. The retirees fled, but the refugees had nowhere to go. They moved into the trailers and stayed put. Once in a while somebody would disappear, as each new magic tide twisted the Honeycomb a little more. A fun place to live if you were into that sort of thing.

"How can we find out where Esmeralda lives?" Julie puffed behind me. "I only know she lives in the Honeycomb. I don't know where exactly."

"You hear that whooming? The Honeycomb changes all the time so they have to have some sort of beacon. It's probably at the entrance, which should be guarded by somebody. We're going to go there and ask nicely where Esmeralda lived."

"What makes you think they'll tell us?"

"Because I'll pay them."

"Oh."

And because if they don't tell me, I will pull out my Order ID and my saber and make myself very hard to ignore.

I wasn't wild about heading into the Honeycomb with a little girl in tow, but considering the neighborhood, she was safer with me than without me. I wondered how she got down there in the first place . . .

"How did you get down into the Gap?"

"We hiked from the Warren. There's a trail." A little light went off in her eyes. "But I probably can't find it now. So if you send me back, I'll just wander around without any water or food."

Why me?

The street turned slightly, bringing us into view of wide-open chain-link gates. Just in front of them a man in faded jeans and a leather vest worn over his bare chest sat on an overturned oil drum. An unlit cigarette drooped from his lips. To the left of him sat an old military truck, its back end pointing toward the gate. Despite rust stains and dents, the truck's tires and canvas top looked to be in good condition. The canvas probably hid some heavy-duty hardware, a Gatling gun or a small siege engine.

On the other side of the man sat a huge rectangular tank. Soft emerald-green algae stained the glass walls, obscuring the murky water within. A long section of metal pipe stretched from the tank and disappeared beneath the twisted remains of a trailer.

The man on the drum leveled a crossbow at me. The crossbow looked a lot like a good old-fashioned, flat-sided Flemish arbalest. The prong gleamed with the bluish-gray shade particular to steel, not the brighter, pale aluminum of cheaper bows, meaning the bow's draw weight probably ranged to two hundred pounds. He could put a bolt into me from seventy-five yards away and he wanted me to know that.

Whoom. Whoom.

An arbalest was a decent weapon, but slow on reload.

The man eyed me. "You want something?" The cigarette remained stuck to his lower lip, moving as he spoke.

"I'm an agent of the Order investigating the disappearance of witches belonging to the Sisters of the Crow coven. I was told the head witch lived in the Honeycomb."

"And who is that?" He pointed to Julie behind me.

"Daughter of a witch in Esmeralda's coven. Her mom's missing. You wouldn't know anything about that, would you?"

"No. You got an ID on you?"

I reached for the leather wallet I carried on a cord around

my neck and took out my Order ID. He motioned me closer. I
approached and passed it to him. He turned it over. The small
rectangle of silver in the lower right corner of the card
gleamed, catching a stray ray of the sun.

"Is that real silver?" he asked. The cigarette drew an elaborate pattern in the air.

"Yes." Silver took enchantment better than most metals.

The man gave me a quick glance and rubbed at the silver
through the clear plastic coating. "How much is it worth?"

Here we go. "You're asking the wrong question."

"Oh yeah?"

"You should be asking if your life is worth a square inch of
enchanted silver."

He gave the card another cursory glance. "You talk big."

I snapped my hand at his face. He shied back and I handed
his cigarette back to him. "These things can kill you."

He stuck the cigarette back into his mouth and returned my
ID. "Name's Custer."

"Kate Daniels."

The canvas shielding the truck shifted, revealing a lean
Latino woman next to a black cheiroballista. Built like a giant
crossbow, the cheiroballista was small but accurate and delivered with amazing power. It could put a bolt through a vehicle
door at close range. The Latino woman gave me a hard stare.
She had the kind of eyes one gets after life hammered out all
softness.

I held her gaze. Two can play the staring game. "I'll pay for
the information."

"Hundred."

I passed two fifties to Custer. Bye-bye, phone bill.

"Trailer twenty-three," she said. "The yellow one. Head
left, then turn right when the path forks."

"If I have to take anything, I'll write a receipt."

"That's between you and her. We don't want any shit from
the Order."

I held another twenty out. "Know anything about Esmeralda?"

The woman nodded. "She was power hungry. Liked to

scare people. I heard she tried to enter one of the older covens, but she played the game too much and tried to take over, so they kicked her out. She's been threatening to 'show them all' ever since. Last I heard she made her own coven. Don't know how she managed that—she wasn't well liked."

She took the twenty and pulled the canvas closed.

Custer tossed me a ball of telephone wire.

"Use it. Stuff changes around here. We get geeks down from the University of Georgia trying to study the 'phenomenon.' They go in and never come out." His eyes lit up with a wry spark. "Sometimes we hear them calling out in the walls. Looking for a way back from the *Outside*."

"Ever try to find them?"

"You're asking the wrong question," Custer's face split into a happy grin. The cigarette performed a pirouette. "The question you should be asking is what they look like when we do."

Oh boy. I tossed the wire back at him. "No thanks. I could hear that damned whooming even in death. What's making the noise?"

Custer reached over to the tank on his left and knocked on the glass. A dark shadow flickered in the tenebrous water. Something struck the far wall with a thud, and a huge head, as wide as a dinner plate, brushed against the glass. Mottled black and slimy like a toad's spine, it rubbed its blunt nose on the algae. Tiny black eyes stared dull and unseeing past me.

The head split in half revealing an enormous white mouth. The folds on the side of the head trembled, and a low sound rolled through the Honeycomb. *Whoom!* The creature scraped its broad nose against the glass once more and whirled, impossibly fast. I caught a glimpse of a clawed foot, a flash of a long muscled tail, and then it was gone, back into the churning water.

A Japanese salamander. Big one, as tall as Julie at least.

"Whomper," Custer said and waved me on with a dismissive flick of his hand.

CHAPTER 6

THE TWISTED PATH TOOK US DEEP INTO THE HON-
eycomb, into the maze of twisted trailers. As I passed, I
sensed people beyond the windows watching me. Nobody
came out to say hello. Nobody wanted to know what my business was. I had a feeling that if I stopped and asked for directions, I'd get no answer. If someone wanted to snipe me from
behind one of those misshapen funhouse-mirror windows,
there wasn't a hell of a lot I could do about it. Julie felt it, too.
She kept quiet and scurried in my footsteps, casting wary
looks at the trailers.

Ahead the path ran into a tall tower of debris and split,
flowing around it. The tower itself, a contorted monstrosity of
trash and metal junk, rose to nearly forty feet. Near the top it
tapered to a slender point merely five feet across before widening abruptly into an almost square platform. As I stopped to
gape at it, two furry animals the size of a cat but equipped
with long chinchilla tails and shrew snouts scuttled up the
rubble and vanished in some hidey-hole.

I kept moving, my thoughts returning again and again to
the hole in the ground at the Sisters' gathering place. The pit
bothered me. Any bottomless hole in the earth would bother
me, especially this close to a flare. I was afraid something had
come out of that hole and odds were, it wasn't friendly.

The Sisters of the Crow had broken the first rule of witch-
craft: don't dabble. Either do it right, or don't do it at all. Before one ever tried to cast a spell, one had to prepare for the
consequences.

Had they been worshipping the Goddess, an embodiment

of nature, a kind of all-purpose amalgam of benevolent female deities popular with cults, little harm would have come
to them. The Goddess, much like the Christian God, was too
all encompassing and benign. But they had worshipped the
crow, which pointed to something dark and very specific. And
the more specific the god, the less wiggle room its worshippers had. It was the difference between telling a child, "Don't
do anything bad while I'm gone" and "If you touch this vase,
I will ground you for three days."

Until I identified the crow, I had to fly blind. Unfortunately,
everyone from Vikings to Apaches had a corvid in their
mythology. Crows created or swallowed the world, delivered
messages for a handful of gods, served as prophets, played
tricks, and if they were Chinese, lived in the sun and had three
legs. Nothing at the site had pointed to any particular mythos.
Not even Bran—no accent, no meaningful peculiarities in
clothes, no nothing.

What I needed was a big fat clue. A mysterious note laying
it all out. A deity popping out of thin air and explaining it to
me. Hell, I'd settle for an annoying old lady with a knack for
solving mysteries.

I actually stopped and waited for a second to see if a clue
would fall out of the sky and land at my feet. The Universe de-
clined to oblige.

Trailer twenty-three stood twenty yards to the left of the
tower, the first story in a cluster of three trailers. Kindly described by the woman as "yellow," the trailer's color matched
that of cloudy overnight urine. It smelled like urine too, although I couldn't pinpoint whether the stink came from the
trailer itself or from the heaps of trash surrounding the cluster.

A series of runes in black and brown ran along the side of
the trailer. On closer look, the brown was uneven and flaking
off. Blood. I wondered what poor stray had to die for Esmeralda's lovely decorative display.

A rusted metal porch that looked like it must've been a
sewer grate in its previous life led to the front door. It buckled
under my weight, but held, and I made it to the door.

"Wait, what about those?" Julie pointed at the runes.

"What about them?"

"Aren't they magic? Mom told me Esmeralda said she had a spell on her trailer that would cut your fingers like glass."

I sighed. "It's a chunk of a ballad from the last page of the Codex Runicus, an ancient Nordic law document. Very famous. It says 'I dreamt a dream last night of silk and fine fur.' Trust me, if there was a ward on this trailer, the Honeycomb would've gobbled it up by now."

I examined the lock. Nothing fancy, but I was never good at lock picking.

Footsteps. Coming toward us, three pairs. And something else. Something sending ripples through the volatile fabric of the Honeycomb's magic. Julie felt them too and ran up the porch to me.

The footsteps drew closer. I turned slowly. Three men were approaching the trailer, the first stocky and thick across the shoulders, the other two leaner. The taller of the leaner guys carried a long chain wrapped around his arm. The other end of the chain disappeared between two trailers. All three looked suitably menacing. The chain carrier hung back, side-stepped an eddy of magic, and jerked the metal links.

A local shakedown team. Out in force, three on one, plus whatever it was on the other end of the chain. They knew where I was headed, they knew I had money, and they knew who I worked for, otherwise there was no need for the three of them to intimidate one woman.

Thank you, Custer. I'll remember this.

"Larry, Moe, and Curly?" I guessed.

"Shut your mouth, bitch," the thinner man said.

"Now, now." The thicker bravo smiled. "Let's be polite. I'm Bryce. That over there is Mory and my buddy with the chain over there is Jeremiah. We're just here to make sure you pay your way. Or the thing will get ugly. And nobody wants that."

"Move on," I said. "I already paid for the information."

"From where I'm standin', you didn't pay enough. Make it two fifty: another hundred for the entrance fee and some to us for the trouble of walking here." Bryce put his hand on the cop baton thrust into his belt. "Don't make this hard. You got a little girl with you. You wouldn't want anything to happen to her."

Julie hid behind me.

Bryce smiled like a pit bull before a fight. "The more we work, the higher the bill will run. Time to be smart about this."

The chain trembled. An eerie metallic rustle came from behind the trailers. Jeremiah leaned back and tugged the chain. A hoarse growl answered him. The chain snapped taut and his feet slid a little.

Judging by Bryce's eyes, they wouldn't leave until someone bled. I still had to try. "You think you're tough guys," I said, moving off the porch to the ground. "I can respect that. But I do this shit for a living. I've had a lot of practice. You won't get more money out of me."

"This here"—the beefier bravo stomped his foot in case I failed to get his point—"is our fucking turf. Keep running your bitch mouth, and I'll put something in there to shut you up."

The chain slacked, and metal links rattled on the ground, as something large moved toward us. A clawed paw bigger than my head appeared from behind the trailer, followed by a grotesquely muscled shoulder. Another paw emerged, and a dog trotted into view. He had to be over thirty inches at the shoulder. Muscle bulged on his forequarters and barrel-wide chest, so broad that his hips seemed disproportionately narrow by comparison. His square head sat low on his shoulders as if he had no neck at all.

The dog jogged forward with a faint metallic jingling, like loose change shaking in a pocket. Long blue-gray spikes protruded from his chin. Another row of spikes ran along his spine to the long tail, forming a crest.

The dog halted and stared at me with intense aquamarine eyes. Rage shivered in the wrinkles of his flat muzzle. His maw gaped open and the beast showed me his teeth, long, jagged, and gleaming. He tensed, legs thrust wide, chest open. His spikes snapped upright with an iron click. All over his body metal needles stiffened, like raised hackles.

Nothing kills a party like an oversized metal hedgehog.

Bryce and Mory shuffled to the flanks, giving Jeremiah and his puppy room to work. Mory was out of my reach, but Bryce ended up only eight feet away. They'd done this before. One small flaw in their reasoning: there was thirty-five feet between me and the dog, and the chain would slow him down.

The puppy jerked his head and roared.

"The money, skank," Jeremiah said.

"No."

Jeremiah shrugged the chain loop from his arm. The links hit the dirt with a thud.

The dog charged.

I moved, pulling Slayer from its sheath. I slammed its pommel into Bryce's throat, while hooking his left leg with my right. He toppled. Before he hit the ground, I spun, clamping the metal feather with my fingers and jerking it from the knife sheath. It cost me a fraction of a second—I couldn't afford to cut myself, not with the Honeycomb's magic swirling around us—and I caught the dog in midleap. I stabbed the feather shaft into his vicious beryl eye, twisted past him, and hammered a kick into Jeremiah's gut. He tried to pitch forward, but I swept behind him and caught his throat against Slayer's blade.

Everything stopped.

The dog let out a long surprised whine and went down with the jangle of carelessly tossed coins. Bryce squirmed on the ground, clawing the dirt, trying to breathe. Mory stared at me, his mouth open. Jeremiah gulped, Slayer's blade sliding a little on his Adam'a apple. On the trailer's porch Julie stood petrified, face slack like a melted rubber mask.

"What the fuck?" Mory said, bewildered. "What the fuck happened?"

"What happened is the three of you made me kill a dog for no reason."

A drop of sweat slid from Jeremiah's dark hair and rolled down his unshaven neck. A two-millimeter change in the angle, and the enchanted saber would bridge the distance between him and his wings. I was pissed as hell and keeping my hand steady proved an effort.

"I paid my fee, and you, greedy assholes, decided to shake me down a second time. And threaten my kid, while you were at it. What the fuck is wrong with you? Are you at all human or did this place leech all decency out of you?" My voice was low and growling. I knew I was wasting my breath talking.

Bryce finally sucked in a breath and moaned.

"You killed my dog," Jeremiah said, his voice high with disbelief. "You killed my baby. Jesus Christ. You killed my dog."

They were done. I took my blade from his throat. Jeremiah sank in the dirt. His face stretched. He put his hand over his eyes. I walked past him to the dead dog. It lay in a glistening metal heap, great paws unmoving, ruined eye bleeding crimson. What a waste.

Bryce got to his knees and stood up shakily.

I pulled a piece of gauze from my pocket and wiped Slayer's blade. "I'm going to break into this trailer so I can find this little girl's mother and Esmeralda, or whatever her real name is. While I'm doing that, why don't you go and get some help. However many you think it will take to get the job done, and then you can have a do-over. I'll be right here. But this time, I'll cut to kill human, not dog. And I'll enjoy it. In fact, you would be doing me a favor."

He took a step back.

I glanced at Julie. "Come."

She scurried in front of me to the door. I walked up the metal stair and hammered a kick to the lock. The frame splintered with a sharp crack and the door flew open.

Julie ducked inside and I followed her into the gloomy house of the head witch.

CHAPTER 7

———◆———

THE PLACE STANK OF ROTTING CITRUS AND OLD socks. Julie clamped her nose. "What stinks?"

"Valerian extract." I pointed to the dark stain on the wall. Glass shards studded the floor below—looked like Esmeralda hurled the vial against the wall. "Our head witch had trouble sleeping."

Narrow to the point of inducing claustrophobia, the trailer lay steeped in gloom. Blood-red tattered drapes hid the windows. Julie picked up a flyswatter off the narrow counter separating the tiny kitchen from the rest of the space and used it to push the curtains open. Smart kid. Who knows what the hell was on those curtains.

In the light of the afternoon, the trailer looked even sadder. A beat-up fridge took up most of the cooking area. I opened the fridge. Years ago I had bought a perpetually cold egglike object, which the seller had called an ice sprite egg. I have never seen an ice sprite, although there were rumors of a swarm in Canada. The egg cost me a pretty penny, but I hung it up in a small sack in a corner of my fridge, and it kept my food partially frozen through the magic waves. Esmeralda had used a cheaper, "friz-ice" method: chunks of enchanted ice, sold for a small fee by Water and Sewer Department. They melted about twenty times slower than regular ice. The trouble with friz-ice was that eventually it did melt, and it had done precisely that, and some time ago too, leaking all over the ritualistically beheaded black chicken on the middle shelf. The sickeningly sweet stench of decomposition slapped my face.

I gagged on putrescence and shut the door before I vomited

onto the chicken corpse. Chopping off chicken heads when you're worshipping a bird took some balls. Either that or Esmeralda was an equal opportunity dabbler and tried other magics on the side.

The kitchen held no clues, and I headed to the opposite side of the trailer. I passed a small immaculate bedroom on my left: bed made, no clothes strewn on the floor. An equally pristine bathroom followed, and then I stepped into what should have been the final room.

The Honeycomb had expanded the room, pulling the ceiling up and widening the walls. The grimy linoleum floor ended with the hallway. The bottom of the room consisted of packed dirt, and it sloped to the center, where an iron cauldron sat. The curve of the floor and the bloated ceiling made the room look nearly spherical.

Past the cauldron, at the opposite wall sat a wicker chest. Next to it stood a concrete picnic table. The table was stained with blood.

Behind me Julie shifted from foot to foot.

The magic sat over the cauldron in a big tense knot, but I sensed no wards. I took a step onto the dirt. The room shimmered a little but remained as it was.

I approached the cauldron and lifted the lid. The greasy stench of burned fat and rancid broth assaulted me.

"Ugh!" Julie stumbled back.

My eyes watered. My stomach churned and squirted acid into my throat. I swallowed it back down, took an iron ladle from the handle of the cauldron, and stirred the nauseating brew. Chicken bones, with shreds of rotting meat still clinging to them. No human. Thank God for small favors.

The magic wave died. The technology regained its control, snuffing out the knot of magic above the cauldron.

I slapped the lid back onto the cauldron and moved on to the altar. A few black feathers had stuck to the blood. A long curved knife, sharpened to a razor edge, lay on the table. Black runes, etched with hot wire, covered the handle of the knife. The pieces clicked together in my brain. Now the chicken in the fridge made sense.

Julie finally braved the room. "Is that human blood?"

"Chicken."

"So what, she did voodoo or something?"

"Voodoo isn't the only religion that uses chickens. Europe has a very long tradition of divination using bird entrails."

She looked blank.

"You behead a chicken, cut it open, and try to foretell the future by how its guts look. And sometimes"—I used the knife to raise a blood-spattered rope from behind the altar to show her—"you don't kill the chicken first."

"That's just sick. What kind of people did that?"

"Druids."

Julie blinked. "But druids are nice."

"The modern Order of Druids is nice. But they didn't start out that way. Have you ever seen any girl druids?"

She shook her head. "They're all guys."

"So why was Esmeralda messing around with druid rituals?"

Julie stared at me. "I don't know."

"Neither do I."

I had a feeling that she had done it because someone had instructed her to do so. The sick premonition that had made me shiver at the edge of the pit returned full force. The deeper I got, the less I liked this.

I crouched before the wicker chest and opened it, half-expecting more grisly chicken remains. Books. MacKillop's *Dictionary of Celtic Mythology*, *Myths and Legends of Ancient Ireland* by McClean, *Awaken the Celt Within* by Wizard Sumara, and *Mabinoghen*. Three books on Celtic rituals and one about King Arthur.

I handed the *Awaken the Celt* to Julie. Of the four, it was by far the easiest to read and it had pretty pictures. I grabbed *Myths and Legends* myself, hoping Esmeralda underlined the important passages. I turned to the index and came to a page with three bloody fingerprints in the middle of the *M*'s. Esmeralda had dipped her hands into the chicken blood and didn't wash them before reading the books. Did she feel anointed? I studied the lines by the prints: Mongan, Mongfind,

Morc, Morrigan . . . Oh shit. I flipped the volume to articles starting with *M*. Please don't be Morrigan, please don't be Morrigan . . . A big fat bloody fingerprint on the two-page spread on Morrigan.

Why me?

I felt like throwing the book against the wall. Found a good goddess to worship. *"Bestoloch."*

"What does that mean?" Julie asked.

"It means 'imbecile' in Russian. Looks like your mom's coven worshipped Morrigan. She isn't a nice goddess."

She thrust her book in front of me. "What's wrong with him?"

On the page, a giant of a man swung a huge sword. Gross bulges broke all over his body, the monstrous muscles swelling above one shoulder, threatening to envelop his head. His knees and feet twisted backward, his colossal arms could've brushed the ground, his mouth gaped open, and his left eye thrust out of its orbit. A glow, indicated with short strokes of the ink pen, radiated from his head.

"That's Cú Chulainn. He was the greatest hero of ancient Ireland. When he got really mad during battle, he went into frenzy and turned into that thing. It's called warp spasm."

"Why is his head shining?"

"Apparently he got very hot during the spasm and after the battle people had to dump water on him to cool him down. In one story he jumped into the cauldron filled with water and the cauldron broke . . ."

I stared at the cauldron in the middle of the room.

Julie tugged on my sleeve. "What?"

"Hold on a minute." I approached the cauldron and took the iron handles.

"Too heavy," Julie said.

I grunted, picked it up, and moved it aside. The lid shifted a little, spilling the rancid broth, thankfully not on me.

Under the cauldron lay a small pit. Narrow, barely large enough to permit passage to a small animal, maybe a dog the size of a beagle. The edges were smooth, the circumference perfectly round, as if sculpted with a knife. I looked into it and saw darkness. The odor of earth and the cloying stench of decay rose from the gloom.

Déjà vu.

Julie pried a clod of dirt from the ground and headed for the pit. I caught her.

"But I want to know how deep it is."

"No, you don't."

She dropped the clod with a sneer. I obviously plummeted a few notches on her cool people meter.

Three small impressions marked the sides of the pit forming an equilateral triangle—the tracks from the cauldron's three legs. Just like the tracks at the coven's meeting place. The big pit in the Gap was missing a cauldron. And a huge one at that.

CHAPTER 8

———◆———

BRYCE AND CO. HAD DECIDED AGAINST THE RE-
match, and we left the Honeycomb unmolested, carrying Esmeralda's books. Custer had wisely chosen to make himself
scarce. From Trailer twenty-three to the chain link gates, we
didn't see another living thing.

It took a good hour to cut around the Honeycomb through
the Warren to where Ninny still patiently waited for me by a
pile of mule poop. I loaded Julie onto the molly. White Street
was only fifteen minutes away, but she looked tuckered out.

"Where are we going?" she asked.

"Home. What's your address?"

Julie clamped her lips shut and stared at the front of Ninny's
saddle.

"Julie?"

"There is nobody there," she said. "Mom's gone. She's all
I have."

Oh boy. Could I turn a momless, hungry, tired, filthy kid
loose on a street with night approaching? Let me think . . .
"We'll swing by your house and see if your mom made it
home. If not, you can bed with me tonight."

Mom wasn't there. They had a tiny house, tucked in a corner of a shallow subdivision branching from White Street.
The home was old, but very clean, all except the kitchen sink
full of dirty plates. Originally it must've been a two bedroom,
but somebody, probably Julie's mom, had built a wooden par-
tition, sectioning off a part of the living room to make a tiny
third room. In that room sat an old sewing machine, a couple
of filing cabinets, and a small table. On the table rested a

half-finished dress, light blue, in Julie's size. I touched the dress gently. Whatever faults Julie's mother may have had, she loved her daughter very much.

Julie brought her picture from their bedroom: a tired woman with loose blond hair looked back at me from the photo with brown eyes, just like her daughter's. Her face was pale. She looked sickly, exhausted, and a decade older than thirty-five.

I made Julie help me with the dishes. Under the plates I found a bottle of Wild Irish Rose. White label. It stank like rubbing alcohol. It was also famous for sending the drinker into wild rages.

"Does your mom ever scream at you or hit you when she drinks?"

Julie stared at me in outrage. "My mom is nice!"

I threw the bottle away.

Two hours later we dropped Ninny off at the Order's stable. The magic, after holding off for a good few hours, resumed hammering Atlanta in short bursts. The afternoon bled into the evening. I was tired and hungry. We headed north through the tangle of streets, to the small apartment that used to belong to Greg and was now my home when I stayed in the city.

I CLIMBED THE NARROW STAIRWELL TO THE THIRD floor, Julie in tow. The magic happened to be up, and the ward clutched my hand as I touched the door and opened it in a flash of blue. I let Julie into the apartment, bolted the door shut behind us, and pulled off my shoes.

Julie wandered past me. "This is nice. And there are bars on the windows."

"Keeps the bad guys out." The lack of sleep finally caught up to me. I was so freaking tired. Worn out. "Take your shoes off."

She did. I rummaged through the closet and came up with an old box of my clothes Greg had kept since the time I had stayed with him after my father died. Fifteen-year-old me was a lot bigger than thirteen-year-old Julie, but the clothes would have to do.

I tossed the sweatpants and a T-shirt at her. "Shower."

"I don't do showers."

"Do you do food? No shower, no food."

She stuck out her lower lip. "You suck, you know that?"

I crossed my arms on my chest. "My house, my rules. You don't like it, the door's over there."

"Fine!" She headed for the door.

Good riddance. I clamped my teeth, hoping I didn't say it out loud, and went into the kitchen. I washed my hands with soap at the sink and searched the fridge for vittles. The only thing I had was a big bowl of cold low country boil. Me, I'd eat it cold: corn on the cob and shrimp were good cold anyway, and I was hungry enough to stomach the cold potatoes and sausage. Julie, on the other hand, might want it warm, preferably with butter.

To warm up or not to warm up? That was the question.

The sounds of rushing water announced a shower starting. She'd decided to stick around. I put a big pot of water on the gas burner. Magic did screwy things to all sorts of ordinary objects, but thankfully, the natural gas still burned. If all else failed, I had a small picnic heater on top of the fridge, together with a jug of kerosene for it.

I had almost finished picking out all of the shrimp, when a very thin, angelic-looking child walked into my kitchen. She had fly-away caramel hair and large brown eyes on a sharp face. It took me a full minute to recognize her and then I collapsed, laughing.

"What?" The little elf-baby looked taken aback.

"You're very clean."

Julie pulled my sweatpants up before they slid off her butt. "I'm hungry. We had a deal."

"Watch the water for me. When it starts boiling, put everything in except the shrimp. Don't eat the shrimp, it's better warm, and don't let the water boil over and drown the gas while I take a shower."

I gathered a heap of clothes and crawled into the shower.

There was nothing better than a nice hot shower after a long day. Well, maybe a hot shower followed by hot sex, but my memory in that department was getting a bit fuzzy.

It took a while to get all the dirt out of my hair, and when I popped into the kitchen, the water was boiling. I hooked a piece of corn on the cob with a giant fork. Steaming hot. Good enough. I dropped the shrimp into the pot, let it boil for a quarter of a minute or so, turned the gas off, and dumped the whole thing into the strainer.

The magic fell. On, off, on, off, make up your mind already. "Ever had a low country boil?"

Julie shook her head.

I put the colander in the center of the table and put salt and a stick of butter next to it. "Shrimp, sausage, corn on the cob, and potatoes. Try it. The sausage is turkey and deer meat. I was there when it was made. It doesn't have dog or rat in it."

Julie snagged a piece of sausage, tasted it, and attacked it like starving wolves were snapping at her food. "Thish ish good!" she announced through a mouthful of food.

I barely had a chance to finish the first cob, when a knock echoed through the door. I looked through the peephole. Red.

I opened the door. He glanced at me, eyes narrowed into tiny slits. "Food?"

Kate Daniels, deadly swordswoman and rescuer of hungry orphans. "Come in. Wash your hands."

Julie burst from the kitchen and threw her arms around him. Red stiffened and put one arm around her.

Her face over his shoulder took on a sweet dreamy look. Her mother's disappearance had to have hit her hard, but losing Red would crush her.

"I missed you!" she said softly.

"Yeah," he said, his face flat. "Me, too."

Twenty minutes later I had two full kids and no boil. That meant I'd have to cook something tomorrow. Oi.

"Let's talk." I pinned Red to his chair with my stare. I did deranged quite well, when the occasion required. Strangely, most of my opponents didn't faint and crash to the ground from my stare, but Red was young and used to being bullied.

He froze. I didn't like to intimidate adolescent street urchins, but I had a feeling he would bolt at the slightest opportunity if I played it nice. "Tell me what you know about the coven."

"Nothing."

"You took Julie to their gathering place. How did you know where it was?"

"I didn't spill, I swear." Julie paled a little.

Red kept his gaze locked on me. "Same as I found this place. Got some of her mom's hair off a brush at her house. Made a charm, spilled some blood, and let it lead me."

Julie's mom had to be alive at the time he cast his spell. Shamanistic spells were life-tied; to sense a dead body required a much more complicated ritual and the kind of power Red probably didn't have. Not yet anyway.

"You went there by yourself first." It was a guess, but I saw the confirmation in his eyes. "What did you see there, Red?"

His fingers twitched. He turned slightly to the right, hiding the side of his face from me.

"Let me see the right side of your neck."

He swallowed.

"Now."

Red turned. Three long gashes marked his neck from the earlobe all the way down to the collar of his rags. A thin line of yellow pus gathered under the puffy red edges of the wounds.

Not so good. I reached over and touched his head. He jerked back.

"Sit still, knucklehead."

He felt feverish. I reached into the fridge and took out a jar of Rmd3 from the middle shelf. Red's eyes flickered to the brownish paste and back to me.

"What's in there?" Julie asked.

"Rmd3. Better known as Remedy."

"It's the stuff the People carry. I don't need it." Red shifted in his seat.

I looked at his face and saw the decisive thrust of the adolescent jaw. No intelligent life there. I turned to Julie. "It's an herbal treatment for the infection he has brewing on his neck.

This is the South-Pacific variety, the best one there is. It can cure the necrosis you get from the undead and takes care of all sorts of nasty infections." I set the jar on the table. Real kava root, and pine-leaf geebung, and a half dozen other things. Expensive, but well worth it.

"I don't need it," he repeated.

"Shamans who topple over in the middle of the street from fever don't live to grow up."

"Take the Remedy, Red." Julie moved the jar to him.

He stared at it as if it were a snake, reached in, and slathered some on his neck. The paste touched the wounds and he winced.

"What clawed you?"

"Creatures," he said. "Odd life. Didn't feel right. Very *powerful*."

He pronounced "powerful" with respect, almost reverence, tinted with longing. The way an alcoholic ordered his favorite poison after a long dry streak, tasting the name on his tongue.

"Lust for power is a dangerous thing," I said.

He bared his teeth at me. A little feral light danced in his eyes. "You only say that because you have some. People who have power never want anybody else to get it."

Julie tugged on his sleeve. "But you have power. You're a shaman."

He whirled to her. "What good is it? The gangs still knock out my teeth and take my food. So what if I can make them piss blood the day after? Next time, they'll just kill me and be done with it. I want real power. Strength. So nobody fucks with me."

"I can give you what I have," Julie said in a small voice.

"Not yet," he said. "Let it grow bigger."

What was going on between the two of them? The way they looked at each other gave me the creeps.

"Tell me about the creatures that hurt you."

"They were fast, with long hair. The hair grabbed me like it was alive. They were afraid of the bowman."

"Tell me about the cauldron."

Red twitched as if shocked with a live wire, burst from his seat, and ran out the door. Julie was sitting closest to the door, and she beat me to the stairs by a quarter of a second. She dashed down, and I forced myself to stop.

They were kids.

Life had beaten them until they had nearly turned wild. They had no refuge, they trusted nobody except each other, and I would be damned if I were going to go down there and threaten Red with a beating to scare the truth out of him. Enough was enough. If they came back, they came back. In the meantime, I'd figure it out my own way.

I went back into the kitchen and ate a piece of sausage off my plate. Through the window I could see Red and Julie on the street. They stood close together, his dark head against her blond. As I watched, the tech hit. The electric lamp came on in the living room, bathing the apartment in a comfortable muted glow. Down on the street, the lone surviving lamp shone from the top of the post, illuminating the kids. They moved to the left, just beyond its light. The faces of the new world: a street shaman and his girlfriend. Starved, feral, magic.

They talked while I finished my plate and drank my water. Finally Red pulled something from his pocket and put it around Julie's neck. Probably a charm.

Julie hugged him. He sort of stood there, very rigid, while her arms were locked around his neck. He probably didn't want to look weak in public. Dread crept up on me. Why was it that watching these two gave me a bad feeling?

Kind of like imagining me with Max Crest.

If Greg had still been alive, I wouldn't have given Max a second glance. Greg's death had hit me harder than I thought it would; I was lonely, scared, and desperate for a warm, loving guy to come home to. For someone to lean on. Max just happened to be at precisely the wrong place at the wrong time. Our relationship had been doomed from the start, because it was based on grief, and unlike love, grief eventually passed. Now that time had filed off the sharp edges, I felt no jealousy toward Myong, nor did I feel any longing for Max. I didn't miss him. Yet every time his name came to mind, I felt a vague unpleasant sensation, not guilt exactly, but something akin to embarrassment.

Ugh. I wanted to take the whole thing, wrap it up, stick it in a box, and drop the box off a pier. If I had never run across Max Crest again, I would've been perfectly happy. But now I had to arrange his wedding. How the hell did I get myself into these things?

Speaking of the wedding. I tried the phone, got a dial tone, and called the number Derek had given me.

"Southeast office," a female voice answered.

Either I had gotten the wrong number or boy wonder was moving up in the world. "Derek, please."

The phone clicked and Derek's voice came on the line. "Yes?"

"You have a secretary?"

He laughed. "No, it's just Mila. She screens the calls. What can I do for you?"

"I have the packet."

"Awesome!" He checked himself and continued in a more even tone. "When can I pick it up?"

"I'll drop it by tomorrow."

"Did you beat the shit out of him?"

Ha! Derek was still in there, under the Mr. Cool Pack Wolf veneer. "Sort of. You're right, he disappears. He also regenerates while he's gone."

Julie came back into the apartment. She was wearing a small monisto: a necklace of coins and tiny metal charms. She paused in the hallway, testing the waters, decided I wasn't going to explode, slid back into her chair, and checked the bowl for more boil. Only potatoes were left. She took a handful and ate them, licking her fingers.

"I have a favor to ask." I moved the butter and salt closer to her.

"Anything I can do," Derek said.

Julie was watching me covertly, probably trying to gauge if any fussing was forthcoming.

"I need an audience with his furry Highness." *I can't believe I'm saying this.*

"I can't believe you're saying this, after all the bitc—yelling you did when I called you for the Spring Meet. I distinctly remember 'never see that arrogant asshole again' and 'over my dead body.' "

"Spring Meet was optional." After working with the Pack to dispatch the Red Point Stalker, I was granted the Friend of the Pack status, which apparently came with such benefits as being invited to ceremonies. Hell, if I transgressed in their territory, the shapeshifters might hesitate a couple of seconds before they shredded me into Kate sushi.

"Myong?" Derek's voice gained a slightly disapproving edge.

"Derek, yes or no?"

"Yes, of course," he said smoothly. "I'll let you know the time and place."

We made parting noises and I hung up.

"Who was that?" Julie asked.

"My teenage werewolf sidekick. We're going to see him tomorrow."

"You know people in the Pack?"

"Yep. There is a spare toothbrush in the vanity . . ."

"What's the vanity?"

"Vanity is taking too much pride in your appearance. It's also the cabinet in the bathroom which has a sink and a drawer. Where the toothbrush is."

Her face grew long. "Do I have to?"

"You bet."

CHAPTER 9

———◦◦◉◦◦———

I PACKED JULIE INTO MY BED, GAVE HER MY BLAN-
ket, and unrolled an old army sleeping bag on the floor. The
magic had reclaimed the city. I had dimmed the feylanterns
already, and the only light in the apartment came from the
outside, a silvery glow from the light of the new moon mixing
with the weak radiance of the bars affected by the magic of
the defensive spell.

Somewhere far away, a wolf howled. I could always tell a
wolf from a stray dog—the lupine howl sent shivers down my
spine. I thought of Curran. The scary thing was, I was kind of
curious about seeing him tomorrow.

What was wrong with me? It had to be hormones. A pure-
ly biological problem. I had an overload of hormones that
clouded my normally rational thinking, causing me to have
fanciful notions about gray-eyed homicidal maniacs . . .

"I can sleep on the floor," Julie offered in a sleep-tangled
voice.

I shrugged. "Thanks, but I'm used to it. When I was a kid,
my dad made me sleep on the floor. He was afraid I'd have
back problems like my mom." I unzipped the bag and laid it as
flat as I could. The wards and bars made my apartment into a
little fortress, but you never knew. Somebody could teleport in
and fill me full of bolts while I untangled my legs from the
sleeping bag.

"Is she nice?"

"Who?"

"Your mom?"

I stopped, an afghan in my hands. Like a little knife,

twisted into my chest. "I don't know. She died when I was very young. My dad loved her so she must've been nice."

"So both your mom and your dad are gone? You have no family left?"

"Yeah."

"Kind of like me," she said in a small voice.

Poor kid. I came over and sat on the corner of the bed. "I know my mom's dead, because my dad saw her die, and I know my dad's dead because I was there when we buried him on a hill behind my house. I visit his grave all the time. But we don't really know anything about your mom. I didn't see her body anywhere. Did you see her body?"

She shook her head and stuck her face into the pillow.

"Well, there you go. No body, no proof she died. Maybe she somehow got teleported to a strange part of the city by that Bran idiot and now she's walking home. Maybe she's there right now. We'll just have to keep looking."

Julie made a sad kittenlike noise.

What do I do now?

I scooped her up, blanket, pillow, and all, and scooted her close to me. She sniffled. "The People probably turned her into a vampire."

I petted her hair. "No, Julie. The People don't just grab women off the street and make them into vampires. That's illegal. If they started doing that, the cops and military would exterminate them in a blink. They have to account for each vampire and they only want specific people for it. Don't worry, your mom isn't a vampire."

"What if she is?"

Then I'll walk into the Casino and there will be hell to pay. "She isn't. If you want, I'll call the People tomorrow and check on it."

"What if they lie to you?"

Boy, this kid had a major hang-up on vampires. "Look, you have to remember that vampires are mindless, like cockroaches. They are just vehicles for the Masters of the Dead. If you see a bloodsucker and it's not ripping everyone to shreds, there's an actual human being riding that vamp's mind. That human being has a family, probably has kids, cute little Master of the Dead babies."

She swiped a tear and tried a weak smile.

"The People have dozens of vampires. The People don't need to kidnap anyone. They have an applicant list a mile long."

"Why would anybody want to be a vampire?"

"Money. Let's say you have an incurable disease. Vampirism is caused by a bacterial infection, which transforms the victim's body so much that a lot of those diseases become irrelevant to the final vampiric organism. In other words, it doesn't matter if you have colon cancer—your colon is going to shrink into twine after a month of undeath anyway. So you apply to become a vampire. If you're selected, you'll be offered a contract that authorizes the People to infect you with the Vampirus Immortuus. Basically, you let the People kill you and use your body after death. And in exchange, the People will pay your beneficiaries a fee. A lot of poor people think that it's a good way to leave their families with a little bit of money after they are gone. It takes a week and a stack of paperwork to make a vampire, and the whole thing is reported to the State Undeath Commission. Making a vamp against a person's will is illegal, and they won't do something that would land them in prison for just one vamp. Listen, why don't you tell me about your mom? It might make it easier for me to find her."

Julie hugged the pillow. "She's nice. She reads books to me sometimes. Just the booze makes her tired and I leave her alone. Go outside or something. She's not like an alcoholic or anything. She just misses my dad. She only drinks on weekends, when she doesn't have to work."

"Where does she work?"

"Carpenter Guild. She used to be a cook, but the place got closed down. She's a journeyman now. She says once she makes carpenter, we'll see real money. She said that about the coven too and now she's gone. She always worries about money. We've been poor for a long time now. Ever since Dad died."

She drew a little circle on the pillow with her hand—the circle of life. Something the shamans did when they mentioned the deceased. Picking up Red's habits.

"When Dad was alive, he used to take us to the coast. To Hilton Head. It's nice there. We went swimming and the water was really warm. My dad was a carpenter, too. A piece of the overpass fell on him. Just squished him. There was nothing left."

Sometimes life just kept punching you in the teeth, no matter how many times you got up. "The pain gets better with time," I told her. "It always hurts, but it gets better."

"People keep saying that." Julie did not look at me. "I must be unlucky or something."

One of the worst things for a child is to lose a parent. When my father died, it was as if my world had ripped open. Like a god dying. Part of me refused to believe it. I so desperately wanted to put things back the way they had been. I would've given anything for another day with my dad. And I was so mad at Greg for not being able to wave his hand and make it right somehow. Then little by little, it set in: my dad was gone. Forever. No turning back. No amount of magic would fix it. And just when I thought the pain had dulled, my mind would betray me and bring Dad back to life in my dreams. Sometimes I didn't realize that he was dead until I awoke and then it was like a punch in the stomach. And sometimes I knew in my dream that I was dreaming, and I woke up crying.

But back then, I still had Greg. Greg, who dedicated his life to making sure I would be fine. Greg, who took me in. I didn't have to live on the street. I didn't have to worry about money.

Julie and her mother didn't have that luxury. Qualified carpenters were paid well, because woodwork was magic-proof. The death of Julie's father must have destroyed their lives. It knocked them down and they just kept sliding lower and lower. It would've been easy to keep rolling until they hit rock bottom. I hugged Julie to me. Her mother must've loved her a great deal, because she picked herself up and she started climbing. She had fought her way into the Carpenter Guild, which couldn't have been easy with all the competition out there. She became a journeyman, which was a hard step up from apprentice. She was trying to keep her daughter off the street.

"You never told me your mother's name."

"Jessica," Julie said. "Her name's Jessica Olsen."

Hold on, Jessica. I'll find you. And I'll keep your baby safe. Nothing will happen to Julie.

As if sensing what I was thinking, Julie squirmed closer to me and we sat quietly, cloaked in the warm night.

"Tell me about the coven. Was your mom in long?"

"Not long. Couple of months. She said they were worshipping a great goddess and we'd all be rich soon."

I sighed. When we found Esmeralda, she and I would have a nice long talk. "You don't really get rich from worshipping. Especially not Morrigan."

"What kind of a goddess is she?"

"Celtic kind. Old Irish. There are a few versions of her, so I'll tell you what I think might be close to the truth. Morrigan is three goddesses rolled into one. She changes depending on what she wants to do. Kind of like putting on different outfits. It's called having divine aspects. Sometimes she is the goddess of fertility and prosperity and her name is Annan. I'm guessing that's the aspect your mom worshipped. Annan also guides dead people to their resting place in the Otherworld. That's the place where the Celtic dead live. The second aspect is Macha. She oversees kingship, governance, and horses. The third aspect is Badb, the great battle crow." I paused. In light of Julie's missing mom, mentioning that the Badb drank the blood of the fallen and reveled in the slaughter was not a good idea.

"I've forgotten what the first one is called." Julie's voice gained a slight sleepy thickness. Excellent. She needed sleep and so did I.

"It doesn't really matter. They're all Morrigan."

"Who did she battle?"

"Fomorians. That's the thing to remember about gods: they always have someone to fight. Greek gods fought Titans, Viking gods fought Frost Giants, and Irish gods fought Fomorians, the sea-demons. Morrigan kicked a lot of butt, and finally the Fomorians were driven into the sea." My Celtic mythology was a bit rusty. I'd have to brush up the first chance I got. Nobody could hope to remember all of the mythological heavyweights, so the trick wasn't to know everything. The trick was to know enough to figure out where to find the rest.

"So why can't you get rich worshipping her?" Julie yawned.

"Because Morrigan doesn't grant wishes. She makes deals. That means she always wants something in return." Only fools made bargains with deities.

She closed her eyes. *Good. Sleep, Julie.*

"Kate?"

"Mmm?"

"How did your mom die?"

I opened my mouth to lie. The response was automatic: I hid my blood, I hid my magic, and I hid the truth of where I came from. But for some odd reason, the lie didn't come out. I wanted to tell her the real story. Or at least a part of it. I never spoke of it and now the words itched my tongue.

What's the harm? She was only a child. It would be like a twisted good-night story. She would forget it by morning.

"I was only a few weeks old. My father and mother were running away. A man was chasing them. He was very powerful and evil. My mother knew that of the two of them my dad was the stronger one. She was slowing him down."

My voice shook a little. I didn't expect the words to be so hard.

"So my mother gave me to my dad and told him to run. She would delay the evil man as long as she could. He didn't want to go but he realized it was the only way to save me. The evil man caught my mom and they fought. She stabbed him in the eye, but he was very powerful, and she couldn't kill him. And that's how my mother died."

I tucked the blanket around her.

"That's a sad story."

"It is." It's not finished, either. Not by a long shot.

She patted the afghan still on my lap. "Did you make this?"

"Yes."

"It's nice. Can I use it?"

I put it on her. She kicked the blanket off and wrapped herself in the afghan, like a little mouse nesting. "It's soft," she said and fell asleep.

A VOICE SPREAD THROUGH THE APARTMENT, PURE like a crystal bell, sweet like honey, soft like velvet. *"Girl . . . Want girl."*

I opened my eyes. The magic was up, setting the bars on the windows aglow with ethereal bluish light. I saw Julie slip into the hallway, a ghostly, silent shape in the darkness of the night-drenched apartment.

"Girl . . ." It was coming from the outside.

My fingers found Slayer's textured hilt. I took it, rose, and followed her.

"Need girl . . . Girl . . . Want girl . . ."

Outside the kitchen window, a pale shade floated an inch from the glass and my ward. Female, with a delicate, almost elven face and a heartbreaking body, she looked into my house with lavender eyes. Her skin glowed with a faint silver radiance. Improbably thick, long hair streamed from her head, coiling like tentacles. *"Giiiirl,"* the creature sang, stretching her arms to the window. *"Neeed . . . where, where?"*

Hi. And what kind of screwed-up beastie would you be?

On my kitchen table, crouched atop a crumpled curtain, sat Julie. She had worked the window latch open and was trying to pry the mechanism securing the iron grate.

I put Slayer down and took Julie by her waist. She clutched at the bars.

The creature hissed. Her jaws unhinged with reptilian flexibility, baring rows of anglerfish teeth in a black mouth. A strand of her hair whipped at the window, aiming for the kid. The ward reacted with a pulse of angry carmine. The creature jerked in pain.

I pulled on Julie. "Julie. Let go."

Julie snarled something wordless and charged with fury. I

dug my heels in and pulled harder, throwing all of my strength and weight into it. Julie's fingers slipped and I almost crashed to the floor. She kicked, struggling like a pissed-off cat. I dragged her off into the bathroom, dumped her into the tub, and slammed the door shut behind us. With a howl, Julie launched herself at me. Her nails raked my arm. I grasped her by the back of the neck, forcing her down into the tub, and opened the cold water tap. She writhed under my hand, spitting and biting. I dunked her under the stream and held her there.

Gradually her convulsions subsided. She whimpered and went limp.

I shut off the water to a trickle. Julie drew a long shuddering breath and sobbed. Slowly tension leaked from her muscles. "I'm okay," she gasped. "I'm okay."

I pulled her from the bathtub and put a towel on her head. She trembled and hugged herself.

I opened the door and glanced out. The lavender-eyed thing hovered by the kitchen window, her eyes fixed on the door. She saw me and hissed again.

"Girl . . . Come . . . Want . . ."

Julie sank to the tile, squeezing into the narrow space between the toilet and the bathtub, chopstick legs sticking out. "She was in my head. She's trying to get back in right now."

"Try to shut her out. We're safe behind the wards."

"What if the magic falls?" Julie's eyes widened in pure panic.

"Then I'll cut her head off." Easier said than done. That hair would grab me like a noose. It's hard to cut hair unless it's held taut.

"Girl?"

"Shut the hell up!"

Why Julie? Why now? Was that thing her mother, turned into something by the coven's magic?

"Julie, does that thing look like your mother?"

She shook her head, locked her arms over her knees and began to rock. She could only move an inch or two squeezed into that narrow space. "Gray. Muddy, sliding, shifting, nasty purple gray."

"What?"

"Gray like the skeleton. Nasty . . ."

"Julie, what's gray?"

She looked at me with haunted eyes. "Her magic. Her magic's gray."

Oh God. "What color is a werewolf's magic?"

"Green."

A sensate. A living m-scanner, who could see the magic, very rare, very valued. I had her with me the whole time. I knew there was something magic about her, but between metal dogs and infected boyfriends, I never got a chance to ask. "That thing, she's gray and purple? Did you say purple? Like a vampire?"

"Weaker. Pale purple."

Purple was the color of undeath. If the creature was indeed undead somehow, she had no consciousness. Someone had to control her, the way Masters of the Dead controlled the vampires.

"Julie, you have to come out. I can't protect you if you're here hugging the toilet. Get up."

"She'll get in. She'll kill me. I don't want to die."

"You will die if you stay here." I held out my hand. "Come on."

She sobbed.

"Come on, Julie! Show that bitch you have some backbone."

She bit her lip and took my hand. I pulled her up.

"I'm scared."

"Use it. It will keep you sharp. In the Honeycomb, why didn't the magic grab you?"

It took her a second to shift gears. "I blended. I made it think I was the same as it was."

"Blend with me, then." Mimicking a different type of magic would camouflage Julie's mind, forcing the creature to concentrate on the magic object instead. Like hiding a weak light in the flare of a strong one. That thing couldn't target her mind if it couldn't sense it.

She shook her head. "I can't. I've tried already. Your magic's too strange."

Shit. Another side effect of my screwed-up heritage. It

wasn't enough that I had to burn my bloody bandages so nobody could identify me, but now I couldn't even shield a little kid. What did I have that she could blend with? There were a half dozen enchanted artifacts in Greg's collection but nothing that exuded enough magic to hide her.

Slayer.

"Stay here."

I dashed to the kitchen, swiped Slayer off the table, and sprinted back to the bathroom. Julie's face had gone blank. I thrust Slayer into her hands and barked, "Blend!"

Awareness snapped back into her eyes. I felt the magic creep to the blade. Julie's breath came out in ragged gasps.

A barely perceptible change took place within the magic field. She took a deep breath. "Okay," she said. "Okay."

The creature screeched in frustration.

I hugged Julie to me. Physical danger I could deal with, but having Julie turned into a zombie would've screwed things up beyond repair. As long as we could keep that bitch out of my kid's head, we had a chance. She clamped the sword with both hands, face pinched, concentrating on the blade.

I steered her to the doorway. "Let's go."

We stepped from the bathroom. The creature's lavender eyes focused on Julie. It licked the ward, burned its tongue on the crimson, and recoiled.

I tried the phone. Dead. Why me?

"Giiirl. Want, want, need . . ."

"You okay?"

She nodded.

The magic crashed. I took Slayer from Julie and tried the phone again. Still dead. Fuck me.

The creature's hair fell lifelessly about her. She clutched onto the bars to keep from falling. Yeah! Choke on tech, you piece of crap. No tentacle hair for you.

The creature thrust her legs against the wall and heaved. The bars bent with a long, tortured screech.

Julie darted into the bedroom. Now wasn't a good time to hide. First rule of bodyguard detail: know where your "body" is at all times.

The creature heaved again. The bars parted.

I stepped into the kitchen. First I'd deal with my lovely new window ornament and then I'd go and dig Julie out from under the bed.

Julie reappeared with her knife in her hand. Her fingers shook, making the point of the dagger dance. She planted herself behind me and bit her lip.

They *would not* get this girl. Not today. Not ever.

Boom!

Something hit the door with a solid thump. Julie jumped.

"Steady. The door's solid. It'll hold." At least for a few minutes. I stepped deeper into the kitchen and moved a chair out of my way, giving myself space to work.

At the window, the creature tasted the air with her tongue like a snake and thrust her head into the gap.

Boom!

I jumped onto the table and sliced her head off in a classic executioner stroke.

The head thudded on the table and rolled to the floor. The body froze halfway through the bars. Thick reddish slime slid from the stump of the neck in a slow gush. An oily stench of rotten fish and bitter, stale seawater spread through the room.

I picked up the head by the tangle of hair and stuck Slayer's point into the left cheek. The flesh sagged a little, liquefied by the saber's magic. Nothing as obvious as what the blade would do to a vampire, but Slayer's magic affected it. Thin tendrils of smoke rose from the saber's blade. Julie was right. Definitely an undead, but not as undead as a vampire. Perhaps, she was just mostly undead. Could you even be mostly undead?

Boom!

The door splintered, vomiting chunks of wood onto the hallway carpet. I dropped the head, grabbed Julie by the shoulder, and shoved her to the left, behind the wall.

The last of the wood fell from the frame. A twin to the creature I had just shortened by a head stepped into my apartment, half-hidden by the black hair drooping to her ankles.

The magic surged back up, banishing technology. My spell flared shut, two seconds behind the monster. Life wasn't fair.

Pale silvery fire ran down the creature's hair. The glossy strands shivered, stretched . . .

I shifted my grip on Slayer.

Coils thrust, catching the door to the bathroom. Slowly the hair parted, revealing flesh that glowed like a beacon. Feeble radiance shimmered along the creature's skin, elusive yet hypnotic, like a swamp light, like a glimpse of a mermaid beneath the waves. She held out her hands. The glow rippled down her ankles and spread in a ghostly, gossamer semblance of a fish tail.

"Girl?" Her voice floated. *"Girl?"*

"No girl! Get out of my house, you crazy bitch."

The creature leaned forward, her arms ready for an embrace, her lavender eyes full of cold amethyst fire. Thin, flexible . . . Ten to one, I had pulled Bran's bolts out of her sister's skeleton.

A dirty stream of liquid wet the table under my feet. I chanced a glance at the body behind me. Only a puddle left. I've never seen that before. I knew my sword—it made vampiric flesh into goo, but not that quickly.

The creature spread her hands. Curved claws slid from her knuckles, dripping red slime. Claws that would make long gashes, just like the ones on Red's neck. He must've gotten a mere brush, because judging by the size of those claws, she could rip my heart out with one swipe. The hair grabbed, the claws shredded, and rows of needle teeth finished the job. She was a complete package.

The creature advanced, slowly, taking her time. Why not? I was cornered. Nowhere to go except outside to a three-story drop. I took a step back and bumped my elbow on the wall, near the fridge.

The hair snapped like a whip and caught my thigh. I sliced it, severing the strands, swiped the jug of kerosene off the top of the fridge, and sloshed it over her.

The creature hissed. I dropped the sword and brought my arms together. The hair clamped me and pulled, off the table, across the kitchen, closer and closer to the claws. She didn't notice the matches in my fingers until a whiff of sulfur announced a fire being born. The hair whipped in panic, lassoing me in crushing coils. I dropped the burning match into its depth.

It caught all at once. The fire surged, bright orange and hot. I tore myself free.

The creature screeched and flailed within the inferno. Something popped with the dry hiss of lard dripping into a fire. She stumbled back, crashed against the bathroom door, splintering the wood, and threw herself across the hallway into a mirror. She smashed into it again and again, breaking the glass into smaller and smaller pieces, until at last they showered from the frame.

I picked up Slayer. Stand still for a moment, and I'll cure all your problems.

The blaze belched a cloud of smoke, and the greasy stench of cooked fat filled the room. I gagged. The wealth of the creature's hair burned to ash, and gray flecks rained on the carpet and swirled around me, caught in the draft from the doorway. The creature convulsed, a lunatic sparkler about to go out.

Julie lunged from the kitchen, a knife in hand, and dived into the flames, burying her blade in the creature's stomach. Oblivious, the monster shook, gripped by a wave of spasms. Julie hacked, swinging wildly, carving chunks from the still burning body. All remnants of restraint fled from her eyes.

I grabbed her and pulled her to me, away from the fire. "Enough!"

Julie heaved, swallowing air in shuddering gasps.

The creature slammed one last time against a wall. Its back snapped like a broken twig. Rivulets of gray liquid burst under the charred husk of her corpse. The puddle spread and started shrinking. I ripped a drawer open, pulled a specimen vial from it, and scooped some filthy liquid. I corked the vial—about a third full and there were ash flakes floating in it. Probably contaminated worse than the city sewer. This was not my day.

I put my contaminated evidence on the table next to my saber and turned to Julie. "Let me see your hands. What were you thinking?"

I knew exactly what she was thinking: you or me. That creature had terrorized her. She didn't run. She didn't hide. She made a conscious decision to fight it. That was good. Except that Julie fighting a monster of this power was like trying to stop a trained Doberman with a flyswatter.

Julie's fingers had turned red where the fire had licked them. Probably minor burns. Could've been worse. "There is a tub of A&D ointment in the fridge. Put some on your hands . . ."

The magic blinked: gone for a second and up the next. I glanced at the doorway to check if anything came through. A tall figure stood behind my ward. Tall, slightly stooped, it wore a thin white habit. The deep hood hung over its face almost to its chest. Like a corpse, wrapped in white linen and ready for burial.

A male voice emanated from under the hood, cold, grating, dry like the sound of seashells crushed under a heavy foot. "Give me the child, human."

I had met and killed the puppets and the puppeteer decided to make an appearance. How flattering. I pointed Julie back to the left wall, out of his sight.

"What do you offer for the child?"

"Life."

"Does that come with a possibility of parole?"

That threw him off track but only for a moment. "Surrender the child."

"Life, huh? That's not a very good offer. Shouldn't you at least throw in some riches and a pile of handsome men?"

"Give me the girl," the whispery voice commanded. "You're nothing, human. You're no threat. My reeves shall grate the meat from your bones."

So the hair ladies had a name. I bared my teeth. "Then why waste time talking. Take off that hoodie, and let's go."

He leaned back and thrust his arms up. Bulges rolled under the cloth, spiraling around his chest and sliding over his arms.

A phantom wind stirred his habit. The cloth parted and within its depth I glimpsed an abomination of a face: a narrow fanged muzzle the color of old bruises, two huge round eyes, dead, cold, and alien like the eyes of a squid, and above them in the middle of the forehead, a soft pale green bump, palpitating like some grotesque heart. Twin streaks of gray ichor leaked from the bump, carving wet paths between the cruel eyes.

Tangles of green burst from the sleeves of the habit and split into tentacles that fastened above the door and raised Hood off the floor. He hung suspended in the tentacle net. The bump pulsated faster. His whisper flooded the apartment, so strong it soiled my skin. *"Asssiiisssssst . . ."*

The magic burst from him in a cannon blast. The ward on my door tore like tissue paper and the blast smashed into me and out of the kitchen window. If the magic had substance, it would've shattered the walls. Shocked by the power, my mind took a second to comprehend that wards no longer shielded the door or the window behind my back.

A coil of black hair grabbed my waist and jerked me back with awesome force, pulling me to the broken window. I smashed into the twisted bars. Fiery pain raked my back and bit deep. I cried out.

A strand of black hair whipped my arm. Julie froze, her eyes wide in panic. The hair pulled me harder and harder, constraining my chest. I couldn't shift a muscle. A steel band crushed my lungs. I would pass out and it would get Julie.

"Kiill . . ." Hood rasped. Teeth bit into my shoulder and let go. The reeve screeched, burned by my blood.

She was undead. Pilot her like a vampire. I reached for her mind and hit a wall of Hood's defense. Impenetrable.

The hair squeezed. Out of options.

The pain slashed my back. I strained and let out a single word. *"Amehe."* Obey.

The power word tore from me in a flash of agony as if my insides were suddenly ripped from my stomach. The wall shielding the reeve's mind shattered. Hood howled in his tentacle net.

The gaping pit that was the reeve's mind opened before me. I took it into my fist and squeezed. The hair noose loosened. The hair still held me, but the crushing pressure had vanished.

I looked through the reeve's eyes and through my own. Through this strange double vision, I saw Julie curled on the floor in a tiny fetal ball. Hood stared at me. I sensed him waiting in the deep recesses of the reeve's mind. He brimmed with hate, not just for who I was but for what I was. He seethed, his rage barely contained, a malignant terrible creature who wished the end of humankind. Disgust swelled in me, an instinctual xenophobic response, so strong, it threatened to overwhelm all reason.

I forced the hair to unwind. It let me go slowly, hesitantly. Even with a power word, I wouldn't be able to hold the reeve for long. The moment I fumbled, Hood would seize control.

I stepped aside and pulled the reeve through the bars, through the window, into the kitchen.

Watch this, you sonovabitch.

Obeying my unspoken command, the reeve rammed the wall head-on.

Hit. The drywall crumbled, exposing the hard brick.

Hit. A red stain spread.

Hit. Her skull cracked like a dropped egg.

You won't get my kid, you hear me?

The reeve drew back for a final blow, red and gray slime spilling from her head. Hood's presence fled. A second later I sent her into motion and bailed too, before the dying mind could drag me under.

Hit.

A flood of filthy liquid washed the wall.

My back burned as though molten glass was poured into the wound. The room wavered slightly. I clenched my teeth and raised my sword.

Hood waited in the doorway. The way was clear. No magic walls separated us.

I smiled slowly, showing him my teeth. "Three down. One to go. Come."

The tentacles contracted, drawing the net tighter. I leaned forward a little, light on my toes, ready to charge.

The tentacles detached, rolled into the sleeves and under the hem of the robe, and Hood fled, as if swept from the doorway by a gust of wind.

I looked down in time to see Julie's legs disappear under the table.

CHAPTER 10

—◦◦◦—

I DUCKED UNDER THE TABLE AND ALMOST TOOK A
dive. My head swam. Purple circles flared in my eyes, blocking the view of the house, as sharp pain seared my back. Not
good.

"Julie, we have to go."

She hit the wall with her back. "You're like them. Like the
People."

"No. Completely different." *Exactly like the People. I'm so
like the People, that if you knew, you'd run away screaming.*
"We have to go, Julie. We can't stay here. There might be
more of these things out there and we have a busted door and
a busted ward on the window. We've got to go."

She shook her head.

The pain sliced my spine in half, wringing tears from my
eyes. I couldn't remember the last time something had hurt so
much. I forced my voice to go soft. "Julie, I'm still me. I
swear to you I'll do everything I can to keep you safe. But now
we have to run, before he comes back with more of those
reeve things. Come on, sweetheart. Come on out. Please."

She swallowed and took my hand. I helped her from under
the table.

"That's my girl. Come."

"What kind of magic was that?"

"The forbidden kind. You can never tell anyone I used it or
I'll be in trouble." The power words commanded the magic itself. They were primal words. It wasn't enough to know them,
one had to own them and there were no do-overs: one conquered them or died. The most accomplished mages had two

or three. I had six and I didn't want to explain why. They were my weapon of last resort.

"Your back . . ."

"I know."

There was only one place within reach that offered stronger protection than my apartment: the Order. Under the Order lay the vault. Its wards were impenetrable, and its armored door would take a focused fire from a howitzer to break.

I tried the phone. Still out. There would be no pickup for us from the Order.

A fifteen-minute run separated us from the Order's building. Twenty with the kid in tow. Piece of cake. I could do this. I just needed something to dull the pain. Just for a little bit. And then I'd be fine.

There was a regeneration kit in the bathroom. I took a step toward the door. A streak of heat ran up my spine and exploded into a jagged hot pain in the base of my neck. It ripped at my bones, twisted my tendons, and dragged me down to my knees. I hit the floor hard, dug my saber into the wood, and clung to it, struggling to stay upright. I had a kid to protect.

The room melted out of focus. The walls sprouted fuzz and bent, like waves threatening to drown me. I smelled my own blood. Julie grabbed my arm and sobbed. "You gotta get up. Come on! Don't you die! Don't die!"

"It will be okay," I whispered. "It will be okay."

The magic drained from the world. The tech flared, bringing with it a new burst of pain.

I had to guard the door. It was all I could do.

I WAS DRIFTING IN AND OUT, CLAWING MY WAY through the fog into consciousness, when I felt someone approach. I slashed on instinct and missed.

"You're a fucking mess," Curran's voice said.

Rescued by the Beast Lord. Oh the irony.

"Will she be okay?" Julie's voice asked.

"Yeah," he said. I felt myself being lifted as Curran

scooped me off the floor. "She'll be fine. Come with me. You're safe now."

THE BED WAS UNBELIEVABLY COMFORTABLE. FOR A blissfully long moment I rested, half-drowned in the luxury of soft sheets. The pain had receded, still there, lurking in the small of my back, but dulled and accompanied by the soothing warmth of well-done medmagic. I was alive. That simple fact made me unbelievably happy. As I snuggled deeper into the pillow, I saw a sliver of white on the blanket next to me. I reached over and touched Slayer's blade.

"Awake, my lady fair?" said a familiar voice. Doolittle. The self-proclaimed physician to all things Pack and wild. He sat in a chair by a reading lamp, an ancient, dog-eared paperback on his lap. He hadn't changed a bit—still the same blue-black skin, the same gray hair, and the same small smile. He had patched me up twice during the Red Point Stalker investigation, and there was no better medmage in Atlanta.

I hugged my pillow. "We meet again, Doctor."

"Indeed we do."

"There was a girl with me?"

"She's downstairs. Being entertained by Derek. I daresay she much enjoys his company."

Derek of the huge brown eyes and the knockdown smile. Poor Red didn't stand a chance.

"What was wrong with me?" I didn't insult him by asking about my bloody clothes. I knew he'd burned them.

"You were poisoned. You do test my skills every time we meet."

"I'm sorry. Thank you for saving me."

He shook his head. "I didn't. You were saved by the flare. The deep magic makes all spells more potent. Including those of your humble medmage."

Icy claws skittered up my spine. "Was it really that close?"

He nodded.

I had almost died. I could think of a number of times I had almost died, but never before while a child depended on me for protection. *Great going, Kate. You just had to stand there with your back to the window. Dumbass.*

As soon as I could walk, I had to find a safe place for Julie. The thought of those long claws ripping into her was too much for me.

"Where am I?"

"In the Pack's Southeast office. There was some thought of bringing you to the Keep, but the consensus was you wouldn't make it."

We were repeating the same conversation we'd had ten weeks ago, almost word for word. Except that time I had brought down a crumbling skyscraper on myself and a few hundred vampires.

I grinned. "How did I get here?"

"His Majesty carried you." He grinned back. That part was the same, also.

"Is he burned to a crisp or sliced in half this time?"

"Neither," Curran's voice said. If I had been standing, I would've jumped. He stood in the middle of the room. Behind him a young woman carried a platter filled with four bowls. "However he is quite put out at being awakened from his nap to go and rescue a fool who always bites off more than she can chew."

Doolittle rose hurriedly, bowed, and left. Curran motioned to the table at the foot of the bed, and the woman set the platter on it and left, as well. The door clicked closed, leaving the Beast Lord and me alone in the room.

Oh joy. I hadn't wanted to meet Curran at all, but if I had to meet him, I wanted to be at my best, because he was a mean, vicious sonovabitch, who enjoyed making me squirm. Instead I ended up helpless, in a bed on the Pack's grounds, having been rescued by him. I wanted to fade into the sheets. Maybe I could pretend to fall asleep and he'd leave.

Curran examined me. "You look like shit."

"Thanks. I try." He, on the other hand, looked good. A couple of inches taller than me, broad shouldered and corded with muscle visible even under his T-shirt, Curran moved with a natural grace particular to the very strong and naturally quick. He gave an impression of coiled power, a contained violence that, if released, would explode with terrifying intensity. The last time I saw him, his blond hair had been cropped too short to grab in a fight, but today he wore it longer, showing the beginning of a wave. I had no idea his hair was wavy.

Curran picked up one of the bowls, looked at it for a second, as if considering a matter of some importance, brought the bowl over, and held it before me. The aroma arising from the bowl was heavenly. Suddenly I was ravenous. I sat up and clamped the bowl with both hands. And let go, shaking my fingers. It was the temperature of molten lava.

"Idiot." He set the bowl on the blanket before me and handed me a spoon.

There are times in life when there is nothing better than a hot bowl of chicken soup.

"Thanks." For the soup and for saving my butt again.

"You're welcome."

"Did you get the surveys? They were . . ."

"On the dresser. Shut up and eat your soup."

Curran took Doolittle's chair, brought it over by my bed, and sat. If I reached out with my foot, I could touch him with my toes. Entirely too close for comfort. I moved Slayer closer.

Curran watched me eat. Sitting like this, relaxed, he seemed almost ordinary: a man slightly older than me, kind of on the handsome side. Except for the eyes. They always gave him away. They were alpha eyes, the eyes of a killer and protector to whom the life of a Pack mate meant everything and the life of an outsider meant nothing. He wasn't giving me his hard stare now, merely watching. But I wasn't fooled. I knew how quickly those eyes could drown in lethal gold. I've seen what happens when they do.

Curran commanded over five hundred shapechangers. Half a thousand souls stuck on the crossroads between beast and man, each a spree-killer waiting to happen. Wolves, hyenas, rats, cats, bears, they were united only by two things: the desire to stay human, and loyalty to the Pack. And Curran was the Pack. They worshipped the ground he walked on.

"So that's the secret," the Beast Lord said.

I froze with the spoon halfway to my mouth. That was it. He had figured out what I was and now he was playing with me.

"You okay?" he asked. "Gone a bit pale there."

In a moment he would drop the charade and rip me to pieces. If I was lucky. "Secret to what?"

"Secret to shutting you up," he said. "I just have to beat you till you're half-dead, then give you chicken soup and"—he raised his hands—"blessed silence."

I went back to the soup. Ha-ha. Very funny.

"What did you think I meant?"

"I don't know," I mumbled. "The ways of the Beast Lord are a mystery to a humble merc like me."

"You don't do humble."

At least he still treated me as if I were on my feet, ready to defend myself, instead of being trapped in a bed, eating chicken soup. Speaking of soup . . . I set the bowl aside and looked longingly at the tray. I wanted more. The medmagic made the body burn through nutrients at an accelerated rate, and I was starving.

Curran took a bowl from the platter and offered it to me. I reached for it. His fingers touched mine and lingered. I looked into his eyes and saw tiny gold sparks dancing in the gray. His lips parted, allowing for a narrow flash of his teeth.

I grabbed my bowl and scooted away from him. The hint of a smile curved the corners of his mouth. He found me amusing. That wasn't exactly the reaction I was looking for as the Order's rep.

"Why did you save me?"

He shrugged. "I picked up the phone and there was a hysterical child on the other end, crying that you were dying, and she was all alone, and the undead were coming. I thought it might be an interesting conclusion to a boring evening."

Bullshit. He came because of Julie. Shapeshifters suffered from devastating child mortality, with half their children being born dead and another quarter being killed because they went loup at puberty. Like all shapeshifters, Curran cherished children and he also hated vampires. He probably figured he would kill two birds with one stone: save Julie and stick it to the People.

I frowned. "How did Julie know to call here?"

"Hit a redial button from what I understand. Smart kid. You're going to tell me what you've blundered into."

It wasn't a question, but I determined to take it as such. "No."

"No?"

"No."

He crossed his arms on his chest, making his carved biceps bulge. I vividly remembered those steel-hard biceps flexing as he hoisted me up off the floor by my throat.

"You know what I like about you? You have no sense. You sit here in my house, you can barely hold a spoon, and you're telling me 'no.' You'd pull on Death's whiskers if you could reach them."

Actually, Death wasn't that far out of reach. If I stretched my leg, I could kick him.

"I'll ask one more time, what were you doing?"

It was a pointless battle. Julie didn't stand a chance against Derek. She would tell him everything she knew, which he would then relay to Curran. But I would be damned if I'd let Curran intimidate me into caving in.

"I see. I retrieve the surveys the Pack let slip through its fingers, and in return you bring me here against my will, interrogate me, and threaten me with bodily harm. I'm sure the Order will be amused to learn the Pack kidnapped its representative."

Curran nodded thoughtfully. "Aha. Who's going to tell them?"

Um ... Good question. He could kill me and nobody would ever find my body. The Order wouldn't even investigate that hard; they might just chalk it up to the flare-related craziness.

"I guess I'll just have to kick your ass and break out of here." I bravely drank the rest of the soup from the bowl, abandoning all propriety. *Probably shouldn't have said that.*

"In your dreams."

"We've never had our rematch. I might win." *Probably shouldn't have said that, either.* "Bathroom?"

Curran pointed to the two doors on his left.

I untangled myself from the sheets. I really had to go to the bathroom. The question was: would my legs support me?

Curran smiled.

"What's so funny?"

"Your panties have a bow," he said.

I looked down. I was wearing a short tank top—not mine—and my blue panties with a narrow white strip of lace at the top and a tiny white bow. Would it have killed me to check what I was wearing before I pulled the blanket down? "What's wrong with bows?"

"Nothing." He was grinning now. "I expected barbed wire. Or one of those steel chains."

Wiseass. "I'm secure enough in myself to wear panties with bows on them. Besides, they are comfy and soft."

"I bet." He almost purred.

I gulped. Okay, I needed to either crawl back into bed and cover myself with the blanket or get the hell to the bathroom and back. Since I didn't fancy peeing on myself, the bathroom was my only option.

"I don't suppose you'd mind giving me a bit of privacy for my trip?"

"Not a chance," he said.

I tried to get off the bed. Everything was under control until my weight actually hit my legs and then the room decided to crawl sideways. Curran caught me. His arm hugged my back, his touch sending an electric shiver along my skin. *Oh no.*

"Need some help, ass kicker?"

"I'm fine, thanks." I pushed away from him. He held on to me for a second, letting me know that he could restrain me against my will with laughable ease, and let go. I clenched my teeth. *Enjoy it while it lasts. I'll be back on my feet soon.*

I walked away from him, successfully maintaining vertical position, and zeroed in on the nearest door.

"That's the closet," he said.

Why me?

I made a small adjustment to my course, arrived at the bathroom door, got inside, and let out a breath. That was entirely too close for comfort.

"You okay in there?" he asked. "You need me to come and hold your hand or something?"

I locked the door and heard him laughing. Bastard.

I found a white bathrobe in the bathroom, which permitted me to emerge with some small shred of dignity intact. Curran raised his eyebrows at the robe but didn't say anything.

I made it to the bed, crawled in, and hugged Slayer. While I was in the bathroom, somebody had taken away the soup. I had still had a little bit left in my last bowl.

Outside the window was dark. "What time is it?"

"Early morning. You've been out for about six hours." He fixed me with a hard stare. "What do you want?"

I blinked. "I'm sorry?"

He spoke slowly, carefully shaping the words as if I was slow or hard of hearing. "What do you want for the maps?"

I wanted to hit him in the mouth really hard. "One of the Pack members came to me for help. If I tell you, will you promise not to punish the persons involved?"

"I can't promise that. I don't know what you'll say. You should tell me anyway. I'm curious now and I don't like being out of the loop."

"And have you embark on a bloody rampage?"

"I grow tired of your mouth." Bones shifted under Curran's skin. The nose widened, the jaws grew, the top lip split, displaying enormous teeth. I was staring into the face of a nightmare, a horrible meld of human and lion. If a thing that weighed over six hundred pounds in beast-form could be called a lion. His eyes never changed. The rest of him—the body, the arms, the legs, even his hair and skin remained human. The shapeshifters had three forms: beast, human, and half. They could shift into any of the three, but they always changed shape completely. Most had to strain to maintain the half-form and to be able to speak in it was a great achievement. Only Curran could do this: turn part of his body into one shape while keeping the rest in another.

Normally I had no trouble with Curran's face in half-form. It was well-proportioned, even—many shapeshifters suffered the "my jaws are way too big and don't fit together" syndrome—but I was used to that half-form face being sheathed in gray fur. Having human skin stretched over it was nausea inducing.

He noticed my heroic efforts not to barf. "What is it now?"

I waved my hand around my face. "Fur."

"What do you mean?"

"Your face has no fur."

Curran touched his chin. And just like that all traces of the beast vanished. He sat before me fully human.

He massaged his jaw.

The beast grew stronger during the flare. Curran's irritation caused his control to slip just a hair.

"Having technical difficulties?" I asked and immediately regretted it. Pointing out loss of control to a control freak wasn't the brightest idea.

"You shouldn't provoke me." His voice dropped low. He suddenly looked slightly hungry. "You never know what I might do if I'm not fully in control of myself."

Mayday, Mayday. "I shudder at the thought."

"I usually have that effect on women."

Ha! "Is that before or after they pee on themselves and show you their furry bellies?"

He leaned forward. "I'm leaving. Last chance."

"Myong came to see me."

"Oh," he said. "That."

The muscles on his jaw went tight. We sat in grim silence for several minutes. I waited until I couldn't stand it any longer. "Myong," I said gently.

"You know who she wants to marry?"

She wants to marry my "ex–could have been" boyfriend whom I accused of kidnapping, sexual torture, and cannibalism. "Yes."

"And you're okay with it?"

"Yes."

"Bullshit," he said.

"Maybe I'm not as okay with it as I want to be. But I don't want to keep them from each other." Seeing Myong, well, it stung. I shouldn't have cared that Crest clearly thought she was better than me, but it did bother me a little. She was without a doubt more beautiful, elegant, refined. But she was also so . . . so dying swan. The kind of woman who, if asked to make tea, would return from the kitchen to tell you the water was boiling and expect you to deal with that emergency while she waited demurely next to you.

"I think I've been rather reasonable about this whole situation," Curran said.

"How do you figure?"

"They are still breathing, aren't they?"

Maybe he truly loved her and losing her hurt. Maybe it was his ego talking: a proud alpha, left by a beautiful woman for a normal human, a wimp, pretty much disliked by every shapeshifter who met him. I wished I could make it better for him and for me. But the only way to do so lay through setting them free.

"Please let them go."

He rose. "We'll talk about it later."

"Curran . . ."

"What?"

"You'll feel better if you cut them loose."

"What makes you think it bothers me?" He almost said something else, but changed his mind and left the room.

I felt very alone sitting on the bed by myself. The last time I had felt so alone was when I found out that Greg was murdered.

I untied my robe and laid down. The expedition to the bathroom followed by a tense conversation wore me out. I wanted Curran to let them marry, so I could be done with all of it.

Something moved outside the window. I raised my head. Nothing. Just a rectangular view of the sky, barely brightening before the sunrise. We were on the second or third floor. No trees nearby. I put my head back on my pillow. Wonderful. I'm hallucinating now.

Knock-knock-knock.

A reeve? Couldn't be—those gals didn't knock. I slid off

the bed and walked to the window. No bars. No alarm. I guess when you can smell a drop of blood in five quarts of water, you don't bother with alarms. And only a total lunatic would risk breaking into a house full of monsters. I turned away.

Knock-knock-knock.

Alright, fine. I'll play. The latch on the window was of the old variety, heavy and metal. I'd have to use both hands to get it open. I put Slayer on the windowsill.

Beyond the glass, an empty street stretched into gloom. I unlocked the latch and slid the window up. Below me lay a small ledge, barely more that an ornamental row of bricks protruding from the wall.

Bran popped into existence on the ledge right in front of me. His hands clamped my hands, pinning them to the windowsill. "Hello, dove." He grinned at me. "Look at that: you don't have your pretty knife and I've got your hands. What are you gonna do now?"

I rammed my head into his nose.

"Ow!" He lost his balance, let go of me, arms swinging, and I caught his jacket just as he was about to plummet. My hand brushed the familiar plastic packet. Unbelievable.

I yanked him into the room, swiping the packet of maps from the waistband of his leather pants. The effort nearly dropped me to my knees. I struggled not to fall and growled. "You stole the maps again? Do you have a death wish?"

He blew some blood out of his nose. "I can't fucking believe it. Busted my nose twice in one day. You owe me for this." He surged to his feet and lunged at me.

And stopped when Slayer's blade made contact with his chest. I was weak but I was still fast. "Who are you, what are you doing here, who is Hood, why does he want Julie, and where is Julie's mother?"

"Is that all?" He wiped the red smudge off his lip with the back of his hand.

"Yes. No. Why is the cauldron important, where did it go, how is Morrigan involved, where do you go when you disappear, and why do you keep stealing the maps? Okay, now that's everything."

He pushed a little against Slayer. "I see now. You just want me for my mind. Who's Hood?"

"White robe, tentacles?"

His eyes lit up. "I tell you what, you put the maps right there on the bed. On the count of three, we each grab them. If you win, I'll tell you who he is. If I win, I'll get you."

"Me?"

He winked. "Cute bow, by the way."

I glanced down. Sure enough, my robe had come open. The whole world now knew I had a bow on my panties.

I pulled my robe closed. "You get me for how long? Forever?"

He gave me an appraising stare. "No offense, but you're not that hot. There are other fish in the sea. A night will do."

I had to give it to him, to flatter and insult a woman in one proposition took talent. "No disappearing into the mist to grab the maps?"

He raised his hands. "Fine, fine."

"Swear on Morrigan's name that you'll pay up if I win."

It was a gamble. I watched for his reaction and got it: he hesitated. To him, Morrigan's name carried weight, which meant she was likely to be his patron goddess.

"I swear by Morrighan to uphold the bargain." He pronounced Morrigan oddly, which was probably the right way to say her name.

I tossed Slayer on the bed, never taking my eyes off of him, and put the maps on the sheets. "Back away, three steps."

We stepped back in unison, he to the middle of the room, and I to the wall by the chair.

"On three. One," he said, bending forward like a runner. "Two."

He lunged for the maps. I grabbed the chair and hit him with it. He went down. I hit him again to make sure he stayed that way, stepped over him, and picked up the maps. "I win." Now if only the room would stop spinning, I'd be all set.

He groaned and a torrent of obscenities burst from him.

"Your problem is, you underestimate me because I'm a woman." I nudged him with my foot. "Hood's name?"

"Bolgor the Shepherd, of the Fomoire." Mist swirled and he vanished.

My legs gave out and I crash-landed on the bed. Fomoire? Fomorian. Morrigan's old adversaries. Now the fish stink made sense: of course, a sea-demon would stink like fish. I frowned. Bran served Morrigan and Morrigan and the Fomorians hated each other. That made perfect sense. But what did this Shepherd want with Julie?

The door burst open and Derek charged into the room, followed by two female shapeshifters.

I held out the maps. "Here. That's twice in one day. You owe me."

Derek took the maps from my hands and sniffed them, while the two women checked the window.

"He's gone," the younger woman said.

Derek's face trembled in fury. "I'm going to find him. Nobody does that to us twice."

"What's going on?" Curran stepped into the room.

Derek paled. Good luck explaining that monumental breach of security.

Bran snapped into the room in a corkscrew of mist, jerked my robe open and down to clamp my shoulders, and kissed me. His teeth clicked against mine. I kneed him, but he expected it and blocked with his leg. He realized his tongue wouldn't make it into my mouth and let go. "I'll still get you," he promised.

Curran lunged at him and caught tendrils of mist.

I wiped my mouth with the back of my hand.

"Did he hurt you?" Curran said.

If my eyes could shoot lightning, I would've fried him on the spot. "Depends on how you define hurt. What kind of show are you running here, anyway?"

Curran snarled.

"Very impressive," I told him. "He can't hear you."

I pulled my robe shut, again, climbed into my bed, and covered myself with my blanket. I had had entirely enough embarrassment for one night.

CHAPTER 11

I WOKE UP BECAUSE SOMEONE WAS WATCHING ME. I opened my eyes and saw Julie's face an inch from mine. We looked at each other for a long minute.

"You're not going to die?" she asked me very softly.

"Not right this minute." And, of course, saying something like that usually resulted in immediate demise. I braced myself for a stray meteorite falling through the roof to crush my skull.

"That's good," she said in a voice that suggested anything but happiness.

She crawled on my bed, and curled up in a corner, hands fastened over her knees.

"I got scared. I get scared when Mom goes to work." She put her head on her hands. "And when Red leaves."

"That's a hard way to live."

"I can't help it."

I didn't know what to say. Kids don't usually understand death. They feel immortal and secure. Julie understood the full extent of death the way an adult would, and she couldn't deal with it. And I didn't know how to help her.

"There is something you said to Red that I wanted to ask you about." If I just could figure out the right way to do it. "You said you would give him what you had. What did you mean?"

She shrugged. "Sex. Red knows a ritual that would give him my powers if I do sex with him."

I stared at her, speechless. There were so many things wrong with what she said that my brain experienced a momentary shutdown.

"I don't need it. It's not a big thing. So I can see magic's colors, so what? If I give it to him, he'll be stronger and he can protect us both. I'd do it now, but he wants to wait. He says if we do it when I get fully grown, he'd get more power."

"Julie, do you trust me?"

The question caught her by surprise. "Yeah."

I took a deep breath. "There is no spell that transfers power from one person to another."

"But . . ."

"Let me finish." I sat up and tried my best to adopt an even tone of voice. "There is a witch spell that lets you mimic someone's powers for a little while. And yes, it involves sex, and yes, you can do it in such a way as to make the other person think that their powers are gone, but they aren't. Not really. Your power is who you are. It's in your blood, it's in your bones; it's in every cell of your body. That's why people burn their bandages, because their magic lingers in their blood even after it's separated from their bodies." That's why if anybody ever got their hands on my bloody bandage, I'd have to kill them.

She opened her mouth.

"Let me tell you something about the spell. It's called mirror lock. You know how sex works?"

For a second she struggled between proving to me that I was full of shit and wanting to show off her adult knowledge. The need to impress won. "Yeah. The man puts his stuff . . ."

"Penis."

". . . penis into the woman."

"And what happens at the end?"

"Orgasm."

"And what causes orgasm in a man?" Kate Daniels, the sex-ed specialist. Kill me, somebody.

"Uhhh . . . ?"

"Sperm comes out. He ejaculates."

"That's how you get pregnant." She nodded.

"Now remember that blood has magic? Well, sperm has magic, also. It's the man's seed and it's very potent. Lots of magic. The way mirror lock works, the witch, a woman, has sex with the man. His seed is now in her body and it can stay alive in there for up to five days. As long as the seed lives, she can use this seed to mimic the man's powers. Those powers won't be that strong, but if she has done everything right, she will have them. Now at the same time while she and the man are having sex, she casts spells that numb the man's senses and make him very tired. He feels weak. He can try to do magic, but he doesn't feel his own power. And then the spells wear off and he's back to normal."

I've run across the mirror lock twice, and both times the victims had killed the witches responsible. It was a nasty spell, used almost always for the wrong reasons.

"Do you understand now why it only works when a woman is casting it? The woman's fluids simply don't enter the man's body in a large enough amount for the spell to work the other way."

I watched it sink in. I wished we could have stopped right there.

"Somebody, probably a witch, told Red about the spell. It's a dangerous spell, Julie. Many things can go wrong. Red knows enough about magic to figure out that it's risky and, if he stopped to think about it long enough, he would also figure out that it can only work one way. But he wants the power so much, he didn't even think about it. He jumped on that chance."

She got a hint of where I was headed. "Red loves me!"

"Red loves power more. What kind of boyfriend is he that he would try to rob you of your power? To use you this way? Sex is . . ." I struggled for words. "It's an intimate thing. A loving thing, or at least it should be, God damn it. You should do it because you want to make the other person and yourself happy."

She was blinking back tears. "If I gave him my power, it would make him happy and then I'd be happy!"

It's good that Red was hiding somewhere far away, because if I could get my hands on him right this second, I'd wring his little neck.

"You're a sensate. One in ten thousand. You and your mom always worry about money, right? Julie, with a little training, you could make three or four times as much as I do within a couple of years. People will bring you money in truckloads. They will pay for you to go to school, just so you could tell them what color of magic something is. But even if you had the most useless power in the world, even if all you could do was to make a fart sound with a flick of your fingers, I would still tell you the same thing. You shouldn't give up what you are to make somebody else happy."

"I decide what makes me happy!" She jumped off the bed and stomped off.

"If it feels wrong, it probably is."

She slammed the door. Well, I had managed to handle that one with my usual tact, finesse, and sense of perfect timing. I got up and went to dress and find something to eat.

YOUNG SHAPESHIFTERS DIDN'T HAVE A LOT OF TIME to find themselves. When puberty hit, they had two choices: go loup or go Code.

Going loup meant abandoning all control to blindly follow your body into hormone hell. Loups fed on human meat. They reveled in pain and sadistic perversion, sliding down from one elaborate torture to the next, until a gun, a sword, or claws cured all their ills, or until Lyc-V burned them out. Loups died young and didn't leave pretty corpses.

Going Code meant controlling your every move. Free People of the Code wanted to stay human and went to extraordinary lengths to keep their beast on a short leash. Code meant strict mental conditioning, discipline, accountability, hierarchy, and obedience. All of the things that pretty much drove me crazy.

The individuals emerging from this Code crucible acquired similar traits. They knew their boundaries. They avoided smoking, strong scents, liquor, and spices, as they dulled their senses. They rarely gave in to excess.

Except when it came to food. The shapeshifters ate like pigs. And I did my best to imitate them. I was ravenous and there was no telling when I would eat again.

I was alone in the kitchen—it was past breakfast except by the most lax standards. I had just taken my first bite when Derek walked in and sat across from me. He had an old-fashioned metal coffee can in his hands and a pair of heavy-duty cutters. He pulled a large iron nail from the can and some wire, and proceeded to cut a two-inch strip from the can. I watched him bend the nail into a gentle zigzag. He folded the metal strip into a roll like it was clay and pinched it onto the nail.

It's good to be a werewolf.

"You got a copy of the Almanac around here?"

Derek got up and brought me *The Almanac of Mystical Creatures*. "Thanks."

I thumbed through it while helping myself to some bacon. No Bolgor the Shepherd. No mention of the reeves. I scanned the entry about Morrigan. No mention of the bowman. Of course, if there was, I probably would've known it—I had read the Almanac from cover to cover several times. It rarely got all the details right, but it was a good general guide to things magically delicious.

Shortly after I started on my second plate, Julie appeared and sat sullenly by my side.

Derek added more strips to the nail, clamping them tight, and bound them with wire.

"Derek, if a boy wanted to take away a girl's power by having sex with her, what would you think about it?"

"I'd break something. His leg. Maybe his arm." He squeezed the wire tighter. "Probably wouldn't kill him unless he wanted to make an issue of it."

"What if the girl wanted to give her powers to the boy?" I asked.

"Then I'd think it would be a pretty stupid thing to do." He shrugged. "Can it be done?"

"No."

"Good for the girl. She might get smarter and find a different boy." He released his hold and handed Julie a metal rose. "For you. Kate, if you're done with your plate, Curran wants to see you. He's up on the roof."

I followed him to the staircase and climbed up onto the third floor, where a small foldout ladder led to the square piece of the sky. I conquered the ladder and emerged onto the flat roof of the building.

The roof was filled with assorted free weights. Curran lay on a massive weight bench with a reinforced steel frame. He was working the bench press, raising a bar loaded with weights above him and bringing it back to his chest in a slow controlled movement. He didn't cheat by letting the bar "bounce" off his chest.

I came closer. The bar was thicker than my wrist. Had to be custom made. I tried to count the weight disks on the bar. A normal bar weighed forty-five pounds, and normal disks weighed up to forty-five pounds, also. But these didn't look normal.

I stood to the side and watched the bar rise and fall. Curran wore an old, torn T-shirt, and I could see his muscles pump under the fabric.

"How much are you lifting?"

"Seven hundred."

Alrighty then. I will just stand over here, out of your way, and hope you don't remember my promise to kick your ass.

He grinned. "Wanna spot me?"

"No thanks. How about I just scream verbal encouragements at you?" I took a deep breath and barked. "No pain, no gain! That pain is just weakness leaving your body! Come on! Push! Push! Make that weight your bitch!"

He cracked up. The weight stopped, perilously close to his chest, while he shook with laughter. I stepped up and grabbed the bar. It put me into an incredibly compromising position, since his head was really close to my thighs and the area directly above them, but I didn't want to explain to a rabid Pack how I was responsible for the Beast Lord crushing his chest with a weight bar.

I put my back into it. There was no way in hell I could ever pull it up without him pushing.

The bar crept up very slowly.

"Curran, stop playing and lift."

I looked down and saw him looking straight at me. He had a smile on his face. The sight of me puffing and straining apparently amused him to no end.

He raised the bar up and slid it into the twin forks on the sides of the bench.

I beat a hasty retreat, putting a few feet between him and me. He sat, pulled his shirt off, and used it to wipe the sweat off his chest. Slowly. Flexing a bit for my benefit.

I turned around and looked at the scenery. Having a streak of drool hang from my mouth would seriously cramp my style. Besides, if he full-out flexed, I would probably faint. Or jump off the building.

I needed to get laid. Otherwise my hormones might go on strike and short-circuit my common sense.

Curran came to stand next to me. Before us the broken city grappled with an impending flare. In the distance husks of skyscrapers sagged to the ground. Between them and us stretched the twisted labyrinth of streets, punctured by greenery, where nature had reclaimed the ruins for its own.

Maybe I was imagining things. Maybe he was just wiping off his sweat because he didn't want to be sweaty, not because he was showing off for me. Once again, I was giving myself too much credit.

"What are you going to do with the child?" he asked.

"I'll take her to the Order. There is a vault below the Order's building. It has a two-foot-thick steel door, and it's blanketed in a ward the entire mage division of the Military Supernatural Defense Units can't bust. The safest place in the city right now."

The Order had to own other facilities too, but I didn't rate high enough to know their location or function. I wouldn't have known about the vault either if Ted thought he could hide it from me. If you put a door marked "Authorized Personnel ONLY" and me in the same building, sooner or later I'll try to jimmy its lock to discover what's so special about it.

"You can keep her here," Curran said. "We'll look after her."

"Thank you for the offer. I honestly appreciate it. But

things are hunting her. She'll be safe in the vault and I don't want to be responsible for any deaths."

He sighed. "You do realize that you just insulted me, right?"

"How so?"

"You implied that I can't protect her or my people."

I looked at him. "That's not at all what I meant."

"Apologize and I'll let it go."

I kept my hands firmly on the iron rail before me. Grabbing the weight bar and walloping the Beast Lord upside the head wouldn't be the best diplomatic move.

"I'm sorry, Your Majesty." There. I was civil. It almost killed me.

"Apology accepted."

"Will there be anything else?" *Your Arrogance.*

"No." He picked up an enormous dumbbell and began to curl, working his biceps.

I turned to leave and stopped. He was in a good mood. Relaxed. He didn't wig out at me. Now was as good a time as any. "Myong . . ."

A low warning growl reverberated in his throat. "I said later."

Technically it was later. "I think she loves him very much."

He snarled. "You forget yourself! Drop it."

"She's very passive and she's terrified of you. It took a great deal of courage for her to come and see me."

He tossed the dumbbell aside. It went flying and hit with a loud thud, leaving a dent in the pavement of the roof. Curran strode toward me, eyes blazing. "If I let her go, I'll need a replacement. Want to volunteer for the job?"

He looked like he wouldn't be taking no for an answer. I swiped Slayer from its sheath and backed away from the edge of the roof. "And be girlfriend number twenty-three soon to be dumped in favor of girlfriend number twenty-four who has slightly bigger boobs? I don't think so."

He kept coming. "Oh yeah?"

"Yeah. You get these beautiful women, make them dependent on you, and then dump them. Well, this time a woman left you first, and your enormous ego can't deal with it. And to think that I hoped we could talk like reasonable adults. If we were the last two people on Earth, I'd find myself a moving island so I could get the hell away from you." I was almost to the drop door leading to the ladder.

He stopped suddenly and crossed his arms over his chest. "We'll see."

"Nothing to see. Thanks for the rescue and for the food. I'm taking my kid and leaving." I dropped into the hole, slid down the ladder, and backed away down the hall. He didn't follow me.

I was midway down to the first floor when it finally hit me: I had just told the alpha of all shapeshifters that hell would freeze over before I got into his bed. Not only had I just kissed any cooperation from the Pack good-bye, but I had also challenged him. Again. I stopped and hit my head a few times on the wall. Keep your mouth shut, stupid.

Derek appeared at the bottom of the stairway. "It went that well, huh?"

"Spare me."

"I take it you're leaving."

I stopped hitting my head and looked at him.

"Mind if I tag along?" he asked.

"Why?"

"I want the thief." Derek's face was grim. "He has a thing for you."

A werewolf who can outrun me, who can bend metal into roses with his fingers, and who could grab Julie in case of trouble and take off like a rocket never to be caught by freaky broads with deepwater teeth. Let me think . . .

"Sure. Be glad to have you."

CHAPTER 12

MIRACULOUSLY THE PHONE IN THE HALLWAY OF THE shapeshifters' office worked. As much as I wanted to get the hell out of there, I didn't want to risk leaving on foot.

I got Maxine on the first ring. "Atlanta Chapter of the Order. How may I help you?"

"Maxine, it's me. May I speak to Ted?"

"He's out."

"Out? Ted's never out. Where is he?"

"He's on an errand."

Crap. "What about Mauro?"

"He's out, too. Most of the knights are out."

What in the world? "Is anybody there?"

"Andrea."

Oh boy. "Can I speak to her, please?"

There was a click and then Andrea's voice said, "Hey, Kate."

Hi, Andrea I know you've been attacked by a loup, but can you come to pick up me and my teenage werewolf at a shapeshifter compound? I took a deep breath. Here's hoping she didn't suffer from post-traumatic stress disorder.

"I really hate to ask you this, but I have no choice. I'm trying to escort a little girl to the Order so I can hide her in the vault. I need three horses."

"No problem. Where are you?"

"I'm at the Pack's Southeast office." I cringed a little as I said it. "I'll meet you on the corner of Griffin and Atlanta Avenue. And I have a shapeshifter with me."

She didn't miss a beat. "Sit tight. I'll be right there."

I collected Julie, once again armed with my knife, and we left, Derek in tow.

"Where are we going?" Julie asked as we headed toward Griffin Street.

"To the Order."

Around us the city shrugged off the remnants of the magic-filled night. Technology had hit early in the morning, but the magic waves had flowed and ebbed all night.

"What are we going to do at the Order?" Julie asked.

"The Order's very well fortified. I'm going to leave you there with Andrea. She's a very nice lady."

"No! I'm going to stay with you!"

I gave her my hard stare. "Julie, this isn't a democracy."

"No!"

I kept walking. "I have to go out and look for your mom. You do want me to find your mom, don't you?"

"I want to come with you."

On the corner of Griffin and Atlanta Avenue a crowd blocked the traffic around a crane. A skinny dark-haired girl with the buttery grace of a pickpocket was working the edges of the gathering. She drifted our way. Julie pulled out her dagger and gave the pickpocket a hard look. The girl reversed her course.

The crane groaned. The cable snapped taut, and a huge fish tail reared above the crowd, followed by a serpentine body covered with turquoise scales bigger than my head. The scales glistened with moisture. Something about that fish looked familiar . . . I couldn't recall where I could've seen a three-story-tall fish. Not exactly a sight I would likely forget.

"What is that?"

A balding middle-aged man with a teamster badge on his leather vest turned to me. "The Fish Market Fish."

"The bronze sculpture in front of the Fish Market?"

"Used to be bronze."

"How did it get here from Buckhead?"

"There was a river," a woman on my left said. "I saw it from the window."

"The ground's dry," the teamster pointed out.

"I'm telling you I saw a river. You could see clear through the waves. Like it was made out of ghosts. Never seen nothing like that."

The teamster spat into the dirt. "Yeah, well, we'll see worse before the flare's over."

We stood to the side, away from the crowd, and watched the fish being hoisted up.

"You can't leave me," Julie declared.

Considering our earlier conversation, I would've thought she'd jump at the chance to get me out of her hair. "I want you to think back to when the reeves came."

She paled.

"The reeves are out there. They want you for something and they won't give up. Put yourself in place of your mom. Would you let your daughter tag along with some weirdo woman who is going out to hunt reeves or would you want your baby to be safe?"

Her face fell. "You're not my mom. You can't tell me what to do," she said finally, but her tone signaled the end of the argument.

"I'm a substitute mom," I told her.

"You're more like a crazy aunt who only gets called when somebody needs bailing out of jail," Derek said.

I pointed my finger at him. He grinned.

"Julie, until I find your real mom, I'm in charge of your safety. She loves you and she's a good person. She deserves to be found and to have you be alright. If I found her, but something happened to you, I don't know what I would do." *And if I can't find your mom, she would've wanted you to be safe.*

At the other end of the intersection, Andrea appeared, riding a bay gelding and leading three horses.

I WOULD'VE LIKED TO GALLOP ALL THE WAY TO THE Order, but the traffic was heavy. The city knew deep magic would hit soon, and while the tech was up, they made the best of it. We had to settle for a slow trot.

Andrea rode in the lead, Julie behind her, clutching the reins with white-knuckled panic, and Derek and I brought up the rear. I wanted Derek and Andrea separated as much as possible. When your partner goes loup and tries to turn your stomach into an all-you-can-eat buffet while you're still breathing, you might develop a slight dislike of shapeshifters. Why tempt fate?

"He's actually quite patient," Derek said, drawing even with me.

"Who?"

"Curran."

I nodded. "He's patient as long as everyone plays by his rules."

"That's not true. You've never seen him when he isn't under pressure."

"Being the Beast Lord, I'd imagine he's always under pressure." I sighed. "I didn't mean to aggravate him. It was a matter of bad timing. He was pumped up full of adrenaline after working out, which made him more aggressive than usual. It was the wrong time to bring it up. That's all." That and I couldn't control my mouth in his vicinity. He got under my skin.

"It's the flare, too," he added. "Makes it harder to restrain yourself."

"Look, if you want I'll try to smooth things over if I get another opportunity." Ha! Fat chance of that. After that blowup, I was probably persona non grata in the Pack for life.

I didn't breathe easy until we dismounted in the Order's parking lot.

I swung the door open and motioned Julie inside. "Second floor, my office is first on the left, should be unlocked." She ducked in.

I filled Andrea in on the problem of Julie's missing mom, the reeves, and Hood, a.k.a. Bolgor the Shepherd, while we stabled the horses. Derek stood guard by the Order's door, but I was pretty sure he heard every word. Wolf ears worked much better than human ones, and his were exceptional. "Fomorians," she said. "What's the world coming to?"

"Three things: what are they doing here, why do they want Julie, and what happened to her mom?"

Andrea shook her head. "I have no clue. But then it's not my area. I shoot. I make gadgets work. I'm good with post-Shift resonance theory. Ask me something about folklore, and I draw a blank every time." She grinned. "But I'll keep your girl safe."

"I'm sorry to dump this on you."

She glanced at Derek. "I wish everyone would stop walking on eggshells around me. It needs doing, so I'll do it. I have to stay at the Chapter anyway: it's standard procedure during a flare for one knight to always be present. I'll guard your girl."

I hesitated. If anyone could help me in this situation, it was Andrea. She was a picture-perfect knight and she knew every regulation ever written.

"What's up?" she asked, as if reading my thoughts.

"Should I write up a petition for safe asylum?"

Andrea frowned. "Worried about the Danger to Humanity clause?"

"Yeah."

The good thing about the petition for safe asylum was that any and all knights would protect Julie from any threat, as long as she remained in their custody. But by signing the petition, Julie placed herself into the Order's care, which meant she fell under the imminent danger clause. If she presented an imminent danger to humanity, the knights were duty bound to dispatch her. The Order wasn't in the habit of snuffing out little girls, but I knew that in Ted's mind, at least, the welfare of many outweighed the lives of the few. I had no clue as to why the reeves and the Shepherd hunted Julie. For all I knew, she was some sort of Fomorian-prophesied child destined to destroy the world. Stranger things have happened. I didn't want to find Julie with her throat slit. I'm sure they would make her end merciful and quick, but that hardly seemed like consolation.

Andrea smiled. "The good news is, you don't have to file one. She is an orphan with no known relatives. Under provision seventeen, you can assume temporary guardianship of her due to the fact she can't legally enter into contract. Fill out form 240-m, and she becomes your ward in the eyes of the Order. During the flare, all families of Order personnel can legally seek shelter at the nearest Chapter without being subject to the imminent danger clause. Unless she attacks, they have no authority to neutralize her."

"I don't know if she would sign something like that. She still thinks her mother is alive. And so do I." I hoped, anyway. "It might hammer some unpleasant possibilities home."

"You don't need her to sign. That's the beauty of it—all you need is the testimony of one knight besides yourself who agrees that you're acting in her best interests." She grinned from ear to ear. "And lucky you, you know one."

"Thanks," I said and meant it.

"No problem. This is kind of fun for me—I'm so freaking bored. If magic hits, we'll skedaddle down to the vault, and if the reeves show while the tech is up, I'll use their heads for target practice."

The door burst open. Julie ran headfirst into Derek and flailed in his hands. He grabbed her and lifted her off the ground. "What? Speak!"

She strained and spat a single word. "Vampire!"

IT WAITED FOR ME UPSTAIRS ON MY DESK, A HAIR-less, emaciated nightmare, wrapped in steel-wire muscle and hidden in human skin. It was nude, ugly, and had been dead for three or four decades. Someone had smeared copious amounts of purple sunblock over its hide. For some reason the sunblock didn't disappear but dried into paste, as if the creature had popped a giant bubble of grape gum onto himself.

"You've got to be kidding me."

The vampire unhinged its mouth and Ghastek's voice issued forth. "A pleasure to see you, as always."

It would have to be Ghastek. I wondered if Nataraja, the leader of the People's establishment in the city, had specifically assigned him to interact with me or if Ghastek took that dreadful task upon himself.

Andrea stepped into the office. And suddenly she had two guns and they were pointing at the vamp's face.

"Lovely firearms," Ghastek said.

"SIG-Sauer P226," Andrea said. "Move and you'll go blind."

"Do you really think you could beat vampiric reflexes?" Ghastek's tone was light. He wasn't challenging her, he was merely curious.

A small smile bent Andrea's lips. "Do you really want to find out?"

I shook my head. "She can blow his head off before you finish a twitch. Trust me, I measure speed for a living."

I made a mental note to never fight fair with Andrea. That was a hell of a draw. I was fast but not fast enough to beat her guns and my saber took a lot longer to come out of its sheath than a gun did coming out of a holster. "Fortunately for all of us, we don't have to fight." I smiled at Andrea.

Andrea nodded and guns vanished. "I'll be down the hall."

"Thank you."

She stepped out. I sat in my chair. "Off my table."

The vampire remained where it was.

"Ghastek, either you move him or I will. I don't have to put up with rudeness in my own office."

The undead slinked off the table. "That was not meant as an insult."

"Good, then I won't take it as such. Now, what is it you want?"

"How do you feel? Any broken bones? Open wounds?"

"No. Why this sudden concern for my well-being?"

"No episodes of dizziness? What about a slight prickling in the chest and along the neck? Feels a little like the rush of blood into a limb after it has fallen asleep, except the process occurs from the inside."

I crossed my arms. "Is there a particular reason why you're describing the initial stages of colonization by Immortuus pathogen to me?"

The vampire crept closer. "There can only be one reason."

"I'm not turning into a vampire, Ghastek." It was physically impossible. My blood chomped the vampirism bacterium for breakfast and then asked for seconds. No vampirism for me. No shapeshifting, either.

The vampire took another careful step to me. "May I see your irises, please."

"I'm telling you, I'm not infected. I wasn't bitten."

"Indulge me."

I leaned forward. The vampire reared from all fours and lifted its face to mine. We stared at each other, the corpse and I, with only inches of space between us. Almost touching. I looked into the vampire's eyes, once blue, and now red from the capillaries expanded by the flow of blood brimming with vampiric pathogen. Within their depths lay hunger, a terrible, all-consuming hunger that could never be doused. If Ghastek's control slipped just a hair, the abomination would rip into me, clawing at my flesh in search of hot blood.

At least it would try. And then I would kill it. I'd crush its disgusting mind like a gnat. It would feel good. It would make my day.

I would've liked to kill them all. I would've liked to go up the People's food chain until I reached Roland, their legendary leader. There were things I needed to discuss with him. But our conversation would have to wait until my power grew, because right now he could wipe me off the face of the Earth with a twitch of his eyebrow.

The vampire dropped to the floor.

"Satisfied?"

"Yes."

"You sound disappointed. Does the idea of navigating me after my undeath appeal to you?"

The vampire's face twitched, trying to imitate Ghastek wincing somewhere in an armored room within the Casino's depths. "Kate, that was in poor taste. Although you would make a magnificent specimen. You're in excellent physical shape and well proportioned. I just looked through the stack of applications this morning and half of the candidates are malnourished, while the other half have wrong proportions."

Ghastek in all his glory. Clinical "R" Us.

I sighed. Was there any remote chance that he would get to the point of his visit this morning? Time was a-wasting and I needed to leave to look for Julie's mother. "My schedule is a bit cluttered this morning. I would appreciate it if we could get down to business."

"Our patrol sighted an unusual undead last night," Ghastek said. "Prehensile hair, claws, very interesting power signature."

Claws, huh. I replayed the fight in my mind. The claws only came out when the reeve was closing in for a kill. Two reeves had attacked my apartment within minutes of each other, but the third didn't show up until much later. It was delayed. I took a stab in the dark. "So how quickly did this weird undead dispose of your patrol?"

If Ghastek was surprised, he didn't show it. "Under ten seconds."

"That's a bit sad, don't you think?"

"It was a young vampire. We just got him."

Excuses, excuses. "I fail to see how it concerns me."

"We traced the power signature to your apartment. Which is in a state of advanced disrepair, from what could be seen through the window. Although it does appear to have a new door. I take it the old one was destroyed?"

"In a very dramatic way."

The vampire paused. Here we go.

"The People would like to obtain this specimen."

Knock yourself out. Ghastek was arguably the best Master of the Dead in the city. He had the best journeymen and the best vampires. The look on Ghastek's face, once he wasted several of those prized bloodsuckers trying to capture a reeve only to have it turn into sludge, would be priceless.

"Your smile has a disturbing edge to it," Ghastek observed.

I kept smiling. "I can't help it."

"Since the incident took place in your apartment, the People would like to request your assistance in this matter. What do you know, Kate?"

"I know very little," I warned.

"Share it with me anyway."

The People really wanted a reeve. Perhaps piloting good old vampires just didn't do it for them anymore. "What's in it for me?"

"Monetary compensation."

The day I took People's money would be the day I gave up on being a human. "Not interested. Any other offers?"

The vampire stared at me, his mouth slack as Ghastek assessed his options. I took a couple of forms from my desk, put them into the vamp's mouth, and pulled them up by their edges.

"What are you doing?" Ghastek asked.

"My hole puncher broke."

"You have no respect for the undead."

I sighed, examining the ragged tears in the forms. "It's a personal failing. Have you thought of anything, or can I be on my way?"

"I will owe you a favor," Ghastek said. "Now or in the future, at your request, I will perform a task of your choosing, provided it doesn't require me to cause direct harm to myself or my crew."

I considered. It was a hefty offer. In the hands of an experienced Master of the Dead, a vampire was a weapon like no other, and Ghastek wasn't just experienced, he was talented. A favor from him could come in handy. And even if he got his greedy mittens on a reeve, he would put it through its paces, trying to determine the extent of its powers. The moment it suffered a serious injury, it would turn into sludge. What was the downside?

"Maxine?"

"Yes, dear?"

"Ghastek promised me a favor for my assistance. Do we have any paperwork that would put this arrangement into written form?"

"Yes."

"You're going to have me sign a contract?"

"Yep."

The vampire emitted a series of strangled creaks, and I realized it was trying to reproduce Ghastek's laugh.

DEREK WANDERED INTO THE OFFICE AND LEANED against the wall, his arms crossed.

"Your associate is still alive," Ghastek said, reading through the forms. "Remarkable."

"He's hardy."

The fact that Ghastek's signature looked exactly the way it did when he signed the document in person was a greater testament to his control than any wall crawling or claw waving. I had to admire the degree of his competency. He still made my skin crawl.

"I'm all ears," he said once Maxine took the paperwork back to her desk.

"Two days ago a coven of amateur witches disappeared from their meeting place at the bottom of the Honeycomb Gap. I visited the place on unrelated business and discovered a bottomless pit and lots of residual necromantic magic. Lots of blood. No bodies."

"Go on."

"I picked up the daughter of one of the witches."

"The child that ran into your office a few minutes ago," he said. "I didn't mean to startle her."

"Yes." I didn't particularly feel like explaining that Julie had a vampire phobia and since magic was down, she couldn't detect the vampiric power signature. "She asked me for help. I've extended the Order's protection to her." So don't start getting any ideas. "I took the child to my apartment. During the night we were attacked."

"How many of them were there?"

"Three, not including the navigator."

The vampire went rigid. "There was a navigator?"

"Yes."

"Human?"

"Not exactly."

I described Bolgor the Shepherd, focusing on his tentacles,

and the reeves, going into detail on the hair, claws, and toxic goo on said claws. I explained the sea-demon angle, although I didn't tell him how I got the information. I could've led him on regarding their peculiar dying habits, but a bargain was a bargain so I came clean and expanded on the whole melting into sludge thing. I did gloss over my near demise, shortening it to "I was stabbed in the back, after which I dispatched the reeve and called to my associate, who picked me up and transported me to the medmage." Which was almost true. To the best of my awareness, nobody knew I could pilot vampires, and it was essential for my safety that things remained that way.

The vampire went into statue mode while Ghastek processed the information. The People consider themselves to have a monopoly on all things necromantic. The idea of a third-party navigator running around the city, even if he was a demon, had to grate on Ghastek. "The moniker Shepherd interests me. It could refer to his ability to navigate."

I tapped my nails against the desk. "I strongly suggest you abandon pursuit of the reeves. They turn into goo once critically injured."

"That's truly unfortunate, but I wish to ascertain that fact for myself. Do you have reason to believe this Shepherd would return for the girl?" Ghastek asked. He was wondering if the reeves were the Sisters of the Crow, brought into the undeath by some strange power they had released. I had wondered it, too.

"The girl is in the vault. If he does, he's out of luck."

"What are your plans?"

"I'm going to go and visit an expert who might help me sort through this mess. I understand the Fomorians' desire to annihilate Morrigan, but I don't know how they came to be in the city, what they want with the child, or why they targeted that particular coven. I know that the coven had worshipped Morrigan, but the head witch was performing druidic sacrificial rites in her trailer. The two don't go together."

"Why not go see the Order of Druids?" Derek asked.

Ghastek shifted the vamp a few inches. "No, she's right.

The Druids spent years trying to distance themselves from their heritage. The moment they hear 'sacrifice,' they'll refuse to communicate. It's a PR nightmare. A third party expert would be best."

I rose. "And the sooner I see him, the better. As you always say, it was a pleasure."

"I'm coming with you."

"I'm sorry, I think I misheard."

The vampire spread its arms, the huge yellow claws adding another three inches to its long digits. "Considering the value of my offer, you didn't give me nearly enough. We both signed the contract, Kate. It stated 'full and substantial disclosure of any information pertaining to the creature in question.' What you gave me was by no means substantial."

How do I get myself into these things?

Derek pushed off the wall, his jaw set. I stepped between him and the vampire. "Very well. Feel free to come along. You understand that there is no guarantee we'll encounter any more reeves?"

"Oh, I think we will. You've cost him three undead. I don't know of any Master of the Dead that wouldn't want to get even."

Before we left, I chased the werewolf and the vampire out of my office and changed my clothes. Over the years I've learned to leave extra clothes at convenient places, and my office offered changes of clothes and gear. Pack sweats were nice and all, but after fun games with the reeves' claws I wanted something a bit thicker. I put on loose brown pants and a white heat-gear T-shirt. Made of a quick-drying microfiber, it wicked moisture from my body, keeping me dry and cool despite the heat of the summer. SWAT wore these seamless T-shirts under armor. I added a leather vest, securing the strings tight enough to be able to move, and completed my kick-butt outfit with a pair of combat boots: black leather toes, leather heels, and black nylon mesh sides. Almost light enough to play tennis in.

I spun and kicked at my shadow on the wall, adjusted the left vest seam to hug my body better, and slid Slayer's sheath into the rings along the vest's back.

Next, I took my dog-eared *Craft Chronicle* off the shelf, found the mirror lock spell, put a pencil on the right page to use as a bookmark, and went down the long concrete staircase into the vault. Hidden behind a foot-thick steel door lay five rooms storing everything from weapons and books to objects of minor power, the inventory the Knights of the Order felt was prudent to keep on hand. The foremost room contained a sink, a fridge, sleeping bags, even a closet-sized bathroom.

Andrea was already there, loading firearms and laying them out on the table. Julie froze when I came in. I thought we were past that. I tried my best to grin. "Getting settled?"

"Andrea has jerky and there is pizza." Her voice wilted. Any kid would be thrilled about the pizza. Boy, it just wasn't going too well with me and her today.

"I'm sorry you're mad at me. I brought you a book to read." I put *Craft Chronicle* on the table.

She didn't say anything.

Oh, screw it.

I stepped right across the heavy silence hanging between us and hugged her. "I'll be back soon, okay? Stay here. Andrea is very cool. You'll be safe with her." She looked about to cry. "Who knows, I might come back with your mom." I'd go to hell for making promises like that. Straight to hell with no detours.

"You think so?"

"I hope so," I told her. "I've got my saber and I've got my belt." I touched the belt, equipped with a half dozen pouches containing herbs and silver needles.

"Batman belt!" Julie said.

"That's right, Barbara. Protect the cave while I'm gone."

Julie took the monisto off her neck. "Here. I'm not giving it to you. I'm just letting you borrow it for a little while. You'll bring it back, right?"

"Right." I slid the monisto into a pocket under my leather.

Andrea and I nodded to each other and I went.

CHAPTER 13

WE MOVED THROUGH THE STREETS OF BUCKHEAD AT a brisk pace. Few things looked stranger than a vampire forced to run on the ground. No longer bipedal but still too disjointed to achieve good speed on all fours, it loped forward in a jerky gait, leaping and running, at times pressing low to the ground and at others jumping too high. Its gallop was completely soundless, betrayed neither by a scrape of the claw on the asphalt nor a whisper of an errant breath. A vampire belonged to the night, to the darkness, hidden from the world, a stealthy and deadly assassin. Out here, brazen in the sunshine of early afternoon, in full view of the stately old mansions drowning in verdant greenery, it looked grotesque, unreal, a nightmare come to life.

I watched the vampire and couldn't help but think of Julie. She had this abandoned look on her face. But to make any headway, I had to understand what was going on, and for that I needed Saiman. Hopefully, he would give me enough information to sort through this tangled mess, and then I could go back and check on her. She would be behind the wards. In the vault. Nothing should go wrong.

Something always could go wrong.

But as long as she didn't leave the vault, she should be okay. Nothing should force her to leave. Unless there was a fire. Was there anything flammable down there?

I stopped. That way lay insanity.

The vamp crossed the road in front of us for the fourth time. The Order's horses had been trained to work with all sorts of creatures, but no matter how much you train a horse, it still remained a horse. They didn't like the vampire. They didn't buck, but they danced in place and shied.

"I think he's doing it on purpose," Derek growled under his breath.

"He is. He hates horses," I told him. "Allergies."

The purple vampire loped along on the right side of the street and launched itself at the telephone pole. The undead climbed with a gecko's agility to about twelve feet, took its bearings, and casually jumped down to resume its bizarre gallop. Normally it would snow in mid-June before the People let a bloodsucker out in full daylight. The sunlight blistered their skin within minutes of exposure. Unless, of course, they were smothered in a quarter-inch-thick layer of purple sunblock. I wondered what possessed him to take the risk anyway.

"Ghastek? What happens to the Casino during a flare?"

He took a few seconds before he answered. "Lockdown. The Casino grounds all vampires. All personnel are pulled in and put on high alert. The Casino is shuttered and locked. All nonemergency communication with the outside world is restricted."

If the flare made all magic stronger, than the vampires, in turn, experienced a surge in power. How many necromancers would it take to keep them put? I wasn't sure I wanted to know. Nor would I want to be there when the steel chains holding the bloodsuckers within their stables started snapping.

Ghastek drew parallel to my horse, and she tossed her head back.

"How much farther?" Derek asked.

"Patience is a virtue," Ghastek advised.

"Lecturing a wolf about patience is unwise." That was the first time Derek condescended to addressing Ghastek directly, and his face plainly showed he felt quite soiled by having to stoop so low.

"Should I find myself speaking to an animal for some bewildering reason, I'll take it under advisement."

"Are the two of you finished?"

"Quite," Ghastek said.

"Nothing to finish." Derek shrugged.

I sighed.

"Does our bickering displease you?" The vamp leaped straight up long enough to look me in the face.

"No. My ability to get myself into these situations displeases me. It's a special talent of mine." I turned to Derek. "The expert lives at Champion Heights. We're almost there."

"The old Lenox Pointe?"

"Yes."

"He does alright for himself," Derek said.

"Indeed." And I would have to empty my bank account to pay for the information he would provide.

Magic didn't like skyscrapers. It didn't like anything new and technologically complicated, period, but it especially hated tall buildings. Ever since the Shift, Atlanta's skyscrapers had rocked, crumbled, and fallen, like exhausted titans on sand legs.

Against this new jagged skyline, Champion Heights stood out like a sore thumb. Seventeen stories tall, it towered above Buckhead thanks to the deep pockets of its owners and a complicated spell nobody had thought would work. The spell worked just fine: the high-rise still loomed above decrepit buildings, clouded with haze, shifting back and forth between the brick and glass building and a tall granite spire, as the complex web of spells worked tirelessly to support the illusion which permitted its existence. The cost of maintaining an apartment in Champion Heights approached astronomical.

The magic hit, so thick my heart skipped a beat. Derek clenched his teeth. His face strained, muscles on his forearms bulged, and his eyes flooded with yellow.

The hair on the back of my arms rose. The intense cold fire of those eyes chilled me. He was on the verge of going furry.

"You okay?"

His lips quivered. The fire in his eyes died to its usual soft brown. "Yeah," he said. "Took me by surprise."

The vampire kept galloping as if nothing had happened.

"Ghastek, you okay?"

He offered Derek a smile. "Never better. Unlike Pack members, the People don't tolerate losses of control."

Derek's eyes flashed gold. "If I lose control, you'll be the first to know."

"I'm quite perturbed by the idea."

We turned the corner. A granite crag greeted us, nestled within artfully landscaped shrubs. The crag rose, completely sheer, until it brushed the sky, where snowdrifts edged its scarred weather-worn top. A flock of birds launched themselves into flight from its top, the setting sun gleaming on their backs and wings. They circled the building once and took off for places unknown.

"Whoa," Derek said. "I thought it was supposed to *look* like a rock, not be a rock."

"Our furry companion once again forgets the advance of a flare," Ghastek said.

"If the two of you don't stop, I'll send you home."

The flare had turned Champion Heights into a granite spire. And it wasn't even going full force yet. We were just getting the preview of what was to come.

We dismounted, tied our horses to the rail, and went up the concrete steps to where the entrance used to be. Solid rock. Not even a crevice.

The magic fell.

"Window," Ghastek said.

Three stories from the ground a pane of glass shone, catching the sun.

The bloodsucker gathered itself like a cat and launched up onto the wall, finding purchase on the sheer cliff with the ease of a fly. It turned around, hanging upside down, and offered me an arm.

"I'll climb myself, thanks."

"It will cost us time."

"That's fine with me."

It'd been a long time since I had gone rock climbing. By the time I made it to the window, Derek and the bloodsucker had been waiting for a good minute. Ghastek scooted the vamp to the side to make room for me. "You delayed us. It's simply not efficient."

I huffed. "Spare me."

Derek knocked on the window. No answer. He rammed his fist into the glass. The window pane exploded into the apartment. We climbed into the hole one by one and let ourselves out of the apartment. Neither of us mentioned the illegality of our smooth maneuver.

We made it to the fifteenth floor, and I stole a little break by taking my time to find the right door.

"So what sort of person is this expert?" Derek asked.

"The very intelligent, methodical kind. Somber, even. Saiman enjoys erudite discussions. He's like Ghastek—" With a sex drive. "He's like Ghastek except instead of piloting vampires, he indulges in books and late night debate on the virtues of Mongolian folklore."

"Wonderful." Derek rolled his eyes.

I nodded to the vamp. "The two of you will probably hit it off."

The magic flooded us again. This time Derek was ready—his face showed no change. Ghastek, on the other hand, halted in midrise halfway off the ground.

I unsheathed Slayer. Derek backed away, giving himself room for a leap. If the vamp went berserk, we'd be in a hell of a lot of trouble.

"Ghastek?" I murmured.

"Just a second." His voice sounded muffled.

"Are you losing your grip on him?"

"What?"

The vampire dropped to the floor, regarding me with blood-drenched eyes. "Whatever led you to that conclusion?"

"You froze."

"If you must know, an apprentice brought me my espresso and I burned my tongue on it."

Derek grimaced, disgust practically dripping off his face.

"Can we enter or not?" Ghastek said.

I slid Slayer's blade into the box of the electronic lock. Like many things in Champion Heights, the lock was magic masquerading as technology.

"Anything else we need to know?" Derek asked.

"Just don't stare if he decides to do his thing. He'll draw it out." The memory alone made me queasy.

"What thing?" Derek asked.

"He changes shapes. He's limited to human only, as far as I know, but within that limitation he can assume almost any form."

"Is he a danger?"

His tone had a slightly driven tint to it. His blood oath acting up again. "I met him through the Guild, when I was a merc. On bodyguard detail. I saved his life and now he gives me a discount. Basically, he humors me and tries to get into my pants. He's harmless."

I put my hand on Slayer's blade, fed a little power into the blade, and pushed the door with my fingers. It slid open.

Beyond the door lay Saiman's apartment: an ultramodern backdrop of steel and plush cushions, blending into a monochromatic, almost sterile, whole.

"Saiman?" I called, crossing the white rug.

No answer. A blast of chill air hit me. The enormous floor-to-ceiling window stood open, half of its pane slid aside. Beyond the pane a snow-strewn ledge, barely four feet wide, hugged the building. I stuck my head through the opening. The ledge spiraled to the roof. A trail of footprints led up through the snow.

"IT APPEARS HE TOOK A WALK IN THE SNOW. BARE-foot." I stepped back into the apartment.

"I'll go first," Derek said.

Before I could say anything, he ducked into the opening and headed up the ledge. Damn it. I followed him. Behind me the vamp climbed the cliff. Using ledges and paths was clearly below Ghastek.

Wind slapped me. My feet slid a little and I pressed against the side of the building. I crouched and rubbed the snow with my hand. Under the snowflakes, the ledge was ice. Figured.

The entire city stretched below, so small, it looked almost tidy from this height. Between me and that tidy city lay a dizzying drop. I swallowed. I could do a lot of things but I was pretty sure I couldn't sprout wings and fly. Right after my father's death, when I was fifteen, Greg had taken me to his ex-wife's house in the Smoky Mountains. That was the last time I could remember being this high. It felt a lot different sitting on the edge of a mountain cliff. In fact, compared to crawling up a four-foot ledge made of ice, sitting on a mountain, dangling your feet over the edge, was downright comfy.

Another gust hit me. I gritted my teeth and peeled myself from the wall. Keep moving, wuss. One foot before the other. As long as I didn't think about falling. Or looking down there . . . Boy, that's *high.*

The ground beckoned me. I almost wanted to jump. How the hell did people ever live in high-rises?

Above me female laughter rang out, followed by a low warning growl. Oh crap. Derek. I tore my gaze from the drop and started up the ledge.

I can do this. I just need to keep moving.

The ledge brought me halfway around the building. A large picturesque iceberg blocked most of the view from this side. More laughter floated on the breeze. Something was going on up there. What possessed Saiman to prance around in the snow barefoot anyway? And why was there snow atop the high-rise? It was bloody June, for crying out loud.

I climbed the last few feet separating me from the top. My feet found the solid roof under the blanket of snow. Finally.

I skirted the iceberg and saw Derek. He stood rigid, hands spread wide, his upper lip wrinkled in a preemptive growl. He was trying his best not to touch a blonde whose hands rested on his shoulders.

She was nude. Short, with hair down to her butt, she was proportioned with an almost obscene generosity: round ass, solid thighs, big heavy breasts tipped by pink nipples. Considering the size of her waist, it was a wonder she didn't fold in half under the weight of her boobs. Her skin glowed, almost as if lit from within by sunshine, and so she stood there, naked, unashamed, golden. Sex in the snow. She looked at Derek with huge eyes and purred. "A puppy. Play with me!"

Derek's eyes had gone completely yellow.

Past him, Ghastek's vamp crouched on the edge, making no move to assist.

I swiped a chunk of crusty snow, clamped it into a ball, and hurled it at the blonde. The snowball hit her upside the head, bursting into powder.

"Saiman! Step away from him!"

The blonde whipped her head around. "Kate . . ."

Her body twisted with preternatural fluidity. Female flesh melted like wax and re-formed into a muscle-corded frame. She swept toward me through the snow, growing, twisting, molding, hardening, too fast to follow and then a man wrapped his arm around my waist pulling me to him.

He was tall, perfectly proportioned, and muscled like a Roman statue. The same golden radiance that had illuminated the blonde lit his skin from within. His hair, a deep red streaked with gold, fell to his waist without a trace of a curl. His face was angular, yet masculine, and his grin had a mordant edge sharp enough to draw blood. He leaned toward me and I got a good look at his eyes. They were orange. Radiant, brilliant orange, streaked with pale green that almost looked like the crystals of ice growing on a window during a freeze.

They did not look human.

"Kate," he repeated, pulling me closer. He towered at least half a foot above me. Snowflakes swirled around us. His breath smelled like honey. "I'm so glad you came to visit. I was so dreadfully bored."

That's it. The flare had driven him insane.

I tried to pull away, but Saiman held me tight. There was strength in those arms that I had never expected. If I struggled too much, Derek would go ballistic. A woman wrestling with a naked man who probably outweighed her by eighty pounds tended to trigger onlookers' protective instincts, even if they weren't bound by a blood oath.

"Derek, please go down to the apartment and wait for me at the window."

He just stood there.

"Jealous?" Saiman laughed.

I tore myself long enough from those eyes to stare at Derek. "Please go."

Slowly, as if waking up from a dream, he turned and left the roof.

"What about the vampire?" Saiman asked.

"Just ignore me," Ghastek said. "Think of me as a fly on the wall."

Bastard.

Saiman touched my hair and I felt my braid unwinding on its own. In a moment, my hair framed my face. "What happened to you?" I asked.

He grinned wider. "Deep magic. It sings in my bones. Don't you feel it?"

I felt it. It had pulsed through me like a wild wine ever since this magic wave had hit. Power twisted and wound within me, wanting to break loose, but I had held it in check this long and I wasn't about to let myself off the leash now.

"Can you dance?" he asked.

"Yes."

"Dance with me, Kate!"

And we were off, spinning and twirling through the snow, raising glittering snowflakes with our feet. The snow refused to fall but chased us, following our movement like a light shroud. It was a wild dance, primitive and fast, and all I could do was follow his lead.

"I need some information," I yelled at a strategic moment.

He clamped my waist, picked me up like I weighed nothing, and spun around. "Ask."

"Too complicated for a fast dance."

He set me into the snow and held me close in a classic stance, one hand on my waist, one cradling my fingers. "Then we'll dance slowly. Put your arms around me."

No! "I don't think that would be a good idea."

We moved gently through the snow. "Things are chasing me." Which wasn't strictly true, but considering the circumstances, brevity was a virtue. "They're called reeves. They are undead. Their hair can tangle you up and hold you like a lasso."

"I don't know what they are."

"They are piloted by a tall creature who wears a white habit like a monk. He has tentacles. His name is Bolgor the Shepherd. I was told he's a Fomorian."

"I don't know him, either."

Damn it, Saiman. "What would a sea-demon want in our world?"

"What we all want: life." Saiman leaned in close, his lips nearly brushing my cheek. His eyes drew me in, and I knew that if I looked too long into them, I would forget why I came here.

"This Shepherd's hunting a young girl. Can you research why?"

"I could, but there is too much magic. I can't concentrate. I would rather dance. It's a magic time, Kate! Time of the gods."

The thought of mentioning money briefly popped into my head. But then he always gave me a discount, both because I had once saved his life and because he found me entertaining. He wasn't that interested in money even during normal time, and right now he was simply too far gone.

"Morrigan is somehow involved. And a cauldron," I said.

His face was alarmingly close to mine.

"The Celts have a liking for the cauldrons. Cauldrons of plenty. Cauldrons of knowledge. Cauldrons of rebirth." His breath warmed my cheek. His hands were warm, too. By all rights he should have been freezing.

"Cauldron of rebirth?"

"A gateway to the Otherworld."

He tried to dip me, but I resisted and he smoothly turned the dip into a turn.

"Tell me more about it."

"You should ask the witches. They know. But ask later. After the deep magic wanes."

"Why?"

"Because if you leave, I'll be bored again."

Oh crap. "Tell me more about the witches. Which coven should I ask?"

"All of them."

He slid my hand onto his shoulder. I pulled back, but he already held my shoulders, hugging me tight to him. His huge erection pressed against me. *Great, just great.*

"How can I ask all of the covens? There are dozens in the city."

"Simple." Honeyed breath washed over me. "You ask the Witch Oracle."

"The witches have an oracle?" We had slowed down to mere shuffling now. I shuffled backward, heading toward the end of the roof where the ledge lay.

"In Centennial Park," he said softly. "There are three of them. They speak for all the covens. I hear they have a problem they can't fix."

"Then it's best I go to them."

He shook his head. "But then I'll be all alone."

"I have to go."

"You never stay." He turned his head and kissed my fingers. "Stay with me. It will be fun."

I noticed the ice building around us. If this kept going, we would be encased in an igloo in a matter of minutes.

"Why is the ice growing?"

"It's jealous. Of the vampire!" He laughed, throwing his head back like it was the funniest thing.

I knocked his hands off my shoulders and jumped off the roof.

I landed in a crouch on the ledge and slipped. My back slapped the ice. I slid, rolling down the narrow path. I dug my heels into the snow, grasping at the wall to slow myself down, but my hands slipped. I hurtled along the path, helpless to stop my fall.

The end of the ledge flashed, feet away.

I ripped a knife from its sheath and stabbed it into the ledge. The momentum carried me forward and I jerked to a halt, my legs suspended over the edge. Carefully I flexed my arms and slid myself back onto the ledge, trying very hard not to think of the bottomless chasm yawning at my feet.

Derek grabbed my shoulder, pulled me up, and neatly de-

posited me on the carpet within the apartment. "Some expert," he growled.

"Yeah. Last time I come here." My brain finally realized
that I wouldn't be falling from fifteen stories and impersonat-
ing a pancake on the ground. I scrambled to my feet. "I owe
you one."

He shrugged. "You had it anyway. I just sped it up a bit."

The vampire met us as we untied our horses.

"You dance very well," Ghastek said.

"Not a word. Not another bloody word."

CHAPTER 14

———◦◉◦———

"SO THIS SAIMAN, HE HAS A THING FOR YOU?" DEREK
asked.

"Right now Saiman has a thing for everyone, including
you, from what I saw. He's drunk on magic and bored." I finished rebraiding my hair and guided my horse up Marietta
Street toward the dense forest that used to be the twenty-one
acres of Centennial Park. I really didn't feel like continuing
this conversation.

The magic fell. It would reassert itself in a minute: the
waves had been coming one after another, short and intense.

"It appeared you were definitely his preferred entertain-
ment," Ghastek said.

Asshole. "It didn't matter who was up on that roof, he
would've changed his shape until he found a perfect fit."

"In more ways than one." The vampire cut in front of the
horses again.

"Thank you for your commentary. I noticed you didn't do
anything to help."

"You seemed to have the matter well in hand." Ghastek
sent his vamp galloping forward, ahead of us. When con-
fronted, run away. My favorite strategy.

"Look," Derek said, "all I'm saying is it would've been
helpful to have all relevant information before we walked in
there."

"I didn't have all the relevant information. Had I known he
would be on the roof dancing in the snow, I wouldn't have
gone up there."

"I can't effectively help or protect you . . ." Derek said.

I turned in my saddle. "Derek, I didn't ask you to protect me. I didn't ask you to come with me. If I had realized that you would be imitating Curran the entire time, I would've thought twice about letting you tag along."

Derek clamped his mouth shut.

Ahead of us the vamp turned to the left, loping onto Centennial Drive.

That wasn't a good thing to say. I halted my horse. Derek stopped, too.

"I'm sorry. I didn't mean to snap."

"Who should I imitate, Kate?" he asked softly.

I didn't have an answer.

"Or are you going to give me a load of bullshit about being myself? Who would that be, Kate? A son of a loup and a murderer, who couldn't save his sisters from being raped and then eaten alive by their father. Why would I want to be that?"

I leaned back in my saddle, wishing I could exhale all of the weight that had settled on my shoulders. "I apologize. I was wrong."

He sat still for a long minute and nodded to me. The vamp halted in the street, waiting for us.

"I shouldn't have nagged," he said. "I get like that sometimes."

"It's okay." I sent my horse forward. I knew why he got like that. I've seen him meticulously fold his clothes. His shave was perfect, his hair cut short, his nails clean and trimmed. I bet his room didn't have a single item out of place. When you live in chaos as a child, you strive to impose order over the world. Unfortunately, the world refuses to comply, so you have to settle for trying to control yourself, your habitat, and your friends.

"I'm just worried about a lot of things," I said.

"Julie?" he guessed.

"Yes."

I wished I could have called in to check on them, but I had no clue where I could find a working phone line and with the preflare magic, the phone probably wouldn't work anyway. Andrea had promised to stay with her. Barred from the field or not, Andrea could shoot a squirrel in the eye from across the street.

"It's hard for you," Derek observed. "To rely on other people, I mean."

For a moment I wondered if he had developed telepathy, too. "What makes you say that?"

"You said you were worried about Julie and then your face looked like you had a hemorrhoid attack. Or a really hard . . ."

"Derek, you just don't say things like that to a woman. Keep going this way and you'll spend your life alone."

"Don't change the subject. Andrea is cool. And she smells nice. It will be okay."

Apparently I was supposed to sniff people to determine their competence. "How do you know?"

He shrugged. "You just have to trust her."

Considering that the two men I had most loved and admired spent my formative years drilling into me that I could rely on myself and myself alone, trusting other people was easier said than done. I worried about Julie. I worried about Julie's mom, too. Since I'd gotten the liaison position with the Order, I made it a point to hang out in the knight-questor's office, because I knew next to nothing about investigative work, and he, being an ex–Georgia Bureau of Investigations detective, knew pretty much everything. While there I had picked up a few vital crumbs of information, and I knew the first twenty-four hours of any investigation were crucial. The more time passed, the colder the trail grew. In a missing person case, that meant the chances of finding that missing person alive dropped by the hour.

The first twenty-four had come and gone. The first forty-eight were waving good-bye from the window of the "you suck at your job" train. None of the normal procedures applied in this case: canvassing the neighborhood, interrogating witnesses, trying to determine who wanted the person to be missing, none of it applied here. All the witnesses were missing with her.

I had no clue where Julie's mom had gone. I wished she was safe back at her house. I had left a note on her kitchen table, explaining that I had Julie, she was safe, and asking her to contact the Order. Until she showed, all I could do was to tug on the tail of the only lead I had—the cauldron and Morrigan—and hope there wasn't a woman-eating tiger on the other end.

We turned to the left onto Centennial Drive, following Ghastek's vampire. A solid wall of green towered along our left, blocking the view. Pre-Shift, the park was open and airy, a large lawn, sectioned off by paths and carefully planted trees into predefined areas. You could stand on the lookout at Belvedere and see the entire layout of the park, from the Children's Garden to the Fountain of Rings.

Now the park belonged to the covens of the city. The witches had planted fast-growing trees, and an impenetrable barrier of verdant green hid the mysteries of the park from prying eyes and sticky fingers. The park was larger, as well. A lot larger. It had swallowed several city blocks previously occupied by office buildings. All I saw was a wall of green. It must've quadrupled in size.

The fact that so many covens had banded together to purchase a park was always a puzzlement to me. If you piloted vampires, you belonged to the People, and if you didn't, they would quickly make a very persuasive financial argument in favor of your signing up with them. If you were a merc, you belonged to the Guild, because you wanted 50 percent off your dental, 30 percent off your medical, and access to a Guild lawyer. But if you were a witch, you belonged to your coven, which usually topped out at thirteen members. Witches had no hierarchy outside of their individual covens. I always wondered what different covens had in common. Now I knew: the Oracle.

It's a good thing Saiman was high on magic. God alone knew how much this information would've cost me under normal circumstances. Of course, under normal circumstances, all this mess wouldn't have happened.

The city gave the park some berth but not too much. Across the street the ruins had been cleared and a new timber building rose, proudly bearing a YardBird sign. Under it in big red letters was written "Fried Chicken! Wings!" And lower, "No Rat!"

The air smelled like fried chicken. My mouth filled with drool. The good thing about chicken is that it's hard to disguise dog meat as a chicken wing. Mmmm, chicken. Thanks to Doolittle's efforts, I still had the metabolism of a hummingbird on crack. The fried chicken aroma beckoned me. After the witches. Once we were out of Centennial Park, come hell or high water, I'd get myself some chicken.

The carpenters from the new construction going up ahead had much the same idea. They sat outside at small wooden tables, munched on wings, and watched the afternoon sun broil the streets. Laborers and craftsmen traveled up and down Centennial Drive, feeling the pavement through their worn shoes, staying on the other side of the street, away from the green. The sidewalk peddlers recommended their wares with hoarse voices. Up ahead at the intersection a fetish vendor, a short middle-aged man, danced about his cart, shaking colorful twine and cord charms.

A street sign announced we had reached Andrew Young Boulevard. Judging by the sign's location, the boulevard sliced off the southern chunk of the park, probably cutting straight through Centennial Plaza. Except no boulevard remained. The greenery grew wild, in full revolt against all things that pruned. Leafy branches hung over the path, their shoots lying on the pavement. Rose vines spread in thorn-studded tangles, binding the myrtles and evergreens into a solid mass that promised to leave no skin unbloodied. I'd need a chainsaw to get through there. A machete wouldn't do it. And I didn't even have a machete.

Witches: one. Kate and Co.: zero.

"We seem to be boulevardless," I said.

"I could've informed you of that, had you bothered to inquire." The vamp favored me with a ghastly attempt at a smile, sure to send any normal person to a therapist.

That's right—the Casino was built on the lot of the old World Congress Center. If it weren't for the fifty-foot trees blocking the view, the sky would be gleaming with its silvery minarets. The People and the witches were practically neighbors. Hell, they probably wandered over to borrow a cup of sugar from each other.

"There is an entrance up ahead." The vamp scuttled north, toward Baker Street. The sun chose that moment to strip off a small cloud, filling the world with golden sunshine and setting the vamp's wrinkled purple hide aglow.

"There is just something so wrong about this," I mumbled.

Derek answered with a light growl.

I trudged along the green wall. The air smelled of flowers. Birds chirped.

The greenery dipped. A narrow path burrowed into the green, twisting to the left, like a dim tunnel to the heart of the wood.

Derek raised his nose and inhaled deeply in the manner of the shapeshifters. "Water."

I strained to recall the layout of the park. Baker Street wasn't that far. "Must be the Water Gardens."

The tunnel lay waiting, like an open mouth. Ghastek's vamp edged closer to it. Derek and I dismounted and tied our horses to a twisted rhododendron. I looked into the tunnel. No time like the present.

"Any ideas on how to approach this?" I asked the vamp.

"None whatsoever," Ghastek said.

I sighed and ducked into the tunnel.

CHAPTER 15

I HAD CONQUERED THE FIRST TEN FEET OF THE PATH when the magic hit. It rocked me like a shotgun blast. My breath escaped my lungs in a startled cry, my heart squeezed itself into a hard fist, and I bent over, cradling my chest. The pain released me in a heady rush of power that spread through my arteries, into my veins, into the vessels, into the capillaries, until my whole body tingled with magic. The exhilaration claimed me and lifted me up, as if two wings had thrust from my back.

Around me, deep within the green, flowers opened, glowing stars of white and pale purple. The branches rustled. The vines slithered. An amalgam of scents spiced the air: sweet and honeyed, reminiscent of a rose.

Derek padded out of the green gloom, silent and stealthy on velvet feet and looked at me with wolf eyes from a human face. I fought an involuntary shiver.

The vampire crouched on the side of the path, snug against the greenery, shivering, head tucked to its chest.

The bloodsucker raised its head. Its eyes burned bright red. The vamp mouth opened but no sound issued forth. It showed me its fangs, two yellowed killing teeth. I showed it my saber. *I only have one tooth, but it's a lot longer than yours and it will turn the stringy meat on your bones into pus.*

"No need for alarm," Ghastek said. "He's quite docile."

The vampire slunk from the path, arched its back, and brushed against my leg.

It took every shred of nerve not to recoil. "If you do that again, I'll kill it."

"I was always curious about your aversion to the undead. What is it that upsets you so much?"

"A vampire is a walking corpse. It oozes undeath that makes the living want to vomit, it has no mind, and left to its own devices it would slaughter until there was nothing left to kill. And then it would cannibalize itself. What's there to like, Ghastek?"

And most of all, Roland had made them. They were his creation.

"Their usefulness far outweighs their few shortcomings," Ghastek said.

I motioned with my saber. "In that case, please go first. Let's benefit from some of that usefulness."

Ghastek took the lead, and we went down the path, single file, vampire, a man on the verge of becoming a beast, and me, bringing up the rear.

The canopy dipped so low, I had to nearly crouch. I scooted through, the twigs snatching at my braid, and finally emerged into the clearing.

Tall pines rose straight and smooth like the masts of a gargantuan underground ship. Their branches stretched to each other, filtering the light, muting the sun to a pleasant green gloom. The ground was thick with decades of autumn, and spongy pine needles gave lightly under my weight. The air smelled of moisture. A gentle murmur of water spilling over man-made waterfalls emanated from the left.

The vamp leaped onto the nearest pine and perched twelve feet off the ground, its body nearly perpendicular to the pine's trunk.

"Two o'clock," Derek whispered.

Beyond the pines lay a sunlit glade, sectioned by neat rows of herbs. Between us and the glade stood a woman.

She was on the heavy side, built solid and thick, but without flab. A plain black dress hung off her shoulders, its hem brushing the ground. Her thick arms matched the color of the pine straw. A mask of beaten iron hid her features, a round stylized face with thick locks of hair radiating from it like the sun's corona. On second glance, those weren't sun rays. Sun rays didn't come with scales and fanged mouths.

A Gorgon Medusa mask. My quip about Medusas in the Honeycomb Gap was coming true. Me and my big mouth. Next time I would imagine a warehouse full of fluffy bunnies instead.

"I'm a representative of the Order," I said. "I'm investigating the disappearance of the Sisters of the Crow. This is my associate." I nodded at Derek. "This is my other associate." I nodded at the vampire. "I request to speak to the Oracle."

The woman said nothing. Moments ticked by, like falling pine needles, one after another. In ancient Greece, Gorgon Medusa could turn a man to stone with her gaze. I had a nice big pine to my left. If that mask left her face, I'd make a break for it. Perseus, who finally chopped off Medusa's head, had a mirror shield. I had nothing. Even Slayer's blade was opaque, so no dice there.

She turned and strode into the sunshine. I followed.

THE COBBLED STONES OF THE PATH VEERED LEFT and right in a gentle curve. The witch's black dress swept them clean as she moved. Her mask flared to cover the back of her head like some bizarre motorcycle helmet and all I could see was a narrow strip of her dark skin right above the neckline.

A vast herb garden stretched on both sides of us; flowers and grasses were separated in rows, bordered by a dense evergreen hedge in the distance. Basil, yarrow, mint, brilliant red poppies, yellow cornflower, fuzzy bush clover, white umbrellas of elderberry . . . They never needed to leave the premises to look for wild plants. Most covens used the same herbs in their rituals. Very convenient when the herbs grew right by the gathering place.

My memory claimed that there was a big grassy lawn somewhere here, but beyond the herbal field rose trees, massive dogwoods and oaks tinseled with Spanish moss. The trees looked entirely too old to have grown naturally. I couldn't recall how I knew the lawn had been there, but I remembered it. And the fountains. Many water jets shooting from the ground.

And a woman. A very tall woman who laughed a lot. Her face was a fuzzy blur in my memory.

Derek wrinkled his nose. I glanced at him.

"Animal," he said. "Odd."

"What kind?"

"Not sure."

The trees parted before us, revealing a hill sitting in the middle of a large clearing. More of a kurgan, actually, rising straight up out of the herbs, like a cap of a colossal mushroom. Kudzu and grasses blanketed the hill in a green shroud, but at the very top the bedrock broke through: smooth, polished dark gray marble, tinted with swirls of malachite and flecked with gold.

If I had a marble dome that pretty, I doubt I'd let it get overgrown like that.

The Medusa impersonator circled the hill and stopped. We stopped, too. Ghastek sent the vamp up onto the hill and it perched among the kudzu like some gaunt ghoul.

Derek sneezed.

"Bless you."

He sneezed again, pulled a canteen from his belt and washed his nostrils out.

The guide waited. We stood with her. A light breeze rippled through the tree branches. Birds sang. The sun, highly amused by our presence, did its best to barbecue us.

The vampire sprang straight into the air and landed ten feet behind us. Derek snarled. And sneezed again.

A deep rumble shook the ground. I backed away.

The grassy soil fell away in heavy slabs. The hill quaked and crept up, higher, *higher*. A colossal brown head emerged from underneath the kudzu, the flesh hanging from it in wrinkled folds. Two eyes stared at me, black and shining like two giant chunks of anthracite.

A tortoise.

I quested: not a shiver of magic. No scent of burning grasses associated with illusion. It was an actual living tortoise.

The curve of the gargantuan mouth widened. The jaws

opened and a black maw gaped before us. I braced for a wave of turtle breath, but no discernible scents emanated from the mouth. The mother of all tortoises rested her chin on the grass and held the pose.

Okay, now I'd seen everything.

Our guide bowed her head and pointed into the tortoise.

"In there?"

She nodded.

"You want us to go into the tortoise?"

Another nod.

"It's alive."

Another nod.

"No." Derek sneezed again.

"I must say it's a bit irregular." Ghastek's voice vibrated with excitement. It's easy to be deliriously happy about investigating something, when you're in no danger of being swallowed.

I glanced at the vamp. "How fast can you rip it apart if it eats us?"

"The shell is quite thick. We'd have to exit back through the neck. If it withdraws its head, we'll have to carve through a lot of flesh."

"In other words, if it eats us, we're screwed."

"Crude but accurate."

I faced the guide. "Are you coming with us?"

She shook her head.

Nice plan. Take the gullible outsiders, walk them around for a bit, then feed them to the giant tortoise. The tortoise is full, the outsiders are dealt with, and everybody's happy.

"Derek, what do you smell?"

He stepped forward, took a deep breath, and doubled over in a sneezing fit. My werewolf was allergic to tortoises. Why me?

"Anything sour? Animal breath?"

He shook his head. "Water. And flowers."

I pointed my blade at the guide. "If it eats us, I'll kill it, and then I'll find you."

The guide nodded again. She didn't take a step back and flee in horror. Perhaps I just wasn't scary enough. Maybe I should invest in some horns or fangs.

"I'm going in. You two are welcome to stay outside." I bent my back and took a step into the tortoise's mouth.

CHAPTER 16

THE TONGUE GAVE A BIT UNDER MY FEET. LIKE WALK-
ing on a saturated sponge. Ahead a deeper blackness indicated
the opening of the throat. I bent lower to clear the roof of the
mouth and headed for it.

Behind me Derek sneezed.

"Decided to come after all?"

Sneeze. "Wouldn't miss it."

The throat sloped gently, its bottom flooded with a murky
liquid. Long strands of what looked like algae hung from the
top of the throat-tunnel, dripping more liquid. Hopefully it
wasn't acid. It didn't smell any different from the ordinary
pond water, a touch fishy. I pulled a throwing knife, stretched
and dipped the tip into the water. No discoloration. I touched
the wet blade. My finger didn't melt. Very well.

I stepped into water, slipped, and landed on my butt. Why
me?

The vampire scuttled past me, throwing me a look over its
shoulder. "As always, a picture of refined grace."

"Shut up."

My boots were full of tortoise throat spit.

The vamp took a step and vanished under the water.

I scrambled to my feet.

The vamp's head reappeared. "A bit deep through here,"
Ghastek warned.

Ha! Served him right.

The water came up to my waist. I waded through the tunnel
in the gloom, the quiet splashing of the vampire ahead the
only guide as to direction. Derek's sneezing finally stopped.

The tunnel turned. I splashed through and stopped.

I stood in a shallow pool, among a dense blanket of lily pads. Cream-colored lilies glowed on the water.

An enormous dome lay before me. High above, at its very top, the carapace became transparent, and pale light filtered through, highlighting the translucent ridges of the tortoise shell. The walls darkened gradually, clear at the top, then green with the colors of the grasses and kudzu sheathing the shell from the outside, and finally deep black and green marble. Large rectangles had been cut within the walls, each with its own glyph etched in gold leaf and a name. The arrangement was strikingly familiar, but so unexpected, it took my brain a moment to recognize it.

I stood in a crypt.

A small noise made me turn. The pool ended a few feet in front of me, and beyond it, across the expanse of tortoise shell floor, just past the edge of light, rose a rectangular platform. On the platform waited three women.

The woman on the right could've easily qualified for a center spot in a five-generation family portrait: withered, gaunt, frail. She had seen seventy some time ago. Her thin hair surrounded her head like a nimbus of fine cotton. The black silk of her gown served only to accentuate her age. But her eyes stabbed me with sharp, predatory intelligence. She sat ramrod straight, poised on a heavy chair that was more a throne than a common seat. Like an aging raptor, old but ready to strike at the first hint of blood.

The woman next to her was barely older than Julie. She reclined on a small Roman-style sofa. Black silk streamed from her in folds and curves, so much of it that the fabric threatened to drown her. Sallow, almost translucent against that silk, she rested her head on her bent arm. Her cheekbones stood out. Her neck was barely thicker than my wrist. By contrast her blond hair fell from her head in twin braids, luxurious and thick.

The last woman sat in a rocking chair, knitting an unidentifiable garment from brownish yarn. She looked like she had sucked up all of the flesh the other two lacked. Plump, healthy, with her thick brown hair braided, she watched her knitting with a knowing half smile.

Maiden, mother, and crone. How classic. Double, double, toil and trouble?

I looked above them, to where a large mural darkened the wall. A tall woman towered above the platform, drawn in a simple but sharp style, the kind a genius child artist might employ. Three arms rose from her body: the first held a knife, the second a torch, and the third a chalice with a tiny snake winding about it. To the left of her sat a black cat and a toad. To the right lay a key and a broom.

Before the woman sat a huge cauldron, positioned on the intersection of three roads. Black hounds ran across the walls in both directions, all facing the cauldron.

The Oracle worshipped Hekate, the Queen of the Night, the Mother of all Witches. Although known by her Greek name, she was much older. Her worship stretched through two millennia, its roots buried in the fertile folkloric soil of Turkey and Asia. The Greeks had too much respect to ignore her ancient heritage and her seductive power. They made her the only Titan Zeus had permitted into his pantheon, partially because he had fallen in love with her. She was the goddess of choice, of victory and defeat, of knowledge magical and medicinal, the guardian of the boundary between spiritual and mundane, and the witness to all crimes against women and children.

Underestimating her Oracle would prove extremely unwise.

I felt Derek behind me, waiting. The vampire had left the pool and crouched on its rim. I bowed.

The crone spoke. "Approach."

Slowly I crossed the water. My feet found stone steps and I emerged onto the floor.

"Closer," the crone said.

I took another step and felt the edges of a spell lying in wait. I put my foot down. Derek stopped too, but the vampire advanced past me, oblivious.

The crone thrust her hand at us, fingers rigid like claws.

Chalk lines slid from under the stones as if blown by errant wind, and I found myself locked in a circle of glyphs. Ahead the vampire fell, caught in an identical trap. Derek growled and I didn't have to look to know he was captured, as well.

The crone smirked.

I probed the spell. Strong, but breakable. Should I stay in the circle out of respect or should I break out? Staying in would be a polite thing to do. Breaking out would likely provoke them, but would they deal with me if they could keep me pinned?

"Release me," Ghastek's voice echoed through the dome. "I've come here in good faith."

The crone stabbed her hand to the right. The circle slid, dragging the vampire within it and crashed into the wall with a harsh thud. The crone's eyes lit up with arrogant satisfaction. Well, that settled it.

"This is an outrage." The vampire sprung to its feet.

"Silence, abomination."

The circle slid to the left. Ghastek tried to run, anticipating the direction but the chalk tripped him and pulled him across the stones. She was enjoying herself way too much. She didn't chant, so it had to be a preexisting spell. If I could have sensed at least the type of magic she was using, I might have gotten some idea where to look for the spell, but locked within the glyphs, I couldn't feel a thing outside the circle.

Derek sat down, cross-legged, and settled to wait it all out.

I reached into my belt, pulled the cork off a plastic tube, and tossed a pinch of powder onto the spell. Wormwood, alder, and rowan, ground to fine dust, and iron shavings flittered to the floor in a fine cloud, tiny iron particles glistening as they caught light. The chalk lines dimmed and I stepped out and bowed.

The crone bared her teeth and thrust both hands at me, crushing the air in her gnarled fists.

A wave of chalk slid across the stones to clutch at me. A triple ring. Earth based, too. Iron and wood wouldn't work. Going all out.

"Break that, why don't you!" The crone leaned back, triumphant.

I raised my sword and thrust into the ring, gathering as much of my magic as I could and feeding it into the blade. The enchanted saber perspired. Gossamer smoke slithered from the metal. The magic squeezed the blade.

The first line of glyphs fell apart.

Sweat broke at my hairline.

The second line of glyphs wavered. My hands shook from the pressure. I leaned forward, channeling more power into the sword.

The second circle broke and I nearly fell.

The crone surged to her feet. Her hands clawed the air. Chalk blew at my feet. Three more rings. Shit.

I could use a power word to release myself, but that would mean announcing to Ghastek that I had one. The circle didn't dull his hearing, only his magic senses.

I drew the sword back, blocking the vampire's view of me with my back, and pricked my index finger. A tiny drop of red swelled. I crouched and drew a line right through the four rings. The ward cracked open like a shattered glass.

The crone drew back.

I stepped out and bowed and stayed that way. Out of the corner of my eye I saw the crone raise her hand, after a momentary hesitation. I read reluctance in her eyes. She wasn't sure she could hold me.

She had locked me three times, and three times I had broken out. Three was a number sacred to witches. I didn't want to show Ghastek more power.

The crone's fingers curled.

"Maria, please . . ." The maiden-witch had spoken. Her voice was weak and wilting, yet it echoed through the dome.

The crone lowered her hand with a sneer. "I spare you because she asks. For now."

I straightened and sheathed Slayer.

"I know you." The mother looked at me, her hands continuing to draw yarn with faint clicking. "Voron's child. *Po russki to govorish?*"

I shifted into Russian. "Yes, I speak Russian."

The witch clicked her tongue. "Accent you have. Don't speak Russian every day, no?"

"Don't have anybody to practice with."

"And whose failing is that?"

There was no good answer to that one so I backpedaled into English. "I've come for information."

"Ask," the maiden said.

I'd only get one shot at this. "Two days ago an amateur coven called the Sisters of the Crow disappeared. One of the witches, Jessica Olsen, has a daughter, Julie. Julie is only thirteen. She has no other family. Her mother means the world to her."

They said nothing. I plowed on.

"I know Morrigan is involved. I know there is a bottomless pit at the Sisters' gathering place and a smaller one in their head witch Esmeralda's trailer. I know Esmeralda was power hungry and was performing old druidic rites, but I don't know why. Now the Fomorians are running around the city, led by Bolgor the Shepherd. They want Julie. She's just a child, and although her mother was in an amateur coven, she was still a witch, just like you. Please help me understand what's going on. Help me fit it all together."

My breath caught in my throat. Either they would deal with me or send me packing. Once the covens said no, they meant it.

The mother-witch pursed her lips. "Morrigan," she said with slight distaste, as if discussing a neighbor who failed to wash her windows. "She always has a hound with her."

I frowned. "A dog?"

"No. A man. A scoundrel. A thief and a brigand."

I almost snapped my fingers. "Tall, dark, carries a bow, disappears into mist, can't keep his hands to himself?"

The mother nodded to me with a smile. "Yes."

"I've seen him."

She smiled wider. "I gathered."

When you want to impress the other party with your intellect, state the obvious. Brilliant. I was simply brilliant.

The maiden's voice whispered, intimate, almost as if she

were breathing in my ear instead of reclining on the couch sixteen feet away. "For the knowledge you want, we would ask a boon of you . . ."

The crone leaned back. Her hands rose, spread wide. Magic flared about her like dark wings.

The floor quaked. A long gash split the tiles between me and Derek, and a wave of musky scent wafted forth. A sleek pink liquid spilled from the floor and streamed away from me to Derek and the vampire.

Derek ripped off his clothes. His back arched and the skin along his chest split. For the briefest of moments I saw bare bones shifting and flowing like molten wax, and then muscle slivered over it, fur burst, flaring into lupine hackles, and a werewolf stood within the circle. Six and a half feet tall, with clawed hands large enough to enclose my head and jaws that could crack my skull like an egg. Half-man, half-beast, all nightmare. The shapeshifter warrior form.

I didn't recall drawing Slayer but it was in my hand.

"No harm will come to them," the maiden's wilting voice assured me.

The red wave washed against Derek's ward. Derek raised his deformed jaws. His fangs bit the air. A long eerie howl broke from his lips, a forlorn lament, a song of hunt, and chase, and hot blood on the tongue. It sent my heart fluttering. I gripped my saber.

"You injure him, you die." That fucking crone wouldn't stop me.

"No harm," the maiden promised.

The red fluid circled the ward and surged up to the ceiling, enclosing the ward and Derek within it in a column of streaming fluid. Holy crap.

In a moment the second column encased the vampire.

"They can neither hear us, nor see us," the maiden said.

"What is the boon?"

"The hound . . ." The maiden shifted a little within her folds of fabric.

"Bring us his blood," the crone said.

". . . and all your questions . . ." the mother added.

". . . will be answered." The maiden nodded.

A witch chorus. Lovely.

"Why do you need the blood?"

The crone sneered. "Doesn't matter."

"It matters to me."

"Then you get nothing!"

Crap. I bowed. "Thank you for seeing me. Release my associates and I'll go."

"Why care?" the mother asked.

"Because I won't fetch the blood of someone with that much magic unless I know how it will be used." For all I knew, they could use it to hex him or brew a city-wide plague. I knew they wouldn't lie to me. In the modern world of magic and tech, your rep meant everything.

"Is that your final word?" the mother asked.

It was wrong. Not even for Julie and her mother's sake. Some things should not be done no matter how much you want the goal. "Yes."

"Then leave!" the crone barked.

I turned.

"Wait." The maiden's voice tugged on me with its magic. I faced her.

The hag glared at her. "No!"

"Yes," the maiden whispered. "There is no other way."

She pushed off her couch and pulled off her hair. Her head was bald. The folds of fabric slipped from her body. She stood nude, save for the panties.

The effort rocked her and for a second I thought she would fall.

You could play the xylophone on her ribs. She had no breasts. Her knees protruded, disproportional, too large compared to her matchstick-thin legs. A conglomeration of misshapen ugly bumps thrust over her left hip, creating a grotesque, dimpled bulge of flesh.

She raised her chin. Magic streamed from her. Her voice filled the dome, invaded my ears, penetrated my mind.

"We are the Oracle. We serve the covens. They rely on us for power, wisdom, and prophecy. We keep the peace. We keep them safe. Look to the walls. You will see our bodies there, buried, secure in the womb of the tortoise. Just as we turn to dust, we rise anew in young flesh, for when one of us Three dies, a child is born to take her place."

Her gaze pierced me, her eyes radiant. Above her the three-armed Hekate towered, black on the gray wall. "We are the knife, the craft, and the torch that banishes the darkness."

The crone was the knife, the knowledge had to be the mother-witch, and the torch stood in front of me. The torch that banishes the darkness . . . She was the one with the prophetic gift.

"I foresaw that someone would come. I didn't know who it would be, but I foresaw the coming."

She took a deep breath. "I'm dying. My body is full of tumors and neither magic nor medicine helps. I'm not afraid to die. When I do, within three years another witch oracle will be born to take my place. But she will take several years to blossom into her power. I'm too ill and Maria is too old."

Within the next few years, the Oracle could be down to one witch. And could stay that way for about a decade, until the next witches revealed themselves. I looked to the mother for confirmation. She had put her hand over her mouth and was watching the maiden. Grief distorted her face.

"We aren't trying to turn back nature. We cannot reverse Maria's age. But there's a way to cure me." The maiden swayed. "There is a potion. My very last chance. The blood of Morrigan's Hound heals all. You want to save a young girl? Here is your chance to save one. Save me. Bring me the blood and I'll tell all you wish to know."

The maiden fell back onto her couch. The mother rose and swaddled the maiden's fragile body into the robes. The black silk, luxurious before, now gained the dreadful air of a funeral shroud.

"How much blood?" I asked.

The mother straightened, reached into her sleeve, and extracted a plastic blood collection tube. "This much. Press here and slide up. The needle will pop out. Once you draw blood, the needle will retract. Put the cap on right here and bring the whole thing back to us." She sighed. "You must meet him in the mist. In Morrigan's place. That's where his blood is most potent. And another thing: the blood can't be taken or bought with money or traded for favors. It must be freely given or it will lose its magic."

How in the name of all that's holy was I going to do that?

I walked to the platform and took the tube from her.

"How do I get into the mist?"

The mother reached to her knitting. "Nettle and Hound's hair, knitted together. You know how to do a calling, don't you?"

"Yes." Where did she get his hair?

"You better," she said. "Go now. Sienna needs to rest."

I turned to see the red columns draining, revealing the vampire and the monster that once served as my sidekick. The ward circles shivered and vanished, and Derek padded to me, eyes alight with yellow fire.

CHAPTER 17

———◆———

"OUTRAGEOUS," THE VAMPIRE HISSED.

"What would you have me do?" I stepped out onto Centennial Drive, shook twigs out of my hair, and headed across the street to the chicken joint. Normally I kept away from fried food, but today was different. I'd danced in the snow, crawled in tortoise spit, got locked up in glyphs, and I deserved some fried wings, damn it.

The vampire followed. The patrons eyed it with open suspicion but stayed where they were. Atlanteans for you. A walking undead, no big.

And then they saw Derek. Chairs scraped as a few moved out of the way.

"Derek, you want chicken?"

The bastard offspring of Dr. Moreau's Dog-Man and the Hound of Baskervilles nodded.

"Hey!" A stocky laborer at the nearest table pointed a chicken drumstick at me. "Hey, what the fuck, huh? I can't eat with them here!"

I gave him my hard stare. "I guess you won't be needing your food then."

That shut him up.

I pushed the twenty-dollar bill across the counter and scooped up my change and a basket of fried wings. I was so tired of being broke and hungry. At least for a moment I could be happy and full of chicken. I zeroed in on our horses, tethered back by the tunnel. We could eat on the go.

I dropped a handful of wings into Derek's paw. He stuck one in his mouth and spat out clean bones.

The vampire scowled at me. "Not a single word of protest, Kate! Not one. You simply stood there. I had a certain expectation of cooperation."

The urge to mouth off was almost too much. I squashed it. This was a professional disagreement. "Ghastek, correct me if I'm wrong, but the contract you and I both signed specified that I'm to disclose all of the information relevant to reeves, which I have done."

"Kate . . ."

"May I finish, please?"

The vamp's face stretched in confusion. Boy, I should be polite more often. "Yes."

The magic fell. It crashed, gone so completely my heart skipped a beat. I caught my breath and drove on.

"You decided that the information was not substantial enough and requested to come with me for the sole purpose of learning more about reeves. You chose to interpret the contract that way, but that's not the way it's written. We both know that technically you don't have any ground to stand on."

"I beg to differ . . ."

"I agreed to your presence because I felt it was a fair request, not because I was bound by our agreement. I'm under no obligation to help you. Furthermore, please note that at no point did the contract specify that you or any other representative of the People became part of the Order's investigation into the disappearance of Jessica Olsen. So far, you have done your best to impede this investigation by nearly sabotaging my rendezvous with the witches. As an Order representative, it's my duty to advise you that further attempts to hinder the Order's activities will *not* be tolerated. That said, since I'm also a representative of the Mercenary Guild, if you require protection from the witches, I'm sure we can come to a reasonable agreement on my retainer. I dislike bodyguard detail but since you're an old acquaintance, I'll make an exception."

The vampire stared at me with an expression of utter shock on its face.

"Who are you?" Ghastek said finally. "And what have you done with Kate?"

"I'm the person whose job it is to settle disputes between the Order and the Guild. I have a lot of free time on my hands, and I spend this time reading the Order's Charter and the Guild's Manual. Would you prefer if I went back to my normal mode of conversation?"

"I think so."

"You underestimated the witches, mouthed off, and got punked. Don't come crying to me."

I picked up a chicken wing. Food. Finally.

Derek snarled. It was a low snarl, a deep, threatening warning of barely contained violence.

I turned. Feet wide, back humped, he stood stiff, facing the wall of green that surrounded Centennial Park. His hackles rose, his black lips drew up revealing huge white fangs, and out came another growl. The hair on the back of my neck rose.

I set the wings on the curb and reached for Slayer. My fingers touched the leather of the saber's hilt. Like a handshake with an old friend.

The vampire slunk low to the ground.

I surveyed the trees. From the massive roots to the tops, etched against the garish orange and gold of the sunset, the dense mass of green looked impenetrable.

The first reeve sailed over the green, her translucent skin bathed in red, her hair flaring like enormous black wings, ready to smother.

No smothering today. The tech was up.

Her twin followed. Another, and another. Five. Six, more . . . How many could the Shepherd drive at once?

They were still in the air when I charged. The first reeve came at me, legs pumping, arms flung wide, gliding as if she didn't have to touch the ground.

"Mine!"

The vampire smashed into her, knocking her out of the way, and leaped on her back. The sickle claws hooked the reeve's pale neck. The vamp pulled and tore off her head with a single muscle-ripping jerk.

"They're poisonous!" I yelled for Derek's benefit and aimed for the second reeve. She whipped her hair at me, but I had room to maneuver. I dodged the black mass, and struck diagonally down, guessing there was flesh under the hair. Slayer connected and sliced into meat. It was a textbook slash—I had pulled the entire length of the blade through the wound. Her head drooped, connected to the stump of the neck by a thin strip of skin and meat. She crashed to the ground.

To the left Derek dug into the back of the third reeve with an enormous clawed hand and ripped the shard of her spine free with a brutal heave.

The vampire dashed across the field and beheaded another reeve.

I kept running. The next reeve met me head-on. I slashed again, an almost identical diagonal stroke but coming from the left. She dodged, but I reversed the blade and struck sideways instead. Slayer cleaved the flesh and broke free. Grayish blood sprayed in a fine mist. She toppled over and then another reeve fell on me. Claws scraped the heavy leather protecting my chest, ripping through it. A wall of hair clogged my view. I thrust myself closer to the reeve, right into her teeth. The stench of fish guts washed over my face.

She had expected me to pull away, and her surprise cost her a precious half second. Cocooned in her hair, I hugged her like a lover, and thrust my saber straight up into the soft flesh under her chin. She rocked back. To the left Derek raised his bloody muzzle from the ruined back of the fifth reeve.

"Don't bite!" Dumbass. Perfect wolf for you—isn't happy until he's got poisonous shit smeared all over his teeth.

The vamp had backed the last reeve flush against the trees. "I can't help but point out that they don't deliquesce."

The reeve hissed. Claws broke through her knuckles.

"They melt like the wicked witch of the west when the magic's up."

The vampire glided closer to the reeve. "So you say."

Why wasn't he killing it?

A shiver ran along the bloodsucker's flanks. It hugged the ground. The reeve hissed again and froze, petrified. Convulsions rippled down her long legs.

No. He couldn't possibly.

"You're out of your mind."

"We're only a mile from the Casino. Well within my range." Ghastek's voice sounded distant like it came from the bottom of a barrel. The reeve and vampire shivered in tandem.

"You can't navigate them both!"

"We shall see."

No, we won't. I headed for the reeve, saber ready.

The reeve swayed on her feet and slashed at the vampire. Scarlet lines swelled across the vamp's chest and sealed.

"I'm so glad you decided to play," Ghastek's voice said from the vampire's mouth.

"Hey, would you look at that shit?"

I turned on my heel. The patrons who'd fled at the first hint of trouble had come back and were enjoying the spectacle.

"Clear out!" I barked.

They paid me no mind. Asshole innocent bystanders.

The reeve's mouth gaped open and Shepherd's voice issued forth, dry and sibilant, full of echoes of dead leaves crushed underfoot. "Surrender, human."

"Bolgor the Shepherd, I presume?" The vamp reared.

A spasm gripped the reeve. She crashed to her knees, her shoulders trembling. The Shepherd rasped. "You cannot stop us. The gate of the Otherworld yawns wide. The Great Crow leads the host. Look into the darkness, human, and you will see your death riding to greet you!"

"That's a lovely speech. Almost Shakespearean." Ghastek's vamp rocked forward and the reeve mirrored its motion.

Magic drenched us. Instantly the bodies littering the ground melted into sluice.

The black mass of the reeve's hair snapped. Thick cords bound the vampire, squeezing its throat. The bloodsucker made no move to resist. I was almost to them.

The puddle to the left of me shrunk, evaporating at a record rate, but before it vanished completely I saw it shake and felt the ground kick my feet.

A loud thud came from the right. A rickety wooden wagon at the northern intersection rocked and crashed onto its side, splintering into shards. A hulking figure emerged from the wreck: eight feet tall, green, moving ponderously on colum-nar legs, his head topped by a horned helmet. At least one hundred pounds of chain mail wrapped around his torso. His shoulders would've made Andre the Giant weep. A long meaty tail hung from under the chain mail, shaking as he ran.

"Kneel before Ugad, the Great Crow's Hammer!" The Shepherd hissed in triumph.

Ugad the Hammer, huh? "You've got delusions of grandeur. 'Bubba' would've done him just fine."

The juggernaut stomped toward us. The spectators scat-tered like so many mice. Stunned into sudden silence, the fetish vendor gaped at the approaching monstrosity. He fum-bled at his charms and shook a small circle of ribbon at the monster. Ugad paid it no mind. His right thigh brushed the cart, spinning it onto the sidewalk. Bright charms spilled in a calico mess on the pavement.

The monster accelerated. With a shock I realized he wore no helmet. Those were his horns, growing from the skull cov-ered with swirls of tattoos.

Behind me the vampire hissed. I glanced at it. The reeve had backed away. The vampire sat alone. Ruby-red eyes glared at me full of hunger, unleashed, unchained, all consuming. No navigator rode this mind.

"Ghastek!"

No answer. Ghastek had lost him.

The vamp gathered like a coiled spring, leaped at me, claws poised for the kill . . .

A shaggy body rammed the vampire in mid jump. With a snarl, Derek dragged the bloodsucker down. The vampire sank its fangs into his shoulder.

Ugad bore down on me.

I dodged left and sliced at the tendon in the back of Ugad's knee. The cut should've taken him down, but instead he spun around. A huge tail swung at me, the meaty protrusion at the end whistling like a club hurtling through the air with great speed. I jumped aside and sliced at the tail. The monster moaned and backhanded me. I saw it coming, but caught be-tween his tail and the hand, I had nowhere to go.

The blow swept me off my feet. I flew and landed hard on my shoulder, sliding across the asphalt. The impact numbed my back.

I jumped to my feet and rolled, just as the tail swung over my head. A huge foot chased me and stomped the asphalt where my head was a moment ago. Ugad bellowed in frustration, making the thick network of veins on his neck bulge. So many places to cut. If only I could make him shorter, so I could get up there.

Another stomp. I leaped back.

Ugad swiped at me. I stood still for him. Whatever it takes to get to the target. A shovel-sized hand closed about me, pinning my sword arm, and dragged me up, off my feet, toward Ugad's piggish eyes. My bones groaned in protest.

The monster's face swung into view. His dim eyes lit up with cruel glee under the tangled mess of tattoos on its forehead. *The tattoos . . .*

The jagged lines etched on his scalp suddenly made sense, flowing into a word of power. Pain exploded at the base of my skull and drowned the world in a bright fiery splash. I couldn't breathe, I couldn't scream, I felt nothing. Caught in a typhoon of pain, I wrestled with the word. I had to make it mine or it would fry my mind. I had to say it.

A clump blocked my throat. My voice refused to obey. Pain shot and twisted through my body, as if tiny needles pierced every cell of me. The pain burst and I screamed the word to escape it. *"Osanda!"*

It hurt so much.

I am dying.

The reality rushed at me with crystal crispness. The monster's knees hit the asphalt. White shards of broken bone thrust through the ruptured muscle. Ugad moaned, a sound filled with bewilderment and pain.

Kneel. The word commanded the target to kneel. I had been hoping for "eat dirt and die."

Ugad crushed me, shaking me with the last of his strength. Compared with the pain of the power word, the steel vise of his fingers felt almost weak.

Never mind comparing—kill now, compare later.

I passed Slayer into my left hand and slashed across Ugad's thick neck, opening a wet, red second mouth under his chin. Red and gray blood gushed. The monster's maw gaped open in one last, silent scream. He released me and toppled forward, breaking into liquid as he hit the ground. Greasy fluid splashed me. My lips burned from contact with an alien magic.

I spat, trying to wipe away enough goo to open my eyes and only getting more goo onto my face. I tasted blood sharp with my magic on my lips. A nosebleed. Shit. I fumbled for the gauze, or I'd have to set the whole scene on fire to hide my magic. I pulled it blindly from my pocket and wiped my face, finally clawing my eyes open.

The bloodsucker lay broken, its chest a mess of crushed ribs, a trail of wet, soft clumps that used to be its heart leading from its body to Derek, who sprawled on his back, unmoving.

The reeve hovered over Derek's prone form. Her hair bound his throat. At least forty feet separated us. I would not make it in time.

The Shepherd's whisper emanated from the reeve's mouth. "Surrender or it dies."

I dropped the gauze and slid my hand up my thigh to the throwing dagger on my belt.

"It dies!" the Shepherd hissed.

I hurled the dagger. The blade bit into the reeve's head, popping her eye like a ripe grape. The impact knocked her back and I threw the shark teeth at her, one after another. The short triangular blades punctured her throat and cheeks. She rocked forward, stared at me with the gaping hole of her eye socket, and broke into water.

I ran to Derek, and I put my head on his chest. Heartbeat. Strong, solid heartbeat.

The vamp's blood smeared his whole head. I couldn't tell if he was hurt.

"Derek! Derek!" *God, whoever you are, I'll do anything, please don't let him die.*

His eyelids trembled. Monstrous mouth opened. He sat up slowly.

"Where does it hurt?" I nearly slapped myself. Only the most accomplished of the shapeshifters could speak in half-form. Derek wasn't one of them.

"Everrrryear." The word came out mangled but recognizable.

"Everywhere?"

He nodded. "Okray."

"You're okay?"

He nodded again.

I wanted to cry with relief. My chest felt heavy like it was full of lead. "You can speak in half-form."

"Yeahhh. Veen praaasing."

"Been practicing. That's good." I laughed a little. "That's real good."

He grinned. Bloody shreds of vampiric meat stretched from between his crooked fangs, wet with drool, and I nearly lost my lunch. "Come on, pretty boy, before this place swarms with People, or we'll never get out of here."

I found my gauze, grabbed the horses, and we took off down the street just as the first smear of necromantic magic announced the arrival of the vampiric scouts.

CHAPTER 18

———◦◦◦———

DEREK FAVORED HIS LEFT SIDE. HIS HORSE REFUSED to bear him. I couldn't blame the horse. I wouldn't want his demonic, undead-blood-smeared, wolf-smelling ass riding me, either. But it made us slow.

Three blocks away I commandeered a rickety buggy from an old woman. Commandeered was too strong a word—I flashed my ID and promised her far more money then I had at my disposal. Considering that I still had my sword out and my hair and face were decorated a lovely brown shade of drying blood, she decided arguing too much wasn't in her best interests. In fact, she told me I could have the buggy if I didn't hurt her.

I told her to bill the Order, packed Derek into the buggy, hitched the horses to the back, and drove the big dappled draft horse to the Order.

Within five minutes Derek fell asleep. His skin split, shivered, and a huge gray wolf lay in his place. The beast-form took a lot of concentration to maintain. Left to its own devices, a shapeshifter's body went either man or animal in a hurry. I guess with the flare, the animal must've taken less energy. And that was the trouble with shapeshifters. They were psychotic, fanatically loyal to the Pack, and they needed a nap or a dinner every time they exerted themselves.

But then if I went up against an aged vampire gone berserk, I'd want a nap, too. He killed a vampire. By himself. No help, no magic, just his teeth, and claws, and raw determination. Bloody amazing. I had the next wolf alpha in my buggy. Here's hoping he'd remember me when he made it into the big leagues.

The sunset burned down to nothing. The magic crashed again, hard. Not a trace of it remained, yet the city knew it was there, waiting like a hungry predator in the night, ready to pounce.

My head pounded. My ribs ached with every breath, but nothing seemed to be broken. Thank the Universe for small favors.

Gradually my brain started up, at first slowly, like a rusted watermill, then faster, trying to sort through the nonsense the Shepherd spouted. He had said something about the Great Crow leading the host. A host of reeves could do a lot of damage. I didn't want to dwell on the full implication of that mental picture.

So a host of reeves with the Great Crow in the lead. The Great Crow could stand for Morrigan, except that Bran turned a reeve by the pit into a porcupine, and Bran served Morrigan. Only a man worried about offending his patron goddess would've balked like he did at the idea of swearing by her name.

So Morrigan and Bran on one side, and the Fomorians and the Great Crow on the other. So far we had stayed strongly in the realm of Celtic mythology. I couldn't recall any Great Crows in Irish mythology other than Morrigan. Esmeralda had all those books in her trailer . . . maybe one of them would mention this Great Crow.

It would only take fifteen minutes to detour to my apartment. Derek's breathing was even, he wasn't bleeding, and he didn't seem in distress. I wanted to check on Julie, but fifteen minutes wouldn't make that much difference.

Why did the Fomorians attack me in the first place? That was the sixty-four-thousand-dollar question. First they attacked Red, who had stumbled onto them, or at least so he claimed. Then they attacked Julie. Now they attacked me. Why? What would make them risk a confrontation with a vampire and a werewolf, not taking into account the fact that I had already made three reeves into wet and smelly spots. Revenge? The Shepherd didn't strike me as a hotheaded, "revenge at all costs" type. He was more of a calculating, "friz-ice in his veins" kind of enemy.

I replayed the chronology of the events in my head, trying to find some form of connection. First, Red got jumped by reeves and had his neck scratched. Next, he and Julie went to look for her mother at the Sisters' gathering place. From there, I took Julie home. Red followed us and gave Julie a monisto. The reeves attacked Julie. Then I left Julie in the vault and the reeves attacked me.

That last bit made no sense. An attack on me and Julie in my apartment I could understand. Then, the odds were clearly in the Shepherd's favor. But attacking me the second time, when I had a werewolf and a vampire with me? And out in the open? It's almost as if he had been desperate.

And how did they find me? They didn't track me by scent. Atlanta's streets are too polluted to provide a good scent trail. They didn't track me by sight, either. They would've had to be close to do so, and Derek would've smelled them.

The only way they could have tracked me was by magic.

Red had said that reeve hair grabbed like a lasso. The hair was only active during a magic wave. Then the reeves attacked my apartment, also during the magic wave. And finally, they struck at me just when the magic wave had ended. It was as if an invisible magic scent somehow stained Red, then Julie, then me, and the reeves followed it like hounds.

Red, Julie, me. Was there a pattern here? What could've connected us all? Perhaps Red became polluted with some weird residual magic. Julie touched Red, and I touched Julie, transferring the traces onto myself. But residual magic usually didn't survive technology, and the magic had been shifting like crazy.

Maybe I was thinking about it wrong. Maybe the reeves were tracking something specific. Something that exuded a definite power signature. Something that only acted up during the magic waves, a beacon like Whomper. Something that passed from Red to Julie and from Julie to me. But what?

The monisto. Red gave it to Julie, and Julie gave it to me.

I pulled the necklace out and tried to examine it, glancing at the road once in a while. A simple cord, knotted together from dirty shoelaces. There were probably two dozen coins on it. Let's see, a Kennedy half-dollar, a quarter, a twenty-peso coin, a Georgia peach quarter—wow, rare, a token from the mall carousel with a little horse on it, a Chinese coin with a square hole in the middle—where did he get this one? A miniature, dollar-sized CD marked Axe Grinder III, a video game maybe? A rough disk with a loop in the center to pass the cord through. A Republica NC Pilipinas coin, Philippines? A little triangular charm with a loop on top, inscribed with an Egyptian hieroglyphic symbol. A round coin, too worn to determine if anything was on it originally. A square bronze charm with a rune on it. A Jefferson nickel . . .

One of those was special. Which one? It would have to be one of the older-looking ones. Of course, with my luck, the Shepherd could be a crazy numismatist just dying for a Kennedy fifty-cent piece. Maybe I could set a trap with a handful of change. Here, Shepherd, here boy, look, I have a Susan B. Anthony dollar, you know you want it.

I put the monisto away. I could stare at it all night trying to pinpoint the reeve magnet, or I could just ask Julie, the human m-scanner extraordinaire, which one felt weird to her. If I was right.

I felt no protective spells on the monisto. Perhaps Red found something that belonged to the Shepherd, a charm, a magic trinket. More likely, he stole it and added it to the monisto to hide it. Unfortunately, the object emitted magic, and whoever carried the monisto became an instant reeve magnet. If I was right, Red had realized he was being tracked, and he handed that thing to Julie knowing that the reeves would return to claim it. He didn't give it to her to protect her. He gave it to her to shift the focus off himself, to point them to a new target. Kid or not, that was a lousy thing to do.

By the time I pulled up in front of my apartment building, I was pissed enough to thrash him. Red was a problem. Julie loved him beyond all reason, and he pretty much used her whichever way he wanted. I tied the reins to one of the posts in a metal row set up for precisely that purpose. Something was seriously wrong with Red. I understood why: because he was on the street, alone, hungry, bullied, left to fend for himself. But I'd known street kids that grew up into people with a decent moral code. I had a feeling Red's moral code consisted of one line: Red does best for Red.

I ran up three flights of stairs to my apartment only to find a solid door blocking the way. I had no key.

I ran down to the first floor and banged on the super's door. "Mr. Patel?"

Mr. Patel was the nicest super I had ever had to deal with . . . and also the slowest. Brown like a walnut, with sleepy, heavy-lidded eyes, he moved with luxurious leisure, too dignified to accelerate. Trying to nag him into hurrying up would slow him down to the speed of chilled molasses. It took him a good five minutes to find the key ring, after which he proceeded to climb the stairs with venerable decorum. By the time he finally opened the door and deposited the right key into my palm, I was dancing in place with frustration.

I ran into the apartment, grabbed Esmeralda's books, ran out, slapping the door shut behind me, and rushed down the stairs, passing bewildered Mr. Patel on the way.

THE VAULT DOOR STOOD AJAR.

A single bulb illuminated its round contours, and the door shone with reflected light at the bottom of the narrow stairwell, like an enormous metal coin.

It should've been locked tight.

I descended the gloomy stairs, one at a time, saber in hand. I had smelled wolfsbane out front. Wolfsbane was used to throw shapeshifters off track. Somebody knew I had Derek with me. If it was directed at me, that is.

Derek slept securely on the landing. I had meant to carry him into my office, but I was tired and he'd been eating his Wheaties. He probably weighed close to one fifty in wolf-form. I gave up midway.

Two drops of blood stained the step in front of me. Another glistened two steps lower. I smelled gunpowder. Andrea had fired. Her bullet must have only grazed him, otherwise there would be a body, not just blood droplets. Andrea never missed.

I conquered the stairs on soft feet and stopped with my back to the wall. An odd hoarse breathing echoed through the vault, like a dull saw being drawn against the wood.

I leaned and glanced through the doorway.

A mangled body curled on the floor among shreds of clothes. Deformed or battered, it lay crumpled in a grotesque heap of mismatched limbs, a patchwork of raw beef, red and mud-brown. Another hoarse breath sent tiny echoes scurrying into the corners. Julie was nowhere in sight.

As I stood there, the body turned its head. I saw a clump of blond hair and a single blue eye, the other hidden by a flap of flesh.

Andrea.

I closed the distance between us in a single leap. The dirty patches on her limbs weren't grime. They were fur. Short brown fur, with traces of spots dappling the skin.

Her chest was misshapen, too flat. The skin on her stomach ended abruptly, not torn or cut, but simply falling too short of its goal, as if there wasn't enough of it. The coils of her intestines glistened through the opening. Her left leg melted into a paw, while her right stretched too long, twisting backward. Her jaws protruded, mismatched, her lips way too short, her fangs puncturing her cheeks.

Dear God. The Lyc-V got her after all.

Andrea's left eye focused on me, her iris baby-blue. A long gurgling sound broke free of her throat. "Heeeeelp."

This was beyond me. I've never seen a shapeshifter stuck between forms.

I had to find someone who could help her. Doolittle. But he was back at the Pack Keep. It would take me hours to reach it. Her skin had taken on a sallow, pale gray tint that meant the shapeshifter's body was scraping the last of its reserves dry. Andrea might not have hours.

Wait. Doolittle was loyal to Curran. He'd give her up in a minute. And then the Pack would test her to ensure she wasn't a loup and then she would have to confront Curran. You can't be loyal to Curran and the Order at the same time. The second her shapeshifter status was discovered, she'd be expelled from the Order. Andrea lived and breathed the Order. I might as well let her die.

But if I did nothing, she would die, as well.

Doolittle was out. So was Derek. Who could I take her to?

A tremor ran through Andrea's limbs. Her right foot stretched. Bones crept forward with agonizing slowness. She moaned, her voice charged with so much pain, it sent my heart hammering. Her stomach contracted, her buttocks tightened, and then the convulsion was over and she slumped back onto the floor.

A distinct acrid stench spread through the room. I've smelled it before. A hyena.

The Keep was shared by all shapeshifters, but each clan had its own gathering place, just as each clan had its own pair of alphas. The hyenas had to have their own spot. They weren't nearly as numerous as wolves or rats, but there were enough of them to form their own little pack. I've met their leader—an older woman called Aunt B. I'd rather fight a wolf pack than cross her. She had a bun on her head and a sweet smile, and I was sure she'd be smiling just as sweetly when she tickled my liver with her claws. Hyenas and lions didn't get along. Curran recognized this. They were still his to command, but he left them enough autonomy to solve their own problems.

I had to take her to Aunt B. She was a scary bitch, but I'd rather reason with her than with Curran.

I bent over Andrea. "I'm going to take you to the hyena pack."

Her eye widened. She shuddered, moaning. "No. Can't."

"Don't argue. We have no choice."

I slid my arms under her. Lymph wet my hands. I smelled the sharp odor of urine. She probably weighed close to a hundred and thirty pounds. I locked my teeth and heaved. Her deformed arms clutched at me.

God, she was heavy.

I headed for the vault door.

When I was a child, my father made me run grueling marathons with a loaded rucksack on my back. Back then the only thing that kept me going was knowledge that the pain would eventually end. And so I murmured it to myself now, as I slowly climbed the stairs. Pain was good. Pain would end. Every moment I delayed, Andrea edged a little closer to dying.

I unloaded her into the buggy. "Julie?" I whispered.

"Boy. Shaman boy. Took Julie." Her voice died in a gurgle.

Damn it, Red. At least, without the monisto, the reeves shouldn't be able to find her. "Hang on for me. Stay alive."

I ran back inside, taking the stairs two at a time. Derek was still out like a light. I shook him. "Wake up!"

He snapped at me, his fangs scratching my hand, and instantly was up on his feet, whining in embarrassment.

"Never mind. I need help."

He followed me down and froze midway on the stairs, his hackles up, his back humped, growling and snarling.

"Derek, please. I know it smells weird, but I need your nose. Now. Please."

I coaxed him down the stairs. He gave the buggy a wide berth and looked at me.

"Can you pick up Julie's scent?"

He put his nose to the ground and jerked back as if struck. He backed away, circled the buggy, circled wider, sniffed the ground, recoiled again, and whined.

Too much wolfsbane. Red covered his scent well.

A hushed moan emanated from the cart. Julie would have to wait, because Andrea couldn't. At least I still carried the necklace. If I were right, the reeves would chase me instead of Julie. They were welcome to it. As pissed off as I was, I'd welcome an assault with open arms.

"Change of plans. Take me to the hyenas. We don't have much time. Please hurry."

Derek trotted down the street. I hopped into the driver's seat and we were off. Slow enough to make me fight against the urge to grind my teeth, but we were off.

All was not well in Atlanta. Magic sang through my bones as I piloted the cart through the rubble-framed streets as fast as the draft horse would allow. Strange things flew through the night sky, dark shapes blotting out the stars, gliding without sound. Twice we had to stop—first, to avoid a vampire patrol, four bloodsuckers in a diamond formation, and second to let a phantom translucent bear pass before us. The bear's head was crowned with horns. It looked at the buggy with mournful eyes as rivulets of transparent fire cascaded down its back in a tangled waterfall, and ambled on its way, down the street.

A ghost river ran parallel to the road, its water inky—black and dense like liquid tar. I tried to stay away from it. The things that howled and cried in the night stayed silent. Listening. Waiting. If by some miracle, the pulse of the city could be captured and played back, a single phrase would echo: "A flare is coming, a flare is coming, a flare is coming . . ."

Andrea's convulsions came faster now, every fifteen minutes or so. I knew when one gripped her because she let out a small pain-choked cry that made me wince.

Finally we left the city behind, heading down the familiar road past the ruined industrial district and down the overgrown highway. The night expanded, the dark sky pierced with tiny lights of stars reaching impossibly high. The colors were muted; the shadows darkened; ordinary trees, so mundane and cheerful in the light of day, twisted into gnarled monsters lying in wait for their prey. This was the way to the Keep, the fortress where the Pack gathered in times of trouble.

We passed an abandoned gas station, dark, its door missing, its windows broken. Small, gaunt creatures crawled along the windowsills and slunk in the doorway. Sickening yellow, like pus from an infected wound, they stared at us with glowing eyes and stretched their gnarled clawed hands in our direction, as if trying to rake us from a distance.

Derek trotted down the road in that lazy wolf gait that ate up miles without effort. We reached the tree line. Massive oaks hugged the road, stretching to clasp at each other with their branches. Derek stopped, raised his head to the starry sky, and howled. His cry floated into the night, lingering, haunting, full of sorrow and chilling to the bone. Announcing us. He waited for a long moment, flickered his ears, and trotted down the overgrown road under the shroud of the trees. I followed.

The buggy creaked, the beat of horse hooves steady and measured.

An eerie cackle echoed through the night. A high-pitched, deranged sound, tight like a guitar string about to snap. Lithe shapes appeared, gliding through the brush on both sides. They ran upright, gray silhouettes in the gloom, too tall and too fast to be human.

A shape leaped into the buggy and landed next to me. Red eyes shone in the dark like two stray sparks. A werehyena in half-form was a terrible thing to behold.

"Hi, pretty." His monster mouth slurred the words.

Ahead three hyenas, two in beast-form and one human, circled Derek, hooting and laughing in berserk glee.

The male lunged at me. I twisted to the side, caught him in an armlock, and squeezed his throat, putting pressure on the artery. "I don't want to play. Take me to Aunt B," I said into the round ear.

His clawed hands clasped my arm. "Mmm, hurts so good. Hurt me more."

God damn hyenas.

Ahead Derek snapped at one of the females.

"You need to learn humility." The human hyena uncoiled a whip from her hand. "Come, let me pet you, little wolf."

Shit. I wrenched the hyena male to the left and into the buggy, nose to nose with Andrea. A weak cry escaped from Andrea's lips and washed over the male's face.

"She's dying!" I squeezed the words through my teeth.

The werehyena shoved me aside and screamed, "Open the way!"

The human female put her fist on her hip. "You forget yourself . . ."

"She needs Mother now!" He snarled and she backed away. He turned to me, eyes glowing. "Drive!"

I drove between the hyenas, and they closed ranks behind me, blocking Derek's path.

"The wolf can't pass. It's the law." The werehyena's voice was grim.

"Nothing will happen to him." I loaded as much steel into my voice as it would hold.

"Nothing will."

The hyenas followed the cart. Spurred by their scent, the draft horse picked up speed. Rumbling and creaking, we drove faster and faster, until the buggy bumped and flew over every pimple on the road. The trees parted, revealing a large ranch-style house. I pulled on the reins and nearly lost my arms. Unable to stop, the draft horse thundered around the house and finally came to a stop. The male leaped onto the grass, scooped up Andrea, and ran to the porch.

The porch light came on and Aunt B swung the door open. Middle-aged and stout, with graying hair rolled into a bun, she looked like she should be baking cookies, not ruling a brood of social deviants with a penchant for hysterical laughter and kinky sex.

She took one look at Andrea and jerked her head. "Inside. You, too!"

I ran inside, behind the male. A female in a human shape followed. At least I thought she was female. Aunt B looked out into the night and shut the door.

The male ran down the hallway into a huge bathroom. An enormous tub sat sunken in the marble platform, enough for six or eight to comfortably fit. He padded across the floor strewn with sex toys and fruit, and jumped into the tub, holding Andrea above the surface.

Aunt B knocked some sort of leather and steel contraption off the marble and sat on the edge. "Who else knows?"

"She had a wolf with her," the female said.

"Who?"

"Derek," I told her.

Aunt B nodded. "Good. The boy will go straight to Curran. I can reason with Curran. It's our luck that the Bear is away. As long as none of the older guard find out, we'll be fine."

What the hell was she so happy about? Curran was about as reasonable as a mad elephant.

She leaned over to Andrea. "Stupid, stupid child. You know what you are?"

Andrea nodded. The effort rocked her distorted body.

"It will go easier then. Strip her."

The female leaped into the tub and brushed away the shreds of fabric, still clinging to Andrea's flesh. My stomach clenched. Acid washed my tongue.

"You're going to gag, go outside." Aunt B nodded to Andrea. "I will guide you into the natural form. Your face is turning gray. You know what that means, so concentrate if you want to live. Chest first. Picture two wings growing from your back. Large wings. Spread them, child. Spread them wide."

Andrea's chest bone crawled down. Her shoulders lowered, stretching her chest . . .

I ran out of the house.

CHAPTER 19

———◦◦◦———

I SAT ON THE PORCH. THE DOOR BANGED AND A hyena female sat next to me. Or maybe she was a he. It was hard to tell with hyenas: they were a weird androgynous lot. In the wild, female hyenas were dominant. The hierarchy went females, pups, and only then males. Considering that spotted hyena females grew larger than males and sported a clitoris big enough to rival any male's penis that could, and frequently did, get erections, the hierarchy made sense.

This particular hyena was short and had blue hair that stuck out straight up from her head. She saw me looking.

"Like my do? I'll tell you who did it. Of course, it won't look as good on you as it does on me." She winked.

"I'm sure. So how much does it cost to get a gas burner installed on your head?"

She guffawed and handed me a sandwich. "You're okay. Here, brought you some grub."

I sniffed the sandwich. "So what's in it? Jism? Ground tiger testicles?"

"Salami. Eat it. It's good and you look like you need it."

I didn't think I'd hold it down, but as soon as the first bite hit my mouth, I knew I would want seconds.

"How is she?" I asked between bites.

"She's doing good." The werehyena raised her eyebrows and nodded. "She's one tough bouda."

"Buddha?"

"Bouda. Werehyena. Although if you want to get technical, your girl is . . ." She cut herself off. "If you want to get technical, it's not my place to tell you. Call us boudas. That's the proper way to do it." The bouda sniffed. "Company. I love visitors for dinner."

A familiar man strode from the trees, moving with a purpose. Six two, with skin the color of coffee grounds, he looked like he wanted to punch somebody. A long black leather coat hid most of him, but what little showed of his chest under a black T-shirt suggested he was all muscle. His swagger suggested he was all mean. In daylight on a busy street, crowds did an excellent impression of the Red Sea before Moses at his approach.

He stopped a few yards from the porch.

"Wow, knock me over with a feather. The chief of intelligence himself at our doorstep." The bouda grinned and her smile wasn't friendly.

"Hi, Jim," I said.

He didn't look at me. "The man wants to know what's going on. And he wants her at the Keep. Now."

"Talking about yourself in the third person now, are we?" The bouda smiled.

Jim leaned back, his chin high. "Curran wants information. Don't make me walk into this house uninvited."

The bouda's eyes flashed crimson. She let loose a strung-out hysterical cackle and leaned forward, showing him her teeth. Her face twisted into a hungry grimace. "Make a move, cat! Break the law. Test the jaws of Kuri's daughter, if you dare. I'll smile wide when your bones snap under my teeth."

She snapped at him and licked her lips. Jim's face wrinkled in a snarl. Two hyenas circled from behind the house like sharks, clicking and growling.

I got up and nodded to Jim. "Give me a minute. As a personal favor."

His face gave nothing away. Slowly, deliberately he took two steps back and waited.

Inside the bathroom, Andrea sat on marble, barely visible behind the female and Aunt B. The male bouda ran his fingers through the wet mass of blond hair on her head, searching for something.

"I have to go . . ."

The boudas parted, revealing Andrea. She was covered in short fur, her skin dappled with uniform black spots. I'd never seen a body that proportionate in beast-form, except for Curran's. The only flaw was her arms: they reached down too low, almost brushing her knees. It took me a second to register the fact that she had breasts. Normal human breasts. Most female shapeshifters in half-form had tiny breasts or a row of tits.

She looked at me. Her blue eyes and her forehead said human. Her dark muzzle and jaws signaled hyena. They melded seamlessly into each other. The effect was a revolting but somehow unified whole.

"Found it." The male hooked something with his claws.

Aunt B braced Andrea's head. "Do it."

The male plucked a small dark object from Andrea's skull, sending a few drops of blood flying. She groaned quietly. Aunt B let go, and the male leaned in and licked Andrea's neck gently.

"I do believe Raphael's in love." The female bouda grinned.

Andrea clumped a wet towel to her head and looked at me. "Kate? Where are you going?"

The words came through startlingly clear, her voice completely unchanged.

"Curran wants to talk to me. He sent Jim, and it's best I go."

Andrea took a deep breath. "I'm beastkin."

By the way she pronounced it, I understood the word must have some sort of deep significance but it flew completely over my head. My face must have said as much, because Aunt B folded her hands in her lap. "Do you remember Corwin?"

"The catwere. He died protecting Derek." Lyc-V was an equal opportunity virus. It infected humans and animals alike and stole fragments of its victims' DNA, sometimes inserting human genetic code into an animal. Very rarely the result was a beastwere, an animal that shapeshifted into a human. Most were idiots and died quickly, but some, like Corwin, learned to speak and became individuals in their own right.

Aunt B nodded. "Corwin was a good person. He came here a lot."

"He liked to play," the female bouda added.

"Yes, he did. He was shooting blanks. No harm done." Aunt B looked at me.

"That's to be expected, the beastweres are sterile," I said to say something.

Aunt B's face stretched a bit. "Not always."

"Oh."

"Occasionally, very, very occasionally, they make babies."

"Oh."

Andrea sighed. "Sometimes babies survive."

"You're a child of a hyenawere?" I just blurted it right out. Everybody winced.

"Yes," Andrea said. "I'm beastkin. My father was born hyena."

Now it made sense. She didn't catch Lyc-V from the attack, because she was born into it. "Does Ted know?"

"He might suspect," Andrea said. "But he has no proof."

I shrugged. "I won't tell him if you don't. What happened to Julie?"

"Just like that?" the female bouda interrupted. "It doesn't bother you that she is a child of an animal?"

"No. Why should it? Anyway, what happened to Julie?"

The boudas looked at Aunt B. Aunt B looked at me. "The Code says we're human first. We're born human; we die human. That is the natural form, the dominant form. We must assert it and set it above the beast, because that is the natural way."

"The beastkin are born beast," Andrea said softly. "It follows that beast is our natural form, but as we grow, we lose the ability to become beast, because we're hybrid. Therefore I'm an animal that's crippled at birth. Unnatural."

Oh for crying out loud. "Andrea, you're my friend. I don't have many of those. How you were born, what you look like, what anybody else thinks makes no difference to me. When I needed help, you helped me and that's all that matters. Now, can you please, please tell me what happened to my kid?"

Andrea twitched her nose. A nervous cackle spilled from her and she choked it off. "A homeless boy came to the vault."

"Red."

"Yes. Julie told me he was her boyfriend. He was covered in blood and he collapsed by the door. Julie went hysterical. I opened the door and he threw something at me, a powder." She frowned, exposing white teeth. "I carried a shaman charm in my skull to keep from turning during the flare. Usually I have no trouble, but the magic ran too high. Whatever he did . . ." She raised her hands. "It interfered with the charm. I started turning, but I couldn't finish. He grabbed Julie and dragged her out."

Red made me very, very angry.

"Your sword's smoking," the female bouda said.

"It does that occasionally." My voice sounded flat. That little shit. What the hell was he doing? And where was I going to look for him? The city was full of spots where two street kids could hide. Ten million to one, the reeves would find them before me.

Aunt B leaned forward. "By tradition, all beastkin are killed at birth. If any of the older shapeshifters find out she's here, I'll have a mob at my doorstep."

The male bouda licked his lips. "It might be fun."

Aunt B reached out and casually smacked him on the back of the head.

"Ow."

"Is that Curran's cat outside my door?"

"Yes."

"He's caught Andrea's scent by now and he'll report. You'll have to tell Curran something. It's better not to lie."

"I'll take that under advisement." I walked out.

CHAPTER 20

CURRAN'S HAIR FELL TO HIS SHOULDERS. LONG, blond, luxuriously wavy, it framed his face like a mane. He sat in a room in the Pack Keep, reading a battered paperback under a cone of electric light from a small lamp. He didn't raise his head as Jim ushered me into the room and closed the door.

Just me and the Beast Lord. And the night, spilling into the room through the wide-open window.

Jim hadn't said a word to me on the way over here. I was on thin ice.

"What's the deal with the hair?"

Curran tore his gaze from the book and grimaced. "Grows every flare. Can't help it."

We stared at each other. "Waiting for the Fabio joke," he said.

The fatigue rolled over me in a sluggish wave. When I opened my mouth, my voice sounded dull, stripped of all life and inflection. "I brought a sick beastkin to the bouda house. She's my friend. If you're going to kill her, you'll have to go through me."

He closed his eyes tight, put his hand over them, and rubbed his face. I sat in a chair and kept my mouth shut, letting him work through his pain.

"Why me?" he said finally. "Are you on some sort of mission to fuck up my life?"

"I try my best to avoid you."

"You're doing a hell of a job."

"I honestly don't mean to cause problems."

"You don't cause problems. An unpiloted vampire causes problems. You cause catastrophes."

Rub it in, why don't you. "Look, after this, I promise I'll do my absolute best to stay out of your way. Are you going to murder my friend?"

He sighed. "No. I haven't killed any beastkin, and I'm not going to start now. It's an old, elitist custom. I'd have cut the legs from under it when Corwin found us, but there was a lot of opposition and crushing it without hurt feelings was tiresome and time-consuming. If your friend wants to join the Pack, I suppose I'll have to revisit the issue."

The sword in my sheath kept my spine from bending all the way and I very much wanted to either slump forward or to lean back. Even my vertebrae were tired. I unzipped my leather jacket, shrugged it off, unbuckled the sword, and set it in the sheath next to me. "She wants to hide. She's a member of the Order." He'd figure it out eventually anyway. "I'm going to help her to cover it up. After I find Julie."

"You lost the girl?"

"Yeah."

"How?"

I leaned back. "Her shaman boyfriend snatched her from my friend. He did something that caused her to start shifting, but she couldn't finish."

"Go on."

"I found her, loaded her into a cart, and drove her to the hyenas."

He gave me an odd look. "You drove her from the Order to there through the deep magic?"

"Yeah. We did pretty good except for some weirdness at a gas station."

He thought about it. "How long ago did all this happen?"

"Hours."

"Derek couldn't pick up Julie's scent at the scene?" A slight growl of disapproval crept into his voice.

I shook my head. "The shaman used too much wolfsbane. I'll find her. I just don't know how yet."

"If there is anything I can do, I'll help. Don't get excited. It's not because of you. For the child. If it wasn't for her and the flare, I'd throw your dumb ass out of this window."

"What does the flare have to do with it?"

"I don't want it to be attributed to a loss of control on my part. When I throw you out of the window, I want there to be no doubt the act was deliberate."

Wow, he was pissed.

Now the muted setting made sense: a neutral room, soothing light, a book. The deep magic fed the beast within him. It took a monumental effort of will to restrain it. With the flare so close, Curran was a powder keg with a short fuse. I had to be careful not to light that fuse. Nobody outside the Pack, except for Andrea, knew I was here. He could kill me right now and they would never find my body.

We shared a silence for a long moment. Magic blossomed, filling me with giddy energy. The short waves again. They would ebb in a minute, and then I'd be exhausted.

Guilt gnawed at me. He could control himself in my presence, but I apparently couldn't control myself in his. "Curran, up on the roof . . . That is, my brakes don't work sometimes."

He leaned forward, suddenly animated. "Do I smell an apology?"

"Yes. I said things I shouldn't have. I regret saying them."

"Does this mean you're throwing yourself at my feet?"

"No. I pretty much meant that part. I just wish I could've put it in less offensive terms."

I glanced at him and saw a lion. He didn't change, his face was still fully human, but there was something disturbingly lionlike in the way he sat, completely focused on me, as if ready to pounce. Stalking me without moving a muscle. The primordial urge to freeze shackled my limbs. I just sat there, unable to look away.

A slow, lazy, carnivorous smile touched Curran's lips. "Not only will you sleep with me, but you will say 'please.' "

I stared at him, shocked.

The smile widened. "You will say 'please' before and 'thank you' after."

Nervous laughter bubbled up. "You've gone insane. All that peroxide in your hair finally did your brain in, Goldilocks."

"Scared?"

Terrified. "Of you? Nah. If you grow claws, I might get my sword, but I've fought you in your human shape." It took all my will to shrug. "You aren't that impressive."

He cleared the distance between us in a single leap. I barely had time to jump to my feet. Steel fingers grasped my left wrist. His left arm clasped my waist. I fought, but he outmuscled me with ridiculous ease, pulling me close as if to tango.

"Curran! Let . . ."

I recognized the angle of his hip but I could do nothing about it. He pulled me forward and flipped me in a classic hip-toss throw. Textbook perfect. I flew through the air, guided by his hands, and landed on my back. The air burst from my lungs in a startled gasp. Ow.

"Impressed yet?" he asked with a big smile.

Playing. He was playing. Not a real fight. He could've slammed me down hard enough to break my neck. Instead he had held me to the end, to make sure I landed right.

He leaned forward a little. "Big bad merc, down with a basic hip toss. In your place I'd be blushing."

I gasped, trying to draw air into my lungs.

"I could kill you right now. It wouldn't take much. I think I'm actually embarrassed on your behalf. At least do some magic or something."

As you wish. I gasped and spat my new power word. *"Osanda."* Kneel, Your Majesty.

He grunted like a man trying to lift a crushing weight that fell on his shoulders. His face shook with strain. Ha-ha. He wasn't the only one who got a boost from the flare.

I got up to my feet with some leisure. Curran stood locked, the muscles of his legs bulging his sweatpants. He didn't kneel. He wouldn't kneel. I hit him with a power word in the middle of a bloody flare and it didn't work. When he snapped out of it, he would probably kill me.

All sorts of alarms blared in my head. My good sense screamed, *Get out of the room, stupid!* Instead I stepped close to him and whispered into his ear. "Still not impressed."

His eyebrows came together, as a grimace claimed his face. He strained, the muscles on his hard frame trembling with effort. With a guttural sigh, he straightened.

I beat a hasty retreat to the rear of the room, passing Slayer on the way. I wanted to swipe it so bad, my palm itched. But the rules of the game were clear: no claws, no saber. The second I picked up the sword, I'd have signed my own death warrant.

He squared his shoulders. "Shall we continue?"

"It would be my pleasure."

He started toward me. I waited, light on me feet, ready to leap aside. He was stronger than a pair of oxen, and he'd try to grapple. If he got ahold of me, it would be over. If all else failed, I could always try the window. A forty-foot drop was a small price to pay to get away from him.

Curran grabbed at me. I twisted past him and kicked his knee from the side. It was a good solid kick; I'd turned into it. It would've broken the leg of any normal human.

"Cute," Curran said, grabbed my arm, and casually threw me across the room. I went airborne for a second, fell, rolled, and came to my feet to be greeted by Curran's smug face. "You're fun to play with. You make a good mouse."

Mouse?

"I was always kind of partial to toy mice." He smiled. "Sometimes they're filled with catnip. It's a nice bonus."

"I'm not filled with catnip."

"Let's find out."

He squared his shoulders and headed in my direction. Houston, we have a problem. Judging by the look in his eyes, a kick to the face simply wouldn't faze him.

"I can stop you with one word," I said.

He swiped me into a bear hug and I got an intimate insight into how a nut feels just before the nutcracker crushes it to pieces. "Do," he said.

"Wedding."

All humor fled his eyes. He let go and just like that, the game was over.

"You just don't give up, do you?"

"No."

The magic drained again. A dull ache flared across my back—must've landed harder than I thought. The ache spread to my biceps. Thank you for the squeeze of death, Your Majesty. I slumped against the wall.

"Why are you hell-bent on their wedding?"

I rubbed my forehead, trying to wipe away fatigue and this conversation. "You really want to know?"

"Yes. What is it, guilt, revenge, love, what?"

I swallowed. "I live alone."

"And your point is?"

"You have the Pack. You're surrounded by people who would fall over themselves for the pleasure of your company. I have no one. My parents are dead, my entire family is gone. I have no friends. Except Jim, and that's more of a working relationship than anything else. I have no lover. I can't even have a pet, because I'm not at the house often enough to keep it from starving. When I come crawling home, bleeding and filthy and exhausted, the house is dark and empty. Nobody keeps the porch light on for me. Nobody hugs me and says, 'Hey, I'm glad you made it. I'm glad you're okay. I was worried.' Nobody cares if I live or die. Nobody makes me coffee, nobody holds me before I go to bed, nobody fixes my medicine when I'm sick. I'm by myself."

I shrugged, trying to keep my voice nonchalant. "And most of the time, I like being by myself. But when I look into my future, I see no family, no husband, no children. No warmth. I just see myself getting older and more scarred. Fifteen years from now I'll still drag my beaten, bloody hide to my place and lick my wounds, all alone, in a dark house. I can't have love and family, but Crest and Myong have a shot at happiness. I don't want to stand in the way."

I glanced at Curran and saw something in his eyes—understanding? sympathy?—I couldn't tell. It was there for a brief moment and then he pulled his mask back on, and I was greeted with the impenetrable face of an alpha.

I looked away. I had left a lot out. I had left out the part that explained that being with me meant being in danger, because my blood made me a target. Having sex with me meant sharing some of my magic. Being with a normal person made me selfish, because I couldn't protect them if I was found. Hell, I couldn't protect myself if that happened.

Being with a powerful person made me stupid, because as soon as they figured out what I was, they would either kill me or try to use me to their advantage. I distinctly remembered the first time I realized this. His name was Derin. He was a wizard. I was seventeen and wanting very badly to jump into somebody's bed. His bed looked pretty good. Years later looking back at it, I had to admit Derin wasn't all that, but for my first time, well, it could've been worse.

And Greg did what any good guardian would do: he sat down with me and very gently explained to me why I could never see Derin again. A one-night stand in another town was the safest option for me. Hide your blood. Bide your time until you're strong enough. Trust no one. I had known all of that, I just failed to realize the complete implications of it. My guardian had enlightened me. I hated him so much for it, I had agreed to enter the Order's Academy just to get away from him.

The magic splashed us, strong, intoxicating. Curran's hair shifted and grew another inch.

I knew exactly what drew me to him: if we fought—really fought—I wasn't sure I could win. No, scratch that, I was sure I couldn't win. He'd kill me. Wouldn't even blink. He scared me, and the more scared I got, the louder my mouth became.

"Your turn," I told him.

"What?"

"Your turn. I told you why I wanted them together. Now you tell me why you want them apart." Jealousy, pride, love, all good enough reasons for an egomaniac like you. Take your pick.

He sighed. "She's weak and he's a selfish asshole. He'll use her. She's making a mistake."

I didn't expect that. "But it's her mistake to make."

"I know. I keep waiting for her to recognize she's making one."

I shook my head. "Curran, she begged the ex-girlfriend of her fiancé to arrange her wedding. If she's willing to humiliate herself in that manner, she'll do anything for Crest's sake. She doesn't seem like a person who handles pressure well. If you keep delaying the wedding, you'll just drive her to suicide again."

"You saw the scars?"

I nodded. "People must make their own choices, no matter how wrong those choices are. Otherwise they can't be free."

A careful knock echoed through the room.

"Enter," Curran called.

A young man stuck his head into the door. "It's awake."

Curran rose. "I have something to show you."

Thank God it wasn't a pickup line.

As we followed the shapeshifter down the hall, Curran asked softly. "How are those arms? Sore a bit?"

"No," I lied. "How's your knee?"

A few steps later I decided to put my worry to rest. "You were joking about the whole please and thank you thing, right?"

"Meant every word." A little light danced in his eyes and he very deliberately said, "Baby."

No.

He laughed. "You should see your face right now."

"Don't call me that."

"Would you prefer 'darling'? Or maybe 'cupcake'?" He winked.

I gritted my teeth.

We went down the spiraling stairs into the inner yard of the Keep. The Pack Keep had trouble deciding if it wanted to be a medieval castle or a twenty-first-century prison. Its main tower rose, looming, forbidding, a huge square building, utilitarian to the point of being crude. Jim once told me that it was built by hand with minimal technology and took almost ten years. It probably took a lot longer. The Keep went on for many stories underground.

A solid stone wall enclosed the main tower, carving a chunk from the clearing. I had never been inside the yard before. It was spacious and mostly empty. Some exercise equipment at the far wall. A large storage shed. A water tower. To the right a group of shapeshifters stood by a tall tank full of liquid. The last time I'd seen a tank like that, it contained dark green healing solution Doolittle had magicked, and Curran floated in it naked.

This tank contained clear water. Within the water sat a loup cage: bars as thick as my wrist, laced with silver. Something dark moved in the cage. The shapeshifters moved back and forth. Among them were three near seven-foot monstrosities in beast-form whose shaggy heads blocked the view.

"What is that?" I headed for the cage.

"You'll see." Curran looked smug, like a cat who stole the cream and thought he got away with it.

As we crossed the yard, a dark shape blotted out the stars. A dark outline of a long colossal body armed with huge membranous wings passed in silence high above us and vanished behind the tree line.

It couldn't be. Even during a flare, the possibility of such a creature was too miniscule to contemplate.

The shapeshifters parted before Curran. A familiar glowing body shifted within the cage. A reeve. "How did you . . . ?"

Curran shrugged. "She came sniffing your trail after you left. We had a mild disagreement and I tore her arms off. She didn't die right away, so we stuck her into a loup cage and drove her over here."

The reeve floated in the water, her eyes wide-open. Tiny slits of gills fluttered on her neck. Both arms were present and perfectly functional. She had regenerated.

The reeve's hair clasped at the bars and drew back.

"Doesn't like silver." Jim congealed from the crowd as if by magic.

Curran nodded. "The loup cage was a good idea. Never would've thought of it myself. Good looking out."

The next chance I got an extra gig from the Guild, I'd put

the money into getting the bars for my apartment made from the same alloy. My current bars were supposed to have a decent silver percentage but apparently not enough to have prevented the reeve from grabbing them.

I pulled the monisto from my leather. The reeve snapped to the bars, her lavender eyes fastened on the necklace.

"You want this, yes?" I moved the monisto to the left. The reeve followed it.

I pried one of the numerous knots open, slid the first coin off the cord and tossed it into the grass a few feet away. The reeve remained focused on the necklace. I slid the second coin and flicked it next to the first. No reaction.

"Is one of those special?" Curran asked.

"Yep. Don't know which one."

Third coin. Fourth.

"Hey, mates!"

I'd know that voice anywhere. I wheeled around. Bran stood atop the wall a good twenty-five yards away. He waved the crossbow at us. "What a lovely party, and me without an invitation."

"Get him down," Curran said softly.

Two shapeshifters in beast-form detached themselves from the group and padded to the wall.

Bran grinned. "So you're the big man, yea? I thought you would be taller."

"Tall enough to break your back," Curran said. His face snapped into the "pissed off Curran" mode: flat and about as expressive as a slab of granite. "Come down off the wall and we can visit."

"No thanks." Bran's gaze snagged on the monisto in my hand and jumped to the shapeshifters surrounding me. He wanted the monisto very much, but the odds were against him.

He shrugged and saw the reeve. "What's this then? Here, let me help you with that."

The crossbow snapped up and two shafts punctured the back of the reeve's head, the bolt heads emerging precisely through her eyes. The reeve went liquid.

The door leading to the tower burst open and a group of

shapeshifters charged across the yard. Someone screamed, "He's got the surveys!"

"Got to run!" Bran waved a packet of surveys at us. "Thanks for the maps."

Mist swirled and he was gone.

Curran roared.

CHAPTER 21

WHEN A LION ROARS NEXT TO YOU, AT FIRST YOU think it's thunder. That first sound is so deep, so frightening, it couldn't possibly come from a living creature. It blasts your nerves, freezing you in place. All thoughts and reason flee from your mind, and you're left as you are, a helpless pathetic creature with no claws, no teeth, and no voice.

The rumble dies and you think it's over, but the roar lashes you again, like some horrible cough, once, twice, picking up speed, and finally rolling, unstoppable, deafening. You fight the urge to squeeze your eyes shut. You turn your head with an effort that takes every last shred of your control.

You see a seven-foot-tall monster. It has a lion's head and a lion's throat. It's gray and furry. Dark stripes dash across its tree-trunk limbs like whip marks. Its claws could disembowel you with a mere twitch. Its eyes scald you with gold fire.

It shakes the ground with its roar. You smell the sharp stench of urine as smaller monsters cringe and you clamp your hands over your ears, so you don't go deaf.

Finally Curran's roar rolled to a close. Thank God. I thought of pointing out that Bran couldn't hear him and even if he could, he probably wouldn't faint in mortal terror, but somehow this didn't seem to be the right moment for clever observations. The lion's face quivered and snapped into the familiar chimera of lion and human I knew as Curran's half-form. His voice boomed across the yard. "Search the Keep. Find out how he got in and what else he took."

The shapeshifters cleared with record speed, all except Jim.

I needed to get to Bran. Time was short, the flare was almost on us, and I wanted to find Julie and her mother before it hit full force. But there was no way I could enter the mist with the monisto in my hand. Morrigan's Hound wanted it. There was no way I could leave without it because the Fomorians wanted it, also. They would come for it.

What to do?

Jim looked at Curran. "We have bait. He likes her. He might come to visit her."

Bastard. He screwed me over again and again. Why the hell was I always surprised? I looked to Curran. He was considering it; I could almost see the wheels turning under that mane. "Don't do this. I have to find Julie. I can't stay here waiting for that idiot to pop out of thin air."

Jim reached out to me.

"Put your hand down or lose it." I didn't bother looking at him. "You know me. You know I'll do it."

"We don't need anyone's help," Curran said.

Jim withdrew his hand.

I took a deep breath. I saw a way out of this mess, but it was the kind of way that only a desperate fool like me would take. It was either incredibly smart or incredibly stupid.

I held out the monisto. "The bowman wants this. I saw him looking at it. I trust the Pack to safeguard it for me until I need it." I put it into Curran's clawed hand. "I trust *you* to keep it safe. I don't know why, but it's very important. Both the bowman and the reeves will come looking for it. I can't afford for it to be lost. Do you promise to guard it?"

It was a gesture of utter faith. Everyone knew Bran had breached the Pack's security three times. The fact that I trusted Curran with the monisto would mean more to him than any revenge. I had made it personal. If he accepted it, he would die to protect it.

The golden eyes looked into me. "You have my word," he said.

"That's all I need."

I was free to do as I must. I could keep Bran occupied, assuming I found him, and no reeve would ever best Curran.

"I'm going to the bouda house to check on my friend and then I'm off to look for Julie."

"I'll get you an escort as far as the hyena's territory."

"I can find my own way."

Curran shook his head. "Don't argue with me right now."

Two minutes later I rode a horse to the bouda house, accompanied by four somber-faced werewolves. They left me at the invisible boundary. As one of them kindly explained, each shapeshifter clan within the Pack had an expectation of privacy in their meeting place. The privacy wasn't easily breached by members of a different beast clan.

The same bouda that promised to smile when she crushed Jim's bones waited on the porch. She watched as I dismounted and got Esmeralda's books out of the buggy still abandoned by the house.

"You're back," she said. "I peeked in on your chickie while you were gone. She's hot. Does she like girls?"

"I honestly don't know."

"So what's her kick, candy, music? What does she like?"

"Guns."

"Guns?"

"Yep."

The bouda frowned. "I don't know anything about guns. This isn't going to be work, is it? Bummer. Now I don't know if I want to bother."

She made me think of Curran again. "Men are dumb bastards," I said.

She nodded. "Women aren't much better. Whiny bitches, most of them." She thought about it. "Guys can be fun. I recommend Raphael. He's the most patient one we've got, so he gets lucky more than the others. Although I think your chickie has his complete attention at the moment."

I found Andrea and Aunt B in the kitchen at a small round table, drinking tea. The sight of Andrea bringing the teacup to her hyena muzzle struck me as hilarious. I clamped my mouth shut and tried not to laugh. It had to be nerves.

If she asked for biscuits, I'd lose it.

Andrea saw me and visibly stiffened. "How did it go?"

"With what?"

Aunt B sighed. "She wants to know if Curran's coming to kill her."

"Oh. No, he isn't interested in murdering you. Believe me, right now you're the least of his problems."

Andrea exhaled.

"Please tell me there is coffee."

Aunt B grimaced. "They're already crazy. If I let them have coffee, they'd be bouncing off the walls. We have herbal tea."

I put my books on the table.

"You look like you need some sleep." Andrea put a steaming cup before me.

I needed to find Julie, find her mom, convince a sociopath to donate some blood for the good of mankind, and deal with a tentacled atrocity swaddled in cloth and his rabid mermaids. I needed coffee.

A male bouda sauntered into the kitchen. He wore black leather pants and a leather vest baring a chiseled chest. He wasn't conventionally handsome, the opposite actually: his nose was too long and his face was too narrow, but he had intense blue eyes and black hair combed to shiny perfection, and he used what he had to his best advantage. You knew by some sort of natural female instinct that he would be good in bed, and when he looked at you, you thought about sex.

He glanced at Andrea with an odd longing on his face, switched his attention to me, and offered me his hand. "Sorry about our . . . altercation in the buggy. I was only playing. I'm Raphael."

"The one who likes the hurting." I moved to shake his hand and he reversed it and kissed my fingers instead, singeing me with a look that was pure smolder.

I took my hand back. "That woke me up."

He smiled a picture-perfect smile. "Been a while?"

For some reason, I felt like answering. "Two years. And if you could tone down that smile, I'd appreciate it. Getting weak in the knees."

Raphael took a step back. His face took on the same

concerned look I saw on Doolittle when I assured him I was fine. "Two years? That's entirely too long. If you want, we can take care of that. After two years, it's pure therapy."

"No thank you. Curran already offered to help me with that problem, and since I turned him down, I wouldn't want to cause any friction between you two." The last thing I needed was to set Curran and the hyenas on a collision course.

Raphael backed away with his hands in the air, strategically positioning himself behind Andrea. "No offense."

"None taken."

"Is Curran serious?" Aunt B asked.

She wanted to know if she now had to walk on eggshells around me. For once, I was happy to disappoint. "No, he's just being an asshole. Apparently every time he calls me 'baby,' I look like a red-hot poker is stuck up my butt. Causes him no end of fun." I drank my tea.

Aunt B gave me an odd look. "You know," she said, stirring her tea, "the fastest way to get him off your back is to sleep with him. And tell him you love him. Preferably while in bed."

I smirked and the tea almost came out of my nose. "He'd run like he was on fire."

Raphael rested his hands on Andrea's shoulders. "Still a bit tense?" His fingers began to gently knead her muscles.

"Will you do it?" Aunt B gazed at me over the rim of her cup.

"Not while I'm alive, no. Wait, I take it back. That should be 'hell no.'"

"Has he invited you to dinner, dear? Gifts, flowers, the usual?"

I had to put my cup down, because my hand was shaking too much. When I stopped laughing, I said, "Curran? He isn't exactly Mr. Smooth. He handed me a bowl of soup, that's as far as we got."

"He fed you?" Raphael stopped rubbing Andrea.

"How did this happen?" Aunt B stared at me. "Be very precise, this is important."

"He didn't actually feed me. I was injured and he handed me a bowl of chicken soup. Actually I think he handed me two or three. And he called me an idiot."

"Did you accept?" Aunt B asked.

"Yes. I was starving. Why are the three of you looking at me like that?"

"For crying out loud." Andrea set her cup down, spilling some tea. "The Beast Lord's feeding you soup. Think about that for a second."

Raphael coughed. Aunt B leaned forward. "Was there anybody else in the room?"

"No. He chased everyone out."

Raphael nodded. "At least he hasn't gone public yet."

"He might never," Andrea said. "It would jeopardize her position with the Order."

Aunt B's face was grave. "It doesn't go past this room. You hear me, Raphael? No gossip, no pillow talk, not a word. We don't want any trouble with Curran."

"If you don't explain it all to me, I will strangle somebody." Of course, Raphael might like that . . .

"Food has a special significance," Aunt B said.

I nodded. "Food indicates hierarchy. Nobody eats before the alpha, unless permission is given, and no alpha eats in Curran's presence until Curran takes a bite."

"There is more," Aunt B said. "Animals express love through food. When a cat loves you, he'll leave dead mice on your porch, because you're a lousy hunter and he wants to take care of you. When a shapeshifter boy likes a girl, he'll bring her food and if she likes him back, she might make him lunch. When Curran wants to show interest in a woman, he buys her dinner."

"In public," Raphael added, "the shapeshifter fathers always put the first bite on the plates of their wives and children. It signals that if someone wants to challenge the wife or the child, they would have to challenge the male first."

"If you put all of Curran's girls together, you could have a parade," Aunt B said. "But I've never seen him physically put food into a woman's hands. He's a very private man, so he might have done it in an intimate moment, but I would've found out eventually. Something like that doesn't stay hidden in the Keep. Do you understand now? That's a sign of a very serious interest, dear."

"But I didn't know what it meant!"

Aunt B frowned. "Doesn't matter. You need to be very careful right now. When Curran wants something, he doesn't become distracted. He goes after it and he doesn't stop until he obtains his goal no matter what it takes. That tenacity is what makes him an alpha."

"You're scaring me."

"Scared might be too strong a word, but in your place, I would definitely be concerned."

I wished I were back home, where I could get to my bottle of sangria. This clearly counted as a dire emergency.

As if reading my thoughts, Aunt B rose, took a small bottle from a cabinet, and poured me a shot. I took it, and drained it in one gulp, letting tequila slide down my throat like liquid fire.

"Feel better?"

"It helped." Curran had driven me to drinking. At least I wasn't contemplating suicide.

I SLID THE BEAT-UP VOLUME OF MYTHS AND LEGENDS close and flipped to the index. If I was going to see Bran, it was best to go prepared. I needed a better grasp on this situation. Unfortunately my brain insisted on replaying the memory of Curran offering me soup.

Raphael wrinkled his nose. "Your books smell like chicken."

"They're not mine."

"If you're going to look for Julie, I'll help." Andrea brushed Raphael's hands off her shoulders. "She's my responsibility."

I shook my head. "No, she's mine. There is nothing I can do for her right now. But I can find Morrigan's bowman." I explained the coven and Esmeralda's books, and reeves, and needing Bran's blood, although I didn't go into what it was for. "When the reeves attacked us, the Shepherd mentioned the Great Crow. Let's see . . ."

I ran my finger down the index. No Great Crows. Loads of

Fomorians but no Bolgors or Shepherds. What else? Something had to connect them all. Let's see, what did I have? A Hound of Morrigan, bow, covens, missing cauldron . . .

I found the entry on cauldron: "Cauldron of Plenty, see Dagda." Dagda was Morrigan's main squeeze for a while. "Cauldron of Rebirth, see Branwen." I flipped to the right page. "I will give you a cauldron, with the property that if one of your men is killed today, and be placed in the cauldron, then tomorrow he will be as well as he was at his best, except that he will not regain his speech."

"Any luck?" Raphael asked.

"Not yet."

That was certainly interesting. The reeves were partially undead . . . Maybe they came out of the cauldron of rebirth, somehow. I went back to the index. "Cauldron of Wisdom, see Birth of Taliesin." Anybody with a drop of education on Celtic mythology knew of Taliesin, the great bard of ancient Ireland, the druid who succeeded Merlin. I knew the myth as well as anybody but found the right page anyway just to be thorough. Blah-blah-blah, Goddess Ceridwen, blah-blah . . .

If it was a cobra, it would've struck me.

"What?" Andrea wanted to know.

I turned the page and showed them the illustration. "Birth of Taliesin. The goddess Ceridwen had a son of incredible ugliness. She felt sorry for him and brewed a potion of wisdom in a huge cauldron to make him wise. A servant boy stirred the potion and accidentally tasted it, stealing the gift of wisdom. Ceridwen chased him. He turned into a grain of wheat to hide but Ceridwen turned into a chicken, swallowed him, and gave birth to Taliesin, the greatest poet, bard, and druid of his time."

Andrea frowned. "Yes, I see that the boy was reborn through the cauldron, but so what?"

"The name of the Goddess's ugly son. Morfran: from the Welsh *mawr*, 'big,' and *bran*, 'crow.' The Great Crow."

"This is the guy?" Raphael asked. "The guy in charge of the Fomorians?"

"Looks that way. And more, he is a crow just like Morrigan. Very similar names plus very uneducated witches equals . . ."

"Disaster," Raphael supplied.

The Sisters of the Crow. It was a terrible name for a coven.

Andrea shook her head. "Those idiot Sisters couldn't actually be that ignorant. Fumbling spells—yes, but screwing up enough to accidentally pray to the wrong deity? Morfran and Morrigan aren't even of the same gender."

"Maybe they started out praying to Morrigan, and then fumbled just enough to give Morfran an opening. Maybe Morfran managed to make a deal with Esmeralda. She wanted knowledge and he offered it to her. Taliesin, Morfran's half brother, served as a druid for King Arthur after Merlin. It follows that Morfran was probably also a druid. Who else would've taught Esmeralda druidic rites?"

Andrea leaned forward. "Okay but to what purpose? Why go through all that trouble?"

"I don't know. If you were a god, what would you want?"

I refilled Aunt B's teacup and then my own.

"Life," Raphael said.

"I'm sorry?"

"I would want life. All they do is look down on us from wherever they exist but they never get to take part. Never get to play."

"It doesn't work like that," Andrea said. "Post-Shift theory says a true deity can't manifest in our world."

"You see reports of deities all the time," Raphael said. He was kneading her shoulders again.

She shook her head. "Those aren't actual true deities. They're conjurer's constructs, wicker men for their imagination. Basically magic molded into a certain shape. They have no sense of self."

My brain had difficulty wrapping around the fact that deities actually existed. I knew the theory as well as anybody: magic had the potential to give thought and will substance. Faith was both will and thought, and prayer served as the mechanism to merge them and to catalyze the magic, defining it much like a spoken incantation defined the will of the incantor. Practically, it meant if many people had a specific enough image of their deity and prayed hard to it, the magic might oblige and deliver the deity into existence. The Christian God or the neo-Wiccan "goddess" would probably never gain an actual form, because the beliefs of their faithful were too varied and their power was too nebulous, too encompassing. But something specific like Thor or Pan could theoretically come to life.

I held that "theoretically" like a shield between me and Morrigan and Morfran. Few things are more frightening than the thought of your god coming to life. There is no such thing as privacy between a deity and his worshipper. There are no secrets, no glossed-over failures. Only promises kept and abandoned, sins committed and imagined, and raw emotion. Love, fear, reverence. How many of us are ready to have our lives judged? What would happen if we were found wanting?

Andrea's voice penetrated my thoughts. "First, most people imagine their deity within some magical realm. I mean, what worshipper pictures Zeus strolling down the street with a thunderbolt under his arm? To manifest on Earth would require independent will on the part of the deity. That's a pretty big hurdle right there. Second, deities run on the faith of their congregations like cars run on gasoline. The moment the magic ebbs, the flow of faith cuts off. No juice, no powers. Who knows what would happen to a god? They could hibernate, they could die, they could be jerked out of existence . . ."

In my head Saiman's voice said, *It's magic time. Time of the gods.*

"The magic is simply not that strong and the shifts are too frequent for a deity to appear . . ."

"Unless she does it during a flare," I said.

Andrea opened her mouth and closed it with a click.

"During the flare, when the magic is at its peak for several hours, a deity could manifest and vanish back to its hiding place before the tech hits."

Aunt B set her cup on the table. "If that's so, nothing good will come of it. Gods aren't meant to meddle in our business. Good or bad, we're running things our own way."

I looked at Andrea. "You said something really smart a couple of minutes ago, about the boy being reborn through the cauldron. Manifestation is a rebirth, in a sense. What if the cauldron is Morrigan's way into our world? A cauldron is missing from the Sisters of the Crow's gathering place. I saw the imprints of its legs and it was huge. I don't think even Curran could lift it. Who would bother to take a giant cauldron unless it was really important?"

Andrea sighed. "It makes sense, I suppose."

"One big problem with this theory. I have no clue how the Shepherd and Red's necklace fit into it. Everybody wants the necklace, but nobody will tell me why."

"Where is it now?" Aunt B asked.

"I put it into Curran's hand. He promised to keep it safe." I rose. "I'm going to chat with Morrigan's bowman. Andrea, you wouldn't watch my things for me while I do my hop and dance, would you?"

She got up, moving the chair back with a screech. "You don't even have to ask."

"Why not just ask the bowman?" Raphael said.

I smiled. "Because he's a thief and a liar. The Witch Oracle is neutral and will tell me the truth."

BEHIND THE BOUDA HOUSE LAY A NICE WIDE FIELD. In the middle of the field grew an old oak. Massive, its branches spread so wide they almost touched the ground, it cast a deep shadow in moonlight. Perfect.

"This isn't complicated." I headed to the oak, carrying a big ceramic bowl and a pitcher full of water. "I'm going to do some weird dancing. If all goes well, I should disappear."

"What do you mean, disappear?" Andrea followed me and Raphael followed Andrea.

"Go into the mist. A calling is a very old spell. It's used by witches to find their familiars. Usually it's done in the woods. The witch dances and her magic draws the most compatible animal to her. There are many variations of the spell. Some are tailored to draw a man, although in my experience nothing good ever comes from that one. Some draw the caster to a specific person. It won't work with a normal person, otherwise

I'd be where Julie is right now, but Bran is so saturated with magic, he should be able to pull me to him."

I unzipped my leather vest and put it under the oak. Next I unbuckled Slayer's sheath and handed it to Andrea. Boots and socks followed the leather. Technically the dance worked best when done naked, but I didn't feel like prancing in the nude into Morrigan's Hound's arms. I'm sure he'd be thrilled to see me.

I stood with my toes touching cool slick grass and took a deep breath. I knew how to do a calling. Someone had taught me a very long time ago, so long, I couldn't even remember who or when, and I've seen a couple of them done. I'd just never done one myself.

Andrea sat in the grass. Raphael landed next to her.

I poured water into the bowl, unbuckled my belt, and sprinkled the herbal powders from the compartments into it: lady fern and ash for clairvoyance, and a touch of wormwood to keep interference from curious things to a minimum. A bit of oak, for masculine reference. I had done a shabby job grinding the oak and instead of fine powder a few leaf sections floated on the surface.

I didn't bring my spinner but a few weeks ago I had happened on a very good staff of European ash and promptly defaced it by carving small chunks from the shaft and loading my belt with them. European ash was one of the best woods for a holding enchantment. I dropped one of the ash chips into the water and whispered the incantation.

The makeshift spinner shivered. It trembled like a fishing float when a fish nibbles at the bait, and spun in place, at first slowly, then faster and faster.

"What is it for?"

"It connects the herbs with magic." I pulled my throwing dagger out and gave it to her. "If something goes wrong, drop the dagger into the bowl. Please don't try to dump the bowl or take the spinner out."

"How do I know when something goes wrong?"

"I'll start screaming."

I took off the wrist guard I wore on my left arm. There go

the silver needles. The other throwing knife, the three shark teeth, the r-kit . . .

"How much hardware do you carry?" Raphael raised his eyebrows.

I shrugged. "That's about all of it."

I stepped into the oak's shadow. I was stripped down to my T-shirt and pants, no belt, no sword, no knife. Except for the blood collecting kit and the knitted square of hair and nettle, I carried nothing. I imagined a wide circle in the oak's shadow and dropped the knitting in the middle.

I returned to the imaginary circle boundary and began to dance.

Step by step I made my way around the circle, bending my body, following the dance. Midway through the second circle, a tight line of magic snapped from the small knitted square and clutched at me. It flowed through my head into my feet, splitting into smaller currents where my skin touched the ground, as if I had become a tree. It led and pulled me.

Vaguely I saw the boudas gather from the shadows, drawn to me like moths to a flame. They watched me with glowing red eyes, swaying gently with the silent music of my dance. And then I heard it, a simple distant melody. It grew with every second, heart wrenching, sad but wild, pure but imperfect. It caught me and wormed its way into my chest, filling my heart with what my Russian father called *toska*, a longing so intense and painful, it made me physically ill. It weakened my knees; it sapped my will until only melancholy remained; it made me miss something, what, I wasn't sure, but I knew I missed it keenly and couldn't take another breath without it.

I danced and danced and danced. The charmed boudas dissolved. Mist swirled around me. A dark dog trotted past me through the gloom. Slowly the fog thinned. Through the whiteness I saw a gentle yellow glow beckoning me.

My feet found wet grass and rocks. I heard the quiet splashing and the popping of wood burning in the fire. Sharp salty smoke tugged at me.

A few more steps and I stepped onto the shore of a lake. It lay glossy, black, and placid in the moonlight, like the surface of a coin dipped in tar. A small fire burned in a stone fire pit near the water. Above the fire on a spit was a carcass of some small animal, a rabbit maybe.

I turned. Behind me the forest lay, dark and jagged. The mist crawled away to the trees, as if sucked into the woods.

The attack came so suddenly, I reacted on instinct. Bran lunged at me from the right, and I stepped aside, redirecting his momentum and tripping him without thinking. I had practiced this maneuver so many times, I didn't realize I had done it until I saw him fly past me and land with a splash into the lake.

He whirled in the water and grinned at me. Damn, he was a handsome bastard. I realized he was half-naked. Blue swirls of tattoos painted his chest. When God made that chest, he did it to tempt women.

"No sword this time."

I shrugged. "Yes, but you can't disappear."

"Don't need to." He sprung from the lake, black hair dripping, and ran at me again.

I dodged his hands, kicked him in the knee, and danced away. He launched a quick kick that whistled a hair from my cheek. I swept around him and rammed my elbow into his side.

He hooked me with a quick punch. I took it on the shoulder—it hurt—and swiped his legs out from under him. He jumped to his feet and hopped away. He frolicked like a hyper puppy. Run up, play bite, let himself be swatted down.

"That's no way to treat a lover."

"I didn't come here to sleep with you."

"Then why go through all the trouble?"

"I need some of your blood to save a girl."

He flexed his right arm. Veins bulged. "Some of this blood?"

"Yes."

He winked at me. "I'm sure we can deal."

"No deals. The blood must be a gift or it won't work."

"Keep me warm tonight and maybe I'll be feeling generous in the morning."

I shook my head. "No deals."

He looked to the sky. "You really aren't going to lie with me?"

"No."

He thought about it.

"Considering raping me? Are you that desperate?"

He jerked his head, throwing his hair out of his eyes. "I've never forced a woman. I don't have to. They flock to me."

Oi. "So nice to know you're a gentleman."

"Why would I give you my blood? What's in it for me?"

"Nothing. Except maybe knowing you've done a good deed. You told me you were a hero. Do something heroic."

He walked to the fire and sat. "You're thinking Christian hero, dove. And I'm not a Christian."

A cold breeze wrinkled the lake. I hugged myself. I wanted to ask him about Julie and about other things, but information from him couldn't be trusted. Get the blood, get out. "Just out of curiosity, what is it about me that makes you think I'm dovelike?"

"I bet you coo in bed." His black eyes shone, reflecting the flames of the fire. "Come sit next to me."

"No funny business?"

"I make no promises."

What choice did I have? I came and sat next to him, basking in the warmth of the fire.

He lay back, his head resting on his arm bent at the elbow. He was muscled like a martial artist or a soldier accustomed to running: lean and hard. And he smelled . . . he smelled like a man, the way young fit men sometimes smell of sweat and locker room and sun.

Somewhere far an owl hooted and her cry lingered over the pitch-black water. "What is this place?"

"Morrigan's refuge. It's her home."

"She's here?"

He nodded. "Just not watching at the moment. She sleeps."

"Does Morrigan ever come down to Earth?"

"Why won't you sleep with me? Afraid of your Rambo boyfriend?"

"Rambo is a character in a story. Not real. You didn't answer my question."

He put his arm around me. "Kiss me and I promise I'll talk."

I took his arm off of me. "I don't think so. That would be a slippery slope."

His hand stroked my arm. "Ahhh, so you want me?"

"Maybe a little bit."

He smiled.

"I'm still not sleeping with you."

"Why not?"

I thought of Saiman dancing in the snow. "I have a friend who can change his shape. Imagine any body and he can transform into it. He's invited me into his bed."

He frowned. "Can he do a girl?"

"Yes."

"I might like to watch that."

Men were still men, even if they lived in the mist.

Bran sat up, pulled the carcass off the fire, and stuck the spit into the ground. A knife flashed and he offered me a half-charred leg. "Here. Might as well feed you since you're telling me a story. Don't want to be inhospitable."

"Thanks." I pulled a shred of meat off the legs and chewed. Sweet aftertaste. Rabbit.

"So what is it with you? Saving yourself for marriage?"

I guffawed. "Too late for that."

"Why won't you play nice with your friend then? Seems to me, the man's working pretty hard. How long has he been after you?"

"About a year. He just keeps switching bodies like they were outfits, but no matter what body he wears, I know it's him."

"Don't like him that much, yeh?"

I shrugged. "He doesn't do anything for me. There were times when he came at me with something that might have been fun, if it weren't him. But in the end, I always remember that he isn't interested in me. If I was thrilled, he wouldn't be happy with me; if I was on the verge of suicide, he wouldn't care. I might as well sleep with a blow-up doll. He's only interested because I said no the first time."

"That's why all men are interested."

"True, but with him it ends with my body. Normal men eventually look for companionship."

He shook his head. "No. Women look for that. Men look for bedsport."

I smiled. "If it were so, why did you invite me to sit by you?"

"I figure I'll change your mind."

"You won't."

"So you say."

"When was the last time you had a dinner like this with another person?"

He shrugged. "I don't remember."

"So you just eat by yourself? All alone?"

"What's it to you?" His voice cut with a hostile edge.

"Nothing, just curious."

He poked at the coals with a long stick.

I finished my meat and lay on my back, stretching my feet to the fire. It'd been a long day. I lost Julie and I still had no clue where her mom had gone. At least Andrea didn't die.

I became aware of Bran watching me. Our stares connected and he went down for a kiss, but I put my hand onto his lips. "I don't want to headbutt you a third time. Trust me, if I change my mind, you'll be the first to know."

He sat up, picked up a twig and snapped small pieces off of it, throwing them into the fire one by one. "I don't understand you. I used to be good at this. Good at women. Now . . . You have a forward manner about you."

I frowned. "I don't think I'm that forward."

"You are. Most women are now. Used to be that if a woman sat next to you like this and you fed her, it was understood she would lie on her back for you. Otherwise, why bother? Women now, they are brazen. Forward. They will sit there and they wear tight clothes, but they won't sleep with you. They want to talk. What is there to talk about?"

I sat up and hugged my knees. "Bran, I don't do anything for you, do I? Kind of like my friend doesn't do anything for me."

He stared. "Why would you think that?"

"A feeling I get. Like you're trying to get into my pants because I'm a woman and you don't know what else to do with me. You don't think I'm all that."

He sighed and looked at me. Really looked at me. "No," he said. "I don't. Don't get me wrong, you've got a nice body and all. I wouldn't turn you down if you wanted to spread your legs, but yeah I've bedded better."

I nodded. "I thought so."

"What gave me away?"

"The kiss."

He reared back. "I kiss like a madman!"

"It was a kiss of a frustrated man with injured pride. There was no fire in it." I handed him another twig. "Just talk to me. Pretend I'm a traveler who stopped by your fire. I bet you don't get many visitors. You stay in the mist all the time?"

"I come out to play during the flares." He encompassed the lake and forest with a wide wave of his hand. "I fish, I hunt. Never run out of game. It's the good life."

"So you don't get to enter the real world unless the flare is up?"

"Yeah."

"But the flare only comes every seven years or so. In between years, you're here, by yourself, with no company?"

He whistled. A shaggy shape trotted from the dark and flopped at his feet. A huge, black dog. "Got Conri here."

The dog raised his paws into the air, turning to get his belly scratched. Bran obliged. "If I get bored, I sleep. For years sometimes, until she wakes me up."

I offered my bone to the dog. He took it out of my hands very gently and settled to gnaw it at my feet. I thought I was alone. At least I could go out and talk to other people. "You must've been here awhile, but you speak with no accent."

"The Gift of Gab. One of three gifts she gave me. Gift of Gab: I speak any language I wish. Gift of Health: my wounds are healed fast. And Gift of Aim: I hit what I see. The fourth gift is my own. I was born with it."

"What is it?"

"Admit it was the best kiss you've ever had and I'll tell you."

"Sorry, I can think of a couple better." Or at least one . . .

"Then why do I waste time with you?"

I shook my head. He wasn't a real person. Just a shadow of one with no memories, no ties, nothing but a sex drive, good aim, and wild eyes.

"Where are you from?"

He shrugged. "Don't remember."

"Okay, when are you from? How long have you been here?"

"I don't remember."

I grappled for something, some sort of marker that any person would know. "What's your mother's name?"

"I don't remember."

I looked at the stars. This mission was doomed to failure from the start. Who was I kidding?

"Blathin," he said. "Her name was Blathin."

He grabbed my hand and pulled me to my feet. "Come! I'm going to show you something."

We ran along the edge of the lake into the trees. Ahead a wooden cabin rose, nestled among the greenery, connected to the lake by a long dock. Bran dragged me inside.

A fire burned in the fireplace. To the right a simple bed stood against the wall, to the left a row of chests sat. Carvings decorated the walls: a tree, runes, and warriors. Many, many fighters twisted by the battle spasm and carved with exquisite detail. Under them on the table lay a scroll, depicting a man with a long staff wearing a monk's cassock. He sat on a rock. Beside him mermaids played in sea waves. The Shepherd . . .

Bran grabbed my hand, pulled me to a chest, and swung the heavy lid open. A white cloth covered the contents. He jerked it aside. Human heads filled the chest.

"Oh God."

He scooped a mummified head from the chest by a scalp lock and thrust it at me. "All of them are mine."

This was officially the weirdest version of "come down to my place and I'll show you some etchings" I've ever been hit with.

He threw open another chest. I saw a World War I Kaiser helm next to a black motorcycle helmet splashed with painted flames. How old was he, exactly?

The third chest: blades. Turkish yataghan, a katana, a marine officer's saber with Semper Fi engraved in Old English . . .

"That's nothing!" He tossed the head into the chest, snatched my hand, and pulled me to the back door. It flew open from his kick and he drew me onto the porch.

Behind the house rose a spire of skulls. Taller than me, bleached white by the elements, it bristled with spears thrust through the bone. "See!" He waved his arms, triumphant. "There is more to me. Nobody has that many! My father would shit himself if he saw this!"

No kidding.

"I'm a great warrior. A hero. Each one of those was a fight I won." His face shone with pride. "You're a warrior. You understand, yes?"

So many lives . . . The pile of skulls towered above me. "How old are you?" I whispered.

He leaped over the rail, took a skull from the pile, and put it in front of me. "My first."

The skull wore a Roman helmet.

I sat down. It was too much to take.

He came to sit next to me. We looked at the skulls. Bran hung his head.

I touched his forearm. "What is it?"

"Nobody will ever know. Nobody but you has seen this. Nobody will ever know what I've accomplished. When I finally die, the only one who'll remember me and all this will be Morrigan."

"She's not the sentimental sort?" I guessed.

He shook his head. "It was a fool's bargain we made. I saved her bird, and she told me to choose my reward."

"What did you ask for?"

"Some would've asked for long life, strong sons. I asked to be a hero. To always have plenty to drink, plenty to fight, plenty of women."

The skulls glared at us with empty sockets in eerie silence.

"If you asked for strong sons, she would've arranged for them to eventually kill you," I said. "You can't win."

"Small solace."

"Yeah.

I touched the Roman helmet. The metal felt ice-cold under my fingers. "The magic wasn't in the world when they were around."

"It was dying," he said. "There was just a trickle left. I slept through its death. When I awoke and fell through the mist, the world was on fire."

The first flare . . . So many people had died during that week.

"The little girl, Mouse, you called her . . . I'm trying to protect her and to find her mother. The witches said they would help me but their Oracle needs your blood to heal one of them. It would be a very good thing for her to survive. She means much to many people."

He took the skull away from me and brought it to his face, eyes to eye sockets, teeth to teeth. "What do I care?"

"The Witch Oracle lives through the ages, its members reborn, again and again. If you were to give them your blood, the covens would cherish your memory. Always. You would endure. You would be a hero and you would be known."

He turned to me, his eyes bottomless.

"It would cost you nothing. It would mean everything."

CHAPTER 22

THE MIST VANISHED AND BRAN AND I POPPED out onto the stone floor of the Oracle's dome. Teleportation was overrated. Sure it got you where you needed to go fast, but hanging weightless in the mist gave me a nasty case of vertigo. On top of that, I had to cling tenaciously to Bran to be teleported, and he had trouble keeping his hands to himself.

Torches and feylanterns lit the dome. I hadn't expected anyone to be here but despite the late hour, the three witches of the Oracle waited on the platform, alert and awake. They didn't even blink, when we materialized in the middle of the floor. Apparently, we were expected.

To the left of the Oracle stood four other witches, two about my age and two older. Some of them wore the distinct blue tattoos that matched the swirls on Bran's chest. Witches from Morrigan's covens?

Bran bent over and sneezed. "I hate this fucking turtle." He raised his head and grinned at the group on the side. "Ladies."

The two younger witches went from bewildered to flirtatious in the blink of an eye.

I walked up to the platform and handed the still warm tube to the mother-witch. She took it. "He gives the blood in good faith," I said. "He doesn't expect anything. But I hope the memory of his gift will endure."

The Oracle rose. As one, the three witches bowed.

"See?" Bran jerked his thumb at the three women. "That's how a woman should treat a man. Next time you see me, I want you to do just like them."

"Hell will freeze over first," I told him.

The witches sank to their seats.

"We had a bargain," I said.

The crone glared at me. "A bargain with the likes of you means nothing."

"This might be a hunch, but I think you don't like me," I told her.

Her fingers curled into claws on the armrests of her chair.

"Maria," the youngest Oracle whispered. "Violence isn't necessary. The Oracle never goes back on its word."

"Could've fooled me."

She pointed to the four witches on the side. "They speak for the senior covens of Morrigan. They are here as witnesses. Tell us what you want to know and I will open your eyes."

"Here is what I suspect: Esmeralda wanted power and formed her coven, but she lacked education and training. The coven probably began by worshipping Morrigan, but whether by accident or on purpose, Esmeralda permitted Morfran to insert himself into their rites and take over."

The seven witches focused on me. The atmosphere in the dome grew tense. I plowed on.

"I suspect that Morrigan has the ability to manifest during the flare, when the magic is at its deepest. She does it by using a magic cauldron. Morfran wanted life just as much and either taught Esmeralda how to duplicate the cauldron or had her steal the cauldron that had been in the possession of legitimate Morrigan covens."

Either I had hit the nail on the head or the four representatives of Morrigan got a simultaneous case of serious constipation, because their faces turned red and strained.

"I think that Morfran is in cahoots with the Fomorians, but I don't know why. I need to know what happened after the rite was performed, what happened to Julie's mother, and what's the significance of the necklace the little shaman boy named Red carried."

"Where is the necklace?" Bran suddenly came to life.

"I'm not telling you."

He spread his arms. "Why not? I'm the good guy here!"

"I don't know that. It's a trust issue. Until somebody explains this mess to me, nobody gets the necklace."

"I'll explain." The middle witch of the Oracle leaned back. Above her, the mural shifted. The black lines crawled. The outlines of Hekate grew faint while the cauldron before her solidified.

"Two generations ago at the start of the Shift, Morrigan entrusted her covens with a magic cauldron."

"They did a bang-up job taking care of it," Bran said.

The mother-witch pinned him down with her stare. "Hush."

"We didn't know," one of Morrigan's witches said. "And she hasn't spoken to us since the last flare."

The middle witch silenced her with a wave of her hand. "Now then, the cauldron is her way into our world. Its magic only manifests during a flare. Morfran wanted the cauldron so that he too could experience life. He made a deal with Morrigan's enemies, the Fomorians, the sea-demons. In exchange for their help, he would release them, through the cauldron, from the Otherworld. They're not gods. They need little magic to exist here. They will become his first worshippers in this world."

"But I killed at least ten of them. How many came through?"

"You don't kill them," Bran said. "They don't stay dead unless I leave one of my shafts in them. As long as the cauldron feeds on the magic of the flare, they continue to return to life. The closer they are to the cauldron, the harder it is to disable them."

Great. Fantastic. "Couldn't you have told me this sooner?"

"It's a trust issue," he told me, mimicking my voice. I felt like smacking him.

"Okay, but how did the Fomorians get the cauldron in the first place?"

The witch sighed, folding her hands on her lap. "Through the ages Morrigan's Hounds have protected the cauldron, and only they have power over it."

On the walls the hounds raised their muzzles in a silent howl. Men, just like Bran, stolen from humanity through a fool's bargain.

"The covens of Morrigan thought the cauldron was secure, because nobody but a hound could move it from their gathering place. But they didn't know that years ago one of Morrigan's Hounds strayed."

On the left a drawing of the hound stretched and became a man.

"He left Morrigan for a woman and the terms of his bargain forced her to let him and his progeny live."

Things snapped together in my head. "Red. That little bastard is a descendant of the hound who got away."

The witch nodded.

"That means he can carry the cauldron. He stole the cauldron?"

The four witches of Morrigan looked like they wanted to be anywhere but here.

"I saw the imprints of the cauldron's legs. It's huge. Red's arms are this big around." I touched my index finger to my thumb. "How in the world did he carry it? And how could you not notice the giant cauldron being dragged away?"

"We were so used to it sitting there, it took a little while to realize it was gone," one of the witches said.

"You can shrink it," Bran said. "Small enough to fit in your pocket."

"Or slide onto a necklace. Oh crap. Wait, you said the cauldron is keeping the Fomorians alive, so they have the cauldron. What's on the necklace then?"

Bran shrugged his shoulders. "The lid. The boy stole the cauldron for the witch, but I crashed the party just as they finished the rite and the first Fomorian crawled out. While I was busy being the hero, he took off with the lid."

"What does the lid do?"

"It controls the cauldron."

I fought an urge to grab him and shake him until the whole story fell out. "How?"

"You put the lid on one way and it's the cauldron of plenty. You put the lid on the other way and it's a gateway to the world of the dead. Right after the first batch of Fomorians came through I closed the cauldron, turning it into the cauldron of plenty. It still keeps them alive, but unless they can get ahold of the lid, they can't open the gateway again to let Morfran out."

"What happens if Morfran gets to appear instead of Morrigan?"

He grimaced. "It's a simple bargain, woman. He gets life and the cauldron. They get life and freedom. If he appears, he will release the horde of sea-demons into your city. They want revenge on Man. Use your head to imagine what will happen next."

I looked to the Oracle. "Is he telling the truth?"

The youngest Oracle nodded. "He is."

"One last thing. Why did you keep stealing the maps?"

He sighed. "The cauldron must sit on the crossing of three roads. It won't shrink for the Fomorians, so they had to physically drag it somewhere. There are only so many places where three roads cross. The cauldron of plenty doesn't shine with magic the way the cauldron of rebirth does. Hard to sense where it is. I was misting to each crossing of the roads near the pit, trying to find the cauldron."

That made sense. "Okay. The Pack has the lid," I told him.

He grinned. "This shouldn't be too hard."

Thin tongues of mist swirled around his feet and dissipated into the air. Leaving him standing in the same spot.

"You're still here."

"I know that!" He rocked forward. Mist puffed and vanished. Again. Again. "Something is wrong. You!" Bran pointed at the youngest Oracle. "Find the Shepherd!"

A hint of a smile brightened the youngest Oracle's face, highlighting her fragility. At first I thought she was laughing at the absurdity of Bran's order, but her eyes glazed over, gazing somewhere far, past us, into the horizon only she could see, and I realized that using her gift filled her with joy. She leaned forward, focused, smiling wider and wider, until she laughed. The music of her voice filled the dome, exuberant and sweet. "Found him."

The dome quaked. Steam rose and the far wall faded into early dawn. Under the gray sky, mist drifted, caught on familiar steel spikes that thrust from the ground littered with metal refuse. A Stymphalean bird perched on a twisted spire of railroad rails, crushed and knotted together, as if some giant had tried to tie them in an angler's knot. The Honeycomb Gap.

The mist parted and I saw Bolgor the Shepherd perched on a mound of rusty barrels. A faint breeze stirred the cloth of his monk's habit. A huge hulking silhouette towered behind him, still shrouded in mist, holding a cross. Ugad, fully regenerated. How nice, I could kill him again.

A tall form strode through the mist. The metal refuse crunched and groaned, protesting the weight, and a monster stepped into the clearing. Tall, broad shouldered, wrapped in steel-hard muscle and clothed in gray fur, striped with slashes of darker gray.

Curran.

What the hell was he doing?

"You first," he said. His jaws were big enough to enclose my skull, his fangs were longer than my fingers, but his diction was perfect.

Behind the Shepherd, Ugad shifted the cross forward, setting it down with a heavy thud. I saw a small, thin body stretched on the pole, legs tied, arms spread wide on a crosspiece. Julie. Oh God.

I grabbed Bran by his shirt and dragged him to me. "Take me there now!"

"I can't!" he snapped.

My heart tried to break through my chest. Slayer smoked. Julie's eyes were closed, her color so pale she might have been dead already.

I would have given my right arm to be there now.

Curran raised his hand, displaying charms and coins dangling from his claws.

Bran howled. "What's he doing? Stop, you whoreson! No!"

"The child for the necklace. As agreed," Curran said.

The Shepherd's whisper raised the tiny hairs on the back of my neck. "You shouldn't have come alone, beast."

Reeves burst out from under the metal scrap. They swarmed

Curran, falling onto each other. In a blink he was covered with a mound of squirming bodies.

I clenched my fists, expecting him to break out. Fight, Curran. Fight back. Any moment the bodies would come flying and he'd burst free from the pile of flesh. Any moment . . . My neck constricted as if caught by a garrote. The reeves screeched.

"No, no, no! Damn you, sonovabitch, do something!" Bran hurled his crossbow into the vision. It pierced the image and shattered against the wall.

A jaguar crashed into the Shepherd. He gave no warning, no snarl, no sound at all. Huge fangs flashed and the Shepherd's head drooped to his chest from the broken neck. Jim paused for the briefest of moments, reveling in the kill, and chased after Ugad.

Four beasts darted from the mist, snapping and biting at Ugad's legs. A wolf let out a short snarl.

Huge hands thrust through the reeves and tore them aside. Curran emerged. Red gashes marked his fur. Now I understood the plan: he had expected a double cross and chose to bear the bulk of the assault, buying time for the shapeshifters to retrieve Julie.

The reeves scrambled back to him. He grasped one, tore it in two, and hurled the twitching remnants to the ground. The reeve went liquid. The puddle of its slime twisted upward in a corkscrew and solidified into the reeve. She was once again whole.

"Why isn't she dying?"

"The cauldron's too close," Bran said through clenched teeth.

They couldn't win. The best they could do was to break away.

Curran swiped at another reeve, crushing her head like an eggshell. She went liquid too and re-formed within seconds.

"Stop killing, dimwit! Maim! Maim them, you son of a whore!" Bran yelled.

Two dozen yards away Ugad stomped and spun about, raking at the shapeshifters with his enormous fists. They lunged at his feet, driving him forward, into the metal spikes. Ugad spun. The huge barbed tail swung like a club and smashed a shaggy body. The shapeshifter flew through the air and bounced off the metal shell of a ruined car. The beast crashed to the ground, stunned.

Ugad jumped. As if in a nightmare, I saw his huge foot stomp onto the prone beast and heard the crunch of broken bones. Blood sprayed. The monster turned, leaving a nude human body broken on the ground. I saw the shock of electric-blue hair stained with bright red spray. I clenched my fists. I could do nothing. I couldn't make it stop. I just watched, helpless.

The jaguar leaped onto Ugad's head. The giant hurled the cross aside to pummel at the new threat. The cross spun on its base, teetered, plunged, Julie hanging limp like a ragdoll, about to be crushed. A slight, sand-colored shape leaped forward and caught the cross inches from jagged iron. Andrea ripped Julie off the cross.

A whip of green tentacles struck her, ripping fur and skin from her thigh. Raw muscle, red and wet, glared through the wound. The Shepherd hissed. He was once again whole, his rags flaring about his thin body. Andrea ran. Tentacles slapped her. She cried out. I winced. Andrea kept going.

One step.

Two.

She fell.

Her hand clawed the ground, as she clutched Julie to her, crawling away.

The tentacles scoured her again and again. Andrea curled into a ball, trying to shield Julie with her body.

The wolves broke from Ugad and rushed the Shepherd. Tentacles flailed like green ribbons echoed by startled yelps of pain.

Ugad pummeled at his head, trying to knock the jaguar off, but hit his own horns. The huge cat hung on, his claws wedged. Watery blood drenched Ugad's massive forehead. Jim dug deeper, clawing at the eyes. Ugad charged in a mad rush, crushing the iron under his feet, straight into the forest of metal spikes.

Jim leaped straight up.

The monster's huge body hit a spike.

Jim landed awkwardly, slipped, and slid, rolling down the sheet of corrugated metal. His fur left a long red smear. He tried to rise, but his feet slipped out from under him.

Metal emerged from Ugad's back, awash with crimson. He strained and pushed himself off the spike. Ugad turned, oblivious to the hole in his torso, stomped over to Andrea's prone form, and kicked her. She flew from the impact and crashed into the refuse. Ugad scooped Julie off the ground, an odd, imbecilic expression of satisfaction on his ugly face . . . and found himself looking at Curran.

Little by little, fighting for every inch, bleeding from wounds, the Beast Lord had gained ground. Curran thrust his clawed hand into the hole in Ugad's torso and ripped a red clump out.

To the right, the Shepherd stretched his arms. His robes tore, revealing his thin, awkward body. Tentacles swirled around his shoulders and snapped forward to catch metal spikes. The tentacles contracted and the Shepherd flew past the wolves and clutched at Curran's back. As one, the reeves clumped onto Curran's limbs, exposing the necklace wrapped around his forearm. The Shepherd's icy eyes flared with hungry fire. His mouth unhinged and serrated teeth bit into Curran's arm and the monisto wrapped around Curran's wrist. Coins went flying as the cord snapped under the Shepherd's teeth.

Curran screamed and I screamed with him.

"Idiot!" Bran hit his head with the heel of his hand.

Tentacles whipped. A bloody hole gaped in Curran's arm. The Shepherd withdrew, back toward the hangar. Three of the reeves followed in a gaggle, swiping Julie out of Ugad's arms, while the rest of the reeves clamped onto Curran's feet. The giant stared at Curran stupidly, turned and ran to the hangar, blood spraying from his body.

The wolves fell upon the reeves. Curran shook like a dog flinging water from his fur.

Ugad's body punched through the thin metal wall and

through the gaping hole I caught a glimpse of the pile of crates.

"No!" Bran's mouth gaped open.

Ugad hit the crates head-on. Shards flew, revealing a metal cauldron as tall as me. Bran swore, biting off words like a pissed off dog.

Magic hit in a huge choking tide. The witches went down to their knees. The vision wavered and the dome quaked.

"The flare . . ." the youngest Oracle whispered. "It's here . . ."

The magic crashed into me, and my body drank it in, more and more and more. No head rush this time. No pause. Just power, pure power streaming through me.

The Shepherd hovered over the cauldron. His body doubled over and a gush of liquid spilled from his mouth, carrying a glittering spark with it. The spark hit the cauldron and expanded into an enormous lid. He must have bit it off the monisto and swallowed it.

Curran was almost to them, a trail of broken reeve bodies in his wake.

Ugad gripped the lid and leaned back. His thick arms bulged. With a guttural snarl, he tore the lid free of the cauldron, opening the gate to the Otherworld.

Like a storm cloud with a mind of its own, a blotch of darkness mushroomed above the cauldron. Within that shadow, a deeper darkness appeared, hinting at a humanoid form, huge and misshapen. Two hands thrust from the gloom as if welcoming an ovation. Feet in black boots solidified on the cauldron's rim. Thick forearms emerged into the light, their bulging muscle crisscrossed by shiny strips of scar tissue and dotted with warts. The darkness slunk back, an eager-to-please pet, revealing first a chest in a scalemail enameled black, and then a pale face.

His nose protruded forward, too long, too flat, like the carapace of a horse skull, like an enormous beak, sheathed in a meager layer of flesh and tapering to a sharp, horn-tipped point. Below the nose a massive jaw supported two rows of oversized teeth. One of the incisors jutted like a boar tusk falling just short of touching the left cheek. His eyes, small and white, sat deep under Neanderthal eyebrows. Between the eyes cartilage broke through the skin to form a thin, sharp ridge that vanished into his fleshy forehead.

It was as if the skulls of a horse and a human had somehow been blended into a horrid whole. A human face stretched over the meld, with barely enough meat and skin to cover the bone. This thing could not be man.

Behind him the darkness slithered and gained shape, solidifying into long black hair and a thousand crow feathers, streaming like a mantle behind him.

Morfran.

He raised his hand and spoke a word.

A gray bubble popped into existence by his fingers and began to expand. It swallowed his hand, then his head, then his feet. Instinctively I knew I didn't want the bubble touching Curran.

The Beast Lord hesitated.

"Run, Curran!" The words left me even though I knew he couldn't hear.

The bubble gulped the cauldron.

My heart clenched. "Run!"

Curran turned on his heel and ran, swiping Jim's body off the ground.

"Andrea!" I screamed, but he couldn't hear me.

The bubble hid the Shepherd and the vision faded.

CHAPTER 23

THREE HOURS LATER BRAN AND I RODE UP TO THE pack keep. The witches had lent us the horses and we had ridden them until they were soaked in sweat. Bran seethed. He cursed me for not giving him the lid in time. He cursed Curran for losing the lid. He cursed Morrigan for denying him the mist as a punishment for his failure. He cursed the Fomorians by name, reaching for stronger and stronger words until his curses no longer made sense. I said nothing.

After a half hour of cursing, Bran wore out his voice and lapsed into silence. "The gray bubble we saw is a ward," he said finally. "The Fomorians can only crawl out of the cauldron one at a time. Morfran is buying time to build his army."

"Can we break the ward?" I asked.

He shook his head. "Cú Chulainn himself couldn't break through it. In fifteen hours it will fall and your city will drown in blood. We are riding through the Otherworld because all of them"—he swept his hand past the houses crowding the street—"all of them are dead. We travel through the city of the dead men. All because that son of a whore was trying to save a beggar child."

She was my beggar child. I would've risked a horde of demons to save her, too.

The gates of the Pack Keep opened at our approach. A clump of shapeshifters waited for us in the inner yard. I searched for the familiar figure.

Please. Please make it.

And then I saw him. His hair fell on his back in a mane. I

had missed it, because it was no longer blond, but gray, the gray of his fur in beast-form.

Bran jumped off his horse and strode into the yard, his face twisted. "You! You fucking whoreson!"

Oh shit. "Curran, don't kill him! He's Morrigan's Hound. We need him to work the cauldron!"

I jumped off the horse and chased Bran.

The shapeshifters parted, giving Curran room. A white bandage covered his arm. That was a first.

Bran shoved Curran, but the Beast Lord didn't move.

"You gave it to them! For what? A scrawny street kid! No-body cares if she lives or dies! You've killed hundreds for her. Why?"

Curran's eyes had gone gold. "I don't have to explain my-self to you." He raised his hand and shoved Bran back. Bran stumbled a couple of steps.

I caught him. "Don't do this. You'll get hurt."

Bran pushed free of me and lunged at Curran. Curran snarled, grabbed Bran by his arm, and threw him across the yard.

Morrigan's Hound leaped upright. An inhuman, terrifying bellow erupted from his throat and slammed my ears with an air fist.

Bran's flesh boiled. Muscles swelled to obscene propor-tions, veins bulged like ropes, tendons knotted in apple-sized clumps. He grew, stretching upward, his elbows and knees sinking into engorged muscle. With boneless flexibility, his body twisted back, distended, flowed, melted, and finally snapped into an asymmetric aberration. Bumps slid across his torso like small cars colliding under his skin. His left eye bulged; his right sank; his face stretched back, baring his teeth and a huge, cavernous mouth. Drool sagged from his uneven lips. The one visible eye swiveled in its socket.

Warp spasm. Of course. The fourth gift he was born with. He was a warp-warrior, just like Cú Chulainn. I should've seen it.

"Let's play, little man!" Bran charged Curran.

The Beast Lord twisted out of the way and hammered a

punch into Bran's misshapen gut. Bran grabbed his wrist and tossed him at the wall like a kitten.

Curran flipped in midair and bounced off the wall. A man had started the leap, but what hit Bran was a hashish-induced nightmare of lion and human.

The beast smashed Bran off his feet. Curran snarled, his gold eyes luminescent with rage. His huge, prehistoric maw gaped open and three-inch fangs nearly sheared Bran's nose from his face. The Beast Lord was pissed.

Bran kicked Curran off with two enormous legs, and leaped upright. "Come on, princess! Show me what you've got."

Curran lunged. Bran swung a meaty hand, missed, and took razored claws to his ribs, slicing him like a pear. The wounds bled and closed.

People scattered. Bran swiped the loup cage that once held the reeve and smashed at Curran with it. The Pack King caught the cage. The wound on his arm bled, the bandage long gone. Mammoth muscles bulged across Curran's back and he ripped the cage from Bran's hands and tossed it aside. "Still second best," he growled, his eyes drowning in gold.

They hammered each other, swiping, kicking, caught in a savage contest. Bran managed to land a kick, batting Curran across the yard. The Beast Lord's rebound took Bran off his feet and slammed him into a wooden shed sitting against the wall. The wall gave, and Bran fell through in an explosion of splinters. Curran dived after him. A moment later another section of the wall exploded, pelting the ground with fragments and Bran's warped body stumbled back into the open. He bled from a half dozen places but didn't seem to notice.

"Is that all you got?" When no answer came, he stuck his head into the hole. "Where are you . . ."

The blow sent him hurtling across the yard. As he slid past, I had to jump aside to keep from being crushed. He hit the loup cage with his head and bounced off.

Curran appeared in the gap. Half-lion, half-man, gray mane flaring around his head, his eyes on fire, huge teeth dripping spit, he looked demonic. His roar shook the air.

Bran surged to his feet and charged. Curran caught his lunge, slid back, and ground to a halt. They strained, clenching each other's arms, muscles bulging, teeth bared.

I turned away. I could kill one of them with relative ease, given that they were otherwise occupied, but there wasn't a force on this Earth that would make them stop. I could scream myself hoarse, but until they tired enough to see reason, neither of them would notice my existence. They'd beat on each other until they got tired. They both seemed to be dealing with damage just fine.

If Jim and Andrea were alive, they would be in a medward.

WHEN NOT SURE WHERE TO GO, BARREL FORWARD on pure determination. It was a good motto and it led me to the door of the medward after ten minutes of squeezing my memory dry and wandering through the Keep's maze of hallways and stairs. It took me only a minute to find the right room.

The room lay steeped in gloom, all lamps out except for a small feylantern glowing blue, more of a night-light than anything else. Its soft glow traced the contours of a familiar odd body, stuck on the crossroads between human and hyena.

I stood in the doorway, unable to enter.

"I can smell you, you know," Andrea said. "I have your sword."

Andrea raised Slayer, hilt first, still in its sheath. I came to sit next to her on the edge of the bed and took the sword.

"Not even a thank-you?"

"Thank you," I said. "How are you?"

"I lost Julie. I had her in my hands and lost her."

"I saw. You did all you could."

"You saw? How?"

"The witches showed me and Bran a vision of the fight."

Andrea sighed. "If I had my guns . . . they wouldn't have worked. Jesus, what a clusterfuck we made of it."

"Are you going to make it?"

She sighed. "You're worried about me. Why? I'm beastkin.

I heal fast. The flare is going full force, and the doctor has worked his magic. I'll be up by tomorrow."

"And Jim?"

"Which one is Jim?"

"The jaguar."

"Heavy muscle damage," Andrea said. "Ligaments all torn to shreds. He's in the next room."

I felt like scum. If I stayed any longer, I would scream.

Andrea looked at me from the sheets. "It was a good plan. Curran creates a distraction, occupies them while they key on him, and we grab the girl. Except those bitches wouldn't die and we failed."

"You tried." That was more than I did.

"Kate, I know what you're thinking. You're thinking that if you had watched Julie, she wouldn't have left with Red and we wouldn't be in this mess."

What? "No. Not at all."

"I just want you to know: when I took her off that cross, she was calling his name. Neither you nor I can do anything to break what's between them."

"Andrea, I don't blame you. I don't blame anyone." Except myself. "You went out there and tried against impossible odds and almost won, while I played footsie with Bran in the mist."

I rose. "I'm going to see Jim and then I'll see about sending a runner to the Order, since the phones are dead."

She raised her head from the pillow, her eyes wide. "Why?"

After Bran had run out of curses, he'd condescended to explain a few things to me. "From what Bran says, the gray bubble Morfran made is some sort of ancient druidic ward. Morfran is buying time and working the cauldron, packing the sea-demons into that bubble. When it bursts, they will spill out onto the Honeycomb and then onto Warren. We'll need the knights and MSDU."

Her face fell. "There will be no help, Kate. Everyone's gone. Even Maxine."

"Where the hell did they go?"

"There's an emergency," she said softly. "All the knights

and the Military Supernatural Defense Units are being pulled
to counter it."

"Andrea, in less than twelve hours, Atlanta will be full of
demons. They will kill, feed, and release more demons. What
emergency is more important than this one?"

She hesitated. "I'm not supposed to disclose this. There's a
man. His name is Roland . . ."

I almost punched the wall. "What is he doing that's so
damn crucial? What, is he building another tower? It will fall
like all his other ones. Or did his eye finally grow back and he
decided to have a battle to celebrate?"

Andrea gently closed her muzzle. "Kate? How do you
know that?"

Shit.

"Even I don't rank high enough to know about the eye and
the towers. I was only told because I would be staying behind
alone. You're not even a knight. How do you know this?"

*How do I fix this? I have to kill her. Wait, I can't kill her.
She's my friend.*

"Are you planning on walking into Ted's office after the
flare and telling him that you're beastkin?"

She winced. "No. He'd throw me out. The Order is all I
know."

I nodded. "You have your secrets and I have mine. I didn't
say anything about Roland and you didn't hear anything." I
offered her my hand. "Deal?"

She hesitated only for a moment. Her fingers grasped mine
and I was relieved by their strength. "And I'm not a beastkin.
Deal."

I found Jim in the next room. He sat in the bed, propped up
by a pillow, and sharpened a short thick knife with a whet-
stone.

"You fucking owe me." He showed me his teeth in an ugly
snarl. "You had a beastkin buddy. Didn't tell me. Made me
look like I don't know my business. Made me look like a
fool."

I came in and sat on the edge of his blanket.

"Get the fuck off my bed."

I sighed. "How are the legs?"

"Doc says I'll be walking by tomorrow." He pointed the knife at me. "Don't change the fucking subject."

The same injury would take at least two weeks to heal during normal magic.

"You remember that time you put a rat scout into an apartment above me to spy on me and Crest?" The scout who had heard everything that went on between me and Crest.

"What about him?"

"We're even."

He shook his head and went back to sharpening his knife.

"You still here?" he asked a few seconds later.

"Leaving as we speak." I got up. "Jim . . . Why did you go?"

He gave me his hard stare. "He promised the child she would be safe. The alpha stands by his word and the Pack stands by the alpha. That's how it works."

He went back to his knife, signaling the end of the conversation.

I NEEDED TO FIND A SINK AND SPLASH SOME WATER on my face. A small room to the left looked promising. I entered. No bathroom. No furniture, either. Just a straight shot to a square balcony connected to something with an outside stairwell leading to the left.

The door barely had a chance to close behind me before it flew open with a bang. Curran appeared in the doorway. He was human again, but only in shape. Sweat drenched his face. His hands gripped the door frame as if they still had claws. His yellow eyes glowed with feral need. He snarled, his face wrinkling, and rushed past me to the balcony. He burst outside, leaned on the stone rail with both hands, and stared down below.

Alrighty then.

I followed and rested on the rail next to him. A staircase led up to a parapet connecting the main Keep with a half-built tower to the left. When they finally finished this place, they would have to rename it. "Keep" simply didn't do it. It begged for a more appropriate name like Doom Bastion of Shapeshifter Superiority. Probably with a big sign underscoring the sentiment, in case some dummy failed to get it. *Pack to the Outside World: We don't like you. Stay out!*

And Curran would brood and stalk along the walls.

"Who won?" I knew he would answer that one.

"I did."

"How?"

"Threw him into the smaller water tower. He doesn't like water. He shrunk."

Below us the trees shivered in the morning breeze.

"Do you want it to be your turn now? Do you want to tell me what an idiot I am?" The violence in his voice sent shivers down my spine.

"Hold on, let me make sure there are no water towers around . . ."

He dragged his fingers across the stone rail. If he'd still had his claws, they would've left white scratches.

"You put that damn thing in my hand and I gave it away. I've got no necklace, no kid, two of my people dead, three are in the medward. There is a ward spell over the Honeycomb Gap and scouts tell me it's full of monsters. Impressive performance all around. Go on. Take a shot."

"I would've traded the necklace for Julie in a heartbeat."

He glanced at me. The next moment I was pinned against the wall, his teeth an inch from my carotid. He sucked in my scent, his eyes still flooded with molten gold. His voice was a contained storm. "Knowing all I know now, I would do it again."

"So would I. Let go of me."

He released me and stepped back.

"If you can't save a child, what's the point of it all?" I told him. "Julie's worth saving, and I don't want to buy my safety with her blood. I'd die first."

I leaned against the wall. "I should've put it all together sooner. Better yet, I should've left her with you. That little shit Red couldn't have taken her out of the Keep. I'm sick of being a day late and a dollar short."

Our stares connected and we were quiet for a long minute, united by our misery. At least he understood me and I understood him.

"A fine pair we make," he said.

"Yeah."

In the yard I saw a small figure stumble from the ruins of the water tower. I nodded at him. "He screwed up, too. Bran teleported all over the place like a nitwit looking for the cauldron. It was right there under the pile of crates. The first place he should've looked. We all got outsmarted by a guy with tentacles and his brood of undead mermaids."

Curran shrugged his massive shoulders. "It's never fucking simple. Just once I want it to be easy and neat. But no, there is never a good decision. I pick what I can live with."

We both knew he blamed himself for every last scratch his people got.

The sun broke above the treetops, flooding the world with sunshine, but the staircase shielded us and we remained in the cool blue shadow. Curran pushed away from the stone. "I take it, that gray bubble in the Gap will burst soon?"

"Fifteen hours from the moment it appeared. If Bran can be trusted."

"So around seven tonight. The thief . . ."

"Bran."

"I don't give a damn what his name is. He can close the cauldron, you said. What will that do?"

"How much do you know about what's going on?"

"Everything you told Andrea."

I nodded. "The cauldron belongs to Morrigan. Morfran, the ugly one, stole it from her, so he could be reborn through it. The creature with tentacles, the reeves, and the giant all serve Morfran. They are the advance party of Fomorians, the sea-demons, who are now climbing out of the cauldron. Closing the cauldron will stop more demons from being reborn. Those who are on the field will become mortal. Morrigan will gain the ownership of the cauldron again, which will be the end of Morfran and his happy Fomorian tent revival."

Curran thought about it. "The Honeycombers are moving

their trailers to prevent the demons from climbing up the walls into the Honeycomb. The demons have only one way to go: southwest, along the bottom of the Gap. The Pack will block the Gap. We'll take on the brunt of the assault. Jim says there is a tunnel leading into the Gap from the Warren."

"I know of it."

"That idiot and a small party of my people can go through the tunnel into the Gap, while the demons are concentrating on us. It will put them into the Fomorian rear. With luck, the demons won't even notice him. Can he keep from throwing his hissy fit until he gets to the cauldron?"

"I don't know. You're not impressed by his warp spasm, huh?"

He grimaced. "It's abhorrent. Total loss of control. No beauty to it, no symmetry. His eye was hanging out on his cheek like some piece of snot. No, I'm not impressed."

"I can try to keep a lid on him until we get to the cauldron." I made a pun, but he wasn't in the mood to notice.

"No."

"What do you mean no?"

"No, you're not going with him."

I crossed my arms. "Who decided that?"

He put on his "I'm alpha and I'm putting my foot down" expression. "I decided."

"You don't get to decide. I'm not under your authority."

"Yes, you are. Without you the fight will happen, but without me and the Pack, it won't. I command the superior force, therefore I'm in charge. You and your army of one can put yourself under my authority or you can take a walk."

"You don't think I can do it, is that it?"

"No, I want you where I can see you."

"Why?"

His lip quivered with the beginning of a snarl. His face relaxed, as he brought himself under control. "Because that's how I want it," he said, using a slow, patient voice reserved for rowdy children and disagreeable mental patients. It drove me to the edge of reason. I really wanted to punch him.

"Just out of curiosity, how do you expect to prevent me from coming with Bran?"

"I'll hog-tie you, gag you, and have three shapeshifters sit on you for the duration of the fight."

I was about to tell him that he wouldn't, but his eyes assured me that he would. I wouldn't get my way. Not this time. Good moment for a new strategy.

"Very well. I'll be good, but on one condition. I want fifteen seconds before the fight. Just me between the Fomorian ranks and your people."

"Why?"

Because I had a crazy idea. I wanted to do something that would make my dad and Greg turn in their graves. I had nothing to lose. We might all die anyway.

I didn't answer. I just looked at him. Either he would trust me or not.

"You have them," Curran said.

CHAPTER 24

———◆———

THE PACK HAD SHIT FOR BLADES. IT FIGURED: THEY didn't need them. I went through the weapons in their armory one by one, and found nothing. I wanted a second sword and Curran said I could borrow any one I wanted.

They did slightly better on the armor front. I found a good leather tunic studded with steel diamonds in strategic places. It was black, it fit me, and best of all, it relied on laced cords to adjust the fit. I'd have to have help putting it on and taking it off. I'd never been in a full-out battle before, but I'd survived some vicious large scale brawls and fought my way through a couple of riots. From experience, I knew I would lose myself in a fight and strip out of my armor to improve freedom of movement without ever noticing I'd done it. I needed armor that was hard to take off. Anything with Velcro was right out of the question.

I was ready to give up on the armory, and then there it was, a single-edged blade, about twenty inches in length with a profile wider than, but strikingly similar to, Slayer. Perfectly balanced, with a distal taper, the sword was crafted from a single piece of spring steel with plain wooden panels for the grip. It was simple, unadorned, functional, not a medieval replica, but a modern age, no-nonsense weapon. It was perfect.

I swung it a couple of times, getting used to the weight.

"Two swords," Bran said from the doorway.

His spasm had torn his clothes, and he had cut and rigged the remnants of his shirt and pants into a makeshift kilt, showcasing the world's greatest chest. Too bad the kilt gave me a flashback to Greg's killer. He had worn a kilt, too.

"Can you handle two swords?"

I pulled Slayer from the sheath, lunged at him, drawing a classic figure eight around his body with Slayer, and blocked his arm with the flat of the shorter blade when he tried to counter.

"Fancy. You missed," he said.

"You want something?"

"I thought since we both might die tomorrow, you'd be up for a friendly roll-in-the-hay."

"I might die. You'll be healed."

He shook his head. "I'm not immortal, dove. Do enough damage fast and I'll kick the bucket like the rest of you."

I disengaged and moved past him to the door.

His kilt fell.

"It took me forever to fix this!" He grabbed it off the floor and it fell apart in his hand. I had cut it in three places.

I walked out into the hallway and almost ran into Curran accompanied by a group of shapeshifters. Bran followed me in all his naked glory. "Hey, does this mean no sex?"

Curran's face went blank. I dodged him and kept walking.

Bran chased me, weaving through the shapeshifters. "Get out of my way, don't you see I'm trying to talk to a woman?"

I made the mistake of looking back in time to see Curran reach for Bran's neck as the Hound of Morrigan rushed by. With an effort of will that must have taken a year off his life, Curran curled his fingers into a fist and lowered his hand instead.

I chuckled to myself and kept walking. The Universe had proven Curran wrong: a person who aggravated him more than me did, in fact, exist.

Bran caught up with me on the stairs. "Where are you headed?"

"To a balcony. I want some fresh air." And maybe to doze off a bit. Although I was no longer sleepy. The magic hummed in me, eager to be released. Is this how it would be when the tech finally fell for good? I wasn't sure I could handle that much raw power. I had to hold myself back, as if I was riding a crazed horse at full gallop and the reins kept slipping through my fingers.

Bran strode next to me, completely unconcerned with his lack of clothes. I stepped into the first room I saw, pulled a pair of gray sweatpants out of a chest of drawers—just about every room in the Keep had them, since people who shifted shapes found it convenient to have extra clothes present—and handed the pants to him.

"Can't control yourself?" He slipped into the sweatpants.

"That's it," I murmured, stole the spare blanket and pillow, and left the room.

He followed me to the balcony, where I made a makeshift bed in the recessed doorway and curled up. The stone shielded me from the sun, but I saw it all: the sky veiled with sunshine and touched with feathery smudges of clouds, the bright greenery of the trees, rustling in the breeze, the stone walls, still smooth and warm to the touch. I smelled the honeyed flowers and the light scent of wolves on the breeze. I drank it all in.

Bran perched on the stone rail. "A scrawny street kid. A throwaway human. Now you'll go to war because of her."

"Wars have been started for worse reasons."

He stared at me. "I don't understand."

How do you explain humanity to someone who has no frame of reference? "It has to do with good and evil. You have to decide for yourself what they are. For me, evil is striving to an end without regard for the means."

He shook his head. "Better to do a small wrong to prevent a big one."

"How do you decide what is a 'small' wrong? Let's say, you buy the safety of many with the life of a child. That child means everything to her parents. You devastated them. There is no greater wrong you can do to them. Why would that be a 'small' evil?"

"Because now more of you fools are going to die."

"We fools volunteered to fight. We have free will. I fight to save Julie and to kill as many of those bastards as I can. They came into my house, they tried to kill me, and they crucified my kid. I want to punish them. I want that punishment to be so hard, so vicious, that the next scum who takes their place wets himself at the mere thought of trying to fight me."

Slayer smoked in its sheath, sensing my anger. Normally I'd have to feed it, or its blade would become thin and brittle, but with the magic flowing this strong, the sword would last through the battle and then some.

I pointed to the yard. "The shapeshifters fight to take a stand against a threat and to avenge their dead Pack mates. They fight to protect their children, because without them there is no future. What do you fight for?"

He ruffled the wild nest of his hair. "I have no future anyway. I fight because I made a deal with Morrigan. Without mist, I'll age and die."

"Would aging be such a bad thing? Don't you want a life? A real life?"

He sneered. "If I wanted a real life, I wouldn't have asked to be a hero. When I die, I want to die strong, with a sword in my hand, sheathing it into the bodies of my enemies. That's how a man should die."

I sighed. "My father served as a warlord to a man of unequaled power. This man called my father 'Voron,' which means Raven, because death followed him. Voron had never been defeated with a blade. Had he remained as a warlord to lead the army he had built and trained, the world would be a very different place."

"Is there a point to this tale?"

"He left it all behind for my sake." And he did it all for a child not of his own blood.

"Then your father was a fool and now I know why you're one."

I closed my eyes. "There is no reasoning with you. Let me sleep."

I heard him jump off the rail and land next to me, and then he poked my shoulder with his finger.

"I'm trying to understand."

I opened my eyes. Explaining my moral code really wasn't my forte. "Imagine you're being chased by wolves. You're running through the woods, no settlement in sight, and you come across a baby lying abandoned on the ground. Do you save the baby or do you leave him for the wolves?"

I saw the hesitation in his dark eyes. "I'd leave the little bastard," he declared, a bit too loudly. "Would slow the wolves down."

"You had a doubt."

He raised his hand but I shook my head. "I saw it. You had a doubt. You thought about it for a second. The same force that drove that doubt is what makes us fight. Now leave me be."

I curled up on my blanket and closed my eyes. The wind gently stroked my face and soothed me into calm sleep.

DEREK AWOKE ME A COUPLE OF HOURS LATER. I looked at the sky. The sun rode high—it was just past noon.

I didn't want to die.

Derek's face was grim. "Jim has something for you downstairs."

He took me to the first floor and held the door open for me. I entered a small room, where Jim sat in a chair, testing the edge of that same knife with his thumb. In front of him, on the floor, sat Red. He was filthy. His left eye was swollen shut with a magnificent shiner. A long metal chain stretched from the wall to clutch at a metal collar around his neck. God help you if you offend the Pack, because they didn't need a K-9 unit to find you.

I crossed my arms and looked at him. He was only fifteen. It didn't excuse his betrayal of Julie but it precluded me from doing all of the things I would normally do under these circumstances.

Red squinted at me with his good eye. "You gonna beat me, go ahead."

I leaned against the wall. At the first hint of my movement, he ducked, covering his head. "Why didn't you tell me about the necklace?"

"Because you'd steal it." He bared his teeth. "It was mine. My power! My chance."

"Do you know what happened to Julie?"

"He knows," Jim said.

"Do you feel responsible at all?" I asked.

He scooted back from me. "What the fuck do you want me to say? Am I suppose to make nice and cry and tell you how sorry I am? I took care of Julie. I watched out for her for two years. She owes me, okay? They had their claws on my throat. Right here!" He clamped his neck with his grimy fingers. "They said, you get the girl or die. So I got the girl. Any of you assholes would've done the same. You gonna stand there and look down on me like that, well fuck you."

He spat on the floor.

"If you didn't care for her at all, why did you ask me to guard her?"

"Because she's an investment, you dumb whore."

He wasn't a person, he was just a ball of hate. We could beat him, we could starve him, we could lecture him, but no amount of punishment or education would make him understand that he was wrong. He was lost.

"What are you going to do with him?" I asked Jim.

Jim shrugged. "I'll give him a blade, put him on the field. He can show me how tough he is."

"He'll stab us in the back."

"I'll have people watching him. We found him once, we'll find him again. He stabs someone, I'll skin him alive. Piece by piece." Jim smiled at Red. Most people saw Jim smile only once, just before he killed them. The smile had the desired effect: Red cringed and paled so light, I could see it even through the layer of dirt smudging his skin.

"Objections?" Jim asked me.

"Do what you will."

IN THE YARD, TWO HUGE BUSES ROARED, THEIR ENgines fueled by magic-infused water. That's the trouble with magic-fueled vehicles: they were slow, thirty-five, forty miles an hour max and they made enough noise to wake the dead and make them call the cops. I'd get to ride to the battle on a bus. The Universe had a mordant sense of humor.

I noticed a familiar slender figure. Myong. And next to her, Crest. He looked well: same dark eyes, same clothes, immaculate to the last crease. He was still a very handsome man, with auburn hair and warm eyes. I looked at him and didn't care. The pang of embarrassment was gone. I was free.

"Curran let them go. Released her from all duties to the Pack. She's excused from the fight." Derek wrinkled his lip. "If it was me, I'd make her fight. And then, if she did well, I might let her go."

Crest held the door of a narrow gray vehicle for Myong.

"There, they are off, the happy couple excused from revenge and saving the world. Doesn't it bother you?"

I smiled. "Derek, in life you have to learn to let some things go."

We circled the bus and a wave of vampiric magic hit me. Eight vampires sat perched like statues in front of a Jeep. Curran stood by the Jeep, having a rather animated discussion with the ninth vampire. The vampire saw me.

"Kate," it said in Ghastek's voice. "Your ability to remain alive never ceases to amaze me."

"What are you doing here? As in what are you doing here, instead of being under lockdown in the Casino?"

"Quite elementary, my dear; I've come to get even. That, and the People would like to monitor the full potential of the vampires during a flare in an environment where they are free to inflict unrestricted damage. But mostly, I'm here to get even with the Shepherd. I find retribution to be a worthy cause."

I looked at Curran's face and suddenly I knew exactly who would escort Bran through the tunnel.

CHAPTER 25

THE BUBBLE FILLED THE GAP. SOLID, TRANSLUCENT,
streaked with hairline cracks, it betrayed the faces of monsters
within. Snouts crushed, heavy lips squished, the Fomorians
stood shoulder to shoulder, packed tight like Altoid mints.

We had ridden the buses to the Honeycomb and walked a
trail to the bottom of the Gap. Curran had brought a hundred
shapeshifters, all volunteers. A hundred could block the Gap
long enough to give Bran a chance to close the cauldron. And
if they failed, no number of shapeshifters would make things
right. Curran didn't want to put more of his people in harm's
way. Still, I would've taken more, but nobody asked for my
opinion.

The trail took us along the Honeycomb Gap's edge. I saw
the bloated trailers pulled up tight to encircle the lip of the
Gap, where it touched the Honeycomb. Beyond the trailers
waited the Honeycomb residents, armed with clubs, axes, and
blades. I counted four dog handlers, holding their metallic
charges on the arm-thick chains and two cheiroballistas beyond them before the path took me eastward. Should any
demons make it up the trash- and spike-studded slope, they
would regret it in a hurry.

The shapeshifters had cleared the floor of the Gap enough
to make it serviceable. All the sharp trash had been thrown
against the bubble. It would slow the Fomorians down.

We descended into the Gap. The Pack formed ranks about
a hundred yards from the bubble. The shapeshifters stood
apart, giving each other room to work. A group of women
strode past me, led by a familiar witch: one of the Morrigan

coven leaders. They wore leather and chain mail, carried bows and swords, and their faces were painted blue. With a look of grim determination, they elbowed their way to Curran. They spoke for a few minutes and the witches climbed up the walls, taking position among the refuse above the battle.

It was my turn. I walked up to Curran. "Fifteen seconds."

His eyes shone. "I remember. Try not to die."

"I'll survive just so I can kill you."

"See you in the morning, then."

I moved aside. Behind me Derek had a wide smile plastered on his face.

"Are you babysitting me for the fight?"

He nodded, his smile even wider.

Marvelous.

A chunk of pale gray, like dirty ice, broke from the top of the bubble. With an eerie whistle, it plunged and bit deep into the bottom of the Gap, punching through the rusty garbage. The gray hissed and fizzled, evaporating into thin air. A hush fell upon the field. The shapeshifters trembled in anticipation.

Curran's voice carried over our heads. "We have a job to do. Today we avenge our own! They came here, onto our land. They tortured a child. They killed our Pack mates. Nobody hurts the Pack!"

"Nobody!" answered a ragged chorus.

He pointed at the bubble. "They are not men. There is no human flesh on their bones."

Where was he going with this?

"What happens here, stays here. Today there is no Code. Today you can let go."

They lived the Code. They followed it with fanatical discipline. Obey, perform, account for yourself. Ever diligent. Always in control. Never let go. Curran had promised them the one thing they could never have. One by one their eyes lit amber, then flared blood-red.

"Remember: it's not your job to die for your Pack! It's your job to make the other bastards die for theirs. Together we kill!"

"Kill!" breathed the field.

"Win!"

"Win!"

"Go home!"

"Go home!"

"Kill! Win! Go home!"

"Kill, win, go home! Kill, win, go home!" They chanted it over and over, their voices merging them into a unified avalanche of sound.

Another fraction of the dome tumbled to the grass. As one, the shapeshifters stripped off their clothes. Around me people gripped their weapons. I smelled sweat and sun-warmed metal.

With the ear-splitting roar of a crumbling ice flat, the gray dome fell apart revealing the sea of Fomorians. They shifted forward a few steps and stood silent, a chaotic mass dappled with green, turquoise, and orange, monstrous like an old painting of hell.

"Turn!" Curran roared.

Fur burst along the shapeshifter ranks like a fire running down the detonation cord. Beasts and monsters shrugged their shoulders and bit the air. Curran snarled and rose above his troops, an eight-foot-tall bestial nightmare.

Behind the Fomorian horde, Morfran stood on a small knoll of garbage. He thrust an enormous, double-edged axe to the sky.

The Fomorians bellowed.

A hundred roars answered them from thick furry throats: wolves snarled and howled, jackals yipped, hyenas laughed, cats growled, rats screeched, all at once, and through it all, unstoppable and overwhelming, came the lion roar.

The Fomorians hesitated, unsure.

Morfran thrust his axe straight up. He pretty much seemed to have one sign for everything: poke a hole in the sky.

The front ranks of the horde started forward, first slowly, trudging, then faster and faster. A stretch of trash-strewn ground as long as a football field separated them from us. The ground shook from the pounding of many feet.

"Hold!" Curran snarled.

A low chant of female voices rose behind us. The magic moved and shifted, obedient to the power within the voices. The ground quaked like a giant drum being struck from within. Vines burst before the Fomorian front ranks and slunk along the ground, twisting around their feet, tripping, binding. The demons halted, tearing themselves free.

A witch screamed. Guttural cries answered her. The sky came alive with glittering shapes. The Stymphalean birds took to the air and plunged at the demonic horde. Feathers whistled through the air and howls of pain echoed them as the razor-sharp metal sliced into flesh. Here and there the demonic forms went liquid. The cauldron would bring them back to life. I remembered what Bran screamed while watching the fight in the Oracle's turtle. He screamed, "Maim." If we could maim a large number of them, incapacitating them but not killing, it would work better than dispatching them only to be reborn. We needed to engage their attention, to occupy them and to thin their ranks to buy Bran safe passage.

The demons had untangled themselves from the vines and started forward again, a roiling mass of flesh and teeth and horns.

My cue. I ran forward, light on my feet, farther and farther away from the shapeshifter line. Ahead, the Fomorians swelled before me.

I dropped all the guards. All the leashes, all the chains, everything that ever restrained me through the discipline and fear of discovery, I let all of it go. No need to hide. Magic flowed through me, intoxicating, heady, seductive. It mixed with my bloodlust and I realized that's how my father must have felt when he led his armies into battle. I was raised by Roland's Warlord. I'd dropped my shackles and they would bow to me.

Magic sang through me. Drunk on its strength, I held nothing back and barked a word of power.

"Osanda!" Kneel.

The magic erupted from me like a tsunami. The ground shook as hundreds of knees hit it in unison. The Fomorian ranks collapsed to the ground in a spray of blood and crunch of broken leg bones, as if a giant had stomped an enormous bloody footprint in their midst. My pain was so slight, I barely noticed it. The pressure of magic within me finally eased.

Faced with its vanguard writhing on the ground in pain, the horde halted in horror. I saw Morfran across the field, his disgusting face distinct before me with preternatural clarity, his eyes shocked. I drank that shock in. I reveled in it and I laughed.

"Bring your army, little god! My sword is hungry!"

He jerked as if whipped, and I knew he'd heard me. The axe thrust, pointing at me. He screamed and the horde started forward again. I was still laughing, giddy with so much magic spent so quickly, when the shapeshifters swarmed past me onto the crippled demons.

A hand jerked my shoulder and Derek's face thrust into my view. "Kate! Snap out of it! Kate!"

I laughed at him and unsheathed my swords. Scabbards hit the ground and then I was running.

What happens here, stays here.

A roar arose as the opposing lines of fighters collided like two great ships ramming each other. The first demon swung a blue axe at me. I disemboweled him, almost in passing, and moved on to the next one.

I sliced and cut, my blades biting like two steel snakes with hungry mouths, and no matter how much Fomorian flesh they consumed, it failed to satiate their hunger. I saw nothing, I felt nothing. All melted into the scent and warmth of blood, the scorching heat of the sun, and the liquid lubrication of my own sweat.

They kept coming, enclosing me in a tight ring of flesh. I killed without comprehension, not knowing whom I had dispatched to the cauldron's depths. They were shapes, obstacles in my way to Morfran, and like a well-tuned machine, I mowed them down, unthinking, unrepentant. Every maneuver I tried worked. Every cut found its victim. A curious elation came over me—they were so many and I hoped they wouldn't end. This was what I was born for.

I could go on killing forever.

The ground grew slippery with the fluid of Fomorian death. Slowly a ring of carcasses began to grow around me: we had overloaded the cauldron of rebirth, slaughtering the Fomorians faster than it could regenerate them.

Suddenly the Fomorians broke and fled the gluttony of my swords. The field opened before me. The combatants crashed against each other, thrown back and forth, the lines between attackers and defenders no longer clear. Mad shapeshifters ripped into monsters, their eyes crimson with rage. Witches howled, loosing spells and arrows. The air steamed with blood. The clamor of swords, the pain-laced cries of the injured, the screams of shapeshifters, and groans of the dying melded together into an unbearable cacophony. Above it all the merciless sun blazed, bright enough to blister the skin. This was hell and I was its fury.

I raised my sword and killed again, with a smile on my face.

WHEN I SAW THE SUN AGAIN, IT HUNG ABOVE THE horizon, bleeding crimson onto the sky, puffy clouds soaking in red like bandages on an open wound. We had fought for nearly two hours.

A pair of vampires landed on the mound of corpses.

"Golf Tree, big mob two o'clock, kick lift?"

"Golf Too, Roger."

The vampire on the left grasped the undead on the right, spun and hurled it like a discus. The undead cleared twenty-five feet and landed atop a giant with a shark's head. Claws sliced and the Fomorian went down.

Vampires. That meant Bran had made it.

A body flew past me. I turned and saw him. Grotesque, enormous, he strode through the field, just yards away.

To the left a scaled Fomorian hurled a harpoon. It shot through the air, hit Bran square in the gut, and bounced off. The monster that was Bran grasped the harpoon with a shovel-sized hand and tugged the chain, jerking its owner off his feet. As the Fomorian flew through the air, Bran kicked him like a soccer ball. The blow caught the harpooner's gut and sent him flying.

The Fomorians fell on him four, five at once, and he scattered them like a flock of birds, swinging back and forth, lopping off heads and stomping the bodies like a toddler rampaging in a field of dandelions. As he chased after them, breaking backs and crushing skulls, his upper body began to glow red like a dying coal.

What was he doing? He wasn't suppose to spasm until he got to Morfran. I turned and saw Morfran, right there, practically next to me. In my spree, I had carved my way to him.

Morfran's hands moved, his lips whispering. His eyes tracked Bran. He was casting a spell.

No, you don't.

I charged up the knoll, screaming.

The attack came, sudden and vicious. Morfran chopped at me in a great overhead blow, moving with preternatural quickness, light on his feet. I leaped aside and launched a barrage of strikes, faster and faster, moving around, flashing my blades. Concentrate on me, you sonovabitch.

The axe whistled past me, once, twice. I kept dancing, too fast to catch, but too precise to ignore. I watched his eyes, I watched his feet, I struck at his face to keep him busy. He swatted my short blade aside and cleaved at my side. I saw the axe come in a great shiny arc, a bright star of reflecting sunlight riding its edge. He had expected me to jump back but I went forward, along with the shaft of the axe, to stab at his throat.

It was a cat-quick stab, but somehow I missed. Slayer's point sliced a red line along Morfran's neck, and then his boot rammed my stomach. The world swam in a watery, painful haze. I crashed into the dirt. He was on me in a second. The axe bit into the ground between my legs.

I rolled and lunged from a half crouch, thrusting both swords deep into his chest. My steel met no resistance. Morfran collapsed in a flurry of feathers. I slashed at them, spitting wordless growls like a dog. The feathers streamed between my feet, flowing into the clearing formed by the Fomorians. I chased them, but they were too fast.

In a blink Morfran re-formed. The axe gleamed in his hands. I charged and saw Bran rise behind Morfran. Bran's head glowed bright white. He bled from a dozen places, where huge gashes split his warped body. The heat emanating from him dried his blood into brown streaks on his skin.

"My tuuuurn!" The Bran thing whipped its arm and backhanded Morfran. The Great Crow slid across the trash. Bran chased after him, swinging and kicking in deranged fury, swinging a huge spear he must've taken from one of the demons.

Morfran's axe ripped through the air with an eerie whistle. The hit split Bran's spear shaft in half and plunged into his shoulder. Blood spurted. He wheeled, unnaturally quick, plucked the axe from Morfran's hands, and snapped the wooden shaft.

Morfran's body fell apart into a tempest of floating black feathers. The feathers sucked themselves upward in a reverse tornado and solidified into an enormous black crow. Cold magic flooded us. Devoid of life, it may as well have spilled from outer space through a crow-shaped hole in the atmosphere. Frost licked my skin.

The crow's claw gripped a huge bronze cauldron.

Bran scooped a handful of metal garbage and hurled it. Jagged metal trash bit into the crow, puncturing his neck and back with a hoarse whine. Dark blood rolled from the jet feathers in fist-sized globules. The spheres detached from Morfran's flesh and hung in the air, shimmering in the light of the dying sun.

Bran hurled the contents of his other hand. A single piece sparkled and bit deep into the crow's back—Morfran's own axehead.

The crow screamed.

Like a drop of molten metal, the cauldron fell from his claws. A wail of pure rage sliced across my mind.

Beneath the cauldron's feet the earth sighed, opened like a hungry mouth, and belched more Fomorians into the light. They swarmed Bran.

I hacked into them. Beside me the shapeshifters tore them

to shreds, but there were too few of us and too many of them. I could not longer see Bran—he was buried beneath a heap of Fomorian bodies.

The heap of demons fell apart. Bloody and battered, Bran heaved an ornate lid free of the dirt. It looked so tiny in his giant hand, no bigger than a Frisbee. Enormous pressure clasped me. My chest constricted. My bones groaned. Around me the shapeshifters and the Fomorians fell screaming in pain.

Bran strained. Blood gushed from his wounds and with a terrible bellow he slammed the lid down onto the cauldron.

The pressure vanished. Bran grinned, pulled the lid open, and vanished in a puff of mist. The lid went with him. That's it, I realized. He has returned the lid to Morrigan and now he was done. But we, we still had a field of demons to clear.

"Kate!" The howl made me turn. Thirty yards away I saw Derek pointing a bloody clawed hand behind me. I spun and saw a familiar little figure on the cross, thrust into the ground only yards away. Julie.

I scrambled over bodies to get to her. A shadow fell over me. I looked up in time to see a huge beak the color of polished iron strike at me. Morfran, still a crow. Boxed in by the Fomorians, I had no place to go. I dropped to my knees, ready to plunge Slayer into Morfran's gut. The crow blotted out the sun and froze as huge clawed hands clasped its wings.

With a roar that shook the Fomorians, Curran ripped into the crow. "Go!" he screamed. "Go!"

I went, climbing over bodies, hacking, slashing, cutting, fixated on Julie. To the left, a clump of Fomorians broke from a vampire whose limbs they had torn and charged me.

"Kill the child!" The Shepherd's hiss pierced the clamor of the battle. The Fomorians reversed their course.

Twenty yards separated me from her. I wouldn't make it in time.

Bran materialized by Julie in a puff of mist. He was back in his human form. He hugged the cross and her with it. Mist puffed and all of it was gone. The Fomorians howled in fury.

Bran popped in front of me, his hands empty, grinned . . .

A swirl of green tentacles burst through his chest. His blood splashed me. His eyes opened wide. His mouth gaped.

"Bran!"

He stumbled forward and fell on me, blood gushing from his mouth. Behind him the Shepherd hissed in triumph. I leaped over Bran, and slashed at the bastard's face. Fish eyes glared at me with hate and then the top of his head slid aside and rolled into the dirt. His body stumbled. I cut it again, and again, and the sea-demon fell in pieces to never get up again.

An unearthly cry rang through the field. Curran rose through the carnage, Morfran's huge crow head in his hand. Covered in blood, he thrust the head to the sky and screamed, "Kill them! Kill them all! They are mortal!"

The shapeshifters fell onto the Fomorians. I spun around and dropped to my knees by Bran.

No. No, no, no.

I flipped him over. He looked at me with his black eyes. "I saved the baby. I saved her. For you."

"Mist! Mist damn you."

"Too late," he whispered with bloody lips. "Can't heal the heart. Good-bye, dove."

"Don't die!"

He just looked at me and smiled. I felt a thin line of pain stretch inside me, strained to the breaking point. It hurt. It hurt so much I couldn't take another breath.

Bran gasped. His body went rigid in my hands and I felt the last of him fluttering away.

No!

I clasped onto that last shiver of life. With all of my magic, with all of my power, with everything I was I held on to that tiny fragment of Bran and I would not let it go.

Magic churned around me. I sucked the power to me, driving it deeper into his body, holding on. It streamed through me in a flood of pain and melted into Bran's flesh.

I'm not letting go. He will live. I won't lose him.

"Foolish girl!" A voice filled my mind. *"You can't fight death."*

Watch me.

The spark of Bran's life slipped deeper. More magic. More . . . Wind howled, or maybe it was my own blood filling my ears. I no longer felt anything except pain and Bran.

I pulled harder. The spark stopped. Bran's eyelids trembled. His mouth opened. His eyes fixed on me. I couldn't hear what he was saying. His heart had stopped and it took all of me to keep him.

He looked at me with ghostly eyes. His whisper floated to my ears, each word weak but distinct. "Let me go."

"This is how undeath is made," the voice said.

And I felt deep within me that she was right.

I would not become what I loathed. I would not become the man who sired me.

"Let me go, dove," Bran whispered.

I severed the magic. The line of pain within me snapped like a broken string. It whipped back into me. I felt the spark of Bran's life melt into nothing. Magic flailed in me like a living beast, trapped and tearing me apart to break free.

In my arms Bran lay dead.

Tears burst from my eyes, and streamed down my cheeks to fall on the ground, carrying the magic with them. The soil soaked in my tears and something stirred beneath it, something full of life and magic, but it didn't matter. Bran was gone.

A Fomorian crept behind me, her blade ready to bite into my back.

I rose, moving on liquid joints, turned, and thrust in a single move. The tip of Slayer's blade punctured the Fomorian's chest. It cut her green skin and sliced smoothly through the tight sheet of muscle and membrane, scraping the cartilage of her breastbone, sinking deeper, driven by my hand until it found her heart. The hard, muscled organ resisted for a fraction of a moment, like a clenched fist, and then the blade pierced its wall and bathed in blood within. I jerked the sword up and to the side, ripping her heart to pieces.

Blood drenched my skin. I smelled it. I felt its sticky warmth on my hand. The Fomorian's eyes widened. Fear screeched at me from the depths of her cobalt eyes. This time there would be no rebirth. I had killed her. She was dead, and the realization of her own fate made her terribly, painfully afraid.

It was a moment that lasted an eternity. I knew I would remember it forever.

I would remember it forever because in that instant I knew that no matter how many I had killed and no matter how many I would kill before the day was over, none of it would bring Bran back. Not even for a moment.

I ripped the sword free. Grief saddled me and rode me into the foray. I raged across the field, killing all before me. They ran when they saw me coming, and I chased them down, and I killed them before they could take someone else's friend away from them.

THE NIGHT HAD FALLEN. THE FOMORIANS WERE dead. Their corpses littered the ground, mixed with human bodies of the fallen. In death, witch, shapeshifter, or regular Joe, they all looked the same. So many bodies. So many dead. This morning they spoke, they breathed, they kissed their loved ones good-bye. And now they lay dead. Gone forever. Like Bran.

I sat by Bran's body. His midnight eyes were closed. I was very tired. My body hurt in places I didn't know existed.

Someone had made a funeral pyre. It glowed orange in the oncoming darkness. Thick greasy smoke tainted the night.

I had taken Bran by the hand and dragged him back to humanity, back to free will and choice. And it, no, *I*, had gotten him killed. The fire had left his eyes. He'd never wink, he'd never call me dove again. I didn't love him, I barely knew him, but God, it hurt. Why was it that I killed everyone I touched? Why did they all die? I could have fixed almost everything else, but death defeated me every time. What good is all the magic if you can't hold back death? What good is it, if you don't know when to stop, if all you can do is kill and punish?

Someone approached and tugged on my sleeve. "Kate," a tiny voice said. "Kate, are you okay?"

I looked at the owner of the voice and recognized her face.
"Kate," she said pitifully. "Please say something."
I felt so hollow, I couldn't find my voice.
"Are you real?" I asked her.
Julie nodded.
"How did you get here?"
"Bran brought me," she said. "I awoke in a lake. There
were bodies everywhere and a woman. He pulled me out and
gave me a knife and he brought me over there." She pointed
back to where we had originally formed our lines. "I fought."
She showed me her bloody knife.
"Stupid girl," I said. I couldn't muster any anger and my
voice was flat. "So many people died to save you, and you ran
right back into the slaughter."
"I saw the reeves eating my mom's body. I had to." She sat
next to me. "I had to, Kate."
I heard a faint jingle of chains. Then a crunch of metal under someone's feet. A tall figure came through the smoke.
Nude, except for a harness of leather belts and silver
hooks, her hair falling around her in black dreads, she stood
smeared with fresh blood. The dark red rivulets mixed with
blue runes tattooed on her skin. Her presence slapped me: gla-
cial, hard, cruel, terrifying like a wolf's howl heard at night on
a lonely road.
"It's her," Julie whispered. "The woman by the lake."
Her eyes glowed, streaked with radiant sparks. The sparks
erupted into amber irises, suddenly as big as a house, all consuming, overpowering . . . The black bottomless pupil loomed
before me and I knew I could sink into it and be forever lost.
So that's what the eye of a goddess looks like.
She looked past us and raised her hand to point over my
shoulder. Chains clanked. *"Come!"* I recognized the voice: I
had heard her in my head.
Red peeled himself from the pile of trash. I had known he
was there for a while. He had crept in when the fight was almost over, followed me, and waited there in the garbage,
while I sat by Bran, numb. Probably biding his time for a good
chance to stab me in the back.

Julie startled. "Red!"

I caught her by the shoulder and kept her put.

"You desire power . . ."

Red swallowed. "Yes."

"Serve me and I will give you all the power you want."

He trembled.

"Do you accept the bargain?"

"Yes!"

"Red, what about me?" Julie broke free of my grip. I didn't hold her too hard. This was her last chance to be cured.

"I love you! Don't leave me."

He held his hand out, blocking her. "She has everything I want. You have nothing."

He stepped over Bran's legs and trotted to Morrigan's side like the dog he was. It had come full circle: from the ancestor who had broken free of Morrigan, through countless generations, to the descendant, who willingly put on her collar.

Bran's body had barely cooled. She showed no signs of grief.

I looked at her. "You recognize me."

Chains jingled in agreement.

"We meet again, and I'll kill him."

"Fuck off. She's too powerful for you. She'll protect me," Red said.

"The blood that flows through me was old when she was but a vague idea. Look into her eyes, if you don't believe me."

"We won't meet again," Morrigan promised.

Behind her, mist swirled in a solid wall. It slunk along the ground, licked at Morrigan's feet, wound about Red, and swallowed them whole.

The tech hit, crushing the magic under its foot. Julie stood alone in the field of dead bodies and iron, her face numb with shock.

EPILOGUE

⎯⎯◆⎯⎯

IN THE MORNING, WHEN THE WITCHES CAME FOR Bran's body, they found it sprawled among white flowers. Blazing like small white stars, with centers as black as his eyes, the flowers grew overnight, sending a spicy scent into the air. By the time the day was over, the flowers had been christened Morgan's Bells and a rumor floated person to person that Morrigan was so distraught over her champion's death, she had wept and the flowers sprang forth from her tears.

Bullshit. I was there and the bitch didn't shed a tear.

The witches buried Bran in Centennial Park and built a cairn over his grave. I was told I was welcome to visit him anytime.

The next two days were spent next to Andrea bent over the reports to the Order. We'd plugged every hole, smoothed every bump, and routed out every inconsistency, until she was pure human and I was just a blade-happy merc.

It didn't help that without magic in the world for the next few weeks, we had to resort to conventional medicine. I had a half dozen cuts, a couple deep enough to be bothersome, and two cracked ribs. Andrea sported a gash across her back that under ordinary circumstances would've healed with embarrassing quickness. Postflare, it took its time. She wasn't accustomed to pain and she popped painkillers by the handful.

After Red left, Julie had retreated deep into herself. She gave noncommittal answers and stopped eating. On Thursday I dropped off the last report together with a leave of absence request, loaded her into my ancient gas-guzzling Subaru, and drove down South, toward Savannah, where I kept my father's

house. Andrea promised to smooth things over with the Order
when the knights returned.

The drive took forever. I was out of practice and had to
stop to take a breather. We passed the turnoff to my house
and kept driving down along the coast to a small town called
Eulonia, until we reached an old restaurant called Pelican
Point. The owner owed me a favor or I wouldn't have been
able to afford it.

The restaurant sat on the edge of the river, just before the
freshwater found its way through the reeds and mud islands to
the Atlantic Ocean. We sat in the gazebo by the dock and
watched the shrimp and fish boats meander through the maze
of salt marshes and then unload their catch. Then we went inside, to a small table by the window, and I took Julie to the
seafood buffet.

Faced with more food than she had ever seen at once, Julie
went stiff. I loaded her plate, got us some crab legs, and led
her back to the table. She tried the fried shrimp and the black-
ened tilapia.

When I cracked the second cluster of crab legs, Julie began
to cry. She cried and ate crabmeat, dunking it in melted butter,
licked her fingers, and cried some more.

On the drive back, she sat sullenly in her seat.

"So what happens to me now?" she asked finally.

"Summer's almost over. Eventually, you'll have to go to
school."

"Why?"

"Because you have a gift. I want you to learn and to get to
know other people. Other kids and adults, so you can learn
how they think. So nobody can take advantage of you again."

"They won't like me."

"You might be surprised."

"Is it going to be one of those schools where you live there,
too?"

I nodded. "I make a very bad mom. I'm not home enough
and even when I am, I'm not the best person to take care of a
kid. But I can pull off a crazy aunt. You can always come and
visit me on holidays. I cook a mean goose."

"Why not turkey?"

"I don't like turkey. Too dry."

"What if I hate it there?" Julie asked.

"Then we'll keep looking until we find a school you don't hate."

"And I can come to live with you when I need to?"

"Always," I promised.

THREE WEEKS LATER I DROPPED JULIE OFF AT MACON Kao Arts Academy. Her magic talents, combined with my dismal income, easily qualified her for a scholarship. It was a good school, located in a peaceful spot, with a decent campus that reminded me of a park bordered by nine-foot-tall walls and towers armed with both machine guns and arrow sprayers. I met every member of the faculty, and all of them seemed disinclined to take any crap. They had an empath as a counselor. She would help Julie heal. Can't get better than an empath.

It was dark when I finally made it home. As always after the flare, the magic left the world alone for a while, and I had to make the trip in Betsi, which had stalled on me midway for no apparent mechanical reason. When I finally made it to the front door, I was dog tired. I climbed the stairs in the dusk and saw a bouquet of red roses in a crystal vase on my porch. The little card said, "I'm sorry. Saiman."

I took the flowers and the vase to the dumpster, grumbling under my breath, returned to the door, reached for my key, and realized the door stood slightly ajar.

I pulled Slayer from its sheath and pushed the door open with my fingertips. It swung soundlessly on well-greased hinges. Through the hallway, I saw the living room lamp glowing with soothing yellow light. I smelled coffee.

Who breaks into a house, turns on the lights, and makes coffee?

I padded into the living room on soft feet, Slayer ready.

"Loud and clumsy, like a baby rhino," said a familiar voice.

I stepped into the living room. Curran sat on my couch,

reading my favorite paperback. His hair was back to its normal short length. His face was clean shaven. He looked nothing like the dark, demonic figure who shook a would-be god's head on a field a month ago.

I thought he had forgotten about me. I had been quite happy to stay forgotten.

"*The Princess Bride*?" he said, flipping the book over.

"What are you doing in my house?" Let himself in, had he? Made himself comfortable, as if he owned the place.

"Did everything go well with Julie?"

"Yes. She didn't want to stay, but she'll make friends quickly and the staff seems sensible."

I watched him, not quite sure where we stood.

"I meant to tell you but haven't gotten a chance. Sorry about Bran. I didn't like him, but he died well."

"Yes, he did. I'm sorry about your people. Many losses?"

A shadow darkened his face. "A third."

He had taken a hundred with him. At least thirty people had never come back. The weight of their deaths pressed on both of us.

Curran turned the book over in his hands. "You own words of power."

He knew what a word of power was. Lovely. I shrugged. "Picked up a couple here and there. What happened in the Gap was a one shot deal. I won't be that powerful again." At least not until the next flare.

"You're an interesting woman," he said.

"Your interest has been duly noted." I pointed to the door.

He put the book down. "As you wish." He rose and walked past me. I lowered my sword, expecting him to pass, but suddenly he stepped in dangerously close. "Welcome home. I'm glad you made it. There is coffee in the kitchen for you."

My mouth gaped open.

He inhaled my scent, bent close, about to kiss me . . .

I just stood there like an idiot.

Curran smirked and whispered in my ear instead. "Psych."

And just like that, he was out the door and gone.

Oh boy.

ACKNOWLEDGMENTS

I'm grateful to so many people:

Thank you, Anne Sowards, my editor, for your wisdom, your guidance, and most of all your faith in my ability as a writer. You took a mess and shaped it into a book.

Thank you, Rachel Vater, my agent, for your tireless devotion to your clients. You're the best thing that could happen to a writer's career.

Thank you, Cam Dufty, Ace's editorial assistant and quite possibly the most patient woman the world has ever known, for your help with copyedits and a million other things. I owe you a chocolate martini.

Thank you, Kristin del Rosario, the interior text designer, for the gorgeous layout and for making the book a reality.

Thank you, Judy Murello, the art director, for the spectacular cover design, and thank you, Chad Michael Ward, the artist, for creating fantastic cover art.

Thank you, Valerie Cortes, Ace's publicist, for tirelessly promoting the books in the Kate Daniels series.

Thank you, all of the generous people who have suffered through my beta drafts, for making this book so much better than how it started out: Charlene Amsden, Bianca Bradley, Susan E. Curnow, Shannon Franks, Elizabeth Hull, Jackie M., Jill Myles, Reece Notley, Lizane Palmer, May, S. K. S. Perry, G. Jules Reynolds, Lys Rian, Melissa Sawmiller, Sonya Shannon, P. J. Thompson, Heidi Tallentine, and Amber van Dyk.

Finally, thank you, all of the people who read the Kate series. Your e-mails keep me going.

Turn the page for a sneak peek at the next novel in the Kate Daniels series, *Magic Strikes*

CHAPTER 1

SOME DAYS MY JOB WAS HARDER THAN OTHERS.

I tapped the ladder with my hand. "See? It's very sturdy, Mrs. McSweeney. You can come down now."

Mrs. McSweeney looked at me from the top of the telephone pole, having obvious doubts about the ladder's and my reliability. Thin, bird-boned, she had to be past seventy. The wind stirred the nimbus of fine white hair around her head and blew open her nightgown, presenting me with sights better left unseen.

"Mrs. McSweeney, I wish you would come down."

She arched her back and sucked in a deep breath. Not again. I sat on the ground and clamped my hands over my ears.

The wail cut through the stillness of the night, sharp like a knife. It hammered the windows of the apartment buildings, wringing a high-pitched hum from the glass. Down the street, dogs yowled as one, matching the cry with unnatural harmony. The lament built, swelling like an avalanche, until I could hear nothing but its complex, layered chorus: the lonely howl of a wolf, the forlorn shriek of a bird, the heart-wrenching cry of a child. She wailed and wailed, as if her heart were being torn out of her chest, filling me with despair.

The magic wave ended. One moment it saturated the world, giving potency to Mrs. McSweeney's cry, and the next it vanished without warning, gone like a line drawn in the sand just before the surf licked it. The technology reasserted itself. The blue feylantern hanging from the top of the pole went dark, as the magic-charged air lost its potency. Electric lights came on in the apartment building.

It was called post-Shift resonance: magic drowned the world in a wave, snuffing out anything complex and technological, smothering car engines, jamming automatic weapons, and eroding tall buildings. Mages fired ice bolts, skyscrapers fell, and wards flared into life, keeping undesirables from my house. And then, just like that, the magic would vanish, leaving monsters in its wake. Nobody could predict when it would reappear and nobody could prevent it. All we could do was cope with an insane tarantella of magic and technology. That was why I carried a sword. It always worked.

The last echoes of the cry bounced from the brick walls and died.

Mrs. McSweeney stared at me with sad eyes. I picked myself off the ground and waved at her. "I'll be right back."

I trotted into the dark entrance to the apartment, where five members of the McSweeney family crouched in the gloom. "Tell me again why you can't come out and help me?"

Robert McSweeney, a middle-aged, dark-eyed man with thinning brown hair, shook his head. "Mom thinks we don't know she's a banshee. Look, Ms. Daniels, can you get her down or not? You're the knight of the Order, for Christ's sake."

First, I wasn't a knight; I just worked for the Order of Knights of Merciful Aid. Second, negotiation wasn't my forte. I killed things. Quickly and with much bloodshed.

Getting elderly banshees in denial off telephone poles wasn't something I did often.

"Can you think of anything that might help me?"

Robert's wife, Melinda, sighed. "I don't . . . I mean, she always kept it so under wraps. We've heard her wail before but she was so discreet about it. This isn't normal for her."

An elderly black woman in a mumu descended the staircase. "Has that girl gotten Margie down yet?"

"I'm working on it," I told her.

"You tell her, she better not miss our bingo tomorrow night."

"Thanks."

I headed to the pole. Part of me sympathized with Mrs. McSweeney. The three law enforcement agencies that regulated life in the United States post-Shift—the Military Supernatural Defense Unit, or MSDU; the Paranormal Activity Division, or PAD; and my illustrious employer, the Order of Knights of Merciful Aid—all certified banshees as harmless. Nobody had yet been able to link their wails to any deaths or natural disasters. But folklore blamed banshees for all sorts of nefarious things. They were rumored to drive people mad with their screams and kill children with a mere look. Plenty of people would be nervous about living next to a banshee, and I could understand why Mrs. McSweeney went to great lengths to hide who she was. She didn't want her friends to shun her or her family.

Unfortunately, no matter how well you hide, sooner or later your big secret will bite you in the behind, and you might find yourself standing on a telephone pole, not sure why or how you got there, while the neighborhood pretends not to hear your piercing screeches.

Yeah. I was one to talk. When it came to hiding one's identity, I was an expert. I burned my bloody bandages, so nobody could identify me by the magic in my blood. I hid my power. I tried very hard not to make friends and mostly succeeded. Because when my secret came to life, I wouldn't end up on top of a telephone pole. I would be dead and all my friends would be dead with me.

I approached the pole and looked at Mrs. McSweeney. "Alright. I'm going to count to three and then you have to come down."

She shook her head.

"Mrs. McSweeney! You're making a spectacle out of yourself. Your family is worried about you and you have bingo tomorrow night. You don't want to miss it, do you?"

She bit her lip.

"We will do it together." I climbed three steps up the ladder. "On three. One, two, three, step!"

I took a step down and watched her do the same. *Thank you, whoever you are upstairs.*

"One more. One, two, three, step."

We took another step, and then she took one by herself. I jumped to the ground. "That's it."

Mrs. McSweeney paused. Oh no.

She looked at me with her sad eyes and asked, "You won't tell anyone, will you?"

I glanced at the windows of the apartment building. She had wailed loudly enough to wake the dead and make them call the cops. But in this day and age, people banded together. One couldn't rely on tech or on magic, only on family and neighbors. They were willing to keep her secret, no matter how absurd it seemed, and so was I.

"I won't tell anyone," I promised.

Two minutes later, she was heading to her apartment, and I was wrestling with the ladder, trying to make it fit back into the space under the stairs, where the super had gotten it from for me.

My day had started at five with a frantic man running through the hallway of the Atlanta chapter of the Order and screaming that a dragon with a cat head had gotten into New Hope School and was about to devour the children. The dragon turned out to be a small tatzelwyrm, which I unfortunately was unable to subdue without cutting its head off. That was the first time I had gotten sprayed with blood today.

Then I had to help Mauro get a two-headed freshwater

serpent out of an artificial pond at the ruins of One Atlantic Center in Buckhead. The day went downhill from there. It was past midnight now. I was dirty, tired, hungry, smeared with four different types of blood, and I wanted to go home. Also my boots stank because the serpent had vomited a half-eaten cat corpse on my feet.

I finally managed to stuff the ladder in its place and left the apartment building for the parking lot, where my female mule, Marigold, was tied to a metal rack set up there for precisely that purpose. I had gotten within ten feet of her when I saw a half-finished swastika drawn on her rump in green paint. The paint stick lay broken on the ground. There was also some blood and what looked like a tooth. I looked closer. Yep, definitely a tooth.

"Had an adventure, did we?"

Marigold didn't say anything, but I knew from experience that approaching her from behind was Not a Good Idea. She kicked like a mule, probably because she was one.

If not for the Order's brand on her other butt cheek, Marigold might have been stolen tonight. Fortunately, the knights of the Order had a nasty habit of magically tracking thieves and coming down on them like a ton of bricks.

I untied her, mounted, and we braved the night.

Typically technology and magic switched at least once every couple of days, usually more often than that. But two months ago we had been hit with a flare, a wave so potent, it drowned the city like a magic tsunami, making impossible things a reality. For three days demons and gods had walked the streets and human monsters had great difficulty controlling themselves. I had spent the flare on the battle-field, helping a handful of shapeshifters butcher a demonic horde.

It had been an epic occurrence all around. I still had vivid dreams about it, not exactly nightmares, but intoxicating, surreal visions of blood and gleaming blades and death.

The flare had burned out, leaving technology firmly in control of the world. For two months, cars started without fail, electricity held the darkness at bay, and air-conditioning made August blissful. We even had TV. On Monday night they had shown a movie, *Terminator 2*, hammering home the point: it could always be worse.

Then, on Wednesday right around noon, the magic hit and Atlanta went to hell.

I wasn't sure if people had deluded themselves into thinking the magic wouldn't come back or if they had been caught unprepared, but we'd never had so many calls for help since I had started with the Order. Unlike the Mercenary Guild, for which I also worked, the knights of the Order of Knights of Merciful Aid helped anyone and everyone regardless of their ability to pay. They charged only what you could afford and a lot of times nothing at all. We had been flooded with pleas. I managed to catch four hours of sleep on Wednesday night and then it was up and running again. Technically it was Friday now, and I was plagued by persistent fantasies of hot showers, food, and soft sheets. I had made an apple pie a couple of days ago, and I still had a slice left for tonight.

"Kate?" Maxine's stern voice echoed through my head, distant but clear.

I didn't jump. After the marathon of the last forty-eight hours, hearing the Order's telepathic secretary in my head seemed perfectly normal. Sad but true.

"I'm sorry, dear, but the pie might have to wait."

What else was new? Maxine didn't read thoughts on purpose, but if I concentrated on something hard enough, she couldn't help but catch a hint of it.

"I have a green seven, called in by a civilian."

Dead shapeshifter. Anything shapeshifter-related was mine. The shapeshifters distrusted outsiders, and I was the only employee of the Atlanta chapter of the Order who enjoyed Friend of the Pack status. "Enjoyed" being a relative term. Mostly my status meant that the shapeshifters might let me say a couple of words before deciding to fillet me. They took paranoid to a new level.

"Where is it?"

"Corner of Ponce de Leon and Dead Cat."

Twenty minutes by mule. Chances were, the Pack already knew the death had taken place. They would be all over the scene, snarling and claiming jurisdiction. Ugh. I turned Marigold and headed north. "I'm on it."

MARIGOLD CHUGGED UP THE STREETS, SLOW BUT steady, and seemingly tireless. The jagged skyline crawled past me, once-proud buildings reduced to crumbling husks. It was as if magic had set a match to Atlanta but extinguished the flames before the scorched city had a chance to burn to the ground.

Here and there random pinpoint dots of electric lights punctured the darkness. A scent of charcoal smoke spiced with the aroma of seared meat drifted from the Alexander on Ponce apartments. Someone was cooking a midnight dinner. The streets lay deserted. Most people with a crumb of sense knew better than to stay out at night.

A high-pitched howl of a wolf rolled through the city, sending shivers down my spine. I could almost picture her standing upon a concrete rib of a fallen skyscraper, pale fur enameled silver by moonlight, her head raised to expose her shaggy throat as she sung a flawless song, tinted with melancholy longing and the promise of a bloody hunt.

A lean shadow skittered from the alley, followed by another. Emaciated, hairless, loping on all fours in a jerky, uncoordinated gait, they crossed the street before me and paused. They had been human at some point but both had been dead for more than a decade. No fat or softness remained on their bodies. No flesh—only steel-wire muscle beneath thick hide. Two vampires on the prowl. And they were out of their territory.

"ID," I said. Most navigators knew me by sight just like they knew every member of the Order in Atlanta.

The forefront bloodsucker unhinged his jaw and the navigator's voice issued forth, distorted slightly. "Journeyman Rodriguez, Journeyman Salvo."

"Your Master?"

"Rowena."

Of all the Masters of the Dead, I detested Rowena the least. "You're a long way from the Casino."

"We . . ."

The second bloodsucker opened his mouth, revealing light fangs against his black maw. "He screwed up and got us lost in the Warren."

"I followed the map."

The second bloodsucker stabbed a clawed finger at the sky. "The map's useless if you can't orient for shit. The moon doesn't rise in the north, you moron."

Two idiots. It would be comical if I didn't feel the blood hunger rising from the vamps. If these two knuckleheads lost control for a moment, the bloodsuckers would rip into me.

"Carry on," I said and nudged Marigold.

The vamps took off, the journeymen riding their minds probably bickering somewhere deep within the Casino. The *Immortuus* pathogen robbed its victims of their egos. Insentient, the vampires obeyed only their hunger for blood, butchering anything with a pulse. The emptiness of a vampiric mind made it a perfect vehicle for necromancers, Masters of the Dead. Most of the Masters served the People. Part cult, part research institute, part corporation, all vomit inducing, the People devoted themselves to the study and care of the undead. They had chapters in most major cities, just like the Order. Here, in Atlanta, they made their den in the Casino.

Among the power brokers of Atlanta, the People ranked pretty high. Only the Pack could match them in the potential for destruction. The People were led by a mysterious legendary figure, who chose to call himself Roland in this day and age. Roland possessed immense power. He was also the man I had been training all my life to kill.

I circled a big pot hole in the old pavement, turned onto Dead Cat, and saw the crime scene under a busted street lamp. Cops and witnesses were nowhere in sight. Gauzy moonlight sifted onto the bodies of seven shapeshifters. None of them was dead.

Two werewolves in animal form swept the scene for scents, carefully padding in widening circles from the narrow mouth of Dead Cat Street. Most shapeshifters in beast form ran larger than their animal counterparts, and these proved no exception: hulking, shaggy beasts taller and thicker than a male Great Dane. Past them, two of their colleagues in human form packed something suspiciously resembling a body into a body bag. Three others walked the perimeter, presumably to keep the onlookers out of the way. As if anyone was dumb enough to linger for a second look.

At my approach, everything stopped. Seven pairs of glowing eyes stared at me: four green, three yellow. Judging by the glow, the shapeshifter crew hovered on the verge of going furry. One of their own was dead and they were out for blood.

I kept my tone light. "You fellows ever thought of hiring out as a Christmas lights crew? You'd make a fortune."

The nearest shapeshifter trotted to me. Bulky with muscle but fit, he was in his early forties. His face wore the trademark expression the Pack presented to the outsiders: polite and hard like the rock of Gibraltar. "Good evening, ma'am. This is a private investigation conducted by the Pack. I'm going to have to ask you to please move on."

Ma'am . . . *Oy*.

I reached into my shirt, pulled out the wallet of transparent plastic I carried on a cord around my neck, and passed it to him. He glanced at my ID, complete with a small square of enchanted silver, and called out, "Order."

Across the street a man congealed from the darkness. One moment there was only a deep night shadow lying like a pool of ink against the wall of the building, and the next there he stood. Six-two, his skin the color of bitter chocolate, and built like a prize fighter. Normally he wore a black cloak, but today he limited himself to black jeans and T-shirt. As he moved toward me, muscles rolled on his chest and arms. His face inspired second thoughts in would-be brawlers. He looked like he broke bones for a living and he loved his job.

"Hello, Jim," I said, keeping my tone friendly. "Fancy meeting you here."

The shapeshifter who had spoken to me took off. Jim came close and patted Marigold's neck.

"Long night?" he asked. His voice was melodious and smooth. He never sang, but you knew he could, and if he decided to do it, women would be hurling themselves into his path.

"You might say that."

Jim was my partner from the days when I worked exclusively for the Mercenary Guild. Some merc gigs required more than one body, and Jim and I tackled them together, mostly because we couldn't stomach working with anybody else. Jim was also alpha of the cat clan and the Pack's chief of security. I'd seen him fight and I would rather take on a nest of pissed-off vipers any day.

"You should go home, Kate." A sheen of faint green rolled over his eyes and vanished, his animal side coming to the surface for a moment.

"What happened here?"

"Pack business."

The wolf on the left let out a short yelp. A female shapeshifter ran over to him and picked up something off the ground. I caught a glimpse of it before she stuffed the object into a bag. A human arm, severed at the elbow, still in a sleeve. We had just gone from code green seven to code green ten. Shapeshifter murder. Accidental deaths rarely resulted in detached limbs strewn across the intersection.

"Like I said, Pack business." Jim glanced at me. "You know the law."

The law said that the shapeshifters were an independent group, much like a Native American tribe, with the authority to govern itself. They made their own laws and they had a right to enforce them, as long as those laws didn't affect nonshapeshifters. If the Pack didn't want my help on this investigation, there wasn't a lot I could do about it. "As an agent of the Order, I extend an offer of assistance to the Pack."

"The Pack appreciates the Order's offer of assistance. As of now, we decline. Go home, Kate," Jim repeated. "You look worn-out."

Translation: shoo, puny human. Big, mighty shapeshifters have no need of your silly investigative skills. "You squared this with the cops?"

Jim nodded.

I sighed, turned Marigold around, and headed home. Someone had died. I wouldn't be the one to find out why. It irked me on some deep professional level. If it was anybody else but Jim, I would've pushed harder to see the body. But when Jim said no, he meant it. My pushing wouldn't accomplish anything except straining relations between the Pack and the Order. Jim didn't half-ass things, so his crew would be competent and efficient.

It still bothered me.

I would call the Paranormal Activity Division in the morning and see if any reports were filed. The paranormal cops wouldn't tell me what was in the report, but at least I'd know if Jim had filed one. Not that I didn't trust Jim, but it never hurt to check.

AN HOUR LATER I LEFT MARIGOLD IN A SMALL stable in the parking lot and climbed the stairs to my apartment. I had inherited the place from Greg, my guardian, who had served as knight-diviner with the Order. He had died six months ago. I missed him so much it hurt.

My front door was a sight like no other. I got in, locked the door, pulled off my noxious shoes, and dropped them in the corner. I would deal with them later. I unbuckled the leather harness that held Slayer, my saber, on my back, pulled the saber out, and put it by my bed. The apple pie beckoned. I dragged myself into the kitchen, opened the fridge, and stared at an empty pie plate.

Had I eaten the pie? I didn't remember finishing it. And if I had, I should've taken the empty plate out of the fridge.

The front door had shown no signs of forced entry. I did a quick inventory of the apartment. Nothing missing. Nothing out of place. Greg's library with his artifacts and books looked completely undisturbed.

I must've finished the pie. Considering the insanity of the last forty-eight hours, I had probably just forgotten. Well, that sucked. I took the pie plate, washed it while murmuring curses under my breath, and put it in its place under the stove. I couldn't have pie, but nobody could deny me my shower. I stripped off my clothes, shedding them on the way to the bathroom, crawled into the shower, and drowned the world in hot spray and rosemary soap.

I had just toweled off my hair when the phone rang.

I kicked the door open and stared at the phone, ringing its head off on the small night table by my bed. Nothing good ever happened to me because of phone calls. There was always somebody dead, dying, or making somebody else dead on the other line.

Ring-ring.

Ring-ring-ring.

Ring?

I sighed and picked it up. "Kate Daniels."

"Hello, Kate," said a familiar velvet voice. "I hope I didn't wake you."

Saiman. Just about the last person I wanted to talk to.

Saiman had an encyclopedic knowledge of magic. He was also a shapeshifter—of sorts. I had done a job for him, back when I worked for the Mercenary Guild full-time, and he found me amusing. Because I entertained him, he offered me his services as a magic expert at a criminal discount. Unfortunately, the last time we had met was in the middle of the flare, atop a high-rise, where Saiman was dancing naked in the snow. With the largest erection I had ever seen on a human being. He didn't want to let me off that roof either. I had to jump to get away from him.

I kept my voice civil. Kate Daniels, master of diplomacy. "I don't want to speak to you. In fact, I don't wish to continue our association at all."

"That's very unfortunate. However, I have something that might belong to you and I would like to return this item to your custody."

What in the world? "Mail it to me."

"I would but he would prove difficult to fit into an envelope."

He? *He* wasn't good.

"He refuses to speak, but perhaps I can describe him to you: about eighteen, dark, short hair, menacing scowl, large brown eyes. Quite attractive in a puppy way. Judging by the way the *tapedum lucidum* behind his retinas catches the light, he's a shapeshifter. I'm guessing a wolf. You brought him with you during our last unfortunate encounter. I'm truly sorry about it, by the way."

Derek. My one-time teenage werewolf sidekick. What the hell was he doing at Saiman's apartment?

"Hold the phone to him, please." I kept my voice even. "Derek, answer me so I know he isn't bluffing. Are you hurt?"

"No." Derek's voice was laced with a growl. "I can handle this. Don't come here. It isn't safe."

"It's remarkable that he has so much concern for your welfare, provided that he's the one sitting in a cage," Saiman murmured. "You keep the most interesting friends, Kate."

"Saiman?"

"Yes?"

"If you hurt him, I'll have twenty shapeshifters in your apartment foaming at the mouth at your scent."

"Don't worry. I have no desire to bring the Pack's wrath on my head. Your friend is unharmed and contained. I will, however, turn him over to proper authorities unless you come and pick him up by sunrise."

"I'll be there."

Saiman's voice held a slight mocking edge. "I'm looking forward to it."

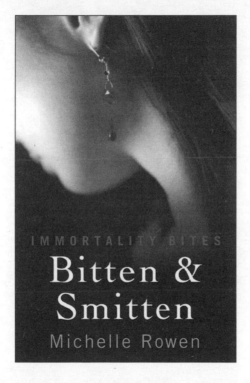

Ilona Andrews is the pseudonym of the husband-and-wife writing team of Ilona and Gordon Andrews. They live in the Smoky Mountains with their daughters and write bestselling books together.

Visit Ilona's website at www.ilona-andrews.com